# BAPTISM OF FIRE

# BAPTISM OF FIRE

## Frank Collins

**Doubleday**

LONDON · NEW YORK · TORONTO · SYDNEY · AUCKLAND

TRANSWORLD PUBLISHERS LTD
61–63 Uxbridge Road, London W5 5SA

TRANSWORLD PUBLISHERS (AUSTRALIA) PTY LTD
15–23 Helles Avenue, Moorebank, NSW 2170

TRANSWORLD PUBLISHERS (NZ) LTD
3 William Pickering Drive, Albany, Auckland

Published 1997 by Doubleday
a division of Transworld Publishers Ltd
Copyright © by Frank Collins 1997

A catalogue record for this book is
available from the British Library.

ISBN 0385 409168

Typeset in Palatino
by Phoenix Typesetting, Ilkley, West Yorkshire.

Printed in Great Britain by Mackays of Chatham, Kent.

For Claire

# ACKNOWLEDGEMENTS

I have changed the names and occasionally the personal details of some of the people who appear in this book. Otherwise, I've told my story just as I remember it. If you were there, it can be painful · to read someone else's account – especially if you've been left out, or if you remember things differently. So to anyone who's upset by anything they read in *Baptism of Fire*, I'd like to say sorry.

I would like to thank the following people, who have helped me in all sorts of ways: Mark Lucas, Bill Scott-Kerr, Ursula Mackenzie, Garry Prior, Ed Christie, Kate Melhuish, Nicky Henderson, Judy Turner, the Collins family: Yvonne; Gary; Michael; Michelle; Revd Alun Price, Revd Rod Price, Revd Rudi Heinze, Preb. Peter Wood, Nick Evens, Andy McNab. There are many others I'd like to thank who cannot be named here.

# PROLOGUE

WE'RE IN THE HEART OF THE NORTHERN IRELAND COUNTRYSIDE. A
Provisional IRA hit team is planning to shoot a man as he leaves his
farmhouse. There's only one place to hide: a small group of bushes
outside the house. We don't know if the terrorists are already in these
bushes. 'Er, what should we do?' asks my lance corporal.

I say, 'I'll go. You stay here and cover me.'

'Frank . . .' He starts to argue, but I get out of the car and walk
towards the bushes. They are 300 metres away across open ground.
In there, perhaps, lurks a terrorist. His gun is trained on me, his safety
catch is off, his finger is ready to make the tiny movement necessary
to kill a man and that man is me. He doesn't want to do it yet. He's
waiting until the last possible moment.

Perhaps I appear unafraid. Perhaps he thinks I don't know he's
there. He's sweating. He must kill me and probably be killed himself.
It isn't easy to murder, even if you're a terrorist. He's crouching in his
bush, perhaps shaking, his heart thudding.

I am afraid. I'm afraid that he'll shoot me in the face. With every
step my body waits, my face waits. My eyes are fixed on the bush and,
although I know I'm moving towards it, I feel frozen with anticipation. I'm waiting to die, he's waiting to kill me. Long, long seconds,
as long as a lifetime.

I am afraid of dying but I am not afraid of death. I'm a Christian
and that means I'm ready for whatever's waiting for me. The prospect
is even exciting. I'm about to embark on the greatest adventure. I'm
about to see God.

I reach the bushes. I stretch towards them and part the branches. Any man here, reluctant to shoot, sizing up the situation, waiting, waiting to kill, can wait no longer. I brace myself for the impact of the bullet.

# 1

IT IS DARK OUTSIDE. WE ARE IN BED, ME AND MY BIG SISTER YVONNE, but we aren't asleep. We're waiting for Dad.

He comes in carrying a bottle of Newcastle Amber and two little glasses. He opens the bottle and pours out the ale in a slow, neat way, which is just how he does his carpentry. Although not in the afternoons. But I know he's good at his job before he goes to the pub. He's a ship's carpenter and I've seen him work. He repaired a piece of skirting board in our house and it was so perfect you could hardly see the join. I'd never thought about skirting board before, never even knew what it was called. It was just there. But now I see that skirting board is a beautiful thing, and that each board is shaped and fitted.

Dad hands us each a glass. They're sherry glasses. Dad says that Amber's a lady's drink. I am not a lady but I'm only five so I'm too young to drink bitter.

Now it's Dad's turn to watch us. I know the way I drink this is important. It tastes awful but I have to drink it because men drink and I'm going to be a man soon, probably a hard man like my dad.

I try to drink quickly and then sort of smack my lips and wipe them with the back of my hand the way Dad does. He looks pleased with me. It's a good moment to ask for something I want.

'Dad, everyone at school's got this record . . . It's called "Ghost Riders in the Sky" . . .'

'It's by Pinky and Perky, Dad,' says Yvonne. She's two years older than me. 'It's really good . . .'

Dad says he'll buy it for us. He's in a good mood. When he's gone

3

we get so excited that we carry on talking in Pinky and Perky voices and giggling a long time after we're supposed to be asleep.

The next day is Sunday. Some people go to church on Sunday but we don't. We have baths. Our bathroom doesn't have hot water so Mam heats some up in her twintub washing machine and then empties the waste pipe into the bath for us. It's full of old Daz which feels scratchy under our bottoms.

Monday is a school day. We do music. I'm picked to play the drums. I bang in time to my second favourite hymn, 'He Who Would Valiant Be'. My favourite's 'When a Knight Won His Spurs'. Mrs Hall plays the tune on the piano and we all join in.

'He who would valiant be, 'gainst all disaster. Let him in constancy, follow the master.'

After school I run downstairs as usual. I'm first into the cloakroom. First! I've beaten all the others. I put on my coat and go outside into the playground. First again! Maybe, if I hurry, I can get home first too. I don't wait for Yvonne. I just run and run. My legs get softer the further I go and I feel hot and there's a banging inside my body like Hammy trying to get out of his cage. But I don't stop. I take my coat off as I turn into our road and drag it along behind me with one hand. It feels heavier than when I was wearing it. Heavy and hot. My face is burning and my eyes are stinging but I'm nearly home now.

I fling open the back door into the kitchen. No Mam. I find her in the living room and plant myself in front of her. I'm first home, Mam. But Mam's on the telephone. She makes appointments for Uncle John. Sometimes she says she's his receptionist and then she laughs at herself. She's got such a nice laugh. Uncle John is a chimney sweep.

When she puts the phone down I say, 'I'm home!'

She says, 'I can see that. What are you doing here?'

'I'm first one back. I ran all the way.'

'First? I should think you're the only one. Look, it's just gone three o'clock.'

I stare at her.

'You're more than an hour early. Your playtime's at three o'clock. Why did you come home in playtime?'

She's seen my coat on the ground now and taken it from me. Coats on the floor are not the sort of thing she likes. I watch her putting it on a peg and suddenly I understand. Suddenly I know why the cloakroom was full of coats and silence and hanging shoebags and no children. It was playtime. It wasn't going-home time at all. My face is already hot from running, but now it gets a different kind of hot. I feel stupid. I want to cry. Mam doesn't shout at me. She's not like the

4

mothers who yell at their children at the school gates. She almost never shouts.

I expect her to send me back to school but she phones and explains and says there's no point me going back now. I hug her. My little brother Gary, who's been watching all this, comes over and hugs her too. But Mam doesn't hang around being hugged. She never does. There's always something important to do.

When Dad gets home, me and Yvonne and Gary are all having our tea. We look to see if he's carrying our record. We look for 'Ghost Riders in the Sky'. But his hands are empty.

Dad sits down while Mam takes his tea out of the frying pan. He tells us that there are going to be some changes. Gary won't sleep with Mam and Dad any more. He and I will share the front room. Yvonne will have our bedroom all to herself and Mam and Dad are going to have a bed in the living room. It will be a big settee by day and turn into a bed at night.

Everyone seems to think that these changes are a good idea but I'm worried. I'm scared that Gary has told Mam how me and Yvonne spit on the bedroom floor every morning so that, when Gary toddles in wearing his teddy bear pyjamas and nothing on his feet, he steps right in it. I wait to see if anyone mentions spit. No-one does.

The next night we wait for Dad to get home with 'Ghost Riders in the Sky'. He's late. Mam is annoyed because she has to go up to the school for a parents' meeting. When at last we hear the door, Dad doesn't appear. He's gone straight into the sitting room. We follow Mam in there and Dad's lying on the floor in front of the three-bar electric fire. Mam sighs and walks round him to the hall. She puts on her coat. We follow her.

'We'll be very quiet while Dad's asleep,' Yvonne assures her. But Mam is tight-lipped. She's pulling a plastic rainhat out of her coat pocket and tying it under her chin.

'Don't bother,' she says. 'He'll be hard to wake.'

It is clear to all of us, even little Gary, that Dad must be very drunk.

'Has Dad lost another job, Mam?' asks Yvonne.

'I expect so.'

Dad often loses jobs when he's drunk but usually he soon finds another.

We sneak in and look at him. He is lying on the floor with his work clothes on. There's a smell in the room which I know is the smell of beer. Dad's face is grey and scratchy and there are black smudges, like crayon, under his eyes. He still has his cap on, although he's lying down. This seems clever to me and I know my father is a very clever

5

man. He is so clever that his jobs require him to go away from home a lot and when he goes I miss him. When he comes back, I want him to talk to me and play with me and make things with me, only me, not Gary or Yvonne, because I'm his first son. I want this probably more than anything else in the world. Even more than a Pinky and Perky record.

We know that nothing will wake him. I can stare at him fearlessly, I can look at his ear lobes and his small hands and his nostrils without him even knowing I'm doing it. The others are staring at him too. Then Yvonne has an idea.

We get some plastic bags and put them over his hands. We secure them with rubber bands. And then we watch. Slowly, surely, it is just as Yvonne has said. The plastic bags get cloudy. They are getting so damp and cloudy that soon we can't see Dad's hands any more. Finally we take them off.

'That', says Yvonne wisely, 'was a scientific experiment.'

We nod.

When Mam gets home she calls us into the kitchen.

'Look what I've found!'

She is standing by an open drawer holding something thin and square. It's a record. It's Pinky and Perky. I grab it and Yvonne grabs it from me. Sure enough, it's 'Ghost Riders in the Sky'.

'I found it in here,' says Mam, 'your dad did get it for you. He must have put it here and forgotten to tell me.'

I am very happy. I catch sight of a strange, knowing look that Yvonne gives Mam. Mam looks away. I don't care what it means. I'm too busy getting the record player out. I move Mam's record collection to one side. They are all from the 1950s and now it is the 1960s. Glenn Miller. Freddie and the Dreamers. Ballroom-dancing records because she and Dad met ballroom dancing. I'm opening the lid and blowing the dust off the needle. We play 'Ghost Riders in the Sky', watching the record make its wobbly circle. We play it again and again. Dad doesn't wake up.

'Our Dad didn't really buy that record. Mam did,' Yvonne tells me later. But I don't believe her.

Dad finds another job and Gary starts school and he and I share the front bedroom. Gary and Yvonne are mates although he's five and she's nine. I don't think I should be the odd one out as I'm seven, right between them in age. Once, they throw Gary's shoes in the fire and when Mam, raising her voice, stands the three of us in a row and asks which of us did it, I start to giggle. I can't help myself. I've done it before in school when the teacher loses her temper and I've done

6

it before with Mam. When people get angry, giggles start deep inside me and they have to come out.

It's not funny to see my mam angry but I'm trying so hard not to giggle that I splutter and once one noise has escaped me I can't control myself. Mam stares at me. Gary and Yvonne stare at me. I laugh and laugh and laugh. I collapse. Mam takes this as a sign of guilt. She smacks my bottom. I stop laughing.

I have a terrible problem, even worse than my laughing problem. I worry about it a lot. It is this: I cannot say the word three. I say thwee. Children at school laugh at me and my dad shakes his head about it. He says, 'Threee. Threeee.'

I watch his mouth and repeat, 'Thweee. Thweee.'

Finally he says that if I can learn to say three he'll give me a pot of jam. This is something I would like. I like jam but most of all I want my dad to give it to me and say, 'Well done, lad.'

Dad goes away working and my mam helps me practise. Three. Three. Three. Then one day, when I'm not even thinking about it, when I'm sitting at the front gatepost watching a football game in the street, I say to myself, 'Three.' That's it. I can say it. One pot of jam for me.

My mam says, 'Little Frank, don't get too excited about that jam.'

'But Dad's going to give it to me and he says I can eat it with a spoon . . .'

'Well he shouldn't, it'll make you sick. He probably won't remember anyway.'

I'm sitting at my gatepost looking out for Dad and when I see him round the corner I practise just a few more times. Three, three, three. Then I run down the street to him.

'Three!' I yell at him. 'Dad, Dad, listen! Three! Three!'

'Hello, bonnie lad,' he says.

'Three! Three!'

'So you've grown out of your baby talk at last.'

'Three! Three!'

'Well that's champion.'

'I practised, Dad. So I could have the jam.'

'What jam, lad?'

'The pot of jam. For learning to say three.'

We're at home now and he's going into the house so I don't hear what he says if he says anything at all.

The next day, there's no pot of jam. Nor the next day. Nor the day after that.

'I don't think he's going to get it for you, young Frank,' says my mother. We're playing toy soldiers. I've got lots of them, mostly Airfix. They come joined together. I have to snap them out of their plastic case and fit them onto their bases. I have big, chunky American Marines, little grey Germans, yellow Japanese samurai warriors and the British infantry. Some of the British soldiers are lying down with their Bren guns. I line them up along one flank. The German commander watches them with his binoculars. He's always first to die. There's a limit to what you can do with a man who never takes his binoculars off.

Tonight my mother has helped me lay out an entire battle. It's taken hours.

I like soldiers, and not just toy ones. Not only do they fight wars but they are nice to us. They have parties and invite Mam and Dad. This is because the army barracks is at the end of our garden, on the other side of the spiky metal fence. The army wants to be friends with all the people in the road, so they hold parties and Mam and Dad go dancing there. They come home in party hats with streamers and they usually bring small presents for us. Once I got a toy trumpet.

I fall asleep knowing two things: that tomorrow my dad will bring me the pot of jam and that when I wake up my mam will have put every single one of my soldiers away.

I'm right about the soldiers. It's Saturday so I decide to go and look at real soldiers in the barracks. It's usually quiet but on Saturdays it can be busy. My dad says that the men there aren't real soldiers, just people who are soldiers in their spare time and their spare time's on Saturday. I try looking through the metal fence but there's nothing much to see as usual. So I go down Redcar Road and turn left on the main road and then left again and stand outside the entrance. There are warehouses and lorries and men shouting to each other and I can hear marching. The sound of all those feet marching in time together is wonderful. I wish I could see it. A soldier in uniform pushes past me.

'Hello, laddie,' he says to me, and ruffles my hair.

When the end of Saturday comes, Dad arrives home cheerful but without the jam. He's in such a good mood that he wants to play. He picks up Gary and runs around the room with him on his back, then he throws him down and picks me up and tosses me over his shoulder. He throws Yvonne into the air and catches her.

'Stop that, Frank, someone's going to get hurt!' says my mother, running around the room after him. 'You've had too much and you'll do someone an injury . . .'

But none of us wants to stop. We don't care how beery Dad smells.

8

He's happy and we're happy too. I know that, even though he hasn't brought me my jam today, he'll bring it soon. I try to imagine him going into a shop and buying it. I fail. But I still know that he'll bring it for me. Every night I go to sleep expecting my pot of jam tomorrow.

Soon it will be Christmas. We help to decorate the tree. It's not a real one. Yvonne says it looks like Uncle John's sweep's brush.

On Christmas morning we wake up early and sneak to the living room. Gary and I whisper to Yvonne that she has to go in first. We hang around the hallway, pushing and shoving each other, but eventually Yvonne gets so cold that she opens the door. There's Mam and Dad, asleep in bed. We sneak round to Mam's side of the bed without waking Dad. Mission accomplished: Mam lets us go to the tree. In the early morning gloom, without its lights on, it looks even more like a sweep's brush than usual. We don't care. We want our presents.

We open them quietly so we don't wake Dad. Football boots. But when I see them I'm disappointed. They're brown leather. My brother has black and white boots, like the Newcastle players wear. I look at his enviously. After a while I decide that my boots are beautiful in their own way. They have hard toecaps and leather studs nailed on. The smell of the new leather is special, too. I open my other presents but I keep getting the boots out of the box to sniff them. They're beautiful boots but right from the start they're the wrong boots. Gary has the right ones.

We're also given a ball, a big brown leather football that smells the same as my boots only stronger.

I don't try the boots on at first. We're waiting for Dad to wake up. When he does we all have breakfast here in the living room and Dad, being nice because it's Christmas, says he'll come out and play some football with us. I'm probably as excited about this as I am about having the boots. I know that Dad played football when he did his national service and won a cup for it too, and I want to be as good as he was.

We start lacing our boots up then and there in the living room.

'You won't be able to wear them in here again,' our mam says, and I'm sad that they won't be new and perfect for very much longer.

When I stand up in them they feel strange. They're very heavy. The studs aren't designed for walking around inside and when I cross the kitchen I slip on the lino and hit my head hard against the stove.

I don't want to cry and I try not to cry but the tears just come.

'Where did you hit yourself?' Mam asks. But my dad stands over me and shakes his head. He tells me to stop that noise. He says I am a big boy and big boys don't cry. He jostles me outside. I'm still sniffing.

It's cold and grey and drizzly out here. Newcastle never looks like Christmas in the old movies they show on television. Our street's just the same as usual except there's almost no-one about today. Red-brick houses, semis with blue slate roofs, identical, stretching as far as you can see. There are low brick walls between the tiny front gardens and the pavement and ours has a gatepost but no gate.

We stand in the road and my dad rolls the ball towards me. I know I'm supposed to kick it. I run forward and kick it square on with the end of my foot and it bounces off the hard toe cap. I thought I was kicking it back to Dad but instead it skims off at an angle through our neighbour's gate. I stand still, staring in disbelief. I'm still sniffing.

My dad shouts, 'No! No! Don't be so stupid!'

He comes up and explains that you don't kick with the toecap. He shows me which bit of the foot to use. He goes back across the street and rolls the ball to me again. I watch it anxiously, waiting for it to reach me. Then I try to kick it the way Dad showed me.

When I look up he's walking back into the house.

He says,'That's it. You're no good. That's it.'

He goes in and closes the front door behind him. I watch him go. So does Gary.

I sit down on the steps at the front of the house and cry, and this time I let myself cry. I don't think about stopping, probably because I know I can't. Dad allowed me two kicks and that was all. After two kicks, I hadn't made it, and I'm a waste of time and not worth bothering with. I mean, ever again. I know that he'll never try to play football with me again. I stare down at my cow-smelly new boots and decide this is the last time I'll wear them.

The day after Christmas we visit Nan and Granda. Nan is Mam's mother. Granda works at Victor Products where machine tools are made for the shipyards. They live in Wallsend, right by the Swan Hunter shipyard and the North East Marine crane. Granda says this is a symbol of the north-east of England and he's proud to live so close to it.

Nan tells us stories. They're good the first time but this is the millionth time we've heard them. The worst one is about her illnesses. She had rheumatic fever when she was my age or even younger and there's something funny about her heart and it's a miracle she ever managed to have a baby because the doctor told her she should never exert herself. If she ever disobeys doctor's orders, then the inside of her chest will go black and mushy, just like black pudding.

I wish she wouldn't tell us this when we're eating drop scones. But she says, 'Just exactly like black pudding. Black pudding! Can you imagine that?' Of course I can imagine it, that's why I want her to stop.

Another story is about the time she had a row with Granda when she happened to be holding a cream cake in her hand. All the time they were arguing she kept saying, 'I'll put this in your face, I will! I will!'

She looks around at us, one by one.

'And do you know what happened?' she asks. Of course we do. 'I did! I put it right in his face!'

She laughs and so do we and so does Granda.

My favourite story is about the war. Nazis were trying to bomb the shipyards and there were German planes flying down Nan's street. They were firing machine guns and dropping bombs and Nan was blown down the hallway, from the front door, where the red step is kept well-polished, bombs or no bombs, to the cupboard at the far end.

She says, 'I was blown right into the cupboard! Can you imagine that? Right down the hallway into the cupboard!'

I like the war stories best. I have an Action Man and this is my favourite toy. But Action Man has been wounded. I show Granda how the ankle joint has snapped and he says to leave it with him. When I go home I feel sad to be leaving Action Man behind. He'll come home smelling of home-rolled cigarettes and Brylcreme like Granda. But the next time I visit, Granda hands me Action Man with a new joint, made of metal and fitting the plastic exactly. I like Action Man even more than before. He already had a scar on his right cheek and now he has a metal ankle as well. He's hard, that's for sure.

There is a death in our family. Hammy hamster is found lying cold and stiff in his cage one morning and we are all in tears. Mam tells us to hurry up for school but we cry while we get dressed.

Mam tells us all to stop crying. Dad's going to take Hammy's lifeless little body away and give it a proper burial on the coast road on the way to work. He'll have a small funeral for Hammy in a field. We stop crying and start sniffing while Mam wraps Hammy in newspaper. Dad's in a hurry and he nearly leaves without the corpse but Mam catches him at the front door with the sad little parcel.

Dad rushes out and a moment later, just about when he must be passing the gatepost, I hear the dustbin lid clang. An awful thought crosses my mind. It's such an awful thought that I refuse to think it again. But when we leave for school I find myself lingering behind the others to open the dustbin and, sure enough, there's a small newspaper package there. It could contain anything, of course. I don't want to find out what's inside it but one of my fingers reaches out and prods it and the newspaper falls open to reveal Hammy. Crying, I run after the others. They think I'm crying about Hammy. Which I am, sort of.

That night, half-scared, half-excited at my own cunning, I ask Dad where he buried Hammy. I look right into his eyes when I ask the question and he looks right back into mine as he lies to me.

There's an air raid shelter in our back garden. It's just a hut really. I like playing with Action Man in there but one day I decide that I'm going to be a carpenter just like my dad and the air raid shelter is going to be my workshop. I'll ask my dad questions about how to do it and he'll show me and then, if I do it right, he'll say to me, 'Well done, bonnie lad.'

Dad is patient. We spend a lot of time in the hut. We don't talk much but we work together and it's nice. Dad shows me how to use a hammer and nails and a saw and I make myself a boat. I'm using some dowel for a funnel. I try to nail the funnel onto the boat by banging a nail straight down the dowel but it splits in two. Dad explains to me all about the grain in the wood, how it's alive and it splits because of the way it grows. Dad loves wood. He brings me home a Stanley saw, a tenon saw. That's a proper saw, the sort a man would use, not one that's especially for children. When he gives it to me I am happy for days because I know that it's Dad's way of saying, 'Well done, bonnie lad.'

When I'm nine years old I want a bike. I've always wanted one. First it was a fantasy, then it was a wish and now it's a necessity. Every boy here in Heaton, and probably the whole of Newcastle, has a bike except me, and I can't even ride one. I sit on the gatepost watching all the other children riding around in Redcar Road. They circle and swerve and make their bikes rear up like horses and do tricks on them or they just go up and down the road without getting bored.

Here's Dad coming home. He's not as big as some other dads but he's a hard fighter and you know it from the way he walks up the street. You know that if you picked a fight with him, you'd lose. Dad never loses a fight. He's the seventh of eight brothers, a family so large that the eldest had emigrated before my dad was even born. And the Collins brothers are hard. Everyone knows it. They are hard men and no-one messes with them. They have a secret, which we don't talk about. We never say it. We never say it inside the house and we never say it to anyone outside. It is very important that no-one ever guesses that our dad is a Roman Catholic.

12

As soon as Dad gets to the gate I start again about a bike.

'Get your hands out of your pockets,' he says, jabbing at me. He never can bear to see us with our hands in our pockets. We might need our hands any minute, if we fall over, or if someone hits us, and they won't do us any good in our pockets.

'But Dad, what about a bike?'

He shakes his head.

'I've told you', he says, 'that we're not having any second-hand bikes in this family and I've told you why.'

Dad's youngest brother had an accident on a bike and it was a second-hand bike which had been broken and repaired. That's why no second-hand bikes are allowed in our family. And we can't afford a new bike. Dad says so. No second-hand bike plus no new bike equals no bike. I know that. But today I'm going to ask again anyway.

To my amazement, Dad stops by the gate and listens to me. There's a silence when I've finished. I watch his face. His eyes are always brown and shiny but today they're only shiny because they're watery, and I can see red veins in them as well. He smells of beer and Brylcreme and tobacco. He has a big moustache. Sometimes he shaves it off but now he has a moustache. His mouth isn't visible beneath his whiskers until he smiles and now, suddenly, he's smiling.

He says, 'All right. You can have a bike.'

I can't believe my ears. I jump off the gatepost. Then somewhere, coming from far in the back of my brain, is a picture. I don't want to look at the picture but I know I have to. It is a picture of a pot of jam. I look away from Dad.

'When?' I ask.

'When what?'

'When can I have my bike?'

Dad says, 'Don't trust me, eh, lad?'

I still can't look at him.

'You get me a pencil and a piece of paper and I'll write it down.'

We go into the house, me leading. I steamroller in, push Gary out of the way, run round my mother, who's not fat but only pregnant, and start rifling for a clean piece of paper by the telephone.

When I find paper and a pen that works, Dad is talking to Mam in the kitchen. The kitchen smells of beer. Mam is busy cooking something and pretending not to listen, although I know she is.

'Told that foreman . . . told him . . . asked him if he wanted to step outside . . . nothing wrong with it at all . . . if a man can't drink eight pints at midday and go back and do a good afternoon's work then he's not a man . . .'

I've heard some of this before. It means that Dad's been sacked again.

'I've brought a piece of paper, Dad,' I say, when he's finished. He narrows his eyes as if I'm out of focus.

'The bike . . .' I remind him.

He remembers then and nods. I hand him the pen and he writes, 'I promise to buy you a bike tomorrow.' He writes slowly and not very neatly but there it is, in his own hand, a promise.

'Thanks, Dad,' I say. Before I can rush out of the room, my mother says, 'What's that, Little Frank?'

I show her the note. She glances at it then looks at my dad and shakes her head with pursed lips.

'It's a promise, Mam,' I say.

She turns away from me. 'He makes a lot of promises. I doubt he'll buy you a bike so don't get too excited.'

But I know he will buy me a bike and the next evening I'm waiting on my gatepost as usual. I'm not staring enviously at the other boys now. I'm studying their technique because later this evening I'm going to be learning how to ride my new bike.

Every few moments my eyes are on the corner and eventually my dad comes round it. He's not pushing a bike. This is a bad sign, but not hopeless.

'Dad, when are we getting my bike?' I ask.

He smiles at me. He has a neat row of even white teeth. Some dads who smoke a lot have brown teeth but my dad doesn't.

'Let me in, lad.' I'm blocking his path. 'Let me in and get me that piece of paper I signed yesterday.'

I run for the paper and present him with it before he can take his coat off.

'Now you read it to me,' he says.

I read, 'I promise to buy you a bike tomorrow.'

Dad starts laughing, a deep roaring sound from somewhere low down in his stomach. I stare at him.

'Tomorrow!' he roars. I can hardly understand him he's laughing so hard. 'And that's what I'll say when you ask me tomorrow!'

Disappointment washes over me. My eyes sting with tears. I am hot and sad and tearful and there is nothing I can do about it.

'Had you there!' he says, cuffing me playfully around the ear. Dad's playful cuffs are always too rough. 'I had you, bonnie lad.'

I go into the kitchen. I'm holding the paper and I'm crying and my mother knows immediately what's happened.

'I told you he wouldn't buy you a bike. I told you,' she says. She doesn't put her arm around me the way she did sometimes when I was small but she looks ready to cry for me herself. She keeps shaking her head.

When Mam's baby is due, we go and stay with Nan and Granda and hear all the old stories. I'm playing on some waste ground by the shipyard when I make friends with a boy called Alan. We find an old piano. It's not all of the piano, just its bones, like a dinosaur relic. We try to lift it. Alan drops his end. I try to get my hand out of the way but fail because it sticks on a nail. Crash. There is a searing pain as the full weight of the piano falls onto my hand.

When we release it we find that one finger is torn and the nail is off. I run back to Nan's house and I'm screaming and bleeding so much that the neighbours all come out. Nan washes and bandages me speedily and then runs up to Victor's to call Granda, who drives me to hospital in his little green Standard Eight car. He hasn't had the car long. He bought it a few months ago after he won £400 on the pools.

At the hospital they try to stitch me with a giant darning needle.

'His skin's too soft,' says the doctor, 'it keeps tearing.'

But eventually Granda drives me home with a big bandage which I show off to everyone.

That night there is a fuss in Nan's living room. Gary and I smell beer before we walk into the room so we know that Dad's here. We can hear the loud voices of uncles and aunts. Inside, there's Dad standing and looking awkward the way he always does with Mam's family. Granda is sitting silently on the settee while Nan stands by the door and cries openly. The room is thick with chatter.

'Has Mam had the baby?' I ask Yvonne.

'She's had two babies,' she tells me.

Twins. Now I know what all the fuss is about. I'm so surprised that I don't think to ask if they're boys or girls. Yvonne tells me anyway. There's one of each.

' . . . had a bet on that it would be another boy . . . no-one's going to tell me I lost my bet . . .' Dad's saying. Dad can bet on almost anything, although mostly he bets on the horses.

'I'll have to sit down,' Nan says. 'It's all too much and you know what could happen if things get too much.'

I think of black pudding. Granda must be thinking the same thing because he says very swiftly, 'Sit here, Tilly.'

Nan sits but she continues to cry. Her voice goes squeaky.

'I don't know how she'll cope. I really don't . . .'

It's difficult to tell if Nan's happy or sad.

Over the next few days we hear a lot about how we have to be good

15

and help our mother. I am excited and want to see our new brother and sister. When we go home, there's Mam with two tiny hairless ratlike creatures. They are to be called Michael and Michelle. Mam asks Yvonne if she wants to hold them and she says no. Yvonne didn't want Mam to have one more baby, let alone two, but you can tell Yvonne really loves them anyway. I hold them, one at a time, and look into their little squished-up faces. I decide I like babies but I don't tell anyone in case they think I'm not hard.

'Do you think Mam's pleased?' I ask Yvonne.

'Shocked, more like,' she says.

There's some shuffling of bedrooms again because we're five children and two grown-ups in a two-bedroom house. Yvonne has to move in with me and Gary in the front room and the twins take her room at the back. Mam and Dad are still on the settee. Yvonne makes it clear that she does not like these new arrangements.

At night, I hear the babies crying and crying. After a while, it makes me want to cry too. I go in to Mam and tell her that the twins are unhappy.

'Do you think I can't hear?' she says, looking at me closely. 'Oh no, Frank, don't you start too.'

I ask if I can pick them up and comfort them but she says no, they have to learn not to cry. Finally I persuade her to let me take them a bottle.

'Did I have to learn not to cry?' I ask her as she heats up the milk.

'I was soft on you,' she says. 'I'd give you a bottle straightaway. I'd just push it in between the bars of your cot and you'd always find it somehow.'

I sit watching her in silence. I don't like the idea of a tiny baby scrabbling around in the sheets looking for his bottle, especially when that tiny baby was me. My mother has seen my face.

'Frank,' she says, 'don't worry about them, babies always cry, it doesn't mean anything.'

I nod and take the bottles in.

# 2

WHEN THE TWINS ARE ABOUT SIX MONTHS OLD, WE MOVE HOUSE. WE move to Whitley Bay. Whitley Bay is a place where many of my mother's relatives live. It is a seaside resort and people who go there on holiday envy the residents who live there all the year round. From now on we'll be residents and people will envy us. We're to have a large house on Beach Avenue and Nan and Granda will sell their house in Wallsend and live in our front room. That way, my mam will have lots of help with the twins. And my dad is going to start a new life. He's going to stop working for other people and be his own boss so no-one can sack him unfairly again. He and Uncle John the chimney sweep will go on a course together which will teach them how to install central heating. Then they'll have their own central heating business.

At Whitley Bay we find ourselves at the heart of Mam's family. We not only share a house with her parents but we're surrounded by more aunts and uncles and cousins than you can count. Auntie June (whose husband John is going into business with Dad), and Auntie Alwyn (who's married to Uncle Tom), are not Mam's sisters but her cousins and her very best friends. Mam's cheerful. She doesn't smoke so much and she gives up Senior Service and smokes Embassy instead, which have filters. She dyes her hair at the front. It's exactly the same colour as mine, sort of blondy-ginger. I wonder if this is a coincidence.

Mam and Dad and June and John and Alwyn and Tom are so

pleased to be one big family that they decide we'll all take holidays together.

They buy a cottage in Scotland for £100. Of course, it's not the Ritz. It's semi-derelict, with bushes growing into one of the rooms and no electricity. In the morning we prime the pump and water comes up from the well. Uncle John was always being asked to take things away from customers' houses when he was a chimney sweep and now he's brought all those things here. There is junk everywhere but some of it is good junk. We build a tree house of old doors and a railway track with angle iron. There are bikes, most of them large. I learn to ride at last. My bike is so big that I have to ride with my legs through the frame and my whole body leaning over the side. I don't care because I'm finally cycling. We cycle for miles in a big traffic-slowing throng.

There are six adults and ten children and all the children sleep together in one big room on mattresses. We have a wonderful holiday. Mam's happy too. Most of the time I don't think about it, but I have an uneasy feeling about Dad. He doesn't fit in properly with the other grown-ups. Uncle Tom likes to go trout fishing and Uncle John heads for the hills and walks up and down them but Dad doesn't go anywhere. Except the pub.

In the evening we all go to the pub and the children have crisps and lemonade in the garden. Uncles bring aunts little red drinks or half-pints of shandy and they sit at a nearby bench, talking in a lazy holiday sort of way. It's how the other people in the garden are drinking too. All except my dad. He doesn't talk much. He thinks chit-chat is for women. He especially doesn't talk when he's drinking because for him drinking is a serious business and he's a professional. He expects to get ten pints in before closing time and the others aren't thinking of having more than a pint and a half.

From the children's table I can see Dad shuffling and wriggling as he tries to pace his drinking to the other's. He usually stands at the bar, so he doesn't much like sitting in the garden. But his glass is always empty long before anyone else's. In the end there's a sort of unspoken agreement that he'll get up and help himself to extra rounds. My mam frowns at him but he does it anyway.

Back at Whitley Bay, Dad learns to drive. He's learning to drive the van which used to hold Uncle John's sweep's brushes but now will be full of central heating equipment for the Advanced Heating Company. That will be the name of the company. The Advanced Heating Company.

Somehow Dad passes his test but he's not a good driver. We

18

children crouch in the back, almost fainting from the petrol fumes, and when he drives right into a roundabout instead of around it, there is panic. Kids and the loose battery and tools are bumping about all over the van.

'It's all right, don't panic,' yells my dad, laughing at us.

I expected Whitley Bay to be a soft sort of place after Heaton. After all, there's a woman here with bleached blond hair which she tints pink and trotting alongside her is a poodle with its hair the same shade of pink. Then next day you see them and they're blue. That just wouldn't happen in Heaton.

I've already been in a few fights in the playground at Ravenswood Juniors in Heaton. I don't look for fights but avoiding them is sissy. I expect that Whitley Bay's probably not the sort of place where boys fight much but on my very first day at school I'm proved wrong. My cousin John and I are challenged by a boy named Monkey. He is called Monkey for a very good reason. He looks like one. He doesn't have a tail but his ears stick out and this makes it easy to hold onto his ears and bang his head against the playground. He doesn't challenge us again. He knows we're hard.

Mam gets Dad to decorate our new house nicely. He's not earning any money while he's on his course, so maybe Granda's giving us some of the money from his pools win. The house is terraced but it's huge, with a room for Yvonne and one for the twins and one for me and Gary and one for Mam and Dad. It has a front garden with grass which no-one mows. Nan and Granda have the big front room and Granda and Dad make a bed that pulls down from the wall at night.

Next door is our living room, with a wall gas fire which Dad surrounds with plywood, made to look like real wood. This is where Mam hangs her horse brasses. Her brass collection makes birthday presents easier for us, except we can't afford real horse brasses. We get the gilt-covered plastic sort instead. She's very pleased, and hangs them up anyway. Mam and Dad's bed settee has been recovered in fashionable black leatherette. There's a new carpet with bright colours and bright wallpaper and Mam's pleased with it all.

Gary and I go to judo. I'm always last to be picked for the football team at school but now I've found out that I'm good at judo. I wear a white belt. Gary's not far behind me and we're picked on by Mr Campbell to give demonstrations to the class. The club goes to school fêtes and open days and soon we're asked to join in these demonstrations. Sometimes boys join the club because they've seen us demonstrating.

We practise at home, throwing each other onto the black leatherette

19

settee. One night we're walking home from the dojo down the back lane, joking and arguing, when over Gary's head in the black night sky I see a shooting star. It's winter and the sky's full of stars anyway but this star's spectacular. It doesn't twinkle, it blazes. All the other stars look pale as it crosses from one side of the universe to the other in a perfect, slow arc. I am open-mouthed at its beauty.

'Look!' I say to Gary. 'Shooting star!'

He laughs. 'Huh! You're not catching me out like that. I know there's no shooting star.'

I'm so busy staring, I can't even argue with him. When eventually it burns itself out, I'm still staring.

'Good acting,' says Gary, 'but it doesn't fool me.'

'It was amazing,' I tell him and he shrugs. I decide I'll always remember that shooting star. Already I look back at my time in Newcastle and there's lots of things I can't remember, little things like what pattern our bedroom wallpaper was. I commit the shooting star to memory.

The next time I'm in the back lane, something else happens. I notice a man hanging about. Hanging about in the back lane's not what men do. It runs along behind a high brick wall at the end of our yard and children play there and grown-ups park there, but men do not hang around there.

The man's coughing and shuffling. He's waiting for someone. 'Get lost, lad,' he tells me when he sees me. I pretend to saunter off but instead hide behind a car.

A minute or so later, someone else arrives. It's another man. They're both about my dad's age, or maybe a little younger.

The first one says, 'I didn't think you'd turn up.'

The second says, 'Well I'm here so let's get on with it.'

And to my amazement they start to fight. One kicks the other, who grabs his leg and almost immediately it seems they're locked in a frenzy of flying fists. They punch and kick and they're soon rolling on the ground, wrestling one another with a ferocity which shocks me. No opportunity is missed to aim a blow at the other's face or kick him in the knees or drag his head back by the hair. The speed of this fight is breathtaking.

I fight myself these days. With boys at school, with Gary, with my cousin John. I twist his toes and he kicks me but nothing we do is like this.

I forget that I'm supposed to be hiding and openly stare at the two men hammering each other. I know my dad fights. I'm scared to think of him fighting like this. I want to run out and tell them to stop but

I'm too frightened and, anyway, nothing will stop them until one of them wins.

I am unable to turn away, although their fight is making me feel sick and scared. Eventually one lies bleeding in the road. He has lost. The winner kicks him around a bit and then walks off. I stay behind the car, too scared to come out. The man lies in the road. Eventually he gets up and walks unsteadily away, in the same direction as the first man. There is a pool of blood in the back lane.

At home, I find Mam in the living room. She's sewing name-tags onto Yvonne's school uniform. There's a cigarette lying smoking in the ashtray with a ring of lipstick around it. She stands up to get her scissors and I do something I haven't done for years. I do it without stopping to think – if I think about it then I won't do it. I walk up to her and try to put my arms around her. I want her to cuddle me like she did when I was small, like she does the twins. Immediately, she pushes me away.

'Watch out for the scissors,' she says.

'Mam . . .' I try to hang on to her. But she shoves me harder. 'Come on, Frank, you're too old for that now,' she tells me.

I go upstairs. I don't tell her about the two men fighting but I tell Gary and I tell my girlfriend. She's at junior school with me. Her name is Rachel and she's very well-developed, so well-developed that some people think she must be fourteen. I buy her a Crunchie bar and a Bounty. These are posh chocolate bars with proper paper wrappers and I buy these to show her how I feel about her. We take our chocolate bars and walk for miles down the beach together. Rachel is introducing me to the facts of life. Some of the other girls at school have done the same but the way they set about things reminds me of the way the two fighters set to in the back lane. But Rachel's not like that.

At judo, I get my yellow belt.

Soon after this there's another fight in the back lane. No adults this time, just kids from our street. There are a lot of boys living here and some of them are hard. The hardest are probably the Stevensons. They're poorer than us and they're a big family like us and, like us, the last born after a big gap were twins. Joe Stevenson is about my age and once he put Domestos in his twin brothers' orange juice. They drank it and had to go to hospital. It shows how hard he is.

In the Stevensons' backyard there are nearly always rubber pants and stinking, dripping nappies hanging on the line which Mrs Stevenson puts there straight from soak. It makes you suspicious of eating anything at the Stevensons'. When they have a birthday party, there are banana sandwiches. We all think of what's hanging on the line outside and look at the sandwiches and then at each other and we say, 'No thank you, Mrs Stevenson.'

Today a small group of boys is fighting. I want the lad Joe Stevenson's fighting against to win so I kick Joe's head a few times. A few minutes later, Mam appears. Usually she's gentle but today she's angry. She says, 'Get in here, Frank, just get in here!'

Mam pulls me into our yard and I say, 'What's wrong? I'm not fighting!'

'Gary just came in and said you kicked Joe Stevenson.'

'Only a couple of times.'

'Well, don't! Just don't! His mother'll be round here for me! Do you want her to pull my bloody hair out?' I stare at Mam because she doesn't usually swear. She doesn't even say bloody, which is almost not swearing.

'That woman'll kick my face in! Do you want me to get my head kicked in? For heaven's sake, Frank, think before you go for one of the Stevenson boys.'

I see she's frightened and say I'll try never to punch a Stevenson. I know she's right about Mrs Stevenson. Most of the mothers in our road will continue the fights their children have started. That's one reason my mam isn't like the other women around here. She'd never start a fight or get into one but Mrs Stevenson's always doing it. She's a big, angry woman who says bloody all the time, and Mam is terrified of her. If Joe and I had a punch-up, Mrs Stevenson would certainly come round and drag Mam out by her hair and beat her up. It's also true that Joe's big brother would come round for me. You don't just fight a boy around here, you fight his whole family. Only the dads stay aloof. They have fights but these are different, more scary fights, usually away from home.

At judo, I get my orange belt.

My friend John volunteers us onto a course. It is called the Royal Marines Acquaint Course. We are going to join the marines for a weekend of adventure and fun. The only trouble is that you're supposed to be over fifteen and we're only eleven. However, the Royal Marines see how keen we are and decide to pretend we're fifteen.

The marines take us to Arbroath in Scotland where we roar around the bay in inflatable boats with big engines. We go to the ranges and shoot with big rifles. We watch films. We abseil down cliffs. The best thing of all is sliding down a rope from a clifftop on one leg, attached by a clip at our waists, with our arms held wide. The bigger boys flail about but John and I plunge recklessly down, our hands waving, into the arms of some big marines beneath us. By the end of the course, we have proved how hard we are. There is no question in our minds. We are going to join the marines.

Next time Gary and I go along to our judo class something is different. At first we don't know what it is. People aren't standing in their usual places and doing the usual things. We notice at once that Mr Campbell isn't there but we think he's just talking to a parent in the office or on the telephone or doing something grown-up. But we feel uneasy. We stand around, not getting changed the way we usually do.

A woman approaches. She's wearing a black belt.

'Have you heard the news, boys?' she says. We stare at her black belt and don't say anything.

'Mr Campbell. I'm afraid he's dead.'

We stop staring at her belt and look up at her face instead. She is trying to be kind but she's told a lot of people this news and maybe there was a softness the first time she said it but the softness has gone now.

'He was killed on his motorbike.'

Our friend and teacher Mr Campbell is dead. I try to imagine him lying in the road without breathing or moving or rolling, but I can't. Mr Campbell is a black belt who can get out of anything. If he falls off his motorbike he can roll. He knows how to roll. How can he be dead?

The woman is our new teacher. By the end of the lesson we've decided we don't like her. We go back next week but the week after we make an excuse to each other and miss the class. Without even talking about it, we give up judo.

I take my eleven-plus. I know how important it is to my mam that I pass. She wants all her children to go to grammar school and have a good education. Even my dad does some spelling tests with me. None of the words come up in the exams. When the results come through I am relieved that I have passed and Mam is pleased. Now I'll go to Whitley Bay Grammar with Yvonne, but first there is the long summer.

We all go to Scotland and when we come back Whitley Bay is teeming with holidaymakers. Gary and I hang around with our cousins including Jackie, my favourite cousin. She is pretty and John and I fight over her a bit.

We spend every day on the beach. We go snorkelling. Sometimes I catch lobsters with little hooks which I take home and put in the fridge.

'Ugh, it keeps waving its feelers at me!' shrieks Yvonne every time she opens the fridge. Finally Mam takes it to work in a plastic bag and the chef pays her £2, a pound for Mam and a pound for me.

Usually, I catch a plaice or two. I put on my fins, my mask and my snorkel and walk down the beach carrying a flattened dinner fork secured to the end of a long bamboo pole. The holidaymakers laugh at me but I ignore them and stride into the sea.

I know what I'm looking for. The plaice buries himself in the sand so well that only his eyes are visible. I snorkel along looking for eyes and when I see some I can usually discern the faint outline of the fish under the sand. I think, a-ha.

I have to move quickly because a plaice keeps perfectly still until you're almost upon it and then can just disappear at the last moment. Today I've lost one that way and I'm not going to lose another. I plunge my dinner fork into it rapidly, slip my hand beneath it and pull the flicking fish up to the surface. I spit out my snorkel and try to discern where in its big, amorphous shape its head is. Then I bite it, hard. A quick crunch kills it. I slip it into my trunks and swim on. By the end of the afternoon, I have three plaice to take home to Mam.

Trailing back from the beach, our plastic sandals gritty, our towels wet, and my plaice cold, we pass the church. There's nothing unusual about that, but today the door is open. Without discussing it, our group wanders into the churchyard and towards the door.

Gary and I are alarmed. We try to head the others off but the mood has seized everyone and they are now determined to go into the church. We follow. Inside, the atmosphere is cool and gloomy. Some of the others stretch out on pews. Gary and I stand in the doorway, one foot in the porch, so that we're not really in church. We watch Jackie march down the aisle towards the altar. There's some sort of silver cup up there and I stare in horror as she drinks from it. Jackie will put almost anything in her mouth, including worms. But I am sure this is holy water and that she is not supposed to touch it. I am relieved when we leave. Our family doesn't go in churches and religion is never discussed. It is a taboo subject. The Collinses are, emphatically, not religious. But somehow we know that the church is a powerful place. I know that my dad used to go, but that's because his family is Roman Catholic. I like to tell myself that Dad's not a Catholic any more but I've heard people say that if you're born Catholic you stay one for life. Probably this is why we don't have religion in our family.

Dad and Uncle John have been in business for a few years now. Dad went on the central heating course and said he didn't learn anything. I can imagine Dad telling the instructors how to install central heating. Then he and Uncle John started advertising and going out on jobs. They install microbore heating. This is a revolutionary system which consists of a network of thin, cable-like pipes.

Uncle John and Auntie June have a cat called Lulu. She is a small tortoiseshell, much loved by our cousins John and Alwyn, but she is no ordinary cat. She is practically a partner in the heating business. Dad and Uncle John take Lulu to people's houses and attach a string to her collar. They take up a floorboard and shove Lulu down into the underworld below the floor. Then they pull up a floorboard on the other side of the room and call Lulu. She crosses the underworld and sneaks out, threading a piece of string where the pipe will be installed. All Dad and Uncle John have to do is feed it through.

I have seen Lulu at work and I think she is a brilliant cat and that it was a clever idea to use her. I wonder if this is what they learned on their course. But I am worried that Dad's income rests on Lulu's furry paws. I have a suspicion that the Advanced Heating Company isn't using advanced methods.

Unfortunately, some of the customers have found that microbore is not so revolutionary as promised. The way Dad and Uncle John install them, the pipes tend to whistle noisily. Some people have called Dad and Uncle John back but there is nothing they can do about the noise.

Occasionally this summer, cousin John and I accompany our fathers on jobs. I like watching Dad work in the morning but, as soon as it's twelve o'clock, he puts down his tools and goes to the pub. I see how much this annoys Uncle John, who works on with us.

We take a short break and then continue working hard until the lady of the house brings us a tea tray. We're crouching on the bare floorboards over the tray when Dad comes in.

Uncle John and John and me and Lulu all look up at Dad but we don't say anything. Uncle John especially doesn't say anything. We know Dad has probably downed ten pints: he doesn't expect to drink less than eight at lunchtime. But he is not drunk. He does not slur his words or stagger and he never, ever swears. I have never seen him do the sort of things drunks on TV do but I know he has been drinking because his eyes are different. Also, he's talkative. He tells us about the horses he backed and the winner and how it was a terrible shame another was withdrawn before the race. We watch him in silence.

Dad picks up a hammer and nails. He is going to do a skirting board. I remember how, when we lived in Newcastle, he made and fitted the missing piece of skirting board so well that it seemed like a work of art. That must have been in the morning. Now it's afternoon and he doesn't care. His elbows fly and sometimes the hammer misses the nail and when the skirting board is in place it doesn't look right.

He prepares to drill a hole through a joist. He explains to me and John that one of the rules of joinery is that you never, ever put a wood-boring bit into a power drill.

'Why not, Dad?' I ask.

'Because it bores,' he says.

I catch sight of John and Uncle John exchanging glances. The glances say that my dad had ten pints at lunchtime.

'Now, you don't ever do this, but I'm going to,' he tells me. 'You couldn't hold it, it'd run away with you. But I'll be all right.'

He plugs in the power drill and switches it on. Woosh. The drill has turned into a frenzied beast. Dad is wrestling with it but it's defeating him, whirling round and round and round. Suddenly the power lead snaps and there's a big flash. Then everything in the room is still and silent. We all look at Dad except for Lulu who is hiding behind John and has smashed one of the lady's tea cups in her terror.

'See,' says Dad, 'I told you never, ever to do that.'

Uncle John still doesn't say anything but by now there's tension in the room and everyone can feel it, perhaps even including my dad.

Sometimes I envy my cousin John his dad. Uncle John intervenes in our disputes and he always backs John and Alwyn. Dad never backs us. He just tells us to sort out our quarrels. And Uncle John looks the way a dad's supposed to. I know because sometimes we all go to the new heated indoor swimming baths on a Sunday morning and Uncle John is big and handsome and hairy-chested the way a dad should be. Our dad is small and pale and bony and there's no hair on him anywhere. And Uncle John likes beautiful things. He tells me how much he likes the mountains and the sea and all sorts of things that Dad's never even thought about. Uncle John really wants the Advanced Heating Company to work. He doesn't want to go back to chimney sweeping.

I look at my dad now, fumbling away with his tools, dropping nails, trying to joke with Uncle John, some joke about the horses which Uncle John isn't laughing at, and I love him very much. But I decide not to go out on any more jobs with him.

I'm not surprised to learn, a few months later, that Uncle John and Dad have had a big row and that their business is over. Uncle John is not speaking to Dad, he has vowed never to speak to him again. I don't learn this from Dad or from Mam but from cousin John. He's careful how he tells me and I feel he's not telling me everything. I nod and don't ask any questions. I wonder if Mam and Auntie June will still be best friends.

# 3

I AM BORED AT WHITLEY BAY GRAMMAR. NOT BORED BECAUSE I'M SO clever but because none of it's interesting. At first I am good at Maths and English and Biology but after a while Maths and English aren't interesting either. That leaves Biology. We have a lot of homework and I often don't do it. I mean to and sometimes I get my books out in front of the television but very often the homework just doesn't get done and I go to school anxious about it.

Mam and Dad are always out in the evenings now. Dad is at the pub. Mam's at the pub too but in a different sort of way and at a different sort of pub. She works in a posh seafront hotel with carpets where men sometimes wear ties and are polite to the bar staff. It's not the sort of place Dad goes to. Yvonne says it's funny that Dad's on one side of the bar spending it as fast as Mam can make it on the other side. But Dad works sometimes too. He gets jobs on building sites as a carpenter. They never last long.

Outside school, life is more interesting. I have joined the Army Cadet Force. We meet in an old, round-roofed, corrugated iron hut on Monday evenings. We wear Second World War uniforms: woollen battledress with blouson tops. I think I look like the hero of some old black and white movie. I wonder if their uniforms itched like ours do. When we do tactics on the old railway line we have to tie our legs in with pieces of string above and below the knee, so that they don't rustle and reveal our position to the enemy. Sergeant Major McFarlane shows us how and says they did it in the war. It still seems silly to us.

The hut has an armoury and we're given old Lee-Enfield .303 rifles which are so heavy and have such a kick that we use our berets to protect our shoulders when we fire them. Our targets are made of wood but shaped like men.

I am quite a good shot but I am not quiet and respectful the way Sergeant Major McFarlane likes us to be. I know, without him telling me, that he does not think I'm army material. I am too cocky. Whenever we do section battle drills and are told to move up on the enemy in a group, I can always think of better ways to do it, and do it alone, sneaking from bush to bush. Sergeant Major McFarlane, who is working from a manual, does not appreciate my contribution. Some of the lads with rank don't like me either. A lance corporal reports me for cheekiness.

We do drill for about half an hour whenever we meet.

'Squaaaaaad!'

We brace up. Stomach in, chest out, shoulders back, head up. I am barrel-chested, which exaggerates the pose.

'Squaaaaaad . . . 'Shun!'

Up comes the left leg until the thigh is parallel to the ground, and then down, hard. We are shown how to drive our left foot into the floor. Hands to sides, look forward.

'Riiiiiiiight turn!'

To the count of one-two-three-one we pivot on the ball of the left foot and the heel of the right.

'By the left! Quiiiiiiiiiick march!'

Left foot forward, right arm forward, left arm back. Hands to shoulder height, thumb out . . . we freeze in the first position and our positions are checked.

Painfully, raggedly, we learn drill and take to the streets. One day we march past Gary and one of his pals. They shout something but I don't look at them.

I'm good at drill. But, unlike some of my friends, I am not promoted.

The ACF organizes a trip to Minden in Germany. Mam scrapes and saves so that I can go. Last year she saved and saved for Gary's school trip to Belgium, this year it's my turn. It will be my first trip abroad. We're going to stay with the Green Howards and Mam buys me cord trousers and a matching cord jacket to wear when I'm out of uniform. I wish it was denim but Mam won't let me wear denims, she thinks they look rough.

Mam has also given me a wallet. I've never had a wallet before, let alone one with £18 in it.

One other boy's going from the Whitley Bay ACF and we wait outside the army hut early in the morning for the coach to come for us. I wait in my new clothes, with my wallet tucked into my coat pocket, knowing it contains £18. I feel grown-up. Eighteen pounds is more than a lot of soldiers earn in a week. I know this because at the cadets' hall there is a recruiting poster which tells you that you can earn £17 a week if you join the army, or £19 if you stay for nine years. So I am standing outside the hut thinking that I am a soldier with a week's wages in my pocket and forgetting that I am only twelve years old.

We take the boat to the Continent and then there's another long coach drive. When we arrive we are shown into a real barracks where we fall asleep. The next morning there is breakfast in the NAAFI and later, much later, I remember my wallet. I have no recollection of seeing it after breakfast, when I shuffled it around on the table wondering where in my uniform to put it.

I realize that I must have walked out of the room without it. For all my pretending to be a grown-up, the truth is that I'm not used to carrying a wallet around with me.

I go back to look, and of course there is no sign of the wallet or the £18. I am shocked and tearful. However, I know that big boys don't cry. The last thing I am going to do is shed tears in front of all the hard soldiers in Minden. We go out with them on exercises in armoured personnel carriers, and they show us their rations and all the things soldiers do. I should love every minute of this. But I spend the whole week wanting to cry. I have a lump in my throat for the next six days. I keep remembering how hard my mam worked to earn me that £18.

Without money, I'm left out of a lot of the activities. The other boy from Whitley Bay is a well-off lad who always looks smart. He says I can go out into town with him but all I can do is watch him buying things in the shops. I remember that when Gary went to Belgium he came back with a little souvenir for everyone. Then the boy has a drink and something to eat and I watch him devour it.

The Green Howards take pity on me. They see I'm left alone in the barracks in the evening.

'Come on, mate,' say a few of them. 'We can't have you sitting in there by yourself all night, come and have a beer with us.'

They take me to the bar and buy me beer. They are very kind and think the best way to console me is to share their primary interest with me. This is pornography. There are movies and magazines.

'Seen this, mate?' they say. 'Take a look at this.'

What they show me turns my face bright red. At first I am

29

fascinated and excited by it. The shamelessness of those healthy bodies and smiling faces is thrilling. All my life I've been told to cover up. My dad shyly hides his pale, pasty body behind his towel as long as he can at the swimming baths. And here are people enjoying, even revelling in, their own nakedness. I wish I could study the pictures, some of which are in remarkable anatomical detail, but I know I'm on trial. The men are watching me. They show me progressively more hard-core pornography until I'd like to ask them to stop. But of course, I can't admit that I don't like it. I try to look relaxed but it's difficult not to be shocked. I remember the word obscene. Now I understand it. This is obscene. It's like a circus but without the joy or humour. I try to look cool in my grown-up cord jacket. Seen it all before. But I haven't, and I don't want to. If only some of my pals were here and we could just laugh about it, everything would be all right. But I am alone with these men and, although their intentions are kind, I feel as if this is some horrible test.

The soldiers say, 'Get the kid a pint. We don't know who nicked your wallet, mate, but it wasn't us.'

They are nice and I try to smile at them.

When I get home my brothers and sisters crowd round me, behind them my grandparents, and behind them, hardly visible, is Mam.

'What did you bring us?' says Gary.

I know now that after not crying for a whole week I will have to give in to the tears and I run upstairs without replying. I can hear the silence in the hallway when I've gone. I throw myself on the big double bed I share with Gary and cry at last. The door opens and it's Mam. She sits on the bed and looks at me. I wish she'd put an arm around me but she doesn't. I know that Geordie boys don't cry, I know that, but it's a while before I can stop.

'What is it, pet lamb?'

I tell her about the money and she says, couldn't I have phoned home? I know that she'd have done anything to get me more money. And I know how she saved long and hard for the first lot and how it was gone in one careless instant.

'What about the other lad from Whitley Bay, he must have had some money?'

'It was his money.'

'Why didn't you ask him to loan you some?'

'I couldn't.'

'Why not?'

'He could have offered.'

30

'Perhaps he was waiting for you to ask.'

'Well, we'd have had to pay it back, Mam.'

'We'd have managed. You shouldn't have been too proud to ask him, pet lamb.'

I lie sniffing on my bed trying to avoid thinking about this. Later I go down and the others are nice to me and don't mention that I haven't brought any souvenirs back.

When Remembrance Sunday comes around, the cadet force tells us we have to go to church in our battledress uniform. After the service we'll march to the cenotaph on the seafront for the wreath-laying ceremony. I hear this news and know that I cannot possibly go to the church service. This is something that the Collins family don't do, except for weddings and funerals, and even then they look uncomfortable.

I tell the boss, Captain Cole, that I don't go to church. He stares at me and then says that, on this occasion, I'll be going. I say that I didn't join the army cadets to go to church and he tells me that this is a Church parade and I am expected to go.

On Sunday I head for the church but I don't go inside. I don't wear my uniform. When the other boys come out to march to the seafront, I walk beside them, laughing, mocking and pointing. They arrive at the cenotaph and stand to attention and I giggle and make silly comments. I know this is foolish. I know that Sergeant Major McFarlane has seen me. And I know I should be there with the other boys, looking smart and serious in my uniform.

The 'Last Post' is played. A haunting sound. The notes hover around the cenotaph, held in the still, foggy November air. The sea is crashing quietly behind us and the sad melody seems to drift out towards it. I am moved by the music, by the solemnity of the occasion, by the old man who stands upright at the back of the onlookers with tears running down his cheeks. I slink away before the ceremony is over.

The next day we meet at the iron hut as usual. The sergeant major marches me into the captain's office where I stand to attention. Captain Cole is a young man with a moustache. He tells me my behaviour yesterday was unacceptable. What do I have to say for myself?

I know the two men are angry with me. I look at their faces, one lined and troubled, the other fresher, with a colder anger. I look at them both and open my mouth to speak but instead of words what comes is my old enemy, laughter. It bubbles up within me but, after a fight, I somehow manage to restrain it. However, nothing, nothing,

31

will stop my face from contorting itself into something which I know to be half-smirk, half-smile.

Both men visibly redden. The old sergeant major's face starts to swell. They were probably intending to let me escape with a ticking-off but my response is escalating the situation. I want to explain that I can't help it, I always laugh when people are angry with me. But I can't explain because I know that if I open my mouth I'll giggle.

'Well? What have you got to say for yourself? Your behaviour is absolutely unacceptable, it's a disgrace and all you can do is —'

This does it. I know that if I work hard I can usually wipe the smile off my face but not when I'm standing to attention, not when people are as angry as these two men. It's going to happen. I wrestle but finally I give in. My laughter arrives with a force that cannot be contained. It escapes. I laugh and laugh into an awful silence. The two men are now both bright red, their faces bulging, fury glittering in their eyes.

When I pause for breath the captain says, 'Collins, you're meant to be a soldier but you're not behaving like a soldier. It's time for you to reconsider your position in the Army Cadet Force.'

I never go back. I know that if I want to I can, all I have to do is apologize, but I no longer want to. They phone to tell me to bring my uniform back if I'm not coming to parade. I don't do either. Finally Sergeant Major McFarlane calls at the house. I feel hot with embarrassment as Mam runs around finding bits of uniform for him.

Granda has a car accident. Someone runs into the side of the old Standard Eight and Granda is very shaken. He's taken to hospital for an X-ray where he is told that, although there are no ill effects from the accident, he has lung cancer. He seemed well enough until now but, as soon as he's told he's ill, he becomes ill. Day by day, he starts to wither before our eyes.

Dad has a new job. He's stopped looking for carpentry work because of his hips and gone on the sick instead. But he has a job in the evenings now and it's a good job for a hard man like Dad because he can drink and fight while he works. He's a bouncer at a nightclub in town.

In the day he sleeps until the pubs open and then he goes out with his pencil behind his ear and the *Sun* under his arm. When he gets there he drinks his pints and does his crossword and picks out today's winners. He's very successful on the horses. We older children see little of him but he sometimes spends time with the twins. He talks to them and plays with them like an indulgent grand-father. Michael in particular dotes on him. Michael's big and slow,

Michelle's small and quick. Dad's intimacy with them makes me a little jealous because it's what I always wanted. I've begun to realize that now it's too late.

Yvonne and Gary and me all have to get ourselves up and ready for school. Mam and Dad have to sleep in because they're working all evening. Nan and Granda are awake (we know because we can hear Granda coughing and coughing in the front room) but they don't come out. It's cold and grey and cheerless early in the morning and we move round slowly. I can hear Yvonne in the bathroom. Gary's still in bed. There's a system of regular kicks and thumps which I give him to get him out of bed.

I'm first downstairs and so I'm first to smell the burning. It's not like burning toast, it's a strange dry, metallic smell. It's like an experiment in the chemistry lab. I pass Dad, slumped asleep in the armchair by the boiler. He's supposed to fill the boiler with coke at night but he's forgotten and it's gone out. I rush past him to the kitchen where the kettle's making a strange new sound, an off-key version of its usual whistle.

Beneath it, the gas flame burns. There is no water in the kettle, in fact, there is hardly a kettle at all. It is half burnt away like a face in a horror movie. I turn off the stove without touching it.

When I turn back to Dad I see that his face is covered in blood. He is in a deep and drunken slumber and I can't wake him. It is clear he came in last night, put the kettle on the stove and then fell asleep.

The others come down and stare at Dad. The blood is coming from his nose. His mouth, which is slightly open, is smeared with blood. He probably has less hair than he used to, and it's probably greyer. Is he smaller? He's very old. He's practically retired, now he's given up his day job to go on the sick. He's almost forty.

Michael comes downstairs and starts to cry when he sees Dad's bloody face. I tell him he should be proud of Dad for being such a hard fighter.

'If Dad looks this bad, imagine what the other bloke looked like!' I say. 'There must have been six of them and I bet they all came off worse.'

Michael still runs, sobbing, up to Mam. I follow him to explain. At first Mam can hardly open her eyes. She says something comforting to Michael. She's wishing he'd go away. She murmurs nothing in particular because she's really asleep. Finally I say, loud and clear, 'Mam, Dad's downstairs with blood all over his face.'

She opens her eyes.

'There's a lot of blood but he's not too bad really.'

'What's he doing?'

'Asleep. He's been in a fight.'

Mam yawns but says nothing. She's never said anything bad to us about Dad. But lately there have been arguments in our house and a coldness between Mam and Dad that wasn't there before.

Michael whines again and Mam pulls the covers and swings her legs out of bed. She puts an arm around Michael.

'Don't worry, we'll soon put him right,' she says.

Yvonne's already left and my friend Daniel's waiting by the front door for me.

Whitley Bay Grammar is a huge, mixed school. It's almost new, made of glass and concrete. I approach it each morning without interest or enthusiasm. I assume that in September Gary will come here too, but early in the summer something happens that upsets my mam a lot. Gary fails his eleven-plus. Mam cries and cries and before long Gary and Yvonne are also in tears. We have a failure in the family. He'll go to the secondary modern which is just a footpath away from the grammar. It's a bigger, rougher school. There are boys in our road who are obviously destined for the secondary modern, like the Stevensons, but Mam doesn't expect us to fail.

'Look, it's not so bad. There's nothing so great about the grammar school,' I tell Gary. But I know that I wouldn't like to go to the secondary modern. Boys from the two schools beat each other up constantly. If it snows, a snowball fight is guaranteed. The boys there are hard fighters. At junior school I could beat up anyone who hurt Gary, and in the road I still do. But at the new school he'll be on his own.

I'm a hard fighter myself. I'm in a gang which is led by Robbie next door, and Robbie's hard. He has a lot of big brothers and one of them went into the army. That's hard. Then he absconded from the army and the police came for him. That's very hard. You can't get much harder than that. He's our hero.

As Robbie graduates from the gang to the pub, I take over as leader. There are sometimes more than ten of us: me, Gary, Adrian across the road, a couple of Australians who are good fighters, a girl called Marilyn who has long hair but fights like a boy, two new lads who moved into the road and put up a good show when I started a punch-up, my best friend Daniel from school, and two of the Stevenson boys, Joe and Jason.

There are two types of gangs, skins and hairies. We are hairies. This is because we are an old-established gang, inherited from the elder Stevenson brothers and Robbie next door and his big brothers. Skins are newer. We wear flares and denim jackets and never cut our hair shorter than shoulder length. Skinheads have hair which is about a quarter of an inch long. They wear stay-pressed trousers and big oxblood-red boots and braces. A lot of the hard lads from the mining areas outside Whitley Bay have become skins. People who are in, for example, the Boys' Brigade, have to be skins because they have short hair anyway. The Boys' Brigade stay at the end of our road and march around playing the pipes on Sunday morning. We go the long way round to avoid them or they give us a hard time. They shout, 'Hey, girl! Come over here!' and we have to choose whether to ignore them or fight.

As leader of the gang I decide what we're going to do that day. The others have to follow me. If Adrian says, 'Let's go down to the beach,' then everyone says, 'Well, you go on, then.' But if I say we're going to the beach, we go. That's how gangs are run.

We have a variety of activities. We like knives. I have a throwing knife, double-edged and very flat-bladed. Between the back lane and our yard is a high door in the wall and we chuck our knives at it. It's covered in slash marks. Anyone walking down the back lane can tell that someone hard must live here.

We take up archery. This is expensive, so we have to steal from our parents. Adrian manages to net astonishing amounts, £20 a time. I don't much like to steal from Mam but my conscience gets the better of me: I can't let Adrian do all the thieving. Gary and I take money from Mam's purse but we make sure it's just the odd one-pound note.

We buy proper steel-tipped arrows and bows and take the bus to the seafront near the lighthouse. We stand in a circle on the beach. One by one, we fire our arrows high into the air. Twang. Pause. Wait. The arrows are supposed to fall in the centre of the circle but of course they rarely do. We all know they could fall on us. This is a game of bravery. No matter how close an arrow falls, you can't move or flinch. I wonder just what would happen if an arrow lands on someone. I suspect it would go straight down through the middle of their head. Probably they would die. This makes the game exciting. It is thrilling to feel an arrow whistle past you, almost skimming your arms or your head. No-one ever gets hit so I never find out how deadly our arrows are.

We also enjoy playing chicken with knives. One of us stands in the doorway and the others throw knives to see how close they can get without hitting them. And we spray one another with lighter fuel and then flick lighted matches around. All these games are supposed to be dangerous but none of us is ever hurt.

My friend Dan doesn't like fighting much. Now we're in our teens he's suddenly grown into his new nickname, Six Foot. He's a gentle giant, not a fighter or a drunk. But once you're in a gang, fighting is inevitable. When I was in the army cadets there was always a fight if we bumped into the sea cadets. Well, now I'm a hairy and there's a fight if we bump into skins. This can occur anywhere. If you go near an amusement arcade on the seafront, you're likely to end up in a fight because they're always full of skins. In Edinburgh week or Glasgow fortnight we don't venture out much because Whitley Bay's teeming with very tough Scottish skins. But when we go to the disco at the YMCA on Friday nights, we get the sort of fight we can deal with.

First we go and buy a bottle of Scotch from an off-licence which is run by a pair of elderly brothers who we know will sell us anything. We pass the bottle round, swigging at it. It tastes disgusting but we have to drink it. We're not very drunk, just drunk enough to deal with the disco. Sometimes we get Tartan beer but it doesn't do the business so well or so quickly.

Inside the disco, the music's playing. The hairies are Rolling Stones fans and the skins like reggae music. When one of our songs comes on we throw ourselves around like Mick Jagger. Then it's their turn to posture to 'Johnny Reggae'. They stick their thumbs in their braces and move with compressed energy.

Before long, gangs are mixing and there are a few punches being thrown on the dance floor. Of course, there are girls in the disco, and sometimes they come up and dance with us, but the disco is about boys, not girls.

A gang of skins on bikes grabs Gary when he's walking along by himself. They pick on him because he's got long hair and they really knock him around, breaking his nose and blacking his eyes. Gary arrives home in tears and within minutes our gang is out looking for them. We don't find them but our pack instinct is running high and so we grab a pair of kids on bikes with shortish hair.

Gary says, 'Er . . . I don't think that's them . . .' but by now we don't care. We get the two surprised kids off their bikes and give them a duffing over until our pack instinct is satisfied.

One thing I do not do is smoke. Neither does Yvonne and neither does Gary. No-one's told us not to. We only have to look at our parents, at the overflowing ashtrays, the cigarette ends, the fug in every room. There's a smell of cigarettes on everyone's clothes and in their hair. Sometimes it seems to me that we're the only kids in our road who don't smoke but nothing will induce me even to try a cigarette.

The beach gives us space and freedom. In the school holidays we roam for miles along the seafront trying to look hard, although we are often accompanied by Auntie Mary's poodle, Lindy. Poodles are certainly not hard dogs. But we're fond of Lindy so we take her along anyway.

There are gangs of kids on bikes at the beach. I still desperately want a bike. I haven't ridden one since we were in Scotland and we haven't been to the cottage there for years, not since Uncle John and Dad fell out. I know there's no point asking for a bike now. Dad still doesn't approve of second-hand ones and money's too tight to buy a new one. I know money's tight because the bank manager calls a lot. Sometimes in the evening, before the pubs are open, there's a knock at the door. Mam and Dad always seem to know who it is without looking. As soon as the doorbell goes, the whole house changes. Mam's rushing around getting ready for work, Nan's ironing, Dad's lying in the armchair. The twins and Gary are playing with Gary's pet rat. Yvonne's combing her hair. I'm working on my balsa-wood aeroplane. Then the doorbell goes and everything stops.

There's a long pause. Everyone's waiting for someone else to do something about the doorbell.

'You answer it,' Dad tells Yvonne at last.

But Yvonne's talked to the bank manager before and she shakes her head.

'I'm not going,' she says.

Mam looks at me and reluctantly, very reluctantly, I get up. The doorbell goes again. Dad doesn't move.

'Tell him your dad's not here,' says Mam. I can see by the look on her face that she's upset. My mam doesn't like telling lies but she doesn't like the bank manager either.

I go to the door and open it. I know what I have to say. My dad's not here. I open my mouth to speak but the bank manager talks first. He's tall and white-haired and he wears an overcoat. 'Hello, lad. Is your dad home?'

'My dad's not here,' I say quickly, too quickly, almost before he's finished the question.

He gives me a long, hard look. He has piercing blue eyes and he knows I have told a lie simply by looking at me. He frowns. He is not pleased. I look away.

'Not home, did you say?'

He's glaring at me now, his brows are close together and his eyes are wider than before. I'm scared of his anger but I stick to my story.

'I said, my dad's not here.'

Behind me is silence. Not a peep from anyone. Not a squeak from the twins. I know everyone is listening.

'I see. Your dad's not here. How about your mam?'

This is a difficult one. I know Mam won't want me to lie about her and that she'll come to the door if I fetch her. But I don't want her to have to face this man. I know that he's come for something we don't have.

'She's not here either.'

'Both out, eh?'

His voice is raised, a cross between angry and humorous. It is threatening. I am scared.

'Mam's not here.'

'I see. Well, when do you think your dad will be home?'

This is a tricky one, as Dad's sitting a few feet away from me. I pause. I can't think of any answer. I just wish that Dad would get up and come to the door. I don't want to stand here answering questions and telling lies. I can't think of any lie to tell. All the time the bank manager is watching my face closely. He can tell I'm trying to lie and the more he watches me the harder it is.

'I don't know,' I say at last. It's a lame answer but the safest.

'Well, when does he usually get home?'

Again, I'm floundering.

'Well . . .'

Suddenly Mam is by my side.

'Hello, Mr Reynolds!' she says brightly. I wonder if Mr Reynolds knows her well enough to recognize the lines of worry and misery which are suddenly criss-crossed all over her face.

'Mrs Collins! Young lad here said you weren't in!'

'I've just come in the back way from next door . . . What can I do for you, Mr Reynolds?'

She sounds so bright and confident. That's the way she talks to the customers behind the bar in her posh hotel.

'I'm looking for your husband, Mrs Collins.'

'Oooh, I'm afraid he's not here just now, Mr Reynolds.'

This is an elaborate dance. They both know Dad's in.

'That's a shame. When do you think he might be back?'

'I'm not sure but it probably won't be until late.'

'I see. Well, I'll call again later in the week. Maybe tomorrow?'

'Tomorrow might not be a good day . . .'

'Thursday then. I'll be back on Thursday.'

He's already backing away down the path. I feel that Mam has won a victory. Until Thursday.

'Right you are, Mr Reynolds.'

'Will you tell him I'll be here on Thursday?'

'I'll be sure to tell him.'

When Mam shuts the door we stand for a few moments looking at each other.

'Mam, who is Mr Reynolds?'

'Nobody really . . .'

'Well if he's no-one, why won't Dad speak to him?'

'He's from the bank and your dad doesn't want to speak to him.'

I knew it. He's from the bank. He's certainly the bank manager. That's what bank managers are like, big and scary and white-haired, and they know when you're lying.

'Mam—'

But I've asked too many questions.

'Go and see your Granda, Frank,' Mam tells me. 'Take your balsa-wood plane in to show him.'

I make a face at her. It's too much to be asked to lie to the bank manager and to visit Granda all in the space of a few minutes. I know she's said it just to stop me asking questions.

'It's a smashing plane and he'd like to see it,' she tells me.

I fetch the plane and take it to the front room. Granda's lying in his bed. There's a smell in the room that was never here before. It's not unpleasant, but I don't like it. There are rows of pills and medicines on one shelf. And there's a humming noise from the corner. It's the machine which gradually inflates different parts of the bed so that Granda doesn't get bedsores. It happens so slowly that you can't see it. We all try to see the mattress inflating when we visit Granda but there's only the hum of the machine.

'I brought you the plane I've been making. It's almost finished,' I tell him.

He looks at me but he does not speak. He's so small and grey and shrivelled now that I want to cry. I sit down on the chair by the bed.

'Look, Granda . . .' I hand him the plane and he holds it, but he still doesn't say anything.

'See, I cut the frame out of balsa wood and then I covered it with tissue paper. It tore a bit there, just under your finger, but I've covered it with dope to harden it off . . .'

Granda looks down at the plane without blinking.

'It's a Lysander. They used them in the war to drop agents

39

behind enemy lines. It'll carry three people at most, see . . .'

Granda continues to stare at the plane. He does not speak or respond in any way. Is this what a person is like when they're dead? He's not dead but in a way he's already gone.

Suddenly, and without warning, I'm scared. The gas fire's on and the room is very warm but I want to shiver. I find myself fighting back tears. The world seems bleak. I remember Sunday mornings when Nan and Granda lived at Wallsend. We'd go into their room first thing and bounce on the bed. Their bed was a friendly place then, with an orange candlewick bedspread and Granda's knees somewhere beneath it just waiting to be bounced on. And now, this is Granda's bed. It has an old, uncomprehending man in it and that man claims to be Granda.

We sit in silence, Granda clutching my plane so hard that I'm scared he'll break it.

Nan comes bustling in. She can see I'm upset.

'It's all right,' she says, and gently she takes the plane away from Granda. He lets her unwrap his fingers just like a child.

'Bye, Granda,' I say. It's a relief to leave that room. I realize that smell is the smell of death.

I join the others. They are having tea. Nothing is said about the bank manager. I wonder whose turn it will be to answer the door to him on Thursday.

It's hard not to feel miserable. Apart from the bank manager and Granda, the start of term is imminent. Once school starts, I pretend to be sick. I often do this and whatever my mother thinks about it she always lets me stay home.

I am lying on the bed-settee when Dad appears. Mam's busy making sausage sandwiches for lunch.

'What's that boy doing home from school?' are his first words.

'He's ill.'

'What's wrong with him then?'

'He's got a bad stomach.'

'If he's got a bad stomach he won't be eating a sausage sandwich, will he?'

'He has to eat.'

'Well if he's well enough to eat that, he's well enough to go to school.'

And despite the sound of the sizzling and the delicious smell, I say, 'I don't want a sausage sandwich.'

'Oh no,' Dad tells me, 'you've asked for it and your mam's made it and you have to eat it now.'

Dad always makes us eat everything on our plates. We even have to chew our way through gristle, which is impossible and means we end up swallowing it whole.

'Dad, I don't want a sausage sandwich.'

'You'll eat it and you'll eat every bit of it.'

By the time it arrives I really don't want the sandwich but with Dad standing over me I know I have to chomp through it somehow. When he wanders out for a minute, Mam hands me a piece of paper.

'Spit it out, quick,' she hisses. I'm in the process of doing this when Dad comes back in.

'He's to eat it, all of it!' he roars. When I've finished he grins at me.

'There now, if you can eat all that you're well enough to get yourself to school,' he says.

Before half-term it's my best friend Daniel's birthday. I go over to his house and find his parents have given him just what I've always wanted. A Claude Butler racing bike. It's second-hand but beautiful. It means I have to walk to school alone now, because Dan rides. Sometimes he sees me and gets off his bike to walk.

A few months later, on Christmas Day, he invites me over. His parents have given him another Claude Butler racing bike, and this time it's absolutely brand new. I can't understand why anyone would want two bikes. The new one is a metallic turquoise with five gears. It is quite simply the loveliest bike I have ever seen. When I've examined it all over and pronounced it the best, he points over at his old bike. He says, 'This one's for you.'

It takes me a few minutes to realize that he's giving me a Claude Butler racing bike. Of course, it's not Dan, it's his parents who're really giving it. They've understood that Daniel isn't going to enjoy riding his bike unless his friend Frank's got one too. From now on we cycle to school together on our beautiful machines. We leave them in the bike sheds, Dan's locked and mine next to it. This lasts a few months. Then I come out of school to find that my bike is missing. I assume someone's just messing me around and walk all the way home looking for it but there's no sign of it. I realize with a heavy heart that my bike's been stolen. I tell the police. Nothing happens. So it's back to Dan riding and me walking to school.

There's a sale room a few blocks from home where weekly junk auctions are held and in there I catch sight of a bicycle. It's a tatty old racing bike with strange wheels, weird tyres and a grotty leather saddle bag. It's a mess but you can see it's a nice bike underneath.

I take Dan in to see it. He squats down on one knee and peers at it all over.

'Tubs!' he says with approval in his voice. 'And Sprints!'

'What's that?'

Daniel has joined a cycling club. He goes out with them every Sunday and he's learned a thing or two about bikes.

'Tubular tyres and Sprint alloy wheels! They're the business. And Mercians are very good bikes.'

I tell Dad about the bike and he immediately trots out the story about Uncle David having his cycling accident on a second-hand bike.

'No,' he concludes, 'I'll never buy a second-hand one, you don't know their history.'

I persuade him simply to look at the bike. I'm surprised when he agrees to come to the sale just to see who buys it. The auctioneer opens the bidding, someone waves a hand and then, to my amazement, Dad joins in. He just straightaway puts another 50p on the top. I turn to look at him in surprise and admiration. The bidding continues, Dad barely nodding to the auctioneer as if he's been doing this all his life. In a way he has, because this is just how he signals to the barmaid that it's time to refill his glass.

I am proud and excited. I am red in the face by the time the price has risen to £4.50, that's four pounds ten shillings in old money. The other man withdraws and the bike is ours.

Dad pays and I'm allowed to wheel the bike away. It is mine. He told me I could have a bike five years ago and now, at last, tomorrow's here.

Dad says, 'Now, it's up to you to sort it out and get it on the road.'

Daniel and I take the bike home. We strip it and study it and use his bike as a model and by the time we've put it back together there's not much we don't know about bikes. We spray it with yellow lacquer paint, which doesn't work too well, so we spray it again. I love my bike. I wipe the mud off it and check the valves and adjust it and keep it in one of the outhouses at the end of the yard. It's the bike my dad bought me.

Despite my early experiences on the beach with girls, I don't have many girlfriends at Whitley Bay Grammar. The honest truth is that girls are scary. You have girlfriends for school trips or to walk home with or even to experiment with, but greater intimacy terrifies me.

One girl in particular makes her interest in me clear. She has very hairy legs. The thought of those hairy legs appals me and I avoid her. To spite me, she selects another boy in the class and goes off with him into the nearby fields at lunchtime where she provides services that every teenage boy dreams about. The boy is thrilled and his lunch-

42

hours are the subject of much discussion. But if ever I start to feel I've made a mistake, I just think of her hairy legs.

Granda is very ill now and we have to be quiet around the house. He lies in the front room on the inflating bed and the room is filled with the sound of the machine and his laboured breathing. We don't want to go in and see him but we're told to. We put our hands into his hands. Ours are full and fleshy. His have shrivelled to bone. He lies in silence, holding us. We're embarrassed.

It's the weekend and we're all having our lunch. My grandmother comes in and it's clear she's very upset. No words are spoken. Mam looks at Dad and he gets up and goes out with Nan. We are silent, all of us, including the twins. We hear them going to the front room and a few minutes later they return. Dad sits down gravely. We look at him but he says nothing, just carries on eating his dinner. Finally my mother says, 'What is it?' Our forks are frozen in mid-air.

My father looks up and says, 'He's dead.'

Then he continues the meal as though nothing's happened.

Nan is already sobbing, and we all look at Mam who gets up and runs out. At this cue, we cry in chorus.

'Finish your dinner,' says Dad snappily to us. He doesn't like crying and he can't abide uneaten dinner. He keeps glaring at Mam's full plate. None of us is allowed to move until we've eaten our meal, every single mouthful.

Then Mam comes in with tears running down her wrinkles. She tells us that we're going to Auntie June's. When we come home later, Granda has gone. I don't cry. For me he was gone the night I took him my balsa-wood plane.

I'm not sure the twins are old enough to understand death but they understand how miserable Mam and Nan are. Probably they pick up some of the strain between Mam and Dad too. There are few angry words, just an atmosphere. My father doesn't like atmospheres much and he rapidly exits, his pencil behind his ear, his *Sun* newspaper open on the racing page under his arm.

We don't go to the funeral. We stay at Auntie June's instead and Uncle John takes us out. We go to a timber merchant's and I have a big polythene bag which I fill with sawdust for my mice.

I have quite a mouse-breeding programme going on in the old privy. I spend hours out there. It's the place I go when I'm sad. I really wanted to breed dogs but that's out of the question so I breed mice instead and, like dogs, these mice are good fighters. They are called Rump White and Tans. They are beautiful, large mice, some almost as large as a rat. They can be any colour from head to waist but across

43

the belly they must have a bright blaze of tan and their bottoms must be white, starting in a straight line across their backs. A good specimen is dramatic and looks as if he's wearing a pair of little white shorts. This is what the judges look for when you show them and this is what I'm breeding towards. The perfect Rump White and Tan mouse.

At school, Biology is still the only subject in which I have any interest, especially genetics as this is just what I'm doing with my mice. I have a breeding book, in which I record the date of birth and parentage of each mouse. Then I try to draw the mouse's markings. Each mouse is numbered as well as named. There's Blackie and Champagne and Pop-Eye. After a while I tire of drawing the mice in my book. It's too slow and mouse breeding is a fast business. So when the time comes, I knock them on the head, skin them with a scalpel and hang the skin up in the shed, labelled and cross-referenced.

Male mice are fierce creatures and will fight to the death if you let them. Sometimes, we let them. I keep them apart until the gang feels like watching a good fight and then we put two males in together and see what happens.

Gradually, my mouse collection gets larger and larger. I start in the shed where Dad keeps his bits of wood and gradually expand to take over the old privy. Adrian across the road funds my mice. I have a paper round but Adrian badly wants to do it so he does it and I pay him a pound and keep the rest.

One day I realize that I have 300 mice. I'm not just dabbling in mouse production, I'm a serious breeder. But I still haven't achieved the whole object of my breeding programme: perfection. That dead straight line across the back still eludes me.

I am in the fourth year at school. We have already started some of our O level courses and next year we'll take the exams themselves. I am good enough at Biology, Maths, English . . . but most of the time I'm just not interested. There is a miners' strike, the country is closing down and the school has no electricity. Only in the chemistry labs is there any sign of life. Here the bunsen burners blaze and teachers gather to give us the work which we are supposed to do at home.

I watch television or look after my mice or mess about with the gang but the work never gets done. Yvonne left school in the summer. I envied her, although now she's gone into the civil service and that sounds dull to me. I'd like to leave school and do something exciting.

The minimum leaving age is fifteen and on Bonfire Night I'm fifteen. The thought that I could leave school if I wanted to is nice.

At home, Mam seems upset most of the time. Seeing her upset

makes me miserable. It makes my stomach hurt. Dad moves from club to club, picking up bouncing work here and there and he still draws his sickness benefit. Mam works very hard. She's always busy in the house or dashing off to the bar. But, in spite of all this, the bank manager still calls. I've had to answer the door a few times. Occasionally, Michelle goes. She's not been at school long but she's already tough. I know it's not right for children to talk to the bank manager like this. Mam knows it too.

Sunday night is bath night and we have a rota. It's my turn and I'm just going upstairs for my bath when the shouting starts in the breakfast room. It's rare for Dad to raise his voice. If there's any shouting, and there isn't much, it's usually my mother. But tonight, Dad's shouting. Probably he's been drinking hard as it's Sunday.

'I don't know!' he's yelling, opening the door onto the hallway. He's retreating, but a hand is reaching out to grab him. It's not Mam's but Nan's. Mam's behind her. The two women follow him into the hall below me and Mam's sobbing.

'Frank,' she's saying, 'I can't pay the coal bill.'

'I haven't got any money!'

'The coke shed's almost empty—'

'Money doesn't grow on trees, woman!'

'I work my fingers to the bloody bone and—' Mam's words are lost in her sobs. She never tells Dad off for spending so much time at the pub, never, ever, but now Nan does it for her.

'And you're off drinking it all away!' she yells.

'Keep out of it!'

'No I won't, I won't!' Nan's roaring now. She's marched right up to Dad. I cringe. You don't do that to Dad, he likes a bit of space around him. But Nan's not scared. She looks hard. She doesn't look like the frail little lady whose chest will turn to black pudding if she's the least bit upset.

'Norma works and works and her earnings and my pension don't keep five children and a husband who spends all day at the pub.'

'I don't spend her money.'

'What you earn should go to your family, not the Ship!' Nan's shouting louder than Dad now and she's waggling her finger at him.

'It's nothing to do with you!' he yells.

'Keep out of it, Mam,' says my mother but her voice is lost in Nan's anger.

'It is! It is to do with me, it is! Everything's falling apart here thanks to your ways. We're going to lose the house if you're not careful and it's partly my house. It is to do with me! It is!'

Dad is speechless. He pushes Nan back.

'He hit me! He hit me!' she shrieks. Mam puts an arm around her and pulls her away from Dad. Nan starts to cry too.

I have seen the whole thing from my vantage point on the stairs and I don't think Dad hit her. He just pushed her away. But the two women hold each other, crying as if he had, while Dad grabs his jacket and goes out of the front door, slamming it.

Upstairs, I run the bath water. I add a few salty tears to its volume. So Mam's earnings and Nan's pension are all that keep us afloat. Dad's contributing nothing. But I know he tries to find work and one place he hears about jobs is in the pub. It's not fair to blame him for everything. I sink down under the bath water and close my eyes and hold my breath. All I can think of is Nan and Mam, hanging on to each other and crying at the foot of the stairs.

When a friend called Bob Trimmer calls round the next evening and asks me if I'll run away with him, I say, yes. I say it without thought or hesitation. This simple idea is almost ridiculously attractive, I don't know why I didn't think of it myself. No showdown at school over all the homework I haven't done. No more visits from the bank manager. No more listening to Mam and Dad finding new ways to be angry with each other.

I walk out, shut the door behind me, and Bob and I are free. He's happy too, because he's just had a big row at home. For about an hour we experience a heady sense of release. I hadn't realized how low I'd been feeling until now, but walking down the street without a care in the world is liberating. I hold my head up high and we walk fast to keep the cold at bay.

It's getting dark when we arrive at the seafront. We don't care. We start walking along the coast. We're heading south for London and we know that we'll get there if we follow the coast.

We walk until Whitley Bay and home are just some lights twinkling in the distance. Ahead of us is Blyth Power Station. There's a cruel breeze whipping around our ears from across the water. I look up but it's too cloudy for stars tonight. I try to remember my shooting star instead, the one I saw when I was coming home from judo with Gary when we were both still small enough to be really happy. Eventually, when we've been walking for a few hours, scarcely speaking, Bob suggests that we get some sleep.

We lie down in some sand dunes, the most sheltered we can find, and try to go to sleep. But sleep won't come. There's nowhere to put my head. I can't take my jacket off to use as a pillow because I'll die of cold. The sand is in my hair and it's cold sand with a hint of sea dampness about it. The breeze is getting stiffer and the dune gives us less shelter than we'd hoped. We lie there miserably. I don't want to be the one to suggest going home. I don't expect Bob does either. I'm hungry and I can't stop wondering how we'll get ourselves some breakfast in the morning. I, for one, don't have any money.

'Got any money?' I ask Bob.

He has about ten pence. Not enough for two breakfasts, I think, and so does Bob because suddenly he says, 'Frank, this isn't how we should run away. We've got almost no money, no food . . . I'm not saying we should give up . . .'

'You think we should go home and do it again when we can plan it a bit better?'

'That's it. We should plan it next time.'

Without another word, we get up. Our walk home is sometimes a battle with the breeze. The lights I was so pleased to leave behind now take an age to reach but at last, dead beat, we are passing familiar haunts and landmarks. Bob peels off when we get to his road and I turn up Beach Avenue. There is a police car outside the house. When I walk in I see the clock. Four in the morning. Mam and Dad are sitting there with the policemen. Mam looks pale and tearful. Her eyes have sunk deeper into her head than usual.

Dad is uncomfortable with the policemen. He is sitting on the edge of the armchair, not slumped in his usual manner.

They are not pleased to see me. They are furious. Dad gives me a hiding right there in front of the policemen. One of them says, 'There you go, lad, your dad's dealt with you, that should be enough.'

The next day I am tired but Dad makes me go to school anyway. Nobody asks me why I tried to leave home. I only have to look at Mam to know how hurt she is.

I can't forget the sense of freedom I felt when I walked away from the house that night. Although the whole episode ended in humiliation the short burst of happiness at the beginning reminded me what happiness is. Happiness, I decide, depends on escaping from the worries. I start to ponder methods of escape.

It is Saturday. I go to Kirby's sweet shop, the same place Granda used to send me for his Sun Valley tobacco and packet of Rizla papers. I used to find it annoying sometimes but now I wish that he was around to send me for them again. He'd feed the papers into his little cigarette-rolling machine and I'd watch in fascination. I stand in the sweet shop waiting my turn and missing Granda.

'Bottle of aspirins, please,' I say.

On Saturday night I take the entire bottle. I take them by the handful and wash them down with water from a plastic beaker. When they're all gone, I hide the bottle under the pillow. I half hope that someone will take enough interest in me to ask what I'm doing but, of course, the two people whose interest and attention I want most aren't there.

I hope this works. If I just succeed in making myself ill, Dad will go berserk. He'll be really angry with me.

'How can you be so stupid! A whole bottle! How can anyone be so stupid!'

I imagine him saying it. Even if I take a whole bottle of aspirin and nearly die he's not going to turn into Daniel's parents and start being nice and asking me what the problem is.

I turn out the light and lie in bed waiting for death to come and take me. It's going to be like walking towards the seafront in the dark, I'll have a glorious sense of leaving everybody and everything behind me. No more pain. I fall asleep thinking of shooting stars.

I wake up in the morning with a splitting headache but the first thing I feel is a sense of relief. I haven't died in the night. I'm still here. I have a quiet Sunday lounging about. No-one notices anything different about me.

At Easter I go to the Lake District with my schoolfriend, Guy. It's running away all over again. No preparation, no money. We camp in a field and steal food from shops in Keswick. One day we decide we'll kill our own dinner. We find an innocent sheep and tell it that its number is up. We chase it for hours, finally catching and stabbing it. Then we stare at its warm body wondering what to do next. A brief examination of its fleece reveals uncountable quantities of bugs and creepy crawlies and, whatever we were going to do with it, we decide not to. We go into Keswick instead to steal some food and look, unsuccessfully, for girls.

Lying at night with our cans of beer by our sleeping bags, we talk. Guy has his future all sewn up. He's going to join the army. He'll finish the school year and in the summer he'll join up and he won't go back.

I think of the army. Infantrymen, sneaking from bush to bush, crawling through mud, carrying guns. I could join up in the summer with Guy. In six months' time I could be wearing a uniform and doing all those things instead of going to school. No more school and no more home. No more Mam looking pale and unhappy. No more bank manager. A new life, somewhere else.

'Are you really going to do it? Just leave Whitley Bay and join up?' I ask. It sounds too easy.

48

'I really am,' he says.

'What about your Mam and Dad?'

'They think it's a good idea. They say the army's the place to learn a trade.'

'What sort of a trade?'

'All sorts. They give you tests and tell you what you're good at.'

'Like what?'

'Like anything. I could be a mechanic. A signaller. A chef . . . all sorts, Frank.'

I lie in the dark listening to the tent flapping a bit in the spring breeze. I can't see any point in joining the army to be a chef. You can be that anywhere.

'Don't you want to be the fighting sort of soldier, then?'

Guy thinks a while. I hear him running his fingers through his curly hair.

'Nah,' he says, finally.

When the summer holidays come, I am arrested. I've been into the police station already on a few occasions. My crimes, reported and unreported, haven't been terrible: some shoplifting, throwing eggs at double-decker buses, stealing the perforated zinc vents from pantries for my mice cages, throwing fireworks at cars.

Now I'm accused of breaking and entering. I have climbed up to the top of a department store to steal one of the big perspex domed skylights from the roof. I know the skylights are there because the gang's played games up on the roof without anyone knowing. My interest in Biology continues and I want a garden pond. I think one of the skylights will be ideal. Upside down, it will hold a wealth of creatures and I'll be able to see everything which is going on inside.

I'm making my exit down the fire escape when suddenly there is a penetrating search light on me and a voice telling me that the police are surrounding the building. I'm instructed to come down right away.

I am frightened and, as usual on such occasions, I can feel laughter starting again. I climb down and break into giggles. The policemen aren't amused. I tell them that I'm only stealing the skylight, I'm not interested in breaking into the shop, but of course they don't believe me. They hold me in custody until my mam arrives, tired and angry.

'You stupid idiot,' she says. But she corroborates my story about the garden pond. She tells them I already have a baby bath in the garden full of crabs and fish. Reluctantly, and with many warnings, I am released.

'I've had enough of this, Frank,' Mam says as she walks us briskly out of the police station into the night. I've had enough of it too. I've had enough of everything. A couple of days later, accompanied by Guy, I visit the army recruitment office in Newcastle.

The office is on the main street and behind the desk is a uniformed sergeant. Mam has always gone to great lengths to ensure that we look nice: our school clothes are pressed and never shabby and the house is often draped with our bri-nylon shirts drip-drying. But when I see this sergeant, I realize what smart means. Every button gleams, every inch of him is ironed, every hair of his head is in the right place. He is immaculate. I ask him a few questions and he gives me piles of leaflets to take home. I learn that the army is recruiting very actively now because the school leaving age is being raised and so two years' recruitment is taking place in one.

I drop the leaflets at Dad's feet and ask him what he thinks about me joining the army.

Dad says, 'Not much.'

Dad did his national service in the RAF and didn't enjoy it, except for the football cup he won there.

'Why not, Dad? I'd like to be a soldier.'

Dad shakes his head slowly.

'No,' he says, 'no. For a start, all the forms you'd have to fill in and the questions you'd have to answer.'

Mam's reaction is different. She thinks hard and then says, 'Well, perhaps it will take the army to knock some sense into you.' I detect something like relief in her tone. I realize it will be a relief for everyone if I go. A relief for me to get away from the atmosphere here, a relief for Mam to know someone's keeping me under control.

I read through the leaflets and persuade Mam and Dad to look at a few and then I go back to the smart sergeant to pick up all the forms and go through them with him. I take the big yellow double-decker into Newcastle.

The double-decker goes right past my grandfather's house. This is my father's father. On an impulse I get out at the next stop. He'll be pleased to see me and I can ask him what he thinks of me joining the army.

I barely remember my grandmother, she died when I was quite small and Granda Collins moved out to the old people's houses, a long row of single storey homes here on the coast road.

When we lived in Newcastle, we saw a lot of Dad's father and brothers. Most of my mother's family were a little posher than us and, although we visited them, it was understood that they didn't visit us. Now we live at Whitley Bay, everything's different. We see little of Dad's family and a lot of Mam's.

The last time a group of my uncles visited us was one evening when we were still in Newcastle. Uncle Norman, Uncle Steve and Uncle George. I'd been picked out for free violin lessons at school and I wanted to play my uncles my latest piece, 'Silent Night'. Dad tried to stop me. I knew without him saying so that he thought playing any instrument at all was namby-pamby and the violin was downright girlish.

Uncle George said, 'Come on, Frankie, let the boy give us a tune on his fiddle . . .' and Dad had to give in. He probably cringed all the way through.

At the end I took my violin from under my chin and they all clapped and said nice things. I remember looking around at their beaming faces and thinking that they all looked exactly alike. They were all carpenters like my dad. But as they clapped I noticed that Uncle Norman had big holes in his jumper. I was very worried about him in the way that only a little kid can be, and suggested in a whispered conversation with Yvonne and Gary that we club together to buy him a new one.

Yvonne said, 'Don't be stupid, those are his work clothes.'

I get off the bus now and walk along the big coast road towards Granda's house and the shipyards.

Outside the houses are pots with flowers in and the occasional hanging basket. An old, old man comes to the door and smiles at me. Probably he knows this is a grandchild, although he's not sure which one.

'It's Frank, Granda!'

'Frankie's first boy! Come in, young Frankie!'

He holds the door open. I'd forgotten how much I liked him. After all those sons he's still got eyes which sparkle.

He takes me through to his kitchen. It is cold and not very clean. It's bare except for unwashed tea cups on the draining board. He fills a kettle and puts it on the gas stove. His movements are slow and precise, like Dad's. He tells me that soon his meal will be arriving and I say I won't stay long.

The house smells. It smells of being old. Old carpets, old wood, old furniture, old man. Granda's face is deeply lined but his chin is still prominent among the folds of skin.

'How's your mam and dad? What about that sister of yours, what's her name?'

I tell him I'm doing all right at school and we discuss my mice. That's something he can understand. Fur and feather is part of the local culture. He tells me about Uncle Bill who emigrated before Dad was even born. Uncle Bill has a sheep farm in Australia.

'Granda, I'm thinking of joining the army,' I say.

He scrutinizes me with his sharp, shiny old eyes.

'Are you now?'

He looks thoughtful and takes a sip of tea and so do I. It's too strong for me but I'm not going to tell him that.

'Dad's not much in favour.'

'No,' agrees Granda, as if this is to be expected. 'Well, we're not that sort of family.'

There's a long pause.

'So,' he says finally, 'you want to be a soldier.' His voice is non-committal. I scan the tone of his words and the expression on his face for some small indication of approval. There is none.

A tap at the door. It's Granda's meal arriving, so I go, leaving him with more tea cups to wash. I wait for a yellow bus out on the coast road and while I wait I feel disappointed. I'd hoped that Granda might encourage me to be a soldier. But I can tell he doesn't think it a good idea.

When I get home from the recruiting office with my forms I start serious persuasion techniques on Mam and Dad. Finally Dad agrees there might be some point in joining up if I learn a trade.

'That way,' he says, 'you won't be leaving in a few years' time with nothing to show for it.'

Guy has had his tests by now and the army has suggested he become a lorry driver. I hope my dad doesn't mean this sort of trade. It's hard to imagine anything less like soldiering.

Unfortunately, Mam agrees enthusiastically with Dad's point of view.

'But, Mam, I want to be a soldier.'

'Well if you learn a trade you'll still wear a uniform and do a bit of marching about, I dare say.'

I don't want my soldiering to be confined to a bit of marching about but I can see that the only way out of Whitley Bay is by agreeing to an army apprenticeship.

I go away to the army youth selection centre for two days. A coach picks up a group of us in Newcastle and takes us to Harrogate, where we stay in a modern army apprentice college. I am given aptitude tests and trade tests. I look at the apprentices marching around the big square outside and am impressed. I want to be one of them. One lad comes up and says, 'Don't do it, you'll be sorry!' But nothing can stop me now.

The army suggests that I become a signals operator or a vehicle mechanic. I'm not interested in being a grease monkey but signals sound interesting. I like the idea of learning morse code. It sounds like the trade closest to being a real soldier. My parents, who have been so insistent that I learn something useful in the army, find this acceptable. I can't help wondering what they think I'm going to do with Morse code when I come out of the army but I don't say this and at last my application forms are filled in. My father still can't bring himself to sign them but only one signature is required and Mam supplies that.

Guy, who has completed the application process, comes to the recruitment office with me. It's Saturday and he brings his girlfriend, Sandra. When we walk in, the smart sergeant gives us a big smile.

'Hello, boys!'

'I've brought my forms,' I tell him. He beams at me.

'Good, well, we'll soon have that hair off!'

He's made some comment about my long hair every time I've been in. I grin back at him now and hold out the forms.

'Let's take a look at them, then,' he says.

He shuffles his way through the pages checking all the boxes.

'Good . . . good . . . champion . . . OK . . .' Then he gets to the last section.

'Oh dear,' he says. 'Is that how your mam signs her name?' He shows me the form.

'Oh no . . . she's printed it. Does that matter?'

The smart sergeant has stopped smiling. He nods grimly.

'Of course it matters. She should have printed her name in blocks there and signed it here. But she's printed it here.'

I look up at him, waiting for him to tell me it's all right. But it isn't all right.

'Oh, the stupid idiot!' I say. That's what Mam calls me.

I want to go straight back home and get Mam to sign the forms properly but Guy and Sandra don't want another couple of bus rides. We're footloose in Newcastle on a busy Saturday and the last place they want to go now is Whitley Bay.

They say, 'Get your Mam to bring it in on Monday. She'll come up to town for you!'

'What do you want to do, then?'

'I need some tights,' says Sandra. I know what that means. Sandra and Guy are keen shoplifters. When we've got her some tights, we go to a toyshop and steal a gun. It's a pop gun with caps, a replica of a real gun. We decide to stage a shoot-out. Guy and Sandra go inside a department store and I stay outside with the gun. When they walk out of the store, I yell from across the street, 'Guy!'

Guy turns round and goes for his gun but I start firing before he can get to it. The busy Saturday shoppers pause and then dive for cover. I'm amazed. They think this is a real shoot-out.

Guy pretends that he's been hit and falls down while I run. People give chase and are close to catching me. I stop and say, 'Look, it's a toy gun, we're only playing.'

They're angry so of course I start to giggle. They say they're calling the police. The three of us make ourselves scarce. We had no idea that everyone would fall for it and, although we get around the corner and giggle, there's a nervousness in our laughter.

We go back into some shops and pinch some spray paints, then some more tights for Sandra. This is easy, but I still get a buzz of fear and excitement every time we leave a shop. It's not really stealing until you've left. We've just stepped outside C&A when a store detective tells us to step back in. He asks to see our receipts and of course we don't have any. The police are called and we are taken to the cells.

Later, my mother arrives. She sees me and bursts into tears.

'You'll not get into the army now. You've wrecked your chances. You'll be in bloody borstal instead!'

It's been a high-adrenalin day. The disappointment at the recruitment office, the craziness of our shoot-out, the shoplifting spree and then the police. Now the sight of my mother in tears in another police station is all it takes to make this hard boy cry.

The police have taken statements and my mother has signed pieces of paper. I want to go straight home with her on the bus but she marches me back to the recruiting office.

'No, Mam—'

I don't want to see the sergeant again in these circumstances but Mam says, 'You're coming with me.' By now she's even keener than I am for me to join the army.

I sit looking sheepish while Mam explains what's happened. There isn't a whisper of a smile on the sergeant's face now. He looks at me and shakes his head. It's clear that I've blown it. The army won't take me after this. The sergeant says he's going to talk to the colonel about me but his tone is not encouraging. I leave without saying goodbye. I have a depressing weekend.

On Monday Mam takes me back to the police station as she's

agreed. Guy and Sandra are already waiting with their parents. The chief constable is there and so is the colonel.

The chief constable delivers a terrible talking to. Sandra sits with her hands in her lap looking a picture of innocence. Her parents give me icy looks. It's clear they think I corrupted their daughter.

'But', the chief constable winds up his lecture, 'I'm giving you a second chance.' He's looking at me. 'You're going into the army to see what they can do with you. But you won't get a third chance, I can assure you of that.'

Relief floods over me. I'm in.

The colonel has all the paperwork ready for Mam to sign. She does this carefully. The colonel tells me I'll report to Harrogate, the very same place I did my aptitude tests, in about ten days' time. That modern apprentice college is going to be my home for the next two years.

I return to Whitley Bay under a cloud, Mam refusing to speak to me on the bus. When we pass Granda Collins' house, I look away. I am sad and distressed, especially because I've upset Mam so much. But something deep down inside me, is refusing to be miserable. One little part of me is jubilant. In ten days' time I'll be gone.

Before I leave I go to Uncle Tommy's to buy a sports jacket like the one I saw boys wearing at the army selection centre. Uncle Tommy works in a tailor's. I have less than £20 to spend. Uncle Tommy walks in and out of the coat racks with his tape measure around his neck and shakes his head. Jackets generally cost a bit more. Finally he produces a blue jacket which has been tailor-made for someone else and then, for some reason, not collected by them.

'Hand-finished,' says Uncle Tommy. 'That's hand-stitching. A quality jacket.'

It's a quality jacket but it doesn't fit me. It was made for someone with a much bigger waist. I buy it anyway.

At opening time on Friday night, my dad looks at his watch as usual, puts on his jacket and, instead of walking out of the door, he turns to me.

'Coming, then?' he says.

I sit up and stare at him.

'Come on. Get that jacket on.'

This is an invitation to join him at the pub. I am the eldest son and I am leaving home on Monday and I know without being told that this is my ritual admission to manhood.

Feeling old, I walk with him to the Fat Ox, a pub with a back room at the end of the back lane. The old boys playing dominoes look up and acknowledge us. Drinking friends of my dad grunt at him and make small comments about my presence. The barman serves us at once. No comment is made about the fact that I am a baby-faced boy of fifteen, three years below the legal drinking limit.

Dad stands at the bar. He doesn't talk. He's a serious professional drinker. He buys pints of Double Diamond, one round after another, in steady succession. This is his usual pace but it soon becomes clear that I can't keep up with him. I am overwhelmed by the sheer quantity of liquid sloshing around in my body, let alone its alchoholic content. I know, without being told, that Dad doesn't go to the Gents, not until much later in the evening. That's part of the ritual. You stand at the bar with your pint and you drink it.

Soon there are a few pints lined up for me. Dad helps me out by drinking one of them. He obliges by missing the occasional round. By ten o'clock, the room is spinning, there are exactly twice as many old men playing dominoes as there were when we came in and I am leaning heavily on the bar for support.

'You'd best be getting on before I get into trouble,' Dad says at last. I am released. I am free to empty my bladder and, somehow, get myself home. All I want to do is get home. Home. Dad remains at the bar. He doesn't say goodbye or even watch as I lurch towards the door.

I feel terrible. The back lane isn't the familiar back lane any more but a moving, spinning, vomit-inducing roller coaster. I stagger down it, walking into cars and hanging onto gateposts. Past all the boyhood landmarks, looking bleary and uncertain now I'm a man: the garage where the two men had their fight, the place where I saw the shooting star, the door where we threw knives. Somehow I get myself through our back gate and then into the kitchen. I can go no further. I clatter around looking for the way out until the noise brings Yvonne in.

'You stupid idiot,' she says. She sounds like Mam. Luckily Mam is at work.

She guides me through the breakfast room and upstairs. The stairs look non-negotiable from the bottom but clinging onto Yvonne I finally arrive at the top. And this is all part of the ritual too, of course. A woman has to take care of you when you're helpless as a baby with drink. Yvonne's also learning her role in these customs. She pushes me into the bathroom where I am sick, over and over again. I bang against the sink, stand upright too quickly and fall back against the wall.

Yvonne appears again.

'That's disgusting and it smells disgusting and I'll have to clear it up,' she says. I realize that although I leaned over the toilet to vomit, I've somehow managed to miss.

She cleans me up a little and pushes me into the bedroom, where Gary's asleep.

'You're revolting,' she tells me as I roll onto the bed. I don't care. I'm home and I can go to sleep now.

The next day I feel terrible. Yvonne's not angry with me, Mam doesn't know what's happened and Dad's asleep. But despite it all, I'm happy. I know I've been admitted to a man's world of drinking.

That lunchtime I'm back in the Fat Ox. Not with Dad now, but with Robbie next door and some of his pals. They're all older than me and they've already graduated from the back lane gangs to the pubs. They were in the bar last night and they witnessed my graduation.

Today I don't get drunk. I have a few pints with the lads and then go home. I'm a drinking man, just like my dad, and on Monday I'll be going out into the man's world and leaving Whitley Bay for ever.

# 4

MY HEART IS CRASHING INSIDE MY CHEST LIKE A BIRD FRANTIC TO GET out, my face burns, sweat drips from me in rivers. My legs are supposed to be running but they're detached from my body now. I have no control over them. I've done the assault course again and again and again and this time I know that the wall, looming ahead of me, hanging over me, is insurmountable. I throw myself against it and try lifting my legs off the ground but by now they just ignore me. I hit the wall and slowly, but with little elegance, I slide down it.

The sergeant appears. He's much smaller than me and about twice as wide. He's dwarfed by the wall. He says, 'Get up.'

I say, 'I can't.'

He says, 'Get up and get over it.'

I tell him I can't and he looks at me with complete contempt. I'm a failure and a nobody and that gives him the right to punch me, which he does, straight in the mouth. I can feel his knuckles up against my lips and teeth. My head is jarred back. I hear something scrunch in my neck. After the shock comes the sting, all around my lips and gums, then a duller, more thudding pain.

My amazement takes the edge off the pain, but the effect is immediate. The shock, and perhaps also his contempt, puts the fight right back in me. I feel a surge of adrenalin and know I can go on. I leap over the wall.

I'm in Aldershot. I thought I was coming here on a parachute course. When I arrived a big white number fifty-two was stencilled onto my leg and my shirt. There was a lot of yelling and shouting but no sign of a parachute. Eventually I learned that this is no parachute course but P Company, a training and selection programme. If I pass, I'll still be in the Royal Corps of Signals, but I'll be a signaller for the Parachute Regiment. I've admired the Parachute Regiment ever since they came to talk to us back at army apprentice college. They're real soldiers, and the best soldiers, and if I can't be a soldier then I'd like to signal for them. So I decide to grit my teeth and pass this course, even though I'm ill-prepared for it.

A few days later, I come first on a 10-mile march. By now we're halfway through and the other signallers I work with at RAF Benson have given up and gone home. But the next morning when I get out of bed I feel as though my legs have been cut off just above the foot. When I walk across the room there's a rubber band inside my ankles squeaking every time I move. The pain is considerable. I hobble to the medic, trying not to bend my foot at the ankle, to the amusement of any passing soldiers.

The medic tells me that my Achilles tendons have torn. I know that, although we're almost at the end of the course, I'm finished. I can't pass now. I'm furious with myself, particularly with my body. I can't understand why it's undermined me like this when I was doing so well.

I stagger around on crutches for the remainder of the course. Anxious to join in test week, I check my confidence by climbing up to the high scaffolding in the gymnasium. I can hardly walk, let alone balance. I give up but I don't return to RAF Benson. I don't want to go back a failure. My short army career hasn't been glorious yet. I was at Harrogate army apprentice college for two years and most of my mates were made up to lance corporal or even higher in that time, but not me. I parachuted, dived, climbed and passed all my exams as a signaller but I did not distinguish myself. Now I'm in the man's army. I'm signalling for real. And still I really want to be a soldier.

At the end of P Company we all assemble in a large cinema. They call out each number in turn and tell you whether you're in or not. I'm waiting for number fifty-two. I can hardly breathe, just in case, despite my injuries, they've decided to pass me . . .

'Fifty?'

'Sir.'

'Fail.'

'Fifty-one?'

'Sir.'

'Pass.'

'Fifty-two?'

This is it.

'Sir.'

'Fail.'

Bang. The sergeant's just hit me in the mouth again. The mixture of pain and amazement are almost enough to make me reel.

Fail. I realize that I hate failure and I especially hate being called a failure in public. We Collinses don't fail. Only Gary, the family's eleven-plus failure. He's had to live with that every day. He's left school now but it still matters. He's failed the eleven-plus for the rest of his life and I've failed P Company for the rest of my life and there's nothing I can do about it. Unless I come back again and pass.

I return to RAF Benson at Wallingford where the lads give me a hard time. I resolve to reapply to the Paras as soon as I'm able and next time I'll be prepared. I'll train and return fighting fit.

When I left Harrogate and the boy's army, I spent my last, long, summer holiday in Whitley Bay. Mam and Yvonne and Gary and the twins came to my passing out. They arrived in a minicab, Mam wearing a flowery dress and a hat I didn't know she had. The driver was a colleague from the upmarket bar where Mam works: he's one of the regular minicabs that the bar uses. Dick Short is a friend of the family. He takes the twins to crazy golf and on the way home they stop at his sweetshop where they gorge themselves. Even I have been along to his sweet shop in the holidays for free rations of Curly Wurlys.

We marched around in our uniforms and afterwards there was a wonderful spread in the cookhouse, with big salmons and salads. Then we went to the NAAFI bar. Mam and Dick had a laugh about what Mam was going to drink and, to my amazement, she ended up with a pint in front of her. I'd never seen my mother drink a pint before.

I was issued with a combat uniform and a gas mask to take to my unit. At home, I tried it all on to impress my mother. I thought she'd like to see me looking like a real soldier but instead she sat down and cried. I removed the gas mask in case it was reminding her of the war, but she still wept.

'Mam, this is how we're supposed to fight,' I told her helplessly. There were renewed sobs.

'I wish you'd take that stuff off and never put it on again,' she said. I began to realize then that it's almost impossible to know what's going on inside the head of a woman, even your mam.

My first few days home the family was careful around me, even my father treating me with a new respect. Then, gradually, they reabsorbed me and all the old tensions and difficulties returned. By the end of the holidays I vowed never to return there for more than a few days.

At RAF Benson, I make a new family of my own. I have three buddies and we are an inseparable foursome. I'm so happy being one of the gang that when I'm picked to take part in a special course run by the regimental sergeant major, I'm horrified. It's some kind of leadership course. It's an honour to be selected, my mates tell me, but I'm convinced it's a punishment. The others tease me mercilessly. They tell me that I'm being lined up for promotion. The thought of being promoted over the gang isn't pleasant.

I arrive at the course looking workaday. Of course my shirt is pressed and my boots shine but when I look around at everyone else I'm amazed. Their shirts are perfection, their boots are mirrors.

It soon becomes clear that this is some sort of test. But I don't want to be tested. I don't want to be judged.

I misbehave. I am the class clown and its resident cynic. When we're each asked to give a five-minute talk on the subject of our choice, the others work from scripts and use overhead projectors and various gimmicks. I don't even bother to prepare mine. I ad-lib on the subject of parachuting with my hands in my pockets.

At the end of the course there's a debrief and the RSM tears me apart. I look nonchalant. I'm anxious to show I don't care.

'You've had a chance here, Collins, and you've blown it. Now why?'

I don't know what to say. The RSM stands over me. His uniform is not just pressed but starched. It is literally crisp. He wears brown shoes which are polished to a rank of their own. He is not big but he's lean and fit. He shakes his head.

'Don't you want to be a leader?'

Finally I reply. My tone is casual to the point of insolence.

'Well, I've never really thought about it, sir.'

This is untrue. I've thought a lot about rank and why I haven't been given it. Not in the cadets, not at Harrogate. In both places, my friends were promoted over me. Now, suddenly, I've been selected for a leadership course and my friends haven't.

The RSM glowers at me and I stare back. I am being both arrogant and rude but I've started on this route and I'm determined to finish. He dismisses me. That night, in the bar, I make jokes with the boys about all the stupid things I've said and done on the course. They are left in no doubt of my loyalty.

A few weeks later, promotions come up. All three of my mates are

61

made lance corporal. Everyone else who was on the course is promoted too. But I'm not. I'm still a private.

I realize that it's time to wake up. I want to be in the next round of promotions. I'll smarten up, stop playing the fool, stop answering back, get drunk less often, speak up with my ideas instead of sitting on them. That's my strategy.

I go home to Whitley Bay for five days. That's long enough. I tell them about the places I've been, Norway and Belize, but I am careful not to mention the leadership course. I'd like to tell some of my old friends about it, especially Daniel, but we've already drifted apart.

Dad's found himself a job on a building project and is due to go away for a few months. He leaves while I'm there. The evening of his departure, Yvonne comes into the bedroom. She looks different. Her face, ringed by dark hair, is thinner and paler than usual, as if she's lost weight very suddenly.

'Frank, I've got something to tell you . . .' She starts to cry.

'Don't get upset,' I say. My voice is sharp. It's touching to see someone as tough as Yvonne crying openly but I am not going to be touched. I watch her stonily. I am determined not to be dragged back into the family misery which I left behind.

'I've told the twins. And Gary.'

'Where is Gary?'

'Gone out.'

So what is it? What is it that makes Yvonne cry and Gary go out? I have a sick feeling in my stomach now, the sickness of anticipation.

'Mam and Dad are divorced,' she says. She splutters into tears on the word divorced and I have to ask her to repeat it. I am numb. I don't feel anything at all. I can hardly even hear Yvonne. This is all happening a long way off, somewhere in distant Whitley Bay.

'You mean', I say, 'they're getting divorced.'

'No. No, they're divorced. They've been divorced for quite a while.'

Mam and Dad are already divorced. They've been divorced for quite a while.

'But . . . everything's just exactly the same here,' I protest. I'm saying this because I feel I ought to protest. I don't want to. I don't want to hear any more.

'It happened last year, probably the early part of last year. They kept it secret.'

Mam and Dad divorcing, joined together in one final, enormous secret. I think of last year. My passing out. Were they divorced then?

62

The summer I spent at home, before joining RAF Benson. Were they divorced then?

'Didn't anyone know? Didn't Nan know?'

'Nan knew because she went to court. She was a witness or whatever you have in divorces. She told the judge about Dad.'

I don't want to know what Nan told the judge about Dad or what the judge did or what he thought.

'How could they carry on living here like this, just the same . . . ?'

'They're not any more.'

'You mean one of them's moving out?'

The room lurches a little at the unreality of the idea. This is all happening in Whitley Bay but, unfortunately, I'm in Whitley Bay.

'Well. Dad's gone away.'

'Just for a few months.'

'And next week Mam's marrying Dick Short.'

It's too much. Mam not married to Dad any longer but to the people's friend, the man with bags of sweets for everyone and a crazy golf club, taxi driver Dick Short.

'No.'

'Yes, Frank. I'm sorry. It's true.'

I stare at her. There is a long silence.

'I don't like him much either,' she confesses. 'As far as I'm concerned he can keep his Curly Wurlys and his Caramac and his chocolate eggs. And his crazy golf. But it's Mam. She's had a dog's life with Dad and Dick doesn't drink much and he's got some money. Maybe things'll get better for her now, Frank.'

I nod. I want Mam to be happy.

'What did the twins say?'

'Michael said, "Do we have to call him Dad?"'

'Do they?'

'Mam said they do.'

I watch her face again. It doesn't move.

'But he's not their dad.' I think one of us should say it.

'That's what Mam wants. She's happy, Frank, happier than she's been for years.'

'Yeah. What about Dad?'

'Hard to tell what he's thinking.'

'Did he want a divorce?'

'No.'

'What does he say about Dick?'

'I'm not sure he knows.'

'You mean, he'll come back and find Dick here?'

'Look, I've told you all Mam's told me.'

I lie on my bed. Yvonne goes out and Gary comes in. He lies down. We don't talk.

'Didn't you know anything about all this?' I ask him at last.

'Nope.'

We both lie in silence. We don't even breathe loudly.

'I don't know why you're bothered,' says Gary. 'You're the one who got away.'

The next day everything's just the same except Dad's gone. Mam seems the same as ever. There's only one thing to talk about and we don't.

I return to camp. As soon as I get there I want to phone Mam. I want to say be happy. You deserve it. I don't know how you've stood it all these years. And thanks for never once moaning about Dad to us. You must have wanted to.

I don't make the phone call.

Back at camp I'm not one of the lads any more. They all have a tape and I don't. They iron their stripes enthusiastically. They're regimental sergeant majors in waiting. One of them in particular, Tim, gets career fever and decides to become Napoleon. In these circumstances, a run-in with one of my mates is inevitable, and it's inevitable that it's Tim.

The lance corporals have responsibility for keeping our accommodation block clean and tidy. It's a nice modern block with carpet and wardrobes and we're expected to ensure it's immaculate. We have to vacuum, empty the rubbish and clean the toilets and sinks daily for inspection.

It's 8.10 a.m. At 8.30 a.m. we have to be on parade outside the hangars. Tim, whose new tape has brought him responsibility for about three rooms, flies in.

'Toilets not good enough this morning. Frank, get in there and see to them before work or we'll all be in trouble.'

Has he chosen me because I'm the first man he sees or because I'm his friend and he thinks I'll support him? Perhaps if he'd spoken to me differently I'd rush to clean the toilets. We all have to pitch in. I hate dirty loos and can't understand why people leave them that way but I'll clean them. Not, however, if I'm asked in that tone of voice. Besides, I'm still getting ready for work.

'I'm just getting myself sorted out here . . .' I say.

He looks at me abrasively.

'Well, hurry up. Then go and do them.'

'Yes, Sergeant Major,' I say.

In the toilets, Tim stands in his funny froggy position with his arms out while I start work with my brush. Tim not only drives an Austin-Healey frog-eyed Sprite but he looks like a frog himself. He has bulgy eyes and a funny fishy mouth. If he'd help me clean the toilets, the way he would have a couple of weeks ago, it would be all right. But he doesn't help. He stands there with his sharp, well-pressed tape on, and watches me do the work.

When I've finished one cubicle, he struts in and checks it.

'Hurry up,' he tells me.

I seethe as I scrub. I finish the second cubicle, walk out and offer him the brush.

'I've cleaned half. Why don't you do the other two?' I say.

'Get on with it,' he orders me.

'Nope. I've done mine, now it's your turn.' I wield the toilet brush.

'Look. I'm telling you, Collins, do it.'

There it is: Collins. We used to be friends.

'You do it,' I say. Both my voice and my movements with the toilet brush are getting threatening.

Tim's eyes bulge dangerously. His fishy mouth is stretched into a small, hard, straight line.

'Right,' he says. 'If you don't clean these toilets, I'm going to charge you.'

He turns sharply and marches out of the room. I stand there in disbelief. Have I just been talking to one of my best friends?

I know that as far as the army is concerned, he had every right to behave the way he did and that I could now be in big trouble. I rapidly clean the other two loos and leave for work. I can't believe that my mate would report me, but later I'm paid a visit by the troop sergeant.

'Let's talk about this,' he says matily.

'Tim's been power-mad since he got his tape. He's turned into a little Hitler,' I say. The troop sergeant nods. He's seen it all before. He assures me he's having a word with Tim, too. But he reminds me that Tim has a stripe and I don't and I have to do what he says.

'You know you're in the wrong. Don't get yourself charged,' he urges. I bite my lip and apologize, not very apologetically, to Tim. It's some time before we're friends again.

Until now, my parachuting has been limited by my own terror of jumping into nothingness from a dizzying height. Terror is big and impossible to fight. It is the enemy that can't be seen. Now, I learn to free-fall and love it. In the seconds between jumping and opening my parachute, I experience the thrill of flying. I fly for 3 seconds, then 5 and, finally, 20. Twenty seconds of falling through space, 20 seconds of human flight. At the moment I can't do much with that 20 seconds but I watch the more experienced free-fallers swooping, gliding and making human formations in the air and I know I'm going to be doing a lot more parachuting.

A letter arrives from Whitley Bay. I've been waiting for this. I've phoned home a couple of times but there's never been a reply. I know something's happened and I've been waiting to learn exactly what. Now the letter is here, addressed with a neat but hesitant hand. Mam's.

I tear it open. They've left Beach Avenue and are now living in a one bedroom flat in Tynemouth. Dick owns the flat, in fact he owns the whole house and is negotiating with the tenants for them to leave. Then, says Mam cryptically, things won't be so cramped.

I wonder how many Collinses can fit into a one bedroom flat in Tynemouth. There's a phone number on the letter so I ring it when I hope Mam will be home but not Dick.

To my relief, she answers.

'Where's Dad?' I ask her.

'In the pub, I expect.'

'No, Mam, I mean where's he living?'

'Oh, Beach Avenue.'

'By himself?'

'I suppose so.'

I can't imagine Dad all alone in that big house. Only him, slumped in the armchair, like that morning I came down and found him with blood all over his face.

'Is he all right?'

'Well I think so.'

'Is he . . . has he done anything to . . .' Now I'll have to say this name. I pause. 'To Dick?'

Surely Dad will have a few pints and then decide to sort Dick out. Dick's apparently been having an affair with his wife right under his nose and a Geordie male like Dad isn't going to put up with that.

'No, no, everything's all right.'

But from her tone I know that she and Dick are scared of what Dad might do.

'So . . . how many of you are living in one room?'

'Not one room, one bedroom,' she corrects me gently. 'There's a living room too, Frank.'

'How many of you?'

'Well, all of us.'

66

'What, Nan and Yvonne and Gary and the twins and you and . . .'
I still have to pause before I say it. 'And . . . Dick?'

'That's right and sometimes Michael too.'

Michael is Yvonne's fiancé.

'What about the dog?'

'She's here as well.'

Another blow for Dad. He loves his Staffordshire Bull Terrier. I
want to say why couldn't you leave him his dog? but I can't.

'How long before you get the rest of the house?'

'Not long now. The tenants should be out by the end of next
month.'

'It would have been more sensible if you'd stayed in the big house
at Beach Avenue and Dad had left,' I say.

'Yes,' agrees Mam in a tone which leaves much unsaid. 'But,' she
adds, 'I think he's selling it.'

So, the bank manager finally won.

In the next round of promotions, I get my stripe. At last. I go home,
except that home isn't home any more.

'A lance corporal!' says my mother admiringly. I'm glad of her
ignorance about the army. This is the first promotion in an army
career which started way back in the cadets and if she knew a bit more
she'd have expected a stripe long ago.

Everybody seems happy enough with Dick except Gary, who's had
a few run-ins. Dick and I both make an effort to be friendly but I'm
glad that he's out so much of the time. He's working hard to feed all
the extra mouths. He's a middle-aged bachelor who's been well-cared
for by his mother. Now, suddenly, he has Mam's immense family to
look after. I wonder how he's coping. I sense sometimes that he's
competing with the twins for her attention and occasionally he gets
snappy. But mostly he's on his best behaviour and that's fine by me.
I don't want to know what happens the rest of the time. I don't live
here any more.

Of course I visit Dad.

I take the red bus to Whitley Bay and it's strange walking up
Beach Avenue knowing that most of my family has gone and soon
Dad will be gone too. I was the first to run away. Now they're all
doing it.

But when I see the For Sale sign outside and the overgrown front
path and the curtainless windows, emotion takes me by surprise. I'm
a hard man and I'm standing outside our house about to burst into
tears. I march resolutely up to the front door. Do I stick my old key
in the lock or ring the bell? I ring the bell.

Dad doesn't answer. He probably thinks I'm the bank manager. I realize now that he wasn't, of course, a bank manager. Bank managers don't come to the door in the early evening intimidating children. He must have been some kind of debt collector.

I walk into the hall. It's much the same. The carpet's still torn and faded in the same places. Only the acoustics are different. It's more echoey. I look in the front room. Nan and Granda's room where Granda lay dying on his inflating bed. The room is empty. There are no curtains, the carpet is gone, there are holes in the walls where the shelves were. It's cold. There's a smell here, not Granda's death smell but the smell of emptiness and neglect. The smell of a house where people used to live.

Dad's asleep in the living room. He's lying in the armchair, the only piece of furniture remaining. He doesn't wake up so I walk past him. Empty breakfast room. The coke fire's out. The kitchen looks much the same and so does the bathroom. All the upstairs bedrooms are empty. There's no bed.

Dad hears me coming downstairs and starts to wake up. I stand, waiting for him.

'Where do you sleep?' I ask him.

'Where does it look like?'

'In the chair?'

'In the chair.'

Next to the chair is a pile of *Sun* newspapers, completed crosswords visible.

'Dad . . . where are all your things?'

'They took them.'

'Who?'

'Your mam took some of it. The bailiffs took the rest.'

'What about . . . what about your tools?'

Dad's tools are very important. Not only does he still use them but they're kept in the box he made as an apprentice. It's a beautiful box, a box for life. It's a showpiece for all the different joints and its maker's skill.

'They left me my second set.'

'Your box . . .'

'They took it.'

I shake my head. Dad lights a cigarette. I want to ask him if he's all right but I don't know how to ask my dad a question like that. Instead I say, 'Where will you go?'

'Council have got a flat . . .'

'That's good . . . What are you doing with yourself?'

'A bit of work . . .' He looks up at me and smiles mischievously. 'And a bit of dancing.'

Dad has always been a dapper dresser and a terrific dancer. I just haven't seen him do either of these things very often.

'Dancing?'

'Ballroom dancing, lad. I was rusty at first but you should see me now.'

Of course, that's how he met Mam. Is he looking for another wife? I decide not to ask any more questions. We go to the pub where conversation is not only unnecessary, it's frowned upon. I try to keep up with Dad's rounds but, as usual, I can't. After far too many pints I say I have to go. I lurch to the seafront, pretending I'm sober and walk towards the lighthouse. It's dark and the weather's gusty but a few late holidaymakers are marching into the headwinds all the same. Eventually, I catch the bus back to Tynemouth.

'Went to see Dad,' I tell Yvonne. 'He's living in that house with only an armchair. The bailiffs took everything. They even took his box of tools.'

She shrugs.

'I don't care,' she says. 'I don't care if I never see him again.'

I search her face for signs of humour. There are none. She's telling the truth.

# 5

MY FAILURE AT P COMPANY HAS ALWAYS NAGGED AT ME. NOW I SET about reapplying. And find that I can't. Army rationalization means that 244 Signals no longer serves the Paratroop Regiment. I'm moaning about this one day in the crewroom over a brew when our troop sergeant says, 'Forget the Paras, Frank. Try the SAS.'

I say, 'What's the SAS?'

'Special Forces. Stands for Special Air Service.'

This rings a bell. I remember seeing a small advertisement in the signallers' journal, *The Wire*, 'If you're looking for excitement and adventure . . .'

Harry, the sergeant, is ex-SAS himself. I've never asked him about it but I have noticed out on exercises that Paras, who I've learned to regard as tough and professional soliders, seem to respect Harry's wings.

'Who are they? What do they do?'

'The SAS is the cream of the British army. The élite. They're highly trained, mate, to a degree you can't imagine. Shooting, demolitions, medicine, hostage rescue, jungle warfare . . . proper soldiering, the best.'

That's enough. I want to join the SAS.

'Basically they're trained to work behind enemy lines. Each squadron's divided into troops. The free-fall troop can get in there by parachute. The mobility troop can get in by any overland means. The boat troop attacks from the water. The mountain troop gets the boys round any little obstacles that happen to be in the way . . .'

70

Stop right there, Harry. I want to join the SAS.

'And when they arrive they're capable of carrying out the most dangerous missions. Hiding out for days on end. Destroying strategic targets. Taking the enemy by surprise. Rescuing hostages . . .'

I want to join the SAS.

'They're real professionals. There are officers but the Regiment's different from the rest of the army. The soldiers know what they're doing and the officers let them get on with it . . .'

I want to join the SAS. Would they really take a signaller like me?

'They'll take anyone who can pass selection.'

I want to join the SAS. How do I apply?

Harry tells me I have to do this through Signals HQ in camp. First, I must borrow the two big army books which give the precise entry requirements for courses. Harry warns me that the selection course for the SAS is a hundred times worse than anything I experienced with the Paras.

I go straight to HQ and ask the clerk to let me look at the books. He glares at me.

'Why?'

I stare at my feet and mumble without saying anything. This doesn't deter the clerk.

'What do you want these books for? They're not light bedtime reading, you must want them for a purpose.'

'Well . . . I'm thinking of doing a course.'

'Oh yes? What course?'

I don't want to tell him. I don't want everyone to know I'm thinking of applying to join the élite of the British army. But in the end I have to. His reaction makes the SAS look even more interesting. He bursts out laughing.

'You! Not a chance!'

My turn to ask the questions.

'What do you know about them then?'

'I know those blokes are monsters. People practically die trying to pass their selection course. We had one lad pass once but he could crush nails between his hands until they went right through. Without even flinching.'

'Right through his hands?'

'George Freemantle. He could put nails right through his hands. I don't see you doing that, Collins.'

'Well, let me have the books anyway. And an application form.'

The clerk gives them to me, laughing.

Over the next few days I ask people surreptitiously what they know about the SAS. What they tell me is terrifying. Stories abound about the sheer machismo of these men. George Freemantle's name is mentioned again and again.

I hand my completed application form into the orderly room and wait. Days go by and I hear nothing. Finally I return to the clerk.

'My application form . . .'

'Oh I remember. The SAS.' Big guffaw.

'I haven't heard anything.'

'Well these things take time, give it a chance. SAS men hide out behind enemy lines for days, you know. They have patience.'

Yeah.

Nothing happens and eventually I return again. I have to go back a third time before I'm finally told that my application was turned down because I'm too young.

I must look as disappointed as I feel because the clerk softens his tone for a minute.

'It's a good thing, Collins,' the clerk tells me. 'Going on SAS selection takes months out of your life and you come back feeling a miserable failure. It's just as well they turned you down.'

The next time I see our troop sergeant he asks me about my SAS application.

'They turned me down because I'm too young.'

Harry shakes his head.

'How old did you say you are?'

'Nineteen.'

'You're not too young.'

He phones SAS HQ then and there. It's in Hereford, a place which sounds more agricultural than military. Don't cattle come from Hereford?

'I've got a young lad down here, he's a fit lad and he's nineteen. He's been told he's too young for selection. His name's Collins. Know anything about it?'

There's a long pause while things happen at the other end of the phone.

'OK, mate. OK. Yes, to me here. Good idea . . .'

When he puts down the phone he says that our Signals HQ had never even sent my form on to Hereford. They'd turned me down themselves. Now the SAS is sending the application form direct to Harry who'll give it to me to fill out. Then he'll send it back.

Soon, my posting instruction arrives. A letter informs me which course I'm on, when I'll arrive, what I should bring with me. I'm jubilant, except that it's not until the summer, some months away.

72

'Good thing too, mate,' says Harry, 'you need to start training now.'

My unit's also been sent a copy of the posting order. They realize that I've given them the slip and they're not pleased.

My officer commanding calls me in.

'You're making the wrong move, Corporal Collins. You're doing well. Stay here. Why go to Hereford? It's a hard course and few pass. It won't be easy for you to come back here a failure. Change your mind. It's not too late.'

But I have no intention of changing my mind. The officer tries one last time.

'Have you heard of a lad called George Freemantle?'

'Yessir.'

'He was a hard lad. He could crush nails in his hands. He could run for miles. He passed SAS selection. But he's the only one we've had pass.'

I am determined to be the second. I'm going to become a myth, just like George Freemantle. I'm going to pass this course and then I'll be a soldier, and not just any soldier, but a soldier in the SAS.

'How do I train?' I ask Harry. I know when I tried for the Paras I was unprepared and I'm not going to make that mistake again. I'm only slightly taken aback when he tells me that I must run for at least 10 miles every night with an 80 lb rucksack on my back.

I fill a rucksack with bricks and jerry-cans of water until it weighs 80 lbs. It's hard to lift, let alone run with. Somehow I get it on my back. I lurch from foot to foot, a cross between a stagger and a lope. I want to give up and go home but I'm determined. I'm going to be a real soldier, not just a lad with a Land Rover and a lot of radios.

I manage to go three or four miles, the massive weight rocking from side to side. The straps are thin webbing and they dig deep into my shoulders. The bouncing rucksack has rubbed my spine raw. My knees and ankles ache. My whole body hurts.

The next night after work I wrap foam rubber around the straps and pad my sore spine. Then I go out again.

'You're mad,' the others say. 'Don't do it.'

'I'm going to join the SAS,' I tell them.

And, a true exhibitionist, I manage something like a run until I'm out of the gate. The truth is that it feels even worse than it did last night. Uphill the weight is unbelievable. I feel as though I'm carrying my own body on my back. Downhill is even stranger. My rucksack is pushing me along. I can't stop if I want to.

Another lad in another troop, Jim, approaches me one day. He's training for the same selection course as me. He suggests we train

73

together. I agree. From now on I usually have a running partner.

In another few weeks the misery begins to abate and my body starts to accommodate these new demands I'm making of it.

I keep my full rucksack on the window sill of the block. That way I don't have to lift it up and down, just reverse into it. But the pain of doing up the straps and then taking the weight for the first time each night never goes. Then I have to get down the stairs in the hallway, hanging on carefully as each step jars my knees.

Gradually we increase our speed and distance until we're running 10 miles a night. Our blisters are spectacular.

On barrack-cleaning night there's always an inspection by the RSM, the same man whose leadership course I failed so dismally. Tonight the first thing he notices is my rucksack on the window sill. It weighs 80 lbs and I weigh 128. If I'm very honest, and I prefer not to be, I admit to myself that I wanted the RSM to see it.

He says, 'Whose is that?'

He grabs it to sling it aside but it doesn't even move. It was a small passing gesture but now, suddenly, the rucksack's immobility has made it the centre of the room. All the lads stare at him as he opens it and unpacks it. First he draws out a jerry-can holding five gallons of water. From the side pockets he pulls out bricks. There is silence in the room as he turns around.

'Is this some kind of a joke?' he snarls.

'Sir, it's mine,' I say. He turns to me with hostility.

'Then it must be a joke,' he says coldly.

'I'm training, sir. To go to Hereford.'

He stares at me. His eyes are glassy.

'Hereford?' he echoes in a small voice, pretending it's the first time he's heard of this. 'Hereford! The SAS! You!'

He begins laughing, a mechanical, humourless laugh.

'It is a joke!' he roars. 'It's certainly a joke! Corporal Collins, you aren't going to get to Hereford. You'll never pass.'

And he moves on, guffawing to himself.

'Corporal Collins! At Hereford!' he's heard muttering under his breath as he completes his inspection.

I'll show him.

Perhaps he thinks that failing to lift my rucksack has made him look small because he gets tough and finds a lot wrong in the block this evening. Dust, some rubbish, untidiness. And a few minutes later he discovers girlie magazines in the toilets and I'm forgotten in the consequent furore.

He goes and we all start cleaning busily. When I finally get outside

74

with my rucksack it's dark and late. The clouds are thick, threatening to fall. The wind is strong. It blows in sudden, violent gusts, sending leaves and twigs without warning across my path. I run out of the base. There is no traffic on this stormy night. After a few miles I turn off on to a small country lane, and then another. By now the wind is fierce. It buffets against my legs and pushes me along. I wonder what it will be like to run against it on the way back. The rain starts. It isn't torrential but it falls in bursts. I run on. I feel the rhythmic beat of my feet on the ground, the slight shudder of the rucksack with every step I take. I realize how comforting these familiar movements are. Beside me the trees are waving their branches frantically. And then one falls, just behind me.

The crash is awful. The smallest branches bounce against the road, the larger ones crack and, despite the roar of the wind, I can hear the splintering of wood. I am overwhelmed by a sense of evil. Late at night, in this lonely place, there is evil and I am frightened. It's the first time I have felt such a thing and I don't know what to do except run, run home as fast as I can.

When I get back to the safety of base I lie in bed thinking about what happened. Evil is stalking the world, a palpable presence. Does the devil really exist? I begin to wonder if that's what a soldier's job is: to fight against evil. I now want fervently to get into the SAS. That is what I see the SAS as doing: tough soldiers, fighting evil.

As my time to leave draws near it's clear there's no leaving party organized. I've only been here eighteen months, I haven't finished my posting and, anyway, they think I'll be coming back soon.

I don't want just to drift out of 244 Signals as if it all never happened, so I say, 'Er, what about my silver tankard, then?'

'Oh yeah. Your tankard.'

A tankard and a small party in the NAAFI is hastily organized. The tone is jovial but low-key. I'm the only person there who doesn't think we'll all be meeting again in a few months' time. I say an affectionate goodbye to my good mates but this is low-key too. From the day I decided to apply for SAS selection, our lives started to diverge. They knew I no longer shared their ambitions. I was leaving the brotherhood and our foursome began to disintegrate from that day.

Jim and I drive up to Hereford together to take selection. When we get there we ask the way to the camp and people say, 'Well, why do you want to know?'

'We're in the army,' we say. We puff our chests out and try to look hard.

'Well if you're in the army, you'll know where it is.'

75

We conclude that the people of Hereford are either very protective or very unhelpful. Eventually we find our own way and arrive at an unimpressive camp. It's just a selection of old wooden huts. It looks pre-war. But fluttering overhead is a blue flag with a winged dagger, and that's a fine sight.

There are Ministry of Defence police on the barrier but security is very relaxed. They send us up to Signals where the chief clerk welcomes us all. The sergeant major says that SAS Signals selection will be starting tomorrow.

'What does he mean, Signals selection?' I ask Jim in an undertone. He shrugs. He looks worried.

'Aren't we taking SAS selection?' I whisper. Jim shakes his head in confusion. I look around at the other lads and I can see that they're mostly thinking the same thing.

'Aren't we taking SAS selection?' someone asks out loud, one of the older lads.

The sergeant major explains that we're taking SAS Signals selection. If we pass, then we'll be signalmen serving the SAS. We'll be working closely with them and this will give us a better chance, if we want to try, of passing selection to the Regiment itself in a year or two's time.

Two years. I'm too shocked and disappointed even to return Jim's anguished look. Two more years of radios and ops rooms when the real action's happening outside. Two more years of being what is known in the army as a shiny-arse instead of getting muddy with the boys.

Some of the older lads start to argue.

'If you want to be in the SAS, you've much more chance of passing selection after a few years with us. We can help you through it. You'll have worked with the boys, you'll know the score.'

The protests continue. Finally the sergeant major says, 'You go now or you stay and take SAS Signals selection with us. You've got a choice. Make your mind up.'

I think of RAF Benson and the silver tankard and all the goodbyes. I'm not going back there. I stay. So does everyone else.

It is the summer of 1976 and it is hot. The reservoirs are low, the Brecon Beacons are burning, the grass is brown, the air is languid with unremitting heat, day after day. I turn red as, carrying large rations of water, we navigate our way around the Beacons for a month. This selection process is not too arduous and I'm happy out on the hills. Many of us pass and I, after all my running with an 80 lb rucksack, feel ridiculously overprepared.

We're issued with SAS smocks, windproofs rather than the combat jackets the rest of the army wears. We wear a three-coloured Signals belt with an SAS badge on it and the SAS sand-coloured beret with a Signals badge. On this badge is Mercury, the winged messenger, carrying laurels on his back. It looks as though he's got scales all over his back and this is how signallers are known: as scalybacks or scalys.

I go home and show my mother my uniform but it's just like two years ago when I was going to RAF Benson and wore my gas mask and combat gear for her. She sits down and cries.

The Regiment's just been brought to public attention for the first time in a glut of media horror stories. The prime minister, Harold Wilson, has retaliated against a particularly nasty IRA attack by announcing that he's sending in the SAS and now the newspapers are telling the world just how tough the boys are. It's probably all a tactic to terrify the Irish and it certainly terrifies my mam. The IRA has issued posters of Harold Wilson and the home secretary, Merlyn Rees, holding pistols and looking calculating. It says underneath, 'SAS – State Authorized Slaughter. An SAS man will dance with your daughter, deliver your milk, drive your taxi. Trust no-one. Talk to no-one.'

'You're making a big mistake. Don't do this, Frank,' Mam pleads with me.

I try to explain that I'm SAS Signals and not actually a soldier in the SAS but everyone except Mam seems to want to think I'm one of the hard men and in the end I don't bother to disillusion them. I just try to look mysterious.

'Frank,' says Mam, trying again, 'don't join the SAS. Change your mind. You joined the army for a proper career, not for this sort of thing.'

I turn on her suddenly, savagely, so that I even surprise myself.

'No! I joined the army to escape. To get away from all the fighting and the atmosphere and the misery in our house. That's why I joined the army.'

She stares at me. Shock and hurt register over her face and then she breaks down in tears again. I wish I'd never said it, even though it's the truth.

I take the bus over to Whitley Bay and see Dad in the pub.

'I'm getting married,' he tells me casually. I nearly choke on my pint.

'Who to?'

'Joanna.'

'Jo who?'

'Joanna and don't try calling her Jo for short because she doesn't like it.'

'When, Dad?'

'Next week.'

'But . . . who is she?'

'She's a widow. Works in a shirt factory. Supervisor. Good wage. Two children and a nice council house.'

'How did you meet her?'

I already know the answer to that one. Ballroom dancing. What I really mean is, how did you persuade her to marry you? But Dad's feeling chipper so I wish him lots of happiness before I stagger back to the bus stop.

'Did you know that Dad's getting married?' I ask Mam.

She just smiles.

One family wedding that we all attend is Yvonne's. She hasn't invited Dad but he announces he's coming anyway. He even intends to give her away. Yvonne insists Dick's going to give her away. The situation threatens to turn nasty and I'm given a special job at the wedding: to stop Dad from punching Dick.

I'm wearing my platform shoes and cream suit with flared trousers and I am the height of fashion. I hope fists don't start flying after Dad's had a few beers, or my suit will suffer. But everything goes smoothly. Dad mutters and moans a bit but keeps well away from Dick. He and Mam don't speak to each other.

To my mother's horror, SAS Signals are sending me straight to South Armagh. But first I have a few weeks of Northern Ireland training in Hereford. This is soldier training, so I enjoy it a lot. I'm allowed to play at being a green soldier with mud on my boots. I'm shooting down at the ranges. I'm learning about tactics and weapons. I'm happy.

A week later, we're sent across the water and I'm out on the streets of Belfast with a rifle completing my training. I'm alert, careful, and I don't overreact. Of course, the public don't know I'm nothing but a signaller, they think I'm a real soldier. I'm in a four-man patrol and I talk to a little boy on a street corner who's playing with a razor blade.

I smile and say: 'Let me have that!'

He looks up at me with something like the hatred which his parents no doubt show for the British army and shakes his head. He says, 'No!'

He reminds me of Michael, or, more likely, Michelle, when they were small and obstinate. I chat to him until he gives me the razor blade and his mother appears from nowhere and starts to drag him away.

I show her the razor. 'He found this and started playing with it . . . I took it off him . . .' My words die away. She glares at me and walks off with her son.

My whole life suddenly fits in a rucksack, or bergen as they're called here. Back at RAF Benson I was mostly in a three-quarter ton Land Rover with a cooker in the back and everything I could possibly need to hand. Now I travel light. But, wherever in the world I go, I know that I'll still be spending the next two years in ops rooms.

I join B Squadron at Bessbrook Mill in South Armagh, down on the border. It's a massive, Yorkshire sort of a mill, a big red-brick ware-house of a building. The windows are blanked out and on top is a false roof made of poles and wires to catch mortar bombs. It is surrounded by a high steel fence. Drive out of the gate and you are straightaway in enemy territory. The countryside is beautiful but systematically ruined by breeze-block bungalows with Spanish hacienda-style porches. This is because the police won't come down here to enforce any planning regulations. We're in bandit country.

I share a tiny room with the other scalys, eight of us in bunks. Our gear's kept in our bergens on our beds, only our washing and shaving kit are out. We're working with SAS men and living with them in close proximity. At night we're drinking with them or watching TV with them. As they learn to trust me they tell me more about what's going on. But I am never left in any doubt that they are in the Regiment and I am nothing but a scaly to the Regiment. Close friend-ship isn't possible.

Off-duty, there is little to do but drink. We scalys are locked up in our big mill, seldom getting out, serving the men who are taking part in the action but never seeing any ourselves. It's not surprising that there's a lot of heavy drinking. When a Royal Army Pay Corps staff sergeant is sent over to Bessbrook to check on the bar accounts and sort out a few pay claims, he is put in the spare bunk in our tiny room. He is allocated the bed no-one will sleep in, which is the bunk under-neath Jim. There is a very good reason we won't sleep there. Jim is incontinent when he has been drinking heavily. I have already been in the army long enough to know that this is by no means an uncommon problem. The RAPC man is furious the next morning and wants heads to roll.

He says, 'I woke up wet. I didn't know where it was coming from so I tasted it and found it was salty. So, I jumped out of bed and I slipped on something else on the floor. A pool of vomit!'

When we're working we're in another small room. Perhaps it's eight by eight. It's cluttered with desks and connected by a hatch to the ops officer's room. He's in there surrounded by maps and pieces of paper telling him who's in a patrol, where it is, what it's doing. He has information on every callsign as well as all the other codes and passwords supplied by the patrol leader before he goes out on the ground. He comes to the ops room after his briefing and fills in the briefing sheet without giving too much information. I don't have access to what's actually going on most of the time – I'm only a scaly.

Our room, in which I'm generally working solo, has a big map of the province, coded up for different areas. We have information sheets from the ops officer telling us which patrols are out and who's in them, and we have three handsets on different radio nets.

Even when nothing's happening and I'm sitting around reading a newspaper and making the boss cups of tea, I'm still expected to ensure that each patrol checks in hourly. If they've missed a call I try to contact them and, if they aren't contactable and miss a second call, someone has to go out and see that they're all right. Patrols are always being compromised.

Suddenly I hear a whispered voice coming up on the radio, 'Hello, zero, this is three-two-alpha, over.' It's no help to the guy if I yell when he's whispering so I whisper back, 'Zero. Send, over.'

'Ident three-two-alpha, chalkdust.'

'Zero. Chalkdust, over.'

I check the codeword list and it says that chalkdust means compromise. I call the boss next door, 'Boss, three-two-alpha's been compromised!'

The boss sticks his head through the hatch.

'What's going on out there?'

Over the radio I say, 'Three-two-alpha, this is zero. Roger your chalkdust, send sit rep, over.' Sit rep is a situation report.

'Three-two-alpha, woman out with two dogs, have to move, gone green army towards location four-one.'

This is a familiar compromise situation: dogs are always sniffing SAS men out. Cows are even worse. They spot the boys in a field and they'll stand in a circle all around them for hours on end. Going green army means that, once discovered, the patrol gets up, dusts itself off and says casually to the surprised dogwalker, 'British army. We'll be on our way now.'

Despite the public relations exercise in Britain telling us there isn't a war on here, we know there is. Anyone Irish is the enemy. We don't discriminate between terrorists and civilians, to us they are all potential killers and, when another soldier dies, the battle hots up.

Within a week of arriving here I get to the point where I'll do almost anything to get out of Bessbrook Mill. I'm jubilant when I'm told I can go out on patrol with the resident batallion, who happen to be marines. Although we're living separately from them at the mill, we're masquerading as one of their companies. When we go in and out we often wear marine berets, although the long hair, age, and non-standard weapons the boys are carrying probably gives the game away.

I'm in marine's uniform checking cars when we stop a carload of young lads who are coming from the south to work in the north. They're all about our age, that is, under twenty-one. They're on edge and so are we in this bandit country. We do the routine check of car numbers against names and one of the Irish lads, irritated by the delay, makes the mistake of saying, 'Come on, you know who we are, now let us go.'

We say, 'You're not going anywhere unless you walk around the car on your knees.'

They stare at us.

'With your hands on your head,' adds someone.

The anger and hostility in the Irish boys' eyes bore into us but we choose not to notice it. They are the enemy and they have been cheeky to us. They protest, but we are powerful because we have guns. We can hold them for an hour, if we like, and stop them getting to work. We can hold them all day and lose them their jobs. We can do anything we want to.

With as much dignity as they can muster, they put their hands on their heads and crawl around the car on their knees. We jeer and laugh. When they get up their knees are dirty and one boy is bleeding a little. They get into their car without speaking and drive off.

We laugh again.

We also carry out eagle patrols. A helicopter swoops down and drops us in a road to stop and check all cars and then after half an hour it returns and takes us away. These unexpected snap checkpoints can catch terrorists off their guard.

Our road check is causing traffic queues. There are irritated faces peering from a long line of windscreens, which we ignore. We are deliberately slow. One elderly man gets out of his car and walks up to us. He says, 'I'm in a terrible hurry, can you possibly let me go on now, boys? I served with the British army during the war.'

A lad who could be his grandson instructs him to get back in line.

The man says, 'Boys, I'm in a hurry and I've already been stopped once, about a half an hour ago.'

The lads say, 'Leg it, mate. Back to your car and wait with everyone else.'

Finally it's his turn. He drives his car up to the checkpoint. We get out our spanners and say, 'We're searching your car for explosives.'

He stares in horror as we proceed to take his engine apart and throw the pieces in the bushes. He turns red in the face and begins to shout.

'I fought for the Queen! I fought Hitler for your generation! I risked my life for your country.'

We look at him as if he's speaking another language. To us he's just an Irishman, a red-faced, shouting Irishman. He is exploding with fury, with frustration, with powerlessness. He threatens to report us but, as we very well know, there is no-one to report us to.

Finally the helicopter comes down to pick us up and we have a good laugh about him. The marines have already lost a few men on this tour and every single car driver down there is a hated enemy. There seems to me to be nothing wrong with the patrol's behaviour. I'd like to forget the angry old man but, to my surprise, his red face, his spitting rage and frustration, all come into my head occasionally for no good reason back in the ops room.

In the bar at Bessbrook I tell some of the SAS lads what happened. The signallers laugh and so do most of the soldiers. But a few of the older men shake their heads. Someone tells us that it's not what soldiering is all about. But it's hard to agree on just what soldiering is about these days.

The Regiment is in a process of change, even a new boy like me can pick that up. There's a difference between some of the more recent recruits and the old guard. The SAS are traditionally tough guys and tough fighters, with well-defined objectives. They wear green and the enemy wears brown and the boys run up hills and kill them. But here in Ireland things are different and some of the men don't like it. There are a lot of resignations in B Squadron during and after this tour. The older men are sometimes tempted by the high sums they can command for security work outside, and they are fed up with the plain clothes undercover jobs here. Morale is low because they are hamstrung by rules and restraints they're unused to. This isn't the work they trained for and they don't enjoy it.

Whenever there's a chance to get out of the mill, I jump at it. An unusual opportunity comes up. There's an SAS man who can't drive and he's looking for someone who can to sit with him while he practises for his test. Of course, none of the men want to go out with him so he asks for a scaly. I offer to go. The soldier's nickname, not very reassuringly, is Thumbs.

Although it's only a driving lesson, no-one ventures out of the mill unarmed. I'm carrying a little 7.65 Walther PPK. It's not a spectacular gun but it can kill someone if it has to and it's the sort James Bond uses. We drive around the dark country lanes, occasionally catching an animal in the headlights, when suddenly we round a bend and drive smack into a group of men in hoods and an unidentifiable uniform. They wave us down and we join a line of cars which the men are checking in a paramilitary sort of way. We've already made sure we know where the legal checkpoints are today and, anyway, this is obviously an ivcp, an illegal vehicle checkpoint.

This situation would be funny if it wasn't so dangerous. Here's an SAS man who can hardly drive stuck like a fly in a spider web. And his back-up man is a scaly. A very good driver might have been able to swing around and escape, but not a learner. Ivcps have cut-offs which you drive past without noticing. If you turn round and try to go back, the cut-off shoots you.

So we sit, sweating in our trap, waiting for one of the hooded men to get to our car, realize we're members of the security forces and shoot us. We strain our eyes trying to find something which will identify whose checkpoint this is.

There's a codeword for an ivcp and we get on the radio and send it. I can even manage a grim smile as I imagine what's going on in the ops room. Jim's sitting watching TV, he notices that nine-five hasn't called in and suddenly he gets this codeword. He doesn't recognize it and when he checks it he has to double-check it. Then he rushes to the ops officer yelling, 'Ivcp! Ivcp!' and suddenly the nice quiet evening is full of people running, asking who's out there.

'It's who? *Who?* Oh no! It's Thumbs and a scaley!'

Then they're organizing a team and weapons to come and help us out while Jim tries to rustle up the Quick Reaction Force.

Thumbs and I sit in the little car with our hearts thumping as the hooded men gradually work their way down the line towards us.

'What's happening?' Jim keeps asking over the radio.

'Can't tell.'

'How many men?'

'Can't tell . . . maybe three or four . . .'

'What are they armed with?'

'Can't tell . . . no, wait, there are some sort of rifles . . .'

But now we have to switch off the radio as the balaclavas are too close. We have our guns ready but keep them hidden as the men are sure to shoot if they see them.

Then we are able to discern that they're all carrying the same kind of self-loading rifles, British army issue. We know at once that this is an Ulster Defence Regiment patrol which has had a few beers and got out of control and set up its own checkpoint.

When they reach the car we flash up our IDs.

'Security forces. Who are you?'

At this point we hope our theory is correct because if they're Provos then we're dead.

The UDR men are clearly taken aback.

'You're not meant to be here, you'd better thin out. Security knows you're about now,' we warn them.

They disappear and we get on the radio.

'Stand down, stand down, it's UDR.'

'What! Who are they? Did you get their names?'

We haven't taken their IDs but the men are identified later anyway and given a good rifting. Thumbs drives us straight back to Bessbrook. We agree he's had enough practice for one night.

# 6

AT THE END OF THIS TOUR I GO BACK TO HEREFORD FOR THREE OR FOUR weeks. I live in camp and my social life is based at a local parachute club. There are a lot of wild young men and, to my delight, women. I've already brought a few girls here but it's boring for them to hang around while I jump. The only solution is to meet someone who likes jumping too. Of course, I want to womanize, I'm barely twenty-one. But in my heart of hearts, I want more. I want romance. I want to be loved and hugged. I want warmth and affection. I've had a few girlfriends. Now it's time for me to fall in love. But who with?

I often stay overnight at the club. We drink hard until about 2 a.m., then get our names up on the chalk board to jump first the next morning. We're up early, ignoring our hangovers, to push the aircraft out of the hangar. The first jump on a cold, grey morning is a mixed thrill. It's minus twenty up in the air, the pilot's wearing hats and scarves and gloves and all the clothes he can because there's no door in these little aircraft. We stick our fingers in the vents to try to keep them warm. Then we jump. Weather permitting, we jump all day, party for much of the night, then jump all day Sunday.

I'm really learning to fly now. There's an art to controlling your body as it plummets through the air. Gradually, like learning some new dance, I begin to increase my speed, to decrease it, to track to the left and the right with the ease of a bird.

We make human formations in the sky, small groups of us. Before we skydive, we dirt dive. The club has a plywood mock-up of a plane out on the grass by the hangar and we bundle into it.

'Cuuuut . . . OK, out the door!'

'Ready, ready, three, two, one . . . go!'

We leap out of the make-believe plane and onto the ground, looking ludicrous with our arms out, pretending to fall when we're actually standing, pretending to fly into position when we're actually walking. On the grass, we link hands to form a Snowflake, a Doughnut or an Accordion. I'm working my way towards the black belt of free-fall, Category Ten.

Once the plane gets up to altitude, we crouch by the door, waiting to jump. There's usually a moment when that old enemy, terror, reappears. I'm going to fall through the air from 10,000 feet. I don't want to do it. But anticipation replaces fear. I'm not going to fall through the air, I'm going to fly through it.

I dive out of the plane, and the rush of the air feels like a trusted friend. Now I know how to use that air. I see the others getting into position far beneath me. I put my arms back and send myself down towards them fast, like an arrow. As I get closer I swoop in a little, arms out, decreasing my speed with the drag. I hold out my hands to link with the others. Joining the formation is high-precision flying.

Then, when my altimeter reads 3,500 feet, it's time to go. We break the Snowflake, turn, straighten our legs, push our arms back and track fast away from each other to clean air where there's no chance of parachutes or people colliding. There's just five seconds to find clean air and open my canopy. A return of terror. I'm down to 2,500 feet now. Any malfunction of the main parachute will take 10 seconds to sort out and by that time I'll be down to 1,000 feet with only 5 seconds to go before I hit the ground. The ground's rushing towards me at a speed that's surreal. I pull the cord. Bang. Over my head there's a canopy, a tightening around my shoulders, my speed drops and I float to earth.

On Monday, it's back to work in camp and, in the cookhouse, there's an extra 200 men today. They're fresh-faced hopefuls who are here to take SAS selection. They look big and tough and ready for anything.

Each day, there are fewer of them. I watch in alarm as men go out in the morning on trucks and then come back bandaged and nearly crippled. Selection is obviously far worse than anything I was prepared for when I came here and I rapidly realize it was just as well that I didn't try it.

Within a week, there's only 100 men left. Another week, and there's only 50. Soon, there are only 10. I am shocked at the state of some of the men when they quit. What happens to them out there on the

Beacons? How do they get broken? Some are tearful with disappointment.

All this time I've been assuming that I'll wait my two years and then take selection and pass. Now that assumption is swept away. The horrible prospect of a lifetime of scalyhood opens up before me. I resolve that if I don't get into the Regiment in two years' time, I'll leave the army.

Not long after I've decided I'm ready to fall in love, that's exactly what I do. Her name is Philippa.

She is the daughter of an ex-SAS man and spends a lot of time at the club with her father and brother. She's a college student and a very good free-faller. Apart from the family interest in free-fall, she benefits from a phenomenon that we call Pretty Girl Progression. This means that men always want to jump with the pretty girls and they get a lot of experience and progress quickly.

Philippa is small, athletic and dark-haired. If she has any idea how I feel about her, she doesn't show it. We go out a few times: she doesn't rebuff me but it's hard for even someone as love-crazed as me to delude myself that she's really interested in me. However, the night before I fly out to Oman I stay with her family. She sleeps upstairs and I sleep downstairs but she gives me a goodnight kiss to remember and on the strength of this I take all my hopes to Oman with me. By the time I get there I can think of little else but Philippa. I do my job and I do it well but every spare corner of my mind is Philippa's and at night, in my dreams, I'm all hers.

I write to her. I declare my love in full and, I hope, poetic terms. I reveal more of myself than I have ever revealed to anyone, even Daniel from Whitley Bay. I try to make these letters comic and upbeat but they are engulfed by emotion. I can only submit to my feelings in astonishment.

Our reason for being in Oman is of little interest to me. I know that the war here with Yemen has just ended. I know that the SAS and other regiments have been actively involved in that war for about seven years. It's gone unnoticed and unreported by the media but the Regiment's role in this predominately tribal conflict has been significant and some of the battle sites have gone down in Regiment history as places of great heroism. Although the war is over, the SAS has remained here. We enjoy a close relationship with the *firqas*, armed hill people who patrol with us. Officially we are known as BATT, the British Army Training Team. Unofficially, we are still active in the interests of the Sultan of Oman.

Diplomacy is important when dealing with the *firqas*, but when a headman expresses an unhealthy interest in me, my diplomatic powers fail me. Unfortunately, one of the soldiers, Freddie Porker, smells cash.

'Hey, Blondie,' he says. 'The chief's offered three thousand rials for you.'

'Oh yeah?' Freddie Porker's not a man you want to cross but my tone says I'm not interested in a night with the chief.

'C'mon,' says Porker, 'three thousand rials is about eight thousand pounds. That's a lot of money.'

'Yeah,' I agree morosely. I can't believe that Porker is going to try to talk me into this one.

'Listen. We'll take the money and what we'll do is rescue you before nightfall.'

Porker squints at me. He already has deep crow's-feet from crinkling his eyes into the sun. He's a Regiment veteran, and when he takes off his shirt you can see operation scars all over his body like a patchwork quilt. His eyes are very blue.

'Look,' I protest, 'what happens if you're late?'

'We won't be late, Blondie.'

'Well just suppose you were late. It could get very painful for me, Porker.'

'We'll split the money fifty-fifty. That's fair. That's four thousand pounds for you. It takes a scaly a long time to earn that much and you'd earn it in a few minutes.'

I shake my head. No dice.

Porker strides off muttering about scalys. I hope he forgives me. He has quite a reputation as a hard man of the Regiment. He is called Porker because of a famous incident when he was doing the combat survival phase of selection. In this test, men are turned loose in the hills without provisions and told to get to a rendezvous point, all the time evading the hunter forces which are out to capture them. Porker stumbled across a farmyard and thought it was a likely source of food. He didn't know that the hunter forces happened to be billeted at the same farm. Porker broke into a pig pen and stole a piglet. The sow made such a commotion that the hunters went out to see what was going on. Freddie Porker rushes off with the piglet under his arm, hotly pursued. He realizes he's going to be caught and so he decides he may as well eat some pig first. He rips the back leg off the piglet and throws the rest of the animal, squealing, over his shoulder. As he runs, he gnaws on the back leg. The lads in the hunter force found the pig with its leg ripped off, witnessed Porker's exit with the missing leg in his mouth and decided that there was no way they wanted to catch this man. Porker had earned both his place in the Regiment and his nickname.

The biggest excitement of this Oman trip is the arrival of a letter from Philippa. I go back to my tent and tear it open. The letter says that it snowed today. Her mother's unwell. The cat's hurt its tail. Something about a new parachute. Nothing about love. I read and reread her words, scanning the lines for some gentle allusion to her feelings but it seems she doesn't have any. There's also no acknowledgement of the declarations I've been making to her. At the end it says love, Philippa. I fasten my hopes on this. But when I get back to Hereford, Philippa is going out with Bob. He's a new boy at the club. He's in the Regiment as a soldier, not a signaller, and he's tall and charming and handsome. I only have to look at Philippa to know that she feels about him the way I feel about her. I sink into a deep, hopeless misery.

Over in Northern Ireland again, I'm still locked away in the scalys' room. But this tour is more exciting. The SAS is now working province-wide, not just confined to the violent border area. I'm an experienced signaller and I've worked with the boys for a while now and I'm trusted. Gradually they tell me a little more about what the patrols are really doing out there. And some of the jobs are exciting.

There are car chases and close-target surveillance ambushes and shoot-outs. The signallers have to be able to deal with fast, abbreviated communications. It's no good repeating, 'Say again, over. Say again, over . . .' when the boys are in a tight spot. I have to be able to talk to them without panicking, and to find out what they need – like the Quick Reaction Force – fast. With a mixture of guesswork and experience I often have to work out where they are and what they're saying. This is hard comms and I enjoy it. Not so much as I would if I was actually out there, but I feel part of a team and I know that the success of an operation can be down to good communications.

By now I have total respect for the men I'm living and working with and I desperately want to be one of them. They're mature and professional. All the army things which matter elsewhere seem unimportant to them. They couldn't care less about bulling their boots. They don't salute. In fact they have little respect for officers. They have nothing to prove.

They all know I'm hoping to take selection next year and gradually, as I become more of a team member, they give me tips on how to pass. But there's a hint from some of them that I'm unlikely to do so. I'm not a blade. I have never been a soldier. Most SAS men come

89

from the infantry, most notably the Paras. Frank Collins has spent his army career on his backside.

I start training again. Round and round the base with my heavy bergen on my back. The perimeter is two miles, I do six to ten laps a night.

Deep down inside, I doubt about my ability to pass. When my confidence is at its lowest ebb, I apply to the Metropolitan Police. It's not hard to get in with army experience and if I fail selection, when I fail selection, the Met will be there waiting for me. I may not be a soldier but I've already grasped the principles of good soldiering and one of them is plan your escape route.

Early in the summer of 1978, I start training seriously on the Brecon Beacons. I'm accompanied by my pal Robbie, another signaller with aspirations to throw off his scaly suit. We spend a month's leave getting to know the terrain. We practise navigating and map-reading and at night we sleep under a poncho, a green groundsheet with a pole underneath it.

Philippa has split up with Bob and is going out with another soldier from the Regiment. I begin dating Alice, a doe-eyed sixteen-year-old who has started coming to the parachute club. She's pretty and fun but she's not Philippa. I'll never be a fool for love again. I'll never open my heart like that again. I like Alice but I'm careful, very careful. There are large chunks of me that Alice can't have.

I take Alice home to meet Mam. Gary, who's working in the security world now, installing alarms, is scandalized by the age gap. His big brother, the SAS hero, has a girlfriend who is three years younger than he is. But Mam is charmed by her, probably because she never knows Alice's exact age, and immediately takes her under her wing. Alice is amazed when she and I are allocated the black leatherette settee from Whitley Bay which folds out into a double bed. Alice thinks it's very grown-up to be given a double bed. She doesn't know that Mam is already fantasizing about grandchildren.

Nan takes to her and tells her the old stories. I leave her listening to the one about Nan's chest turning to black pudding and go over to Whitley Bay to meet my dad and Gary for a drink.

'When I came up the coast road,' I remark, 'I thought of stopping off and seeing Granda Collins.' I remember the impromptu visit I paid him when I was thinking of joining the army. That's probably the last time I saw him.

Dad and Gary look at each other. Then Dad says, 'He's dead.'

My pint stops halfway between the bar and my mouth.

'What?'

'He died.'
'When?'
'A few months ago.'
'But . . . why didn't you tell me?'
They shrug.
'Well, you were away.'
'You could have written!'
They look at each other and shrug again. I realize that, just as the family is very firmly out of my thoughts when I'm away, they don't spend a lot of time thinking about me either.

# 7

IN AUGUST SELECTION BEGINS. THIS IS THE MOST ARDUOUS SELECTION procedure anywhere in the British army and probably in the world. The pass rate is sometimes as low as 5 per cent. Nobody's failed in selection: you fail yourself. You know when you can't go on any more.

Some phases will test me, physically and mentally, to my limits, and assess how I cope with that. Other phases are pure training. It's a long process: in the highly unlikely event that I stay the course, I won't be finished before December, five months away.

Just when selection's due to start, I bump into Tony, one of the SAS men I've worked with closely. He laughs at me.

'Are you on selection?'

I nod.

'I'll tell you now. You don't stand a chance. You'll fail,' he says, and walks off chortling. I resolve that I am going to show Tony a thing or two.

On day one we gather in camp and I look around at the others. I am twenty-one, quite a few years younger than the average. Everyone is keen, focused, determined, and fit. I've seen it all before in the cook-house. Within a few weeks, it'll be platform four at Hereford station for most of us, and a large proportion of us will need help getting onto the train.

We spend the first week with an instructor who has a map, shows us where we are on the Beacons, and then asks us to map-read. The routes we take get more and more arduous and we carry progressively heavier weights. In this terrain, in this heat, it's hard. When the ground's flat or uphill, I stride. When it's downhill I run. You don't just have to finish, you have to finish fast.

We're wearing standard army issue DMS, or Directly Molded Sole boots. Keeping even a favourite pair of old boots from torturing you in these conditions is a science. If your boots give way, it's a crisis and if you haven't got a well-worn back-up pair you're finished. Most of the lads are waging war on blisters but my running sore is my bergen, cutting into my shoulders and rubbing against my spine. I use every padding technique I can devise on my shoulders and zinc oxide tape on my raw spine. I have deep cuts which rapidly turn septic.

Each night we burst our blisters and soak our feet in surgical spirit. It's supposed to cauterize the tears but when it hits the broken blisters it feels like holding a lighted match up to my feet. Then I wrap them in zinc oxide tape.

The fourth week is test week. A lot of lads have already given up.

Every morning we're taken out to the Beacons, every night the trucks deposit their shattered, limping cargo back at camp. The pass grade is a C. You can't afford to get anything less, not unless you can make up for it with an exceptionally high grade. Your grades are secret, or they're supposed to be. However, I know some of the instructors, since I've signalled for them, and they leak my marks to me each day.

On day one they tell me I'm graded C. That's good enough.

On day two, I'm given a scrappy piece of paper with a sketch map on it – there's a tree here, a hill there. I'm escaping from a prisoner of war camp and I have to navigate using this flimsy little piece of paper. I take a wrong turning and come in half an hour late. I am graded E. This is a crisis. I am in danger of failing selection already. In the evening, Tony wanders into my hut.

'Still here! Incredible! But I hear you got an E today. You'll be out tomorrow, mate.'

On day three we are taken to a Welsh valley where the grass is long. It's tiring walking through this. We're climbing up and down valleys for more than 20 miles. I have to do well or I'm out. I have a little pocket radio and, no matter how much I tune it, I can find nothing but hymns. Today must be Sunday. So I keep it tuned to the hymns and find myself back in school assembly at Whitley Bay. I thought I wasn't listening, in fact it was a point of honour to treat hymns with complete disdain but now, here I am, singing along. I don't know them all but they're coming at me in sterling Welsh voices and I find myself striding out confidently in time to the hymns. No-one could

93

be less religious than me but this music, out here on the hills, is strangely uplifting. With a spring in my step I score a B today. That's good.

The following day I actually look for hymns on my radio. But they're just for Sundays and all I can find is pop music.

We're dropped off at a checkpoint and given a grid reference. I march to the grid and someone's waiting there in a small tent. It's raining and all he does is stick his head out.

'Number?' he calls.

I supply my name and number. He gives me the next grid reference and away I go. There are no pleasantries and the possibility of a brew doesn't arise. He doesn't even point me in the right direction. I carry my own food, eat as I go, stop, change my socks, have a drink, map-read and get going again. The month Robbie and I spent out on the hills is really paying off now. We're both still in. I know that if I'm to stay in I must get another B today, to compensate for that E. But by now I am taking every day at a time and expecting nothing. I'm just trying to get to evening.

When I reach the final rendezvous the truck is waiting and no-one else is on it. There must be a mistake. I must have missed a grid. I'm out now, for sure.

I give the instructor my name and wait for him to start laughing at me.

He says, 'On the truck.'

'What?'

'On the truck.'

It's a trick. He's going to tell me I've failed any minute. Soon there's the sound of grunting getting closer. A bergen's slung onto the truck and a gaunt figure's walking up the tailgate. It's Sandy, the broken-nosed hard man who's been first back every day. He stares at me.

'What you doing here?' he asks. 'Jacked it in?'

'Er . . . no.'

I've beaten Sandy to the truck. I've definitely missed a checkpoint. I must have done something wrong. But no. When I see the instructor he tells me I've got an A. I'm jubilant. There's no sign of Tony.

The next day I get another C. Last onto the truck is a small, tubby Welsh corporal. He heaves his bergen on board and then himself.

'That's me finished!' he says.

We urge him to continue. There's only one more day to go. It's an endurance march, covering 45 miles over the hills with a 65 lb pack.

'Nooooo,' the corporal says, shaking his head vigorously. 'Noooo.

I'm off. I never really wanted to be in the SAS. I'm only doing this to lose weight and I've lost enough now.'

I look down at his feet and there is blood coming out of the lace-holes of his boots. As he crosses the truck, more blood squelches out of the tops and runs down the sides of his boots.

My neck is now badly scarred by my bergen and my feet are horribly blistered but, compared to some of the other feet in the spider hut, they're doing well.

At 4a.m. the next morning, we're dropped off in the hills. The sergeant major calls out a list of about twenty names. Mine's on it. He takes us aside and says, 'Right, you lot, you haven't just got to pass today, you've got to get an A or a B.'

We all nod numbly. I'm confused because I know my grades and, now I've compensated for the E, I've been hoping a C will get me through today. Evidently that's not good enough. Maybe my immaturity is already counting against me. I steel myself to give the endurance march everything I've got. I wish they'd tell us the times we have to aim for.

My friend Robbie turns to me as we walk away. He knows he needs an A today to stay in. He says, 'That's it, Blondie. I can't do better than a pass.'

I say, 'Come on, Robbie, you can do it!'

Robbie shakes his head.

We start off together and I think I might be able to get him through by encouraging him. This works until we're heading towards the final checkpoint. He's shattered. We're all shattered but I've got a little more fight left in me than Robbie. It's clear he's holding me back. Another lad, Curly, urges me to go on ahead with him.

'Robbie's finished. Give yourself a chance, Ginge, and get moving.'

I hesitate. I know he's right but I don't want to leave my mate. Into my mind comes the RSM's leadership course, back at RAF Benson. I blew it because I didn't want to leave my mates. I'm relieved when Robbie says, 'Go on, Blondie. Go ahead.'

Curly and I march on into the rain. After a few minutes, when we're up the next slope, I look back at Robbie. He's barely moving now. I'm walking but only out of habit and it's not my usual walk. It's mechanical, but the machine is going wrong. I know that my limbs are connected to me because of the pain which comes with each step. But they're not obeying orders any more.

'We're nearly there. We're nearly there,' Curly keeps saying. He's a signaller too, for the Paras. He arrived at SAS Signals selection and got the usual lecture about working as a signaller for two more years and, instead of accepting it meekly, he kicked up a storm. He ranted and raved and yelled until they finally agreed to let him take SAS selection. After the fuss he's made, he knows he just has to pass.

We finish. We're completely spent. Robbie's not far behind. I've finished the 45 miles in 17 hours and 10 minutes. It turns out that 17 hours qualifies for an A, so I get a good B grade. Robbie is just 10 minutes behind me. That means he's only 20 minutes outside an A but that 20 minutes costs him the course.

Tony comes to the spider hut that night.

'So, you're through. Well done. But it's jungle training next and don't think you can win out there, boy.'

Four days later we're off to Belize. The night before we leave, Curly's wife starts to miscarry their baby. He kisses her goodbye, leaves her with the doctor, and catches the flight with the rest of us. You've got to be completely focused on one thing and one thing only to pass this course. Nothing else can matter.

I've been to Belize before. As a signaller, the jungle was something you looked at from the outside, perhaps something you visited for half an hour. Now we're flying over it, low, in a helicopter, and it looks like a massive, bumpy green rug. Any minute now we'll be deposited right in its heart, miles from anywhere.

The helicopter circles and hovers and then lowers itself. When we climb out we find we're on a big log platform. On all sides the jungle slopes away from us. The heat, a wet heat, the sort that sits on your head like a big, hot, bath sponge, has us sweating within moments. The rotors give us a bit of breeze but they're kicking up leaves and dust and chopped twigs, all of it debris from busy machetes. It's a relief when, almost immediately, the helicopter takes off again. Then we're left alone in the jungle, the dense heat wrapping itself all round us.

We each have a bergen to carry, full of everything we'll need, our rifles and a big box of rations.

We walk in single file down a thin trail. It's muddy and impossible not to slip. It's hard to balance when my arms and back and shoulders are carrying so much weight. I estimate that it's 150 lbs. I weigh 140 lbs.

The vegetation reaches out for me, spiky and hostile. I haven't seen anything like these leaves before except possibly small, neat, unthreatening versions on my Auntie June's houseplants back in Whitley Bay. I imagine parting some of the big leaves and discovering Auntie June here in the jungle. The idea is so surreal that I guffaw. No-one notices.

We walk in silence, except for puffing and grunting. Everyone, even the biggest man, is struggling with his box. The heat is wrapping itself around me now, making every step difficult. The overhead canopy is light and birchy, allowing thick growth beneath and everything here seems designed to trip me or grab me. Things fall onto me. I can feel them on my neck but I can't do anything about them. There's something in my boots. So this is the jungle.

Suddenly, through the thick undergrowth, I see a black face. I recognize it. This is Ray, an instructor and one of the few black men in the Regiment. Ray doesn't move or acknowledge me in any way. Our eyes meet and I pass on. As we reach the bottom of the hill I notice a bullet case, empty, lying in the mud. I ignore it. Later, there's a mess tin off to one side.

After about a mile of this, the sound of running water gets closer. We arrive at a small camp which has been set up by a bend in the river. A tree has been felled across the river and this is the only means of access to the camp. It is about 40 feet long. Twenty feet below is water. The log is slippery and somehow we have to balance as we carry our bergens, our rifles and our ration boxes.

On the other side is a collection of amazing shelters made of bamboo with big frondy leaves on the roofs. I don't delude myself that this is for us. The men who've been setting up the camp have made themselves these bed spaces. Now it's our job to make our own. We dump our gear and are told where we can put up our hammocks. We can hear other helicopters overhead bringing more men in. Eventually there are about thirty of us.

We're called together for a talk from the regimental sergeant major. It's his camp. He's the Regiment's top man and he's here to watch us and decide whether he wants us or not.

While we surreptitiously pick the bugs and beasties off our hands and necks he tells us that the move down from the helicopter was appalling. Most of us weren't looking or watching. He instructs us to put up our hands if we saw anything which shouldn't have been there.

Hands go up, including mine.

'What did you see?'

'I saw some ammunition, sir.'

'Good. What about you?'

'Mess tin, sir, hanging on a tree.'

'Yes, anyone else see the mess tin?'

A few hands go up.

'What about this man? Did anyone see him?'

Ray grins and looks at me.

My hand goes up.

'What else?'

An empty round. A knife. A cigarette packet. A pair of binoculars. A machete. I realize I've seen only a few of the props they planted.

I've worked out after that hard one-mile hike that I can never win against the jungle. If it becomes my enemy then I'll lose. I have to find a way to work with it.

We're organized into patrols of five men. The fifth is an officer, also on selection. Each patrol needs a signaller and, not surprisingly, I'm appointed signaller to my patrol.

And so the long ordeal starts. It's an ordeal not because the jungle is such a terrible place after all but because, from now on, whatever we're doing, we're being observed and assessed.

Nights in the jungle are dark. There's little risk of attack then: the enemy's more likely to strike at first light. So by first light we have to be out of our hammocks and in position. It's impossible to sleep well and not difficult to wake up because we're so cold and wet. The idea is that we sleep in our dry gear and after a day or two we know it's worth almost anything to keep our dry gear dry, so that there's something to change into at the end of the day.

In the pitch-black – your eyes can never become accustomed to this darkness so you have to know where everything is – I grope for my bergen and soon locate the cold, wet clothes I took off last night hanging over my bed poles. Somehow I get them on. I am going to put a cold, wet shirt on every morning for a month. Can I stand it? I think of the ops room, with its heater and its charts and its radios. That's the option for me. I put on the shirt.

My dry gear goes in a plastic bag. I can't see the bugs and beasties but I can feel them biting and stinging me. My rifle and belt kit are always to hand, that's one of the first rules. Now I've got everything, I make my way to my position.

It doesn't take long for me to find a position I like. It's an attap, a tree with big palm fronds. I can sit underneath its big umbrella and watch the rain dripping past me. I am well-hidden and keep a good lookout. After a while my attap seems like an old friend, a retreat from the tension of jungle training.

Our combat drills put all the pressures on us that we'd expect in a real battle. As a patrol we advance down a valley, knowing the enemy's out there. Suddenly, a target pops up, sometimes four targets pop up. We're an aggressive, reactive patrol, and we have to take out the target. As we advance, we use grenades. Our lead scout fires off. As bullets fly the shout goes up, 'Enemy right!' The patrol leader directs us, 'Frank, move round!'

Then there's a yell.

'Grenades!'

The rest of the army hardly ever uses grenades in this way. If they throw a grenade they watch where it lands and then get their heads down. Here, we're running forward. We hit the deck at the cry, 'Grenades!' and then we're up and running foward almost immediately, firing on automatic as we go. About a metre away, my mate's doing the same. Twenty yards behind us is another lad who sees where we're going and puts down covering fire.

No wonder the SAS often has training fatalities. The weapons and ammo we're using are all real. It's the only way to learn and we're learning how to win the firefight. Effective enemy fire is taking casualties. It's no good hitting the ground every time a gun goes off. If they're firing automatics you have to keep your head up and fire back because then they'll bottle out. Or you go down fighting. There isn't a man among us who isn't prepared to go down fighting. We want to join the SAS and the SAS don't run away. They fight, they advance, they take casualties. Or they die.

This is hard soldiering and I love it. We learn about close quarter battle techniques, spraying and slaying, ambushes, how to hang mortar bombs in trees, booby traps and the construction of razor-sharp bamboo traps. We learn about speed, aggression, surprise. SAS.

When we're map-reading our way through the jungle we're usually rushing to get to a grid reference in an impossibly short time. We have a lead scout who goes ahead looking for the enemy. This man's all eyes and ears and his rifle's always ready. He's looking for a bent twig, a footprint, a leaf . . . when his hand goes up the whole patrol stops and he goes down on one knee. Number two, the navigator, moves forward. They discuss what they've seen and work out what direction they're going.

The officer leading our patrol has something to prove. His father was prominent in the Regiment and this lad is determined not to fail him. He's a good officer but an appalling map-reader. If I say, 'I think we're here,' he's certain to disagree.

'No, Frank, we're here.'

The whole patrol might back me but he remains adamant. Partly because he's been told to provide some tough leadership.

Previously the SAS, unlike the rest of the army, has been a soldiers' operation. The men were the professionals and the decision-makers and they treated officers as if they were just there to sign the claim forms. Now, backed by a new colonel, the bosses have decided it's time for things to tighten up. Officers are to push their authority more. As a signaller I've already seen the animosity this change is causing: it's even been responsible for a steady trickle of resignations. Even the mighty Freddie Porker has thrown in the towel. So when our officer flexes his muscles, I know what's behind it.

Our officer asserts his right to map-read and we say, 'Well, you're in charge, let's go.'

Soon, predictably, inevitably, we are lost. It's hard terrain to navigate and everyone has problems but our patrol is constantly lost. We arrive back at base hours, sometimes days, after everyone else. They slow handclap us in. We walk behind our officer, signalling to the others that we were lost again and it was his fault. To his credit, the officer always takes full responsibility but, all the same, our patrol becomes legendary for its tardiness. We are all of us convinced that we'll be failed.

Each patrol is shadowed by a member of the directing staff who watches how we're doing and witnesses all our mistakes. Our DS is nicknamed Blot.

As usual, we're lost in the jungle.

'I think we're here,' says our officer, pointing at the map. 'What does the rest of the patrol think?'

He's ready for us to disagree with him as he's nearly always wrong.

We take a look. We're certainly at the junction of two streams. Are they the right streams? The jungle's running with water and there are few landmarks.

'Yep,' we say, 'looks fine to us.'

The officer is taken aback. Not only do we all agree where we are, but it's the right place.

Our DS, however, isn't so sure.

'Wait here,' he tells us, 'I'll just go and check.'

He'll go up the hill for a better view. He takes off his belt kit and starts off.

The belt kit consists of webbing and pouches, connected by a yoke which goes over the shoulders. It can weigh 30 lbs if it's fully loaded. Generally it has six magazines full of ammunition, a first aid kit, survival rations . . . the golden SAS rule is that you must never take off your belt kit. Ever. It's your lifeline and your survival. Even at night, it's never, like your rifle, beyond arm's reach. If a member of the directing staff sees either out of arm's reach, you're out.

Blot starts off up the hill and he leaves his belt kit behind. We exchange glances. But we know it must be all right. He's an instructor and he knows what he's doing. We sit down and wait. The streams trickle and roar. We watch the water, take a nap, relax. And wait. And wait. The instructor's belt kit becomes a sort of presence in our group. He's gone out into the jungle, perhaps he's lost, and he's left his belt kit. People keep looking at it as if it's suddenly going to get up and walk to its owner. We speculate on what might have happened to him. Finally it starts to get dark. We stay put but get out the radio. Naturally it falls to the trained signaller in the patrol to radio back to camp in Morse code that the DS is missing.

Back comes a message. DS missing? Confirm DS missing.

We confirm.

Where did he go?

Map check.

Stay where you are. Wait.

We wait. Finally, at 11p.m., word comes over the net: DS at this location. Return tomorrow.

We put up our hammocks and settle down for the night. We like not having a DS around. The mood is light. He's safe at base and we're relaxing in our hammocks. In the morning we troop back to base. There we learn that the instructor went to the top of the hill and couldn't find us again. He must have turned around a few times and then gone down the wrong side of the hill. He did navigate his way back to base but all he had was a map. No belt kit.

We hand in his belt kit but it never sees Blot again and neither do we. A helicopter has picked him up and he has already been RTU-ed. That means Returned to Unit. He hasn't just been sent home from the jungle, he's been chucked out of the Regiment and then probably the army. His mistake was not getting lost in the jungle. That's forgivable. His mistake was getting lost without his belt kit.

We are all shocked and silent when we learn what's happened. We know that Blot must have been a good soldier to have become an instructor. We are amazed at the ferocity with which the Regiment enforces its golden rules.

One night, when we're slumbering away in our boots and our half-dry clothes, the instructors stage a camp attack. In the black, black night, bleary from our half-slumbers, we have to get out of our hammocks and down to the emergency rendezvous. Naturally my patrol gets lost on the way there. Finally we all meet about a kilometre away at the river and the instructor checks that everyone has their belt kit and their rifle. He need not worry. After what happened to Blot we're not going to let either of them get away.

We're given a grid and told to move there for the night. It's about two kilometres away. We move tactically now, as a big group, all thirty of us crashing blindly through the jungle. This is a horrible experience. Lightless, hopeless, cold, surrounded by creatures that eat us and suck at our blood and drop on us from all angles, tripped by plants, grabbed by small hooks, cut by sharp leaves, scraped by bark, stung and bitten by the great unseen.

We arrive at the location. It's raining hard. We're cold and wet and there's no sheet to cover ourselves with or the ground. So we just lie down on the floor of the jungle and things crawl over us and feast on us all night.

Sleep is fitful and shallow. When the light glimmers, we look around. The first thing I notice is the centipedes, huge ones, and scorpions. Then we move back to camp to be given a quick debriefing.

'Now,' finishes the instructor, 'you've got half an hour to sort your-selves out and get some food and then get back down to the track. Half an hour! You've got to have your kit and be ready for the briefing for the next job in thirty minutes.'

It's at this point that a lot of people give up. They have never been so cold and wet and hungry and utterly miserable. They know there's a helicopter due in a couple of hours. It will take them back to England and their own beds where they can pull the sheets and blankets up over their heads and sleep in perfect comfort for a week if they want to. Do they really want to be doing miserable, jungly things like this for the rest of their working lives? They decide that they don't. They walk over to the instructor and say, 'I've had enough.'

'Fine,' says the DS. 'Flight leaves in a couple of hours.'

No-one tries to talk you out of it. You've failed yourself and no-one's going to tell you that when you get back to your cosy bed in England you'll feel restless and dissatisfied and ask yourself why you left. By the time you arrive in the UK you'll already begin to wonder what was so awful about being in the jungle and why you couldn't put up with a little hardship. The sheer misery of jungle training has already begun to fade. Like any memory of pain, it can't accurately be relived.

As men leave, one by one, I understand them. Each morning I lie to myself: just until tomorrow. You only have to stay until tomorrow. I hear the helicopter taking other men home and I feel nothing but envy.

Just once I almost throw in the towel. It's been the usual early rising routine. I've stumbled to my lookout point for first light, my familiar attap. My friend. In a hostile terrain, where I don't belong, my attap gives me a small measure of security. Today I get to my attap and it's not there. Only a stump remains. Someone has chopped it down.

I am livid. It's possible that it's been chopped down for some genuine reason but much more probable that an instructor has sensed its importance to me. I am beside myself with fury and misery. My attap has gone. I can hardly move for anger. Suddenly the grimness of the camp overwhelms me. There are still two weeks to go. Two more weeks of dry clothes that are never really dry, two more weeks of squeezing into cold, clammy clothes every morning, of getting lost with my patrol, of sweating and being stung throughout the day. I can't go on.

But I do go on. Just until tomorrow. It's like my dad's promise: 'I'll buy you a bike tomorrow.'

Not only do I stop myself from resigning then and there but I somehow manage to hide my fury from the instructors who are, I know, looking for it. Mostly what's on trial during this stage is my personality and maturity. The instructors are actually weeding out the weirdos, the men who no-one would want to work with, the men who get too angry, the men who say too much. Because the jungle reveals the truth about everyone.

The handbook warns that the jungle is neutral and that the biggest mistake you can make is to treat it like the enemy. I've already worked this out. But I have to keep reminding myself of it. Some people never learn it. The jungle closes in on them and suffocates them. They have to get out.

I find the jungle oppressive but gradually, painfully, I learn to live there. I smell of it, I become a part of it. We don't use soap because it smells and we don't shave, we clean our teeth without toothpaste and after a while we begin to look as overgrown and wild as the jungle itself.

Others can't submit to it. We hear stories of patrols who are failing to make their grid on time breaking into bitter arguments. Curly, who left his wife miscarrying her baby, gets into a fight. He's probably not really angry with his opponent. He's probably angry about other things and the jungle has squeezed it out of him.

Our patrol has some minor conflicts when our officer gets over-bearing but mostly we get along amicably. That's because we're all sure that we're going to fail together. Occasionally an instructor joins us to check on us but mostly we're on our own now our DS has been dismissed. We think probably they've already marked us down as failures and don't want to waste too much time on us.

After four weeks, the course culminates in a grand finale. There's a big attack and the patrols have to cover massive distances – over 20 jungle miles in less than six hours, a hopelessly inadequate time allowance. We have to hit targets and write reports and it goes without saying that we are lost again. We can see that we're not going to make the final rv to meet the helicopter which will airlift us out of the jungle and home to our beds. And sheets. And blankets. And showers.

Our patrol's rushing and, to save time, we decide to risk using a river bed. This is a good method of travel because you leave no trail, but it's dangerous. There are slippery loose rocks and sudden very deep pools into which you can just disappear. And you're very exposed. Despite all this, we decide to use the river to make up that lost time.

The risk doesn't pay off. One of the boys slips on a rock and twists his ankle. There is a heated debate about what to do next. It is just possible that this lad is bluffing because he was having trouble keeping up. He says he can't walk but the ankle looks OK. We can call for a casualty evacuation but, if we do, and it's revealed nothing's wrong with his ankle, it will seem that we've concocted the story to get ourselves airlifted out of a tight spot. We agonize for a while. Finally we agree that if his ankle isn't badly hurt then we'll hurt it for him with river rocks. Luckily for him the ankle then starts to swell and turn blue.

I go up the hill to get a good radio signal and call cas. evac. Back at base, they're not too chuffed to hear from me. We're supposed to be at the log platform by now, not miles away down the river.

Soon afterwards I hear the helicopter. I grab my radio aerial, which is 30 feet long, pull it in, stick it in my bergen and rush, as fast as it is possible to rush in the jungle, down the hill. By this time most of the others, including the injured lad, are on board the helicopter. One lad is waiting for me and he lets me go up first.

At the end of a long, long wire, is a loop of orange plastic webbing. The helicopter itself is about 200 feet up. Despite its height, the chopper blades are spraying the river water everywhere. It's noisy.

The other lad holds open the webbing loop for me and I climb into it as though it's a swing, with my bergen on my back and my rifle across my chest. As I start to go up, I spin. As I go higher I turn faster. The centrifugal force is turning me into a mad, spinning machine until I have lost control of my body. I am powerless to remain upright as the weight of my bergen pulls me backwards and my legs flip into the air. I am trying to hang on to the webbing but my bergen is so heavy and I am so dizzy that the force of gravity is beginning to win. I confront the possibility of death for the first time in my life. I have been ill and miserable and frightened before but I have never been so close to death. Beneath my head the jungle canopy is spinning round and round. I know that I cannot hold on much longer and all the determination I have shown over these last weeks slips away from me as the webbing slips gradually from my grasp.

My life is saved by a big hairy hand. One of the instructors grabs hold of me and pulls me into the helicopter. I am more dizzy than I can believe is possible. I cannot think or move. I am numbed by dizziness.

'You all right, Blondie?' asks the instructor cheerfully.

I can't talk. I just sit there while the world spins, as if I'm still on the end of that rope.

A few minutes later the last lad arrives. He, too, is spinning like a top. We all look around at each other. We've all had the same experience. The helicopter crewman who operates the winch is not happy. He wants to know why we're all so incompetent on the end of a rope. Later, our instructors realize. They've forgotten to teach us about helicopter rescues. They simply missed that part of the course in error. We learn that we should have taken off our bergens, hung them on the metal hook, put the orange strap under our arms so it's tight around the chest and then hung onto our rifles. So next time we'll know.

Those of us who have lasted to the end of jungle training fly back to the UK not knowing whether we've passed or failed. I try not to care. But I do. By now I've decided that I want to pass. If I fail at this stage I don't know how I'll plod off into the Met.

The instructor doesn't read passes and fails to us like they did at P Company. He just says, 'Right, these are the names of the men who're going to see the chief clerk.'

The chief clerk issues railway warrants home. After going through hell and giving your all for two months, you're being told you're not good enough and a clerk is sending you off to platform four. I wait for my name on the list, knowing I'm not good enough. I was in the patrol that was always lost.

The instructor finishes the list and I think he's left a name off. I wait for him to say, 'Oh, just a minute, I forgot someone. It's . . . er . . . Collins.' He doesn't say it. I wait, but he doesn't say it because I've passed. I've passed jungle training. I'm through to the next phase.

I feel relieved all over. It's like putting on warm, dry clothes. I'm still in. I'm still here. And there's only one more phase to go.

It's impossible to enjoy all these pleasant sensations for long because of the anguish all around me. The failure rate is high and for many people the sound of their own name on the list is devastating. Some stare straight ahead of them, comatose with shock. Others are close to tears, brushing the back of their hands in swift, swatting movements against their eyes. A few are angry. Others start talking, quickly, compulsively, about nothing in particular. All of them have had just one goal for a long time and now they'll have to readjust their lives, rethink. And I'm not one of them. I'm still allowed to hope.

Tony strolls into the spider hut. He says, 'Well done, mate. I didn't think you'd get this far. Hang on in there. Although you'll probably fail next week.'

Next we learn basic infantry skills, something which is second nature to the infanteers among us, especially the Paras. We may have gone into selection with a few pounds of extra weight but by now we have certainly lost it.

The final month-long stage is combat survival. At this point the course opens out and the men on selection are joined by a number of other students, many of them from foreign armies and other units, particularly the RAF. It's an instructor's course: at the end of the four weeks, we'll have a combat survival instructor's certificate.

Among the newcomers is a huge Norwegian. He's a monster of a man. Even his hair is big. We're learning unarmed combat drills, and I've been unlucky enough to find myself landed with the monster as an opponent. I'm supposed to strangle him. He has huge blond hairs bristling out of his collar and very blue eyes. He takes one look at me and grunts. I'm still sure there's a question mark over me and that I'm going to fail any minute and I'm pretty sure that this minute has come. The instructor is watching us with interest.

I manage to jump for the Norwegian's throat but he just laughs and grabs me with one hand. It's like a cartoon. He simply pulverizes me. He throws me down, picks me up, mangles me and throws me down again like a big cat playing with a little mouse. But I just keep attacking him. He must be eighteen stone to my ten and he clobbers me. Gradually everyone else stops doing their practice strangles and stares at this display. But afterwards the chief instructor says to me, 'Well done, Blondie.'

We're shortly to be taken to the hills and taught how to survive there and a couple of us decide to spend one of our last nights in civilization at a disco. The best disco in town is held in an old cinema and Jerry and I are enjoying ourselves so much that we stay until 'Hi, Ho, Silver Lining' at two o'clock. We decide to take a taxi back to camp.

There's a queue at the taxi rank and we're waiting patiently when a young man walks drunkenly to the front of the line. He says aggressively, 'I'm having the next taxi.'

Jerry and I look at each other and then say, 'Oy! You! There's a queue here!'

He tells us where to go.

I walk right up to him and say, 'Come on, you, back of the queue.'

He sneers, 'Who's going to make me?'

He argues with me and at that moment a taxi pulls up. I tell the young couple at the front of the queue, 'You take it, I'll sort him out.'

Then I hit him. I just give him a few punches and knock him down and then I take him to the back of the line. I'm too hard and fast for him even to begin to fight back. Actually, my hand is hurting a bit but I ignore it and the whole taxi queue claps me enthusiastically. They almost certainly guess that Jerry and I are something to do with the Regiment. We're wearing the standard late 1970s uniform of desert boots and checked shirts and we have moustaches and short hair.

Another taxi arrives and, unbelievably, the drunk walks straight to the front of the queue again and tries to take it.

Jerry says to me, 'OK, mate, my turn now.'

He walks up to the man and lays into him. The drunk starts to get up and Jerry hits him a few more times. There is a lot of shouting but the right people get in the taxi. Then, suddenly, we hear a whistle blow. We look around to see a policeman taking an active interest in the fracas.

Jerry and I know that we'll be straight out of the Regiment before we're even in if we get into trouble with the police. We've passed all the endurance tests, we've survived the jungle, we've finished infantry training and to be chucked out now, just before the last exercise, because of a stupid drunk in town would be beyond imagining.

There is one option. We turn and run.

'You two, stop!' yells the policeman. We hear him radioing for help. We run faster. We run on and on, up the road, through the park. We're running towards the camp, and Jerry takes one route and I take another. I'm wearing a dark jacket which I pull off and throw up a tree. Then, when I can't run any more, I walk along in my light shirt thinking that no-one will recognize me now.

Suddenly behind me I hear, 'Stop! Or I'll let the dog go!'

I turn around and there is a policeman with a big Alsatian which he is barely able to restrain by its collar. I know that he's not allowed to let the dog go unless a serious crime's about to be committed. We were taught that by the police themselves just a few days ago when they'd been practising letting their dogs loose on us and we'd been practising getting away.

I break into a run again. I run hard and fast and very soon I've outrun the copper.

When I get back to camp there are police cars outside.

I stroll in innocently, whistling.

'All right, mate?'

'You haven't seen a couple of lads out there?' asks a policeman.

'No. Nope. Nothing like that.'

I get back in and there's Jerry in bed, snoring not very convincingly. I know he must still be fully dressed under those covers. I get undressed and go to bed and the next day the word's all around the camp: the police are looking for a couple of Regiment lads. There's been a big fight downtown and a bloke's in hospital, badly injured.

My hand's still hurting a lot but there's no way I can see a medic about it now. I suspect a bone is broken. I'll just have to go on combat survival with a painful hand.

The next day we are dropped off in the Black Mountains and taught how to live off the land by trapping, killing, cooking and eating small furry animals. We eat seagulls, squirrels and cabbages. We learn to make coffee out of roasted acorns.

We spend the last week on the run. We are dressed in rags and our bootlaces are taken away from us. We are escaped prisoners of war. Somehow we have to survive and get from rendezvous to rendezvous. There are hunter forces out to catch us. On this occasion a Scottish battalion are the hunters.

The big Norwegian who made mincemeat of me in unarmed combat speaks very little English but he understands that he has to escape. We are taken in trucks to the Black Mountains and he jumps over the tailboard when we stop at traffic lights in Abergavenny and disappears. That's the last we see of him.

When we arrive in the Black Mountains we're given escape maps and told to get ourselves to the rendezvous point. The nights are long, cold and hungry. When I finally get close I'm prowling through a dark wood shortly before dawn when I hear someone else. I freeze and listen. Twigs are snapping, branches are bending. It might be an animal. There's no moon and I can see nothing. My heart starts to thump. With difficulty, I soften my breathing.

The animal, or person, is coming closer. Crash, swish. An animal would have smelled me by now. It's human. I almost stop breathing. Is it one of us, or one of the hunter force, sent out to catch us? There are no codewords or passwords. Somehow we have to smell the difference between a friend and a foe.

He's sensed my presence now and the way he stops, rapidly, nervously, indicates to me that he's more victim than aggressor. I take a bold initiative.

'Who is it?'

'Curly.'

I'd laugh out loud if I dared.

'Curly! It's Frank!'

'Frank!' We've been holding our breath without realizing it and finding each other here is a release as well as a relief.

We immediately sit down and compare stories. Within a couple of minutes we're joined by a third whisper.

'Too loud!'

It's another of the lads. As the night wears on we meet up with other groups of refugees until there's one big gang of us lurking in the woods. We know that there will be an agent arriving soon at the rv who'll give us some information that will lead us to the next rv.

We locate the agent. He's standing in a clearing in the woods. We all agree that we'd be laying ourselves open to capture if we all go forward. Two people offer to get the information. One of them's Curly.

A few minutes later they return. They're holding something.

'It's no good. He wants to see everyone. If you don't go forward, you don't get a cheese sandwich.'

There's a cheese sandwich inside that clingfilm. A cheese sandwich is something every single one of us would die for.

Curly hands me something. 'It's OK, I got you one,' he whispers.

As the next wave of people go forward, there's a yelp and a whoop.

'Now,' someone yells.

'Whaaaaaat?'

'Run!'

The hunter force is after us. The still silence of the woods is shattered by men running, dogs barking, shouting, and torches flashing around the trees.

I run. Without dropping my cheese sandwich. I run as hard as I can. I can't see a thing but I know that, like the others, I'm running towards the river. Branches snap into my face, roots trip me, needles pierce my skin, but nothing stops me. I'm running for my life, stumbling, fighting for breath, jumping, falling and running again.

The trees start to thin a little and the river, wide and curving, is suddenly audible. Soon, I can see it glimmering beneath me. Some of the boys just plunge straight into its deep waters, determined to cross. I slide down the bank and am halted by a tree root. Behind the tree root is a hollow. It's not big but it's big enough for me. I can swing myself in behind it and remain invisible.

I slide into the hole, knowing all the while that I must be caught. If the men don't see me, the dogs will sniff me out. Since I'll certainly be caught I'm going to eat my cheese sandwich before they can take it away from me. It's my first food for two or three days and no-one's going to stop me eating it. I stuff it into my mouth. The sound of my heartbeat and chomping teeth seems to echo around my little chamber. I'm close to not caring now, so long as I can finish my sandwich.

Close by, almost overhead, I hear voices.

'Where'd they go?'

'Across the river.'

The accents are Scots.

'Across that? They must be crazy.'

'I'm not going after them.'

'Not me either.'

I freeze, waiting for the hunters to notice me. If the dogs don't sniff me they'll sniff my sandwich for sure. I turn my head and I can see boots. Torches are sweeping up and down the river. They shine straight on me more than once. But incredibly, miraculously, no-one sees me.

Gradually the voices fade away. I'm alone, cold and wet. And I'm miserable because I ate my cheese sandwich in a few gulps instead of savouring every wonderful mouthful. I am wearing a fetching plastic waistcoat and a jaunty plastic hat, made out of a white Fison's fertilizer bag I found in a field. Sadly my accessories don't match. The waistcoat is tied, and so are my boots, with orange baler twine. In my pocket is a big hunk of mushroom which I know is edible but which I don't want to eat.

My feet get colder and colder until the blood seems to withdraw from them completely. I stay there all the following day and the next night I get out and stamp my feet up and down the river bank but one foot in particular seems to have lost all feeling, except for being wet and cold. In the day I slip back under my tree root. My foot feels as if it just isn't there now. The next night I get up and stamp about again. I know I could die of exposure but I'd rather do that than be caught.

I arrive at the final stage, where capture and 72 hours of interrogation is part of the routine.

There is white noise and a blindfold. They strip me off and then get a woman to laugh at my body. They humiliate me in every way they can think of. They keep me cold and hungry. They try to tempt me with food. But I am determined not to crack. All I can say is my name, rank and serial number.

My Fison's bag attracts great attention from the interrogators.

'So . . . what is this . . . Fison? Tell me what it means?'

'24286081. Lance corporal. Collins. Sir.'

'Perhaps it is some sort of a bag. Perhaps you were carrying something in it. Perhaps that something is very interesting. Come on, tell me what you were carrying in the bag.'

'24286081. Lance corporal. Collins. Sir.'

He knows and I know that it's a hat. I want very much to open my mouth and say, 'It's a hat, you prat.' But if I do those words will cost me the course. After five months of physical hardship and mental hell, muttering a few words can lose you everything.

'It'll be the worse for you if you don't tell me . . .'

'I'm not allowed to answer that question. Sir. 24286081.'

'Shut up!'

Guards make us lean against walls on our fingertips for hours on end. It's impossible to sustain this. Whenever I flatten my hands I feel the crash of a big wooden stick on my back.

'Get up, get up, get up . . .'

The 72 hours might as well be three weeks. All I can say is my name, rank and serial number. All I want is some food.

Then, suddenly, finally, I'm released. It's over. It's all over.

A big pile of food is waiting for me. A doctor inspects me. He tells me that sitting under a tree root for three days has given me trench foot. He gives me painkillers and instructs me to sleep with my feet elevated. He bandages up the deep cut I've acquired from some stray barbed wire. He takes a look at my hand, the one I hurt in the fight downtown. He asks no questions, just tells me that a small bone in the hand has been broken: it's known as a boxer's fracture.

This is the time to catch up on everyone else's story and all the news. I find that some of my mates are still in. A few have cracked under interrogation.

Curly tells me that he was captured at the river by the hunter force. They stripped him and handcuffed him and tied him in a waterfall. It's December. He passed out. When he woke up he was being kicked around a farmyard. The Scots boys asked him more questions and when he only gave his name, rank and number they put him back in the waterfall, where he passed out again. They did this to him three times. Finally they dressed him and threw him off the back of a truck, telling him not to get caught again. It was field interrogation and we both know it never should have happened. The hunter force was abusing its power. We shake our heads. I remember how some of the older men in the Regiment shook their heads in just the same way when I told them about the road checks I did with the marine patrol in Northern Ireland. For the first time, I feel bad about what we did to those civilians. I realize that we abused our power and helped, in our small way, to heighten that conflict.

We also talk about the Norwegian who thought he was escaping in Abergavenny. By all accounts, he is still living rough. There have been terrified reports from old ladies that a spiky monster has been seen eating out of their dustbins. He didn't understand that the game was over or that it had rules and both the police and the Regiment are still out looking for him.

Casually, Jerry and I ask whether the police found the two Regiment lads they were looking for before we left. To my relief I learn that it was all a mistake. There'd been two fights at the same time and it was the other fight which had turned nasty. The police had confused the two. The people in the taxi queue had stopped the police and explained to them what happened. The queue-jumping drunk turned out to be a well-known troublemaker in town and the police kept him in a cell overnight.

Jerry says quietly, 'You should have done a proper job when you punched him the first time. Then the whole thing wouldn't have happened.'

We return to camp and the very next day I am badged. I go to the colonel, who gives me my beret and my blue belt with the SAS winged dagger and badge. The colonel shakes my hand. It is December 1978. I am just twenty-two years old.

I've made it. I am in the Regiment. The undistinguished, un-promoted boy signaller from apprentice college has joined the cream of the British army. No-one is more surprised than me.

I look in the mirror and someone else, someone new, someone in an unfamiliar beret, stares back at me. I know I'm still me, I don't feel any different. But the uniform says I am different.

I'm still going out with Alice. She's very keen for her SAS boyfriend to go to the school Christmas party. She must be joking. One of the drawbacks of having a sixteen-year-old girlfriend is that she still goes to school but there's no way she's going to drag me to a school party. Despite her begging and pleading, I refuse to join her. From now on, it's Regiment first, everyone else second. Including Alice. She goes to the party without me and falls for a sixth-former and that's the end of that. Newly appointed Mr Macho has been thrown over by a girl of sixteen.

I go back to Whitley Bay for Christmas, where I have trouble explaining that, although I was in the SAS before, I'm even more in the SAS now. All the men who are attached to the Regiment, from drivers to signallers, carry something of the SAS mystique. That's the way they like it. Some live a lie, pretending to friends and even family that they're badged members of the Regiment, when really they just push pieces of paper around. Their bluff is rarely called because there's no way of checking.

As a signaller, I've never misled anyone, but my silences did their work. Everyone jumped to their own conclusions. Now that I'm badged, I pay for those silences. No-one understands why I wanted to join the SAS when I was in the SAS already. But they're all proud of me. Even Dad. I look closely at him, standing at his place at the bar of his pub. He's only forty-eight but he's already an old man.

I try to tell my mother something of what's been happening since August but she looks at me blankly. What I am describing is far outside the experience of other people, even my closest family. Now, the other men in the Regiment will become a sort of family. They understand because they've been through it too. Especially people on my own selection. Only they know.

# 8

I WEAR MY UNIFORM FOR THE FIRST TIME WHEN I ATTEND PRAYERS. There's nothing religious about prayers. It's just the squadron's morning meeting. I've attended as a signaller, of course, but now I'm standing with my new troop, the free-fall troop.

I learn that I'm about to return to the jungle in Belize.

I'm determined to prove myself on my first job and show that I'm one of the boys and not just a scaly any more. This makes me tense. Even packing my gear is tense. I want to take exactly the right things. I ask a lot of questions. I pack it the way I've been told, waterproofing everything, but when I get to Belize I find that the four very experienced soldiers in our patrol have just chucked their gear into their bergens without really thinking about it.

This is the first revelation. I spend the next few months trying to do things correctly, the way we've been taught on selection. My patrol gently teaches me to ignore all the rules. They're so lax that I'm amazed. Sometimes they even patrol with their shirts off. They're like something out of *M.A.S.H.* As the new boy, I watch my step with them. The leader is keen to make me feel welcome but one of the men is hostile. He's an old warhorse whose respect has to be won. I tread carefully with him.

The boys carry regulation first aid kit pouches on their belts but they're stuffed full of sandwiches. They tell me to throw away my army issue jungle knife and buy a light, long-handled parang from the locals.

Belize isn't just used for training by the Regiment. We're

114

operational here. We're down on the borders winning hearts and minds, making friends with the locals so that if Guatemala invades as expected we'll be able to penetrate behind enemy lines with their help.

Across the border we plant caches, big boxes made of fibreglass dipped in latex. They're full of food, money and clothing, plastic explosives, anything you might need if you're operating behind enemy lines. The main problem is the termites, which can eat through anything, even fibreglass. And there are local Indians who want the contents of our caches.

Each patrol has a highly trained medic and a man appointed signaller. I'd love to be the medic but, unsurprisingly, I'm the signaller. The medic is the man in demand. We move from village to village, sitting in long huts, taking part in ceremonies and dispensing medical aid. We give routine treatment for worms and other injuries. When a feverish little boy with a badly infected machete cut in his leg is brought to us oozing pus and maggots it's clear that he's about to die. We call in the RAF and have him airlifted to hospital and from now on the headman is our friend.

There's only one other source of western medical aid: an elderly lady missionary. She sometimes turns up on her donkey with her Elastoplast, laughing and looking jolly.

'Are you a Christian?' she asks me cheerfully one day.

''Fraid not,' I inform her, with an apologetic smile.

We're busy doing a boat patrol down the Sarstoon River which borders Belize, Honduras and Guatemala when we're told that a new officer will be joining us. We send back word that he should bring a bottle of rum.

We've abseiled in from a helicopter and cut a landing site so that the next helicopter can bring us inflatable boats. We've been having a great time travelling down the river with our shirts off, calling at villages, doing a bit of fishing. At night, there's a campfire and rum. It's more like Club Med than hard graft. This is something selection didn't prepare me for: enjoying myself.

The helicopter arrives carrying the officer, who is nicknamed Biggles because of his old school, Bomber Command-style derring-do. We have anchored a boat to a sunken tree in a big bend in the river. It's normal for the helicopter to hover at about 200 feet to winch someone down but for some reason the pilot has decided to winch Biggles from about 50 feet. The helicopter comes lower and lower until the river is chopping and sloshing and shaking. The sunken tree floats off and the boat it is holding turns round a few

115

times in the uproar and ends up on the bank with most of its gear tipped out. We are not impressed. It's not his fault, but it's not a good start for Biggles.

He is only made to feel downright unwelcome, however, when we ask if he got the message about the rum.

'Good joke!' he laughs jovially.

We say, 'It wasn't a joke.'

Biggles looks nervous.

'Er, wasn't it?'

'No. And if you haven't brought any rum then you can't have any of ours.'

We sit around the camp fire with our drinks and don't give Biggles any. He makes no comment but we know he disapproves. We're working and shouldn't be drinking. He'd like to assert himself, the way officers are now supposed to, but doesn't dare when he's dealing with lads like these, the old-guard SAS who have years more experience than he has. Perhaps he knows they don't really want him here. It wasn't his fault the helicopter pilot flew too low but if he hadn't joined us it wouldn't have happened.

Once he gets over the shock of our rum punches, Biggles becomes one of the team. We even relent and let him have some of our rum when we think we've punished him long enough. By now his standards have dropped and he takes it. He is, like nearly all SAS officers, a talented man. The officers have to pass not just normal selection but officers' week as well, and it means only the best get through. They come for two years from their own regiments and then return. We men lose any rank we might previously have held: when I joined the SAS I became a private again. The officers come in as captains. They're usually given a hard time by their men, but some of them, like Biggles, deserve it.

We sleep in hammocks, strung between two trees at a height of about 5 feet. Biggles' hammock is always lower than ours. Everyone's asleep one night when suddenly there's a hollering from Biggles, whose torch is on. We all grab our rifles and Biggles explains that a huge animal walked underneath his hammock, lifting it, with Biggles inside right up on its back. He's terrified, but there are no lions or tigers here, only panthers and pumas and they are very shy. Probably it was a wild boar, or tapir. The next night Biggles' hammock is strung about 9 feet up.

In the morning we check there're no beasties in our boots and then use our jungle knives to lift up the flap of our rucksacks because that's where tarantulas like to crawl. They sit there like big, furry,

116

teddy bears with too many legs, and we flick them briskly away.

Over our hammocks we hang a *basher*, which is the Malay word for house. It is just a sheet shelter. Inside is the mosquito net and, since we're non-tactical, we cut poles to provide candlesticks so that we can lie in our hammock reading. It gets dark early in the jungle. We drink our rum then go to bed to read our books, listening to the mosquitos buzzing around outside the net. Unfortunately, Biggles has soaked his net in repellent and when the candle gets too close . . . whoosh! The whole net goes up in flames, lighting the jungle suddenly at night. Biggles gets out unscathed but he has no mozzie net now.

He also hangs his hammock on trees which are just a fraction too thin. The minimum width is five inches and we tell Biggles this but he's an officer and they never listen. We show him how we tie cloth soaked in mosquito repellent around our hammock strings so that the ants which try to march onto us in the night do an about-turn, but he doesn't listen.

For the third time, we're awoken by Biggles' night yells. This time a tribe of monkeys has been moving through the jungle, swinging from the trees overhead. When they're over Biggles he wonders what all the commotion is and shines his torch up on them, which drives them wild, chattering and jumping. The trees his hammock's tied to are so thin that he's tossed out by their activity.

After four months it's time to come home. These have been great months. Without the pressure of selection the jungle isn't hostile any more. It's a living, breathing entity. I can almost live harmoniously with it. It's been far harder to live with my colleagues than the jungle. There's a politics to living in such isolation with a close-knit team of individuals. When to speak and when to be silent. When to laugh. When to confide. Always to appear relaxed, even if I don't feel it, so that tensions don't escalate. I've learned a lot on this tour and most of it hasn't been about soldiering.

As a member of free-fall troop, I have to go on a High Altitude Low Opening (HALO) course. This is a military use of free-fall which enables men to jump behind enemy lines from aircraft flying so high that no-one can even hear them, let alone suspect that parachutists have jumped off the tailgate. In fact, I've already reached Category Ten as a free-faller so I'm already jumping past this standard.

High Altitude is theoretically 28,500 feet but we often jump from 32,000. That's over five miles. Climbing up this high in an un-pressurized aircraft can explode your sinuses if you have a cold and there are rumours that dental fillings pop out.

Our training starts at RAF Brize Norton. We begin with jumps in daylight with no equipment and, by the time they send us away, everyone can leap out of a plane in any conditions with a heavy bergen strapped on. Then we're sent down to Pau in the South of France where the weather is good and we can jump early in the morning and late at night. Below us, in the early morning mist, are the wild crags of the Pyrenees. We finish with night jumps on Salisbury Plain.

Some bad news comes through from Germany, where most of the squadron is taking part in a big annual NATO exercise. Of course, it's Biggles. Jumping into Germany, there was a malfunction on his parachute. He cut it away and used his reserve canopy, but he didn't jettison his bergen, perhaps because he couldn't face the thought of being a leader without his gear. When Biggles crashed to the ground carrying too much weight for a reserve parachute he badly broke his legs. We have flares for emergencies which we're supposed to send up every ten minutes but Biggles was in such agony that he sent them all up more or less simultaneously. It was like Guy Fawkes night in Germany.

At the end of our HALO course we're sent out to Canada to do some troop training. The whole squadron meets high in the Rockies in Banff National Park. The park is closed because it's the season when the bears wake up.

We have a briefing from the park rangers who tell us not to run if we're attacked by a bear. The best thing is to lie down and play dead. That doesn't seem a very satisfactory way of dealing with the problem to us, so we just hope it won't happen.

We aren't allowed guns but we are allowed to carry pocket knives. We wear civilian clothes and practise navigation, walking about 30 miles a day carrying heavy weights.

I love being out in the forest. Every so often the view opens out and there's a lake, still and deep and blue. It's like looking down at the sky. The mountains seem to jump out at you, the air's so clear here.

We've been out a few days and are enjoying the work when we see a pick-up truck with a big crate on the back. A ranger's driving and he shouts, 'Don't worry, boys, just stand still, it's a baby.' By this time we can see there's something moving in the crate.

The ranger walks round to the back of the truck, pulls a lever, runs like a demon, jumps in the truck and closes the door. A minute or two later a paw appears, then a head and then a whole bear gets out. It sniffs around on the ground and stands on its hind legs with its big paws up in the air and its nose poking around enjoying the smells. Forget Yogi and Teddy, this is a monster. It must be over 9 feet tall. I

118

can't guess how much it weighs. We must all involuntarily be holding our breath as it lollops off into the forest, happily not in our direction, because when it's gone there's a collective sigh.

We say, 'That's a baby! If that's a baby, how big are the big ones?'

The park ranger laughs at us. He says, 'Don't worry, he won't bother you if you don't leave any food lying around.' And he drives off, safe in his big pick-up.

That night we camp up, a little group of about eight or ten. We sleep in a circle with some people snug in the middle. I'm right out on the perimeter. We've had curry for dinner and I'm too lazy to wash out my mess tin. I just push it away so it isn't right next to me and go to sleep. In the sharp, cold mountain air you sleep like a baby, but tonight I don't. Something wakes me.

I'm trying to work out what it is. I know it's a sound that shouldn't be there. Then I realize it's my mess tin. I left my spoon in it and the spoon is rattling in a ghostly sort of a way. I half turn and then freeze, remembering the ranger's warning. It's a bear. It's right here beside me eating the remnants of my food. I can hear the spoon banging. When it stops momentarily there's a rustling in the grass, the big rustling of a bear's foot.

I am terrified. My heart is banging away. Any minute now it could come bursting out. It seems amazing the bear can't hear it. My hair is actually standing on end. I start to sweat. I can't believe the bear doesn't smell me. It seems just a matter of time before his big paws will be on me. What should I do? What can I do? If I call the others he might attack. I reach out for my knife but it's pitch-black and I can't see a thing. If I started digging around for it the bear might come up to investigate so I lie still.

Then it all goes silent. We've been told by the ranger how incredibly quietly these enormous creatures can move. I think: he's gone. I begin to get my body under control. The pounding in my heart starts to ease up.

Suddenly, the noise begins again. Fear swamps me again. This time I manage to reach over to my knife and I'm lucky enough to put my hand right on it. I almost manage to turn my head to see exactly where the bear is but the noise stops again. I don't move. I wait and wait but nothing happens. The silence goes on so long that gradually I calm down and begin nodding back off to sleep. I'm almost there when the noise starts for a third time. I lie letting my eyes become accustomed to the dark and then, very, very slowly, I manage to turn so I can get a good view of the monster. I turn. I look. And I look. But there is no bear. There's nothing.

I get out of my sleeping bag and pick up my mess tin. Inside it is a big, fat mouse. It has been running round and round, pushing my spoon around the tin. There never was a bear. But in my mind there was. Imagine if I'd shouted out for the boys. They all would have woken up yelling, 'Where's the bear, where's the bear?' I'd have had to pretend that he'd run off.

The next night I scrub my mess tin out so that it's spotless and I sleep in the middle of the group.

My father on Royal Air Force national service. He later discouraged me from going into the army because he hadn't enjoyed his time with the RAF. Except for the football.

My parents' wedding day. From right: my Auntie June, Grandad Wilkinson, Mam, Dad, Uncle Eddie, Granda Collins and Nana Wilkinson.

My mother, left, on her wedding day, with Auntie June. Auntie June isn't exactly an aunt: she was Mam's cousin and best friend.

Me as a baby. I may look fat but Mam
called me bonnie.

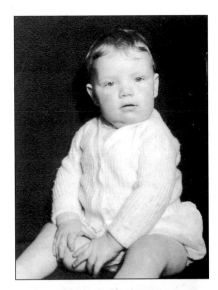

Me, aged about three, with baby Gary and
big sister Yvonne.

Me aged six in my old school tie. We were still
living in Heaton, Newcastle.

Participants in a Royal Marines Commando acquaint course, held in Scotland. My school pal and I were only twelve. I'm kneeling, fourth from the left, trying to look like a tough sixteen year old.

P Company, November 1974. As a young signaller, I thought I'd signed up for the parachuting course but soon discovered I was trying out for the Parachute Regiment. Back left is 'Number Fifty-two, Signalman Collins, sir.'

Looking a little worried, aged nineteen, before my first free-fall jump.

On oxygen at 30,000 feet, preparing to jump HALO with 7 troop.

**Operation NIMROD**

1923 hrs Monday the 5th of May 1980. Embassy of the Provisional Revolutionary & Islamic Goverment of Iran.

JOKER

B SQUADRON 22 SAS BRADBURY LINES HEREFORD

16 PRINCES GATE KENSINGTON LONDON

JOKER

The Operation was carried out by men of the 22 Regiment with the following freed, 5 Terrorists killed

The SAS joker played at Iranian embassy siege in May 1980. One of the lads sketched this and gave each of us one after the siege. *(Drawn by Roy)*

Meeting HM The Queen, 1980. Some time after the Iranian embassy siege.

Claire and I wore jeans and sweaters for our wedding in 1981.

Proud father. Holding new-born baby Charlotte, September 1982.

Family Christmas, 1983.

Free-falling in the USA just before Claire gave up. Me on left, Claire centre.

My troop in the North African desert, 1983. I'm second from the left, Big Al Slater is third from the right. We wouldn't have been smiling if we had known that soon after this picture was taken we would all have to bite the heads off sand snakes and eat them raw.

# 9

I GET BACK TO HEREFORD IN TIME FOR PHILIPPA'S WEDDING. PHILIPPA IS marrying a Regiment lad who's leaving the army to become a lawyer. I think I've just about got over Philippa by now but when I see her looking the radiant bride I'm not so sure. I dance with her. Of course, everyone dances with her. She's the bride.

Soon afterwards, I'm sent off to Ireland. I remember all those months at Bessbrook Mill and the other camps when I was stuck in the ops room and the boys were out seeing the action. Now I'm one of the boys, where the action is.

At last I'm going to be crawling through sewers, hiding in attics, living out for days on end.

My first job is a close target recce. There's a known terrorist living across the street from one of Belfast's many derelict houses. It could be an ideal observation post, but it has to be checked out first. Paul and I are called for the job. It's exciting because the house is in a rough, Republican area.

Paul has pulled a donkey jacket out of the big bin full of civilian coats which we use for undercover work. This is standard wear for undercover soldiers and I've decided it's too obvious. There aren't that many donkey jackets on the streets of Belfast and most of them are worn by soldiers trying to look casual. So I'm wearing a bright blue duvet coat.

Paul takes one look at the coat and reels.

'You're not wearing that.'

'I am.'

'But it stands out.'

'It's just the kind of thing people are wearing.'

'You're crazy!'

'You certainly wouldn't expect an SAS man to be wearing a coat like this,' I tell him.

'Too darn right,' he agrees.

We set off but I can tell he's miffed with me.

Under our controversial coats are little M16 Armalites and in the pancake holsters on our backs are 9mm Brownings. We know we have back-up, one car close by with two men in it, and another further away with four men. This is a hard area.

The lads drop us off a couple of blocks away from the target. We make a jovial show of departure.

'See you! Bye, mate!' Not so loud, of course, that anyone hears our accents.

We walk down the street, chatting and laughing together. The laughter deserves an Oscar nomination because Paul's still furious with me and is actually berating me for the coat. All the time, we're vigilant. We're looking at lads who come out of doors, cars that pull up in the street . . . and I'm pushing the radio button in my hand, murmuring as we chatter.

'Zero, this is Papa Foxtrot One, towards target, passing Green One.' Green One refers to the landmarks we've identified with coloured stickers on a map back at base.

As we get closer to the target I start to abbreviate.

'Foxtrot Green Two.'

The signaller just clicks back.

We get to the target house and wander down the adjacent alley. We look around and Paul says, 'Let's have a look in.'

Casually, we hop over the wall and into the derelict house. We're only inside a few minutes, looking for signs that tramps are in residence, which they aren't. There's a good line of sight to the suspect's house. We take some rough measurements so that we can establish what's possible and decide how the lads will get up to the loft. Rapidly, we exit. Back over the wall and up the street, keeping up the chatter.

People are always taking a look around derelict houses. It doesn't look unnatural for two lads to take a peek inside, especially as we were there for such a short time.

'Papa Foxtrot. Back towards Green One. Pick up fifteen minutes.'

We jump back in the car and return to base. At the debrief, Paul complains about my blue jacket but the others disagree with him.

'He didn't stand out at all,' they say.

Our close target recce report is written up and that night we return. Only now we're in uniform and carrying guns. It's our job to go ahead of the surveillance patrol and check out that it's safe for them to use it. Under cover of darkness we're dropped off near by. We leap over the wall and into the back of the house. It's empty, so we call forward the men who will be staying there.

A big Saracen armoured personnel carrier arrives with a standard green army patrol. Everyone on the streets of Belfast is used to uniformed lads jumping out of tanks and taking a look around. But in the back of this tank are SAS men with bergens who disembark unobtrusively with the rest of the men. Only they don't get back in the tank when it moves off. They're scrambling up into the loft with us, where we remain for a few days watching the target.

It's our job to photograph, using a telephoto lens, everyone who goes in and out of the suspect's house, noting the time. There's the terrorist, his wife, his teenage son and daughter and, importantly for us, their visitors. Whenever the terrorist himself leaves, we trigger mobile surveillance, who follow him.

The days and nights are long on surveillance. A few people sleep at any one time while a few of us watch. There's little eating, no talking, strictly no snoring. There's a bag for all our excrement. It's not glamorous work. In spite of the fact that we're watching a family, with all the tensions and ties of any normal family, it's impossible to see our target any differently from the way a scientist observes a rat in a cage, perhaps because we know we may one day kill him. At the very least our surveillance work will add to an intelligence picture which will prevent him making a terrorist attack, or be used as evidence in court one day.

People come in and out of the derelict house with alarming frequency, and this is nerve-racking. They can't see us, or get to our lair, but we can see them moving around down there. Sometimes there are drunks, or people just talking, but the most nerve-racking are the quiet men who wander round alone. Has the terrorist realized he's being watched? Is this shadow downstairs planting a bomb or setting fire to the place? We're helpless and vulnerable, wrapped in our silence up here.

When it's time to go we exit at night, melting into another green army patrol.

Back at base, I've been reading two books about the occult and the paranormal. I'm by no means the only lad in the Regiment interested in this subject. We live close to death, it's natural for us to have an interest in it and in what, if anything, happens afterwards. Christianity is not for us. All that arcane language, the dos and don'ts, the Lamb of God, and the wimpish priests. But I've dabbled in other religions, mostly with an intent to scorn. I read the Penguin translation of the Koran while I was in Oman, delighting in pointing out any inconsistencies I could find. I've read Buddhist tracts and some Hindu texts just to disagree with them. I haven't even bothered with the Bible. We all know that's the most ludicrous book of all.

Our next job is a terrorist ambush, expected to take place in a factory at about nine o'clock one morning. We have intelligence that the Provisional IRA plans to kill the man who guards the door of the factory. He's part-time UDR.

The troop sergeant takes me to recce the building with him very early in the morning when the factory is still closed. The manager lets us in and shows us around. We agree to put the Quick Reaction Force in a room at the back of the factory. We'll go forward and, if there's firing, they can back us up.

We go back to base to brief the others. One of the lads is known as Bill the Back because he has a bad back which gets better or worse depending on how good a job is. This ambush is considered a good job and Bill the Back's anxious to be in on it. 'I thought your back was bad?' says the troop sergeant beadily.

'Oh no, no, it's fine at the moment,' Bill the Back assures us. 'Just fine.'

'OK, well you can come along,' agrees the troop sergeant.

When we arrive he puts the Quick Reaction Force in the back room, then he asks the manager if he has a big cardboard box.

'Lots of them. What do you want it for?'

'I want to put a man in it . . . Would it look out of place just here in the reception area?'

'No,' agrees the manager, 'there could well be a big cardboard box standing there.'

'Right, mate, in the box,' the troop sergeant tells Bill.

Bill stares at the box and then at the boss.

'In the box? But . . .'

'You said your back was all right,' the troop sergeant reminds him. He has no option. Bill climbs inside.

'Just pop up and give us covering fire,' says the boss.

He and I go in the adjacent broom cupboard. I'm patrol signaller and I soon find a mop and a bucket. I sit on the bucket with my radio. The boss is at the ready.

Nine o'clock passes. No terrorists but we're already exhausted.

People are coming in and out of the factory constantly and we have to be on the alert every time someone passes. Ten o'clock and there's still no attack. We can hear everything which goes on in the reception area. Suddenly, there are footsteps. We stiffen. The footsteps walk right past the broom cupboard and up to the man we believe is a target.

Voices. They're speaking softly but we can hear them loud and clear.

'So . . . where's the SAS, then?'

'They're in the broom cupboard.'

'In the broom cupboard!'

The boss and I exchange pained glances.

'And the box!'

'What, that cardboard box over there! Never! Who'd have guessed it?'

'How long will they stay?'

'Don't know. But they're good. Don't tell anyone.'

'Oh, I won't tell a soul.'

A few minutes later, more footsteps, another voice.

'Is it true the SAS are in the box?'

'Shhh. Don't tell anyone.'

It's obvious to us that the whole factory knows we're here. The boss tells me to radio in.

'Papa Four Zero, this is Four Zero Bravo . . . radio check.'

Nothing.

'Papa Four Zero . . . radio check.'

Still nothing.

I change the battery but still the radio is dead.

'Great,' says the boss.

We're stuck in a broom cupboard with no communications, I'm on a mop bucket and Bill the Back's folded up nearby in his box. There's another voice outside now.

'Are the boys still in the cupboard?'

'Aye, they're still in there.'

'Well, do you think they'd like a cup of tea?'

It's hard not to laugh.

'They've been there for hours. They must be thirsty.'

A few minutes later there's the clink of teacups and the sound of someone sidling up to our cupboard with a tray.

'Pssssssst! Pssssst! Cup of tea, boys?'

At this point the boss gives up. He pushes open the door and says angrily, 'We may as well just forget this job.'

125

'But . . . don't you want any tea?'

The boss walks up to Bill's box and kicks it.

'Come on, get out, we're going.'

Bill unfolds himself. He looks miserable. He groans a bit. We hoist him out.

'Come on, mate, get a move on, I thought you said you didn't have a bad back.'

We put our guns and our radios in our holdalls. We're wearing civilian clothes. We say to the man holding the tea, 'It's OK, the job's off now, we're going.'

We have to walk straight through the factory to pick up the Quick Reaction Force, which we assume has been on the alert all this time, guns at the ready. The factory workers all smile and wave and nod at us. They all know who we are and they're thrilled to see the real SAS. We get to the back room and there's the Quick Reaction Force. They're sitting around, surrounded by cups of tea and cake wrappers and biscuits. They've been fed and watered since eight o'clock. At this point the boss caves in and we have a brew as well. It's obvious why the Provos didn't come today – most of Belfast seems to know that we're there.

For us it's been a bad tour. Within the squadron there are some lives taken and a couple of arms finds and plenty of successful surveillance jobs but we want to confront terrorists – and come out of that confrontation with more men than they do. And this just hasn't happened.

There's a chance that we will, however, on our very last job before the tour ends. We have been working against a particular terrorist team for some time. Intelligence has informed us that they're planning to hit a green army patrol. As they wait, guns at the ready, we are to assault their house. They have a big American machine gun, an M60, which is the point of the exercise. It's lethal and the harm they've already done with it is considerable.

We set off in a civilian van, our hair unkempt and looking ordinary. We drive through a hard area of the city, our minds fixed on our plans. We're going to pile out of the van and assault the house. It will be a surgical attack. No-one who isn't involved – like women and children who may be at home – will be hurt. The rules say that we have to challenge three times, 'Halt, security forces!', unless this would place our own lives or others' in immediate danger. There's unlikely to be room here for a challenge. We might have to shoot.

We have a sledgehammer and we're going to use it to break straight in through the front door of the terrorists' house. We'll also hit the two adjacent buildings, going through the front and out the back so that we can assault the target from each side.

Inside the house we know the players are waiting for the green patrol, arms ready. As soon as we arrive we have to be fast, very fast. Speed, aggression, surprise.

We drive up to the house. My palms are sweating. My gun's ready. I'm wearing a donkey jacket but no body armour. We're almost at the house and about to go in when suddenly, over the radio, comes a message. Stop. Drive right past.

We don't know why and we don't ask questions. We just drive on, put down our guns, loosen our clothing, stretch our legs out. I feel a mixture of relief and disappointment. Today we'd hoped for some sort of body count, or at least a few arrests.

We aren't told the reason, when we get back to camp, but we know that intelligence is good in this area. The Provisional IRA has been well-infiltrated. It's a leaky organization, where people will often talk for money, or simply for glory down at the pub.

Disappointed that we missed the action, we hand over to the next team in and return to the UK. I head straight for the parachute club. I'm going to be here in Hereford for a while now: I have five months ahead of training and that's the longest stretch any member of the Regiment can expect to spend on home turf.

A week later news comes through that the hit we were scheduled to carry out on the terrorist house back in Belfast has gone ahead at last, with the team which took over from us. An officer has been killed in the assault by the very M60 which we were trying to get our hands on. All the terrorists have been arrested and are awaiting trial.

I have already attended a lot of Regiment funerals. The coffin draped in the Union Jack. 'He Who Would Valiant Be'. 'Jerusalem'. 'I Vow to Thee My Country'. 'Fight the Good Fight'. And so on. There's no sermon but a eulogy from a friend. However, there are prayers. We say amen, but most of us aren't listening to the prayers. I'm thinking about the man, his death, the circumstances, anything but the content of the prayers, which has little meaning for me and offers no comfort. Afterwards, at the graveside, the medals and beret of the dead man are presented to his wife or parents, then the flag is folded in a special way and given to them. When the coffin is lowered into the ground, the 'Last Post' is played hauntingly on the bugle. The occasion is significant for us, but it is nothing to do with religion.

Now we're back in Hereford, we're doing counter-terrorist training. And, a familiar story is unfolding. I haven't been promoted again. Promotion may not affect the work you do at the moment, but it makes a difference to your pay packet and your later career. It's normal to be promoted to lance corporal about a year after joining the Regiment. Now another lad has been promoted, and this hurts because he joined the Regiment about six months after me.

I go to the troop sergeant and ask why Steve's been promoted and not me.

He shrugs.

'You're doing fine, Ginge . . .' (I'm called Ginge or Blondie according to the eye of the beholder.) 'You're doing fine but . . . we thought you were going back to Signals.'

My blood feels warmer. It starts to move round my body a little faster. There is an unwritten and unspoken assumption that signallers who leave the Royal Corps of Signals to be soldiers will return in a few years to signalling. SAS Signals benefits from having badged signallers who understand what the soldiers are doing. Once a scaly always a scaly. But I've never wanted to signal. It was only my parents' ludicrous idea that Morse code would be a useful trade which put me there in the first place. That was eight years ago and it seems I'll never shake it off.

'I'm not going back to Signals!' I say, as calmly as I can.

'No need to get heated, Ginge.'

'I'm not!'

'Calm down!'

The Regiment's written off my career because they think I'll only stay a couple of years. Signals is proving harder to escape from than Alcatraz.

'I'm not going back!'

'OK, all right, we get the message!'

A few days later I'm made a lance corporal. But I know this is a paper-shuffling exercise. They're still expecting me back in Signals one day.

On the counter-terrorist team you either train to be an assault trooper or a sniper. The two work in concert: the assault trooper smashes in windows and gets into a building but he's covered by the sniper out on the perimeter who takes out the obvious targets. This time, I'm an assault trooper.

We spend all day learning house assault techniques and hostage rescue. We constantly create fake seige situations in Hereford's own 'killing house'. We learn how to burst into a room, how to take out whoever's there safely, how to deal with prisoners, hostages and bodies.

At this time I don't have a girlfriend. I'm propping up the bar at the parachute club when in walks a striking young woman. She's tall and slim and she has thick, black hair down over her shoulders.

'She's pretty,' I say to whoever's sitting next to me.

'She's training to be a lawyer,' they say. 'So she'll be rich one day.'

Beautiful and rich. What a devastating combination. Unfortunately right next to her is Bart, with his arm around her in a proprietorial way. Bart is wearing cowboy boots. He hasn't got his stetson today but he still looks as though he should be busting open saloon bar doors somewhere in the Wild West – until he orders a drink in a thick Welsh accent. Bart is from a parachute club in South Wales, but he's a regular at Shobdon too. By the end of the evening I've had quite a few beers. I've learned that the girl's name is Claire, that she's Welsh and lives near Newport except during term time when she's up at Manchester University studying law. She's also a keen student parachutist. So far so good. When the bar closes, I'm feeding her peanuts and I've informed Bart that I'm going to take his girlfriend away from him. Bart just laughs.

Soon afterwards, Bart goes off to jump over Florida and Claire and I get together. She comes with me to jump in Belgium and when we return she's definitely my girlfriend.

I am gentlemanly. I leave a message for Bart telling him that he should contact me, and that I want him to know that Claire and I are going out now. When Bart returns, there are rumours circulating that he's not pleased. I go looking for him in all the Shobdon locals without success. Then, one night, when Claire and I are in the club bar, in walks Bart.

It's just like the OK Corral. He's wearing his cowboy boots.

'Here's Bart!' people whisper, and the whole room goes quiet.

He walks straight up to me and says, 'Frank, I think we need to talk outside.'

The silence in the room is deathly now. When a Welsh ex-miner asks you to step outside it can only mean one thing.

We walk out of the hut and to my surprise Bart sits down on a bench in the evening sun. I blink at him. I wonder where we're going to have our fight.

Bart says, in a man-to-man way, 'Come on, mate, let's talk.'

So I join him on the bench.

'I just want to say to you, no hard feelings. The best man won. Now let's shake on it, mate.'

I'm so taken aback by this that I wait for him to headbutt me when I stand up, but he doesn't. We walk back into the bar the best of friends to the amazement and perhaps the disappointment of the drinkers. Bart coldly ignores Claire after this, but, after all, a man has his pride.

It seems to me that this is going to be a serious relationship. But I'm careful. Not since Philippa have I allowed anyone to get really close to me. If I let anyone in, it might, just might, be Claire. But it'll take a long time.

Since I passed selection I've been living with another lad in the Regiment, Jake. Jake is the proud owner of a three-bedroomed semi in town. It's immaculate because Jake's very houseproud. He's also tight. The house has no heating so Jake has bought a small gas heater on wheels. In the morning he gets dressed by it, then wheels it into my room so I can do the same. After that it's switched off until the next morning. There's no hot water because Jake says we can shower when we get to work.

I learn to live with this because I like Jake. He's one of the lads. He props up the bar until late at night, his beer belly hanging over the stool, his shirt-tails trailing behind him and a cigarette at the side of his mouth which waggles when he talks.

'I don't understand, Frank, why I can't pull the really special birds,' he says to me.

'Well, have you thought of tucking in your shirt-tails? And how about a new haircut? Women don't go for pudding basins these days . . .'

Jake shakes his head.

'Women don't care about that kind of thing, Frank. You don't know anything about women.'

When Jake brings a girl home the house shakes with ecstasy until about three in the morning. Then there's a big thump. It's the sound of the woman being chucked out of bed. Whining and pleading follow.

'It's three in the morning! I can't get home now, how can I find a taxi now?'

'Not my problem,' Jake says. Jake is determined that no woman is going to win his heart and get her hands on his house. He does not respect women in general and he is especially unimpressed by Claire because she's a student and, for Jake, that puts her somewhere near the amoeba on the evolutionary scale. He is not going to turn his immersion heater on for an amoeba. When Claire's staying she waits for Jake and me to leave for work. As soon as the car's at the end of the road she switches on the immersion. Then she does the unthinkable. She has a bath. When she's finished, she has to run all the leftover hot water out of the tank because she knows that, as soon as Jake gets home, he'll feel it to make sure it's stone cold.

'There's a woman in the garden and she's almost stark naked,' roars Jake when Claire sunbathes in her bikini.

'Phhhhooof!' This is supposed to be a sound of indignation but it's more like pure lechery. He cannot take his eyes off the girl who only that morning was wallowing illicitly in his hot water. 'I mean, what will the neighbours think?'

'Probably just what you're thinking,' I say. Claire is stunning in the bikini. She is tall and slim and shapely and I can't imagine that all the neighbours aren't lining up to stare at her just like Jake is.

'Phhhhooof!' says Jake again.

Claire commutes down from Manchester to see me most weekends. She's not much enjoying her law course. She talks of leaving the university. She's still beautiful but something tells me that, after all, she's not going to be rich. Not long into the summer term, she skives off Friday lectures and arrives at the house before I'm home.

'Er, is Frank here?' she asks Jake.

'No,' he says, and shuts the door. He has his feather duster and his tin of spray polish and he's busy beautifying his semi.

Claire rings the bell again.

'Well, do you mind if I wait?'

Jake shrugs. He's reluctant. He runs his hands through his pudding basin hair. Finally he says, 'Well, if you want.' He shuts the door again. This time Claire manages to get a foot in it.

'No, Jake. I mean, can I wait inside?'

Jake lets her in at last. I arrive soon afterwards and join her in front of the TV. As we're watching it, Jake bustles in with the Hoover. He plugs it in and starts to run it over the room. Unfortunately, he unplugs the TV to do this.

'Sorry,' I say. 'That's just Jake.'

Claire looks at me and laughs. We're learning to understand each other, me and Claire. In spite of my wariness about getting involved, I am. And I'm finding I like it.

# 10

A COUPLE OF MONTHS INTO THE COUNTER-TERRORIST COURSE, AND we're still in the killing house, firing three, four, five hundred bullets a day and coughing lead smoke because the ventilation system's so poor there.

We break for a brew in the team room as usual. On the radio there is something about a group of terrorists taking over an embassy in London. We notice this, but not much. Then we're back into the killing house in our gas masks.

Soon afterwards we're warned that we're to deploy to London. Since we've heard the news bulletin we can guess why. By now we've listened some more. It's the Iranian Embassy and the terrorists have stormed in taking all the staff hostage as well as the British bobby who was guarding the place and a couple of other UK nationals who happened to be in there waiting for visas. We don't expect for one minute that we'll be called upon to use our training in some London embassy seige. We assume the police will sort it all out before we've even got the gear into the Range Rovers but no, the word is still go.

We drive down to London in the Regiment's white Range Rovers, stopping off at Beaconsfield for a brew. The boss has already flown down in a helicopter. There are about fifty of us in B Squadron and when we've had our brew we expect to be told that the whole thing's over. But the word comes that we're to drive to Regent's Park Barracks.

We go to the barracks and spend the night there. By now we are certain that negotiators will have talked the terrorists round. But in the night we're told that we'll be moving into the building right next to the embassy.

We arrive in a police van trying to look ordinary. We wear jeans and checked shirts and could be tourists or a brass band off-duty. We carry bags, heavy black bags, two each, which might contain cameras and creased trousers or musical instruments. They might, but they don't.

It's dark. I want to stare at the adjacent building but nobody else does. I glance around rapidly and see only police screens. I look where we're going and I'm impressed. I can tell the other lads are too. There's a small stone staircase outside. Inside, another staircase. It's grand. We pause on the ground floor and some of the lads are looking about to see what they can pinch but before they can recce we're led up the stairs. Polished wood, lots of it, and a red carpet.

We're allocated an immense room a couple of floors up. Perhaps people dance here. It must be 100 feet long. The ceiling is ornate. There are chandeliers which throw circles of light onto the walls.

We're called into the adjoining room for the briefing, in case the order comes and we have to go straight into immediate action. The second-in-command gives us the plan without bothering to raise his voice. There is silence in the room. Everyone listens. The pen squeaks on the white marker board when he draws his plan of the next-door building.

Afterwards a few people comment or make suggestions. The officer listens. Sometimes he nods. I'm too new to speak, and I'm still one of the youngest. I keep my mouth shut. I don't talk to anyone on the way out either but return to my gear and start to change.

First on are the coveralls. Black cotton. Then the assault boots. They're scuffed. They don't have toecaps. They're never bulled. Like the greatest of friends, they demand nothing and give everything. I keep them laced loosely and when they're on I pull the laces four times, once at each pair of holes. I like to feel the boots tightening around my feet with every tug. When I've tied them they feel like a part of my body. Now they're on, they'll stay there.

Then my belt and all the kit it carries, the holster and the magazines. There are three magazines on the left leg for my sub-machine gun. I wear my pistol low, above my right knee. I've watched a lot of cowboy movies and we're agreed, me and Wyatt Earp, that the best place to wear your pistol holster for a quick draw is low on the thigh.

For my next trick I pull the fireman's axe out of the bag. It has a small wooden handle which fits my palm nicely. I wear this on the other leg. Then the body armour, a ceramic plate which fastens with big velcro straps at the front. On top of this goes the plastic waistcoat. The pockets clip on and I slip in a few grenades and snap them on. Then the knife. It's a primitive survival weapon but sometimes we have to get primitive. The hood now, black. I pull it back until it is time to stand-to. Last on are the gloves. Thin, green, leather, we all love our aviators' gloves.

I'm unrolling my bed when tea arrives in a big shiny urn. There's a smell of garlic and a couple of bobbies come in bearing trays. They're trying not to stare at us. They're trying to act as if they see rooms full of men wearing gas masks and checking their sub-machine guns every day of the week.

'It's from La Pierre,' they say, putting the trays down and then backing off fast. They tell us La Pierre is a French restaurant down the road and the chef's special today is pork in cream sauce. They thought we'd like that so they bought the lot. We gather around the trays but before we have a chance to taste-test the chef's special we're told to stand-to.

Instantly the room's full of movement. Not fast, panicky movement. It's quick but it's deliberate. People are grabbing their weapons, putting on their belts, fitting their respirators. Nobody runs out of the room but within seconds we're gone. Outside, the policemen who brought us the food press against the wall as we pass. Now they stare.

Everyone goes in their own direction, some upstairs, some down, some along this floor. I go up. There are twelve of us. As we climb the stairs they get narrower and more secret. After one flight they aren't grand any more and after two there's no carpet. We reach the top. It's our first position. We're grouped right under the roof now and a sliding wooden ladder will take us up there when the word comes. But the word doesn't come. We wait.

At first I'm tense and my heart is beating fast but as the minutes go by I relax. My weapon feels a little heavier. It's an MP5, a little Rolls Royce of a machine, smooth with no rough edges. It's my own gun and I know it well. Slowly, quietly, hoping no-one's looking, I check the safety catch. I don't want to be the one to screw up. It's the most public operation yet, there are lines of camera crews at the end of the street and, although I have no interest in the politics of this operation and don't even care who the terrorists are or why they're there, I know that mistakes could have repercussions, serious repercussions, for the Regiment. If anyone makes mistakes, I don't want it to be me.

We wait in silence but it's a noisy silence. The gas masks magnify our breathing and there's a slight echo here on the landing so the whole place sounds like one big dirty phone call. The rubber diaphragms on the respirators click each time we breathe and with every breath I take there is a smell of rubber and traces of old gas. It's a peppery, pungent odour. The lenses steam up a little. I start to get that detached, underwater feeling. I think of yesterday's training exercise, when I last wore this mask. Was it only yesterday? I remember that Claire is coming down to Hereford this weekend. She would have arrived by now and found me gone and known better than to ask where. If she switches on the TV she might guess.

Via my earpiece a voice brings me back here to London. We're being told to stand down.

We return to the long room and wolf La Pierre's pork in cream sauce. Something cold and gooey for pudding. I take off my holster but not my boots and lie down feeling full. Another couple of bobbies have arrived.

'Pizza. From Carlo's around the corner,' they say. 'The boys thought you'd like it.'

I sit up. I can smell the pizza and it smells good. Someone tells him that we've already eaten but the copper shrugs, nearly upsetting the trays, and then puts them down on the floor.

'I was told to bring it in here,' he says.

So we eat the pizza too. Garlic, tomato, wedges of gooey cheese. Bottles of cold water. More tea. Overhead the chandeliers are going tinkle, tinkle. Life's pleasant. I almost forget what we're here for. We've just finished when we're told to stand-to again. This time, I grab a pillow as well as my weapon. We're supposed to be alert up there but I like to think I can be alert and asleep at the same time. It's another false alarm. When we return a copper comes in.

'The outer police cordon hasn't been fed,' he says. 'We bought them pizza from a restaurant down the road.'

'Oh yeah?' we say pleasantly.

'It's not in here by any chance?'

'Oh no,' we say. He looks at us hard and doesn't argue.

Over the next few days we stand-to and stand down again and again. My pillow earns me a reputation and the nickname Forty Winks Frank.

Sometimes my team goes back to the barracks in Regent's Park where we get in a few hours' training and build a model of the next-door building using wood and sack. The abseilers find similar buildings elsewhere in London and go out training in public without anyone realizing why. We get bored. Most of us don't believe we'll be called in next door to do the business and even the TV people are

135

sounding less excited now. Our plan is constantly upgraded. Briefing follows briefing.

Then, suddenly, there's an alert. Television reporters under makeshift lighting start jabbering at the entrance to the street. The terrorists have killed a hostage. There's rustling and readiness. I know the word's going to come soon and when we're told to stand-to again I suspect it's for real. Over the earpiece there are more voices than usual and their pitch is different, more urgent.

I have no idea of the day or the time of day when we take up our first positions under the roof for the umpteenth time but there's something electric in the air which tells me that now, at last, we'll move to deliberate action. It's coded black amber and when I hear black amber, although I'm not surprised, there's a lurching feeling inside my ribs and my heart starts to thud.

Up the sliding ladder. I await my turn and then I'm up so fast that I'm outside before I know it. Out here it's light but not bright. Even through lenses I can tell it's the soft light of an early May evening.

The first thing I see is a London bobby. He's young, fresh-faced and his cheeks look smooth under his helmet. He's been patrolling the roof all day, probably, thinking about what's for dinner, and suddenly here are twelve men in black advancing towards him, dehumanized by gas masks, weapons wrapped around their bodies. Which side are we on? Are we going to kill him? His face goes through an interesting range of emotions from horror to terror. We give him the thumbs-up to reassure him but he's already fingering his radio, so nervous he can hardly work it. Er, are there supposed to be a bunch of men up here with sub-machine guns, er, sir? He's trying to control his voice but it's slipping up and down a few octaves. We tell him as kindly as we can in the circumstances that there is going to be a big bang and he should get his head down. He looks at us in disbelief. He's sweating now.

We are to storm the building from a number of different points simultaneously and my team is going down through the roof. My heart is still thumping. I'm not scared, just scared I'll make a mistake. We've trained for this and we're good, the best. The dry spot in my throat is self-doubt.

We're on the roof of the adjacent building now and the abseilers are already starting to drop their ropes down the front. My team are lowering the detonator onto the roof. While I wait I look across the back of the building, down onto a kitchen, a restaurant kitchen. Perhaps it's Carlo's or La Pierre. A couple of elderly women are standing over the sink. One has her sleeves rolled up. Her arms are frozen in the water by the sight of us. The other is pointing and shouting. A few more people come running into the kitchen, flapping their elbows and shaking their heads like chickens. I cannot resist it. I raise my arm, at the end of which there happens to be an MP5, and give them a jaunty oh-I-do-like-to-be-beside-the-seaside wave.

There's no time to see their reaction. Our ball of plastic explosive is in place, so is the detonator. We're waiting for the go, knowing there should be a delay of a few minutes while everyone else gets into position. When the word comes, I'm to be first in. A ladder will be lowered for me and I'll go down into the building. I'd like to use these few moments to prepare myself but, before we expect it, things are happening. We're waiting for, 'Stand by, stand by . . . go!' but instead we get a voice over our headphones yelling, 'Go, go, go!' This is it. Bang. We hit our explosives device. There's a woomph of smoke and dust.

I feel misgivings. Everyone can't be in position by now, something must have gone wrong. My heart's hammering. I hear the words, 'Go, go, go' again inside my head.

Alpha-three is hooking the caving ladder onto the roof rails for me to climb down but there's a problem: it won't hook. I tell him to hurry but he fumbles some more. It's essential to take everyone in the building by surprise by attacking simultaneously so I decide to go down with the ladder only half-stabilized. Alpha-three stands aside for a moment. I lower myself into the dark hole at the heart of the building. I have never felt so alone.

I'm twenty-four and have smelled my own fear on occasions, but this isn't one of them. Once the action starts and I'm climbing down the rope ladder, hand under hand because it's so unstable, I'm no longer aware of my heartbeat, my breathing. I'm working now.

I'm waiting for my feet to touch the ground. When they do, I'm in half-darkness. There is smoke and dust and the smell of explosives. Silence, for a split second. Then the bang and shudder of the building rearranging itself around our bomb. I can't hear the rest of my team behind me or the other lads storming in through the windows at the front. Am I the only one in? Have the terrorists guessed what's happening? I feel vulnerable. I know the others will be inside in a few seconds but I slide a couple of stun grenades out of their holders and chuck them down the stairwell. They're a spectacular light and sound show. Fairly harmless, but guaranteed to terrify the uninformed.

I enter the telex room. The windows have been blown out. I cover the hall, down on one knee. By now the team has sorted out the rope ladder and my partner, alpha-three, is there behind me. The building is smoking. Perhaps my stun grenades have caused a fire.

When alpha-three taps me on the back, I go. We know the layout of the fourth floor. Our job is to comb this area for people, terrorists or hostages. I burst out, sweeping my gun ahead of me. I stop at each door until my partner taps me on the back. I open it, my gun goes in first, then me, then my mate, and it all happens in a split second. I decide on the instant whether to go right or left and he covers me while I search behind curtains, and I cover him while he searches the cupboards and under desks on his side of the room. We've done this back in Hereford a thousand times. It's like clockwork. He yells, 'Clear, clear, out, out, out!' We shut the door behind us.

Below us is the sound of gunfire, screams, a cloud of CS gas. In my earpiece voices are shouting. Sixty men, one radio channel. What's happening? a voice is saying. The politicians and top brass are anxious for news but they're blocking the channel with their questions. Shut up, someone tells him, we're trying to carry out an operation here.

My mate and I find no-one. One door is locked and alpha-three tells me to shoot the lock. I use my MP5. You'd expect a sub-machine gun to deal with a lock. Guys in detective movies are always shooting them off with 38s, but I feel splinters of brass bouncing off it into my legs and the lock hasn't budged. I use my axe and in a few swings it's off. We open the door. It's empty. It's a loo. I've shot the lock off the ambassador's toilet.

'Congratulations alpha-three-bravo,' says alpha-three.

We've cleared the floor now, our team. The boys upstairs have cleared the fifth. We all go down to the third.

This floor is chaotic. There's a lot of screaming, more gunfire, a strong smell of burning, voices yelling at each other inside my ear.

Someone, I can't tell who, one of the team, runs up to me. My gun is equipped with a streamlight, a powerful torch which is zeroed to my weapon and illuminates the target in the dark. He says, 'You've got a torch, come with me.' I leave my partner as we run downstairs.

He leads me to a door. 'There's a terrorist in here,' he says. 'Not sure if I killed him or not.'

We hit the door. Darkness. Nothing. No noise, no movement. Torches on, I go left, he goes right. I run the beam over the floor and chairs and we advance on the curtains. They're big, heavy velvet curtains and they swish as we rip them down. A yell from the other lad. He's found the terrorist. We both shine our torches on his body. He's dead, fallen back across a sofa, blood on his face, a small sub-machine gun cradled in his arms, grenades strapped to his body. His eyes and mouth are open. Outside, we tell the team leader about the body. We know the next man who goes into that room will be a scenes of crime officer.

We join the human chain on the stairwell. The boys have already started grabbing the hostages and passing them from man to man down the stairs. I seize each warm, sobbing body and throw it to my left. Some of them are trying to hug me, but I am not gentle. We're trained to handle hostages and I know that any one of these grateful, sobbing people could be a terrorist acting as a hostage. And then I pause. I'm holding a man by the lapels. He is wearing a green denim jacket. He has bushy hair. Instead of passing him along, something about him stops me. His eyes aren't saying, thank God, I'm rescued. He's afraid. We look at each other but I can't hesitate for longer, the next hostage is being passed to me. I hand him on. A few seconds later a yell comes.

'That's him! That's Salim!' Salim is the leader of the terrorists. I feel sure that this is a man with the fight gone from him, a man whose bravado has been replaced by terror. But intelligence tells us that he is carrying grenades and he is thrown up against the wall to be searched.

He is shouting, '*Taslim, taslim.*' No-one understands him. The firing begins. His body is rapidly riddled with bullets. A question comes into my head: why so many? But, there's no time to ponder further. The embassy is on fire and we are ushering the hostages out through the back door.

The building blazes. There are big flames in the rooms behind us. Outside in the garden we lay all the hostages down, handcuff them and search them. We are still wearing our gas masks. Anyone who takes off their respirator rapidly puts it back on when they see the TV crews. We climb into police vans and are driven away from Prince's Gate.

When we return to the Regent's Park Barracks we're jubilant. We push aside our life-size model of the embassy. We're too busy finding out who was who behind those masks and who did what. We learn that the order to go came early because one of the abseilers put a foot through a window upstairs and alerted the terrorists to the fact that something might be going on. About three people claim to have shot Salim there on the stairs. Eventually the meaning of his last words is revealed to us: he was surrendering. But for all we knew it could have been an Islamic battle cry, particularly since he was believed to be carrying grenades. Most of us speak at least some Arabic but he was speaking Farsi.

Margaret Thatcher arrives with Willie Whitelaw, the home secretary. It's an emotional occasion: Whitelaw is crying openly. When the bangs, flashes and gunfire started they thought it must be carnage in there. To find that the hostages were alive, we were alive and most of the terrorists were dead was a huge relief for them. The prime minister congratulates us, not in a formal line-up sort of a way but just mingling in amongst us. Then someone shouts, 'It's on the telly,' and we all of us sit down and watch it, including Mrs Thatcher. There are cheers as we see the boys going in.

Later that night, when we're driving back up to Hereford in the Range Rover, we're stopped on the M4 by a police car. We're still wound up and we just want to get back and we've been driving at 110 m.p.h. We have blue lights which we can use in an emergency but going home doesn't really qualify.

The policeman says, 'Bit of a hurry, sir?' and we say, 'Well, yeah.' We tell him we're an army team and give him the special codeword and then watch his face. He says, 'You're the boys!' and he and his copper mate shake us by the hand, congratulate us, and radio ahead, 'The boys are going through, don't pull them no matter how fast they're going!'

Back in Hereford we unpack, derig, clean up and go home. Home for me is Jake's house. Claire's already returned to Manchester.

I phone her and persuade her to come back. I have a week off as the press are everywhere. The other men in the Regiment make no secret of their envy. We just happened to be on counter-terrorist training when the Iranian Embassy seige happened. It could have been any of them and many wish it was. Despite all the training we do, it's possible to spend a whole career in the SAS without seeing any action. Maybe, and this thought is awful, maybe there'll be no more action for me before I leave at forty.

# 11

CLAIRE'S SPENDING LESS TIME IN MANCHESTER AND MORE TIME WITH me. We don't have any money because every last penny goes on free-fall. She's as crazy about parachuting as I am, and she's progressing fast. She has natural talent. She flies with ease. I'm proud of her free-fall.

On her twentieth birthday I give her a card and tell her to go down-stairs, I'll call her when her present's wrapped. Because I can't afford to buy anything I've decided to gift-wrap myself. I get out the paper and the tape. It soon becomes clear that I only have enough for my head. So I wrap my head and call her, a strange, muffled yell. When she appears we laugh like drains. She takes off my wrapping paper and kisses me and says it's a great present. I realize that I've just given myself to Claire. A few months ago, I wouldn't have done that.

When her summer term ends, she pulls the plug on her law course. By now, after a year, she is thoroughly disillusioned. I have an old camper van now and I collect her from Manchester in it. We can't stay at Jake's so we move into another Regiment lad's house until we can find somewhere to ourselves. Living together isn't really discussed. It isn't an issue. It just seems natural and we do it.

I'm getting ready to go on jungle training. The operational order explains what everyone's going to be doing in Belize. Then there's a last paragraph. Lance corporal Collins will stay in the UK to attend a Signals course in Catterick.

I am angry. The long scaly arm is never going to let me go. This course is preparing me for my return because if I pass it I can be made

141

a sergeant of Signals. But I have no interest in being made a sergeant unless I'm a soldier. I protest but am sent anyway.

Claire comes with me and we move into a bedsit in Darlington for the duration of the course. It's not far to Whitley Bay and so, of course, we visit my family.

Dad and Joanna and her two children and Dad's new Staffordshire Bull Terriers are all living in a council house. It's easy to find. The one with the front garden full of big weeds.

'Well,' says Joanna when Dad shows us into the living room, 'I suppose I'll have to put my teeth in now.'

She turns down the volume of the television but keeps *Coronation Street* flickering silently away in the corner. She watches it while she talks to us. Her two children, who are aged around ten, aren't home.

Claire's apprehensive when the dogs start snapping and grabbing and turning round in circles, the way dogs do. Dad grabs one of them.

'Look at the state of this animal,' he comments. Mitch has just been for a walk and has thick mud caked into her paw. Dad cleans the mud out with his finger and then pauses, his mud-encrusted finger hovering.

'What shall I do with this, then?' he asks nobody in particular. 'Here. You have it.'

He wipes the mud across Claire's clean trousers.

Claire stares at me in amazement. Dad watches her closely. He's interested to see what her reaction will be to this humorous gesture. Perhaps he guesses that she doesn't think it's funny.

I say, 'Da-ad . . .'

'It's only mud!' he laughs. But his expression says that now he knows what Claire is: posh.

*Coronation Street* ends and Joanna gets up to make tea in mugs. She brings it in on a tray with biscuits. She's a good sort. She's a supervisor in a clothing factory and she earns enough money to keep Dad and his dogs as well as her own family and she doesn't seem to mind the fact that she's the breadwinner and he's the drinker.

We all try to make conversation but it doesn't come easily. Dad watches the silent television. I can tell that, when the time comes, Claire is glad to leave.

Our visit to Mam's house is almost as difficult. She and Dick are no longer living in Tynemouth. Things have not gone well for them and they have moved to a council house on the coast road. Maybe Dick found he couldn't support such a big family. Maybe he's a bad businessman. The sweet shop's gone bust and he's been working at a sports centre, doing a bit of driving out of hours.

142

A glance at Mam and Dick tells me that their financial problems have taken their toll on the marriage. There's little affection between them now. I suspect that it always was a tug of love between Dick and the twins and somehow Dick's lost and Mam's ended up shielding them from him, which makes him angrier still. Gary left long ago but Nan's still around.

There are strange little reminders around the house that Mam used to be married to Dad and not Dick. Dad's power drill is lying dirty in the pantry, its lead in knots. Dad would never have let it get into that state. He kept his tools tidy.

Michelle and Michael are fifteen now. Michelle plans to stay at school to take A levels, the first of the five of us to do so. Amazingly, she's got religion. She takes her guitar along to the Pentecostal church and sings songs there. Michael and I tease her mercilessly about it.

Michael is a punk. He walks around with a tartan bumflap and his knees chained together. He wears a pair of big army boots and has a rat in his room.

'You can laugh,' he says, 'but this is it, it's here, this is the lifestyle of the future. Punk's here to stay.'

Michael delights our dad because he's a good footballer but academically he's outshone by his sister, who is consistently top of the class. Michael wants to leave school as soon as possible and become an army chef.

'You've got to be joking!' I say.

'No, I've been to the army information centre and found out all about it—'

'A slop jockey! The blokes just want chips, it doesn't matter what you cook them. Imagine a cookhouse out in the field in winter. Big petrol burners, big pots of beans and stew. That's not cooking, Michael. If you want to be a chef, be a chef out there in the real world.'

But Michael's stubborn.

'I want to join the army and get away,' he says. 'I can't stand Dad much longer.'

When he says Dad, he means Dick. That's what he's called Dick all these years. He hasn't seen much of our dad since the divorce. Only Gary maintains frequent and amicable relations with Dad. He goes to the pub with him every Sunday lunchtime.

I take Michael to Catterick to see the cookhouse.

'Look,' I say, as the men push past big pans of sloppy food. 'Can you imagine frying two hundred eggs for this ungrateful lot?'

His eyes are shining. He says, 'Oooh, I'd love it.'

Michael stands behind a hotplate and the chef says, 'Now, we've

143

got curry, rice, pasta, vegetables . . . but all they'll want to eat is chips and we'll end up throwing most of the rest away.'

He's right. The lads head straight for the chips. They have chips with anything. Even chips and stew. As soon as the chips are all gone, the lads are saying, 'Any more chips, mate?'

'Now, do you really want to work in a place like this?' I ask Michael. 'Oh yes,' he says.

Claire and Mam get along but there is none of the warmth that my mother shared with Alice, the last girl I brought home. Claire always keeps her distance. I look at Mam's council house and I think of Claire's big family house in Wales. I know my family has rapidly sensed something which I've never really thought about. We're working class and Claire isn't.

Dick knows it too. He ignores Claire. He strolls in and puts his bare feet up on the table and behaves like a pig throughout our stay. Mam keeps apologizing.

Yvonne is still in the civil service. She's married to a man who's turned out to be just like Dad. He's a hard-drinking Geordie who expects her to bring him his dinner while he watches TV. I don't understand why she lets history repeat itself.

She tells me quietly that she's worried about Mam. I'm worried too. Mam claims to have emphysema. She has to visit the hospital frequently to have her lungs emptied and she looks small and pale and frail. Both Yvonne and I wonder if it's something worse than emphysema. Mam's back to smoking Senior Service and Woodbines.

I learn that she often visits the hospital chapel. The chaplain there has become a friend of hers. I am so astonished by this that I choose to ignore it completely. My mother, who never goes to church and never mentions religion, should not be going to chapel. If this is a sign that she's on the way out, I just don't want to know. If she has beliefs, I don't want to discuss them with her.

Nan's always busy, cooking up her corned-beef recipes. She sits Claire down and tells her all the old stories. I'm very embarrassed by this but Claire sits on the edge of her chair listening politely. The twins start finishing off the stories, they know them so well. Then Nan shows how she can peel an orange at one go. Claire pretends to be impressed but she pretends badly. I wish Nan wouldn't do all this. But I'm grateful to her for trying to be friendly and make up for Dick.

When the Catterick course ends I go to say goodbye to Mam because I'll be leaving for Oman shortly. She looks terrible but she's

144

still working in a seafront bar. It's not quite so posh as the places she used to work but it's nice enough.

At her request we go there for a drink and she introduces us to her customers. She talks, with sly glances at Claire, about how much she'd like grandchildren. And she talks about the chaplain at the hospital. I can't respond. If she's really dying, it seems to me all wrong to start throwing out a lifeline to some God who doesn't exist. I think this is a cop-out. Mam is a strong woman and I don't want to see signs of her weakness.

At the end of the evening we drive her home and I'm amazed that she seems too weak to get into my old camper van by herself. I practically have to carry her in. I realize how much smaller she is than she used to be.

When it's time to go she gives me a hug and a small kiss and I hug her back. It's allowed now I'm grown up, but still only a brisk manly hug. Not a proper, deep-down, loving hug from me to her and from her to me. But I learned long ago that we're not that kind of family.

Mam's cheeks are sunken and wrinkled. There are tears in her eyes. She says, 'Take care of the little ones. Dick won't stay around, and they'll need you when I'm gone.'

This is the talk of a dying woman and I don't want to hear it. I agree at once, rather than discuss exactly how bad things are, or asking if there's anything I can do. I left home a long time ago when things were in a mess and now it's painful to be home again and I want out. I tell her I'll come and see her when I get back from Oman.

Driving down to Hereford, there's a silence in the van. I'm wishing I'd asked Mam more about her illness and let her talk a little more about her religion if she'd wanted to.

I leave for Oman. The war's long over here now but we're still doing a hearts and minds programme, bringing medicine to obscure villages. We're also practising desert warfare. Some of the boys in my troop are doing free-fall out here but, since mobility troop are short of men with signalling skills, I'm to travel with them in their convoy across the desert by Land Rover. Our jeeps are big open vehicles with machine guns front and back.

This is a sandy desert, like deserts in storybooks, with miles and miles of shifting sand, little vegetation, and the odd oasis. Gorilla, one of the Regiment's big moustaches, is patrol leader. We're travelling by night and are not too far from a village when we get a flat tyre. There's no jack in the vehicle. I'm speechless with disbelief. This is mobility troop, which specializes in land transport, and they travel in vehicles with no jack.

145

After a week we reach the sea. We stop by a river running down steep rock and the fishermen appear with their catch. I'm in a tent taking down Morse messages. There's one for 0043. That's me. I'm 0043. This message isn't even routine. It's an immediate. I know at once what it is. I don't think it in words. I just know it in my heart and in my body.

I write down the figures and two of the lads decode them. They're puzzled. They can't quite work it out. Something about someone's mother. Mother passed . . . I know what it is but I carry on taking down the Morse, one ear on the boys.

Then there's a silence. They both go out of the tent. I know why. My message said, 0043. Mother passed away.

Mechanically I copy down the other messages but in my head my own message is still ringing: 0043. Mother passed away.

I am still writing as I blink back the tears.

Gorilla comes into the tent. He's widely acknowledged as a big, angry bear but he comes up to me and puts his great paw on my shoulder.

He says, 'Frank . . .'

I say, 'It's OK, Gorilla, I know.'

When I've finished taking down the messages I walk out of the tent by myself. I don't cry. I'm in the SAS. I can't.

Within an hour a helicopter arrives. The Bell Jet Ranger screams across the desert. It lands by the fishing village and the locals have never seen anything like it. All the children rush out, shouting and pointing. Gorilla shakes my hand.

On arrival in the UK, I go straight to the north-east. There I learn that my mother had lung cancer. The doctors had given her three months to live and she decided not to wait that long. In great pain, she'd taken an overdose of painkillers. She was forty-eight years old.

Dick takes me to see Mam's body at the funeral parlour. I am appalled. She looks terrible because she's wearing some pink frilly dress that isn't her at all. She's so tiny. She used to say she was a pea on matchsticks, because she put weight on but never on her legs. And now here she is, reduced to this small doll. Her face is sunken, her cheeks hollow. But she looks peaceful.

Dick is crying uncontrollably. He strokes her face again and again. I just touch her gently on the forehead. It's not a real person. It's not Mam. I've seen the dead before but am overwhelmed now by the sense that she's gone and this lifeless corpse has nothing more to do with her.

Standing over her body, I think about Mam's life and it seems to me to be a tragedy. A kind, gentle woman who married the wrong man. Twice. She tried to hold things together. She cared for us in her own way, not by hugging us all the time but by earning money for us. It meant she was always busy and never there but it was her way of caring. I understood how she needed to escape from Dad because I'd needed to escape too. I just wish she hadn't escaped to Dick Short. He was a spoilt man with a doting mother. Maybe he'd wanted Mam to be the same with him. Maybe he'd underestimated the cost of taking care of her children. Maybe it would have gone wrong anyway.

Driving home, I stop at a green traffic light and wait for it to turn red before I drive off. Dick stops me.

I realize that, because I left home when I was only fifteen, I've always been Mam's boy. I've always been fifteen for her. I may have misbehaved a bit when I came back but all the usual rebellions and teenage rows just didn't happen. The whole family is for me somehow preserved in 1972. I still think of the twins as six-year-olds, Gary as thirteen, Yvonne as seventeen. And, in the family in my mind, there's no Dick Short, no Joanna.

I feel guilty that I left Mam. She needed support and I went away instead of giving it to her, more than once. I failed her often. How I stole money from her. How I got her to buy me a stereo when I first went to Harrogate instead of giving her some of my wages. How I told her one day that I'd joined the army just to get away and she'd collapsed in a helpless heap of sadness. I should have told her how I appreciated her. But I didn't.

At the funeral everyone is upset. People show it in different ways. Michelle is angry. She says she'll never go back to church. Nan is beside herself with grief. She's always been the frail one, and now her daughter has died before her. She keeps saying, 'It should have been me!'

Auntie June, Uncle John, Auntie Alwyn, they're all there and tearful although Mam didn't see much of them in recent years. A lot of people from Mam's work are there. The last time I saw her, when we took her home from the pub, was my only glimpse of that other life, her working life, where there were friends and jokes and where maybe she was happier.

Of course Dick is there, sobbing. So, to everyone's surprise, is Dad. Dad is devastated. For the first time in my life I see him cry. We walk through the rose garden outside the crematorium and tears run down his cheeks. I realize that, in his own way, he's always loved my mother.

Gary and Yvonne and I stay strong for the sake of the twins and Nan and Dad, all of whom cannot control their tears.

The minister talks about my mother's Christian faith and how he'd come to know her through the chapel. He reveals how she'd sat and talked to him intimately and I'm shocked and even jealous. She never spoke to me like that. And when she did talk to someone, she chose a priest. I feel disappointed in her for copping out. Then I remind myself how familiar she must have been with disappointment.

Afterwards food is served back at the house. Unusually for a Geordie funeral, there's no drink. At Mam's request, only tea and coffee is served. She probably didn't want a fight breaking out. Did she guess that Dad would be there, heartbroken?

I bring up the subject of funding the twins with Yvonne and Gary but they shake their heads. Dick has indicated that he wants to manage. We've all been warned by Mam that he'll leave and we agree to discuss the subject again if and when this happens.

I don't go back to Oman after the funeral. I stay with Claire in the big farmhouse we're now renting together. A couple of weeks later, Michelle phones. She says that a van pulled up outside the house and Dick went out to meet the driver. Then they both walked into the kitchen and started carrying the freezer out.

'What are you doing?' shrieked Nan.

'He's borrowing it,' said Dick.

'But . . .' Nan yelled, 'but . . . it's full of food!'

'Well he's borrowing the food as well.'

Nan started to call Dick names but all he said was, 'It's none of your business, this freezer doesn't belong to you. Everything here is mine.'

That was the start of Dick's systematic sale of all the furniture in the house. With my family still in it.

Michelle is crying and I am very big brother and tell her not to worry, I'll sort it out. I am livid. I can think of a number of ways of dealing with this.

I'm on the counter-terrorist team again. I go into camp to the sergeant major and ask for some time off. I explain, 'There's a problem back home. This man, who's supposed to be a stepfather, is selling off all the family's possessions.'

He says, 'Go home and sort it out, Blondie. Do you want any of the boys to go too? You can take a team up if you like.'

That's the Regiment for you. Once you're in, you're family and your problems are everyone's problems. I'm not sure what the boys could have done for me, but the offer shows solidarity. I thank him and say I'll let him know if I have trouble sorting things out myself.

I phone the solicitor who says that Dick isn't allowed to sell anything in the house while the family's still there. I phone Dick.

'What do you want?' he says.

'Dick, get out of the house. Get out of the house and don't come back. I'm coming up tomorrow and I don't want to find you there. If I do, there'll be trouble.'

The following day I go home and he's gone. Nan and the twins are relieved. They're scared he'll come back but I'm confident we won't hear from him again.

Nan and Michael and Michelle are happy that Dick's gone. Financially, they can cope. Offers of help are refused. Because the twins are so young the council house is rent free and Nan has her pension. If they're entitled to anything, Michelle sees to it. She can go to the council and make mincemeat of the officials there if necessary. She's not sixteen yet and she's formidable. When the school year ends, Michael will be joining the army. That will leave Michelle and Nan. Nan is still grieving. She's supposed to be looking after the twins but it's the other way around.

# 12

CLAIRE AND I HAVE BEEN TALKING ABOUT GETTING MARRIED FOR A while now. I'm not sure how we've drifted into the subject. Marriage isn't something I take very seriously. It's hard to see relationships as permanent. I love Claire but I'm still holding a lot back, just in case she hurts me. But it seems to me that marriage doesn't have to be too great a commitment: we can always get divorced if it doesn't work. Claire's a great friend and good fun and if we're married we'll get an army quarter. Plus, free-falling is my life and it's a passion Claire shares.

We've brought up the subject of weddings with Claire's mother and she has immediately produced a list of family who have to be invited, most of whom Claire has hardly met. Claire's parents are divorced too and the prospect of having warring factions at our wedding is too much.

Then Claire's dad suggests: just go out and get married. Take the money I would have spent on a big wedding and put it down as a deposit on a house.

It's the end of March, 1981. We're driving back after a weekend at the parachute club. On the radio we hear the story of someone who proposed on April Fool's Day. Claire says, 'That's the day I'd like to get married.'

I agree with her that it's a good joke. I try to get us a licence to marry on 1 April but it's too late. The earliest licence I can get is for Friday, 3 April.

We tell no-one except the three parachuting friends we invite to be witnesses, Tony, Geoff and Paul. At the registery office, we are all wearing jeans except for Paul, who wears a suit. The registrar keeps trying to marry Claire to Paul.

Afterwards we buy some cheese and ham and rolls and champagne and go back to the farmhouse we rent. Our three witnesses stay with us. We phone our families to tell them we're married and Claire's mother insists that she wants us to report to her with our wedding certificate. Her father bursts into tears.

The next day the bride, groom and witnesses all skydive together and then we start house-hunting. We find a red-brick semi-detached cottage with roses round the door. It's right out in the country with no bus service, no drains and no bathroom. We agree to live in married quarters in camp until we can get the place habitable.

In quarters, everyone knows everyone else's business. Claire finds herself inundated with invitations to coffee, where she answers endless questions.

'What does your husband do?' everyone asks.

'He's in the army,' she says.

One day a neighbour asks, 'What do you think of my settee?'

It's hideous, a brown corduroy sofa swinging on a chrome frame. But Claire makes polite noises.

'Well, if you like it, you can have it!' says the woman. Claire is horrified. She tries to refuse this gift but the woman insists. Finally Claire gives in and the woman informs her that it will cost £20.

'What's this?' I say when I get home.

'Isn't it horrible?'

'Well, what's it doing here?'

'I paid £20 for it and I hate it.'

She goes into the kitchen to make macaroni cheese, my favourite dish. She cooks it in the oven and then browns it under the grill. But our new grill collapses and the macaroni cheese is plastered all over the floor.

'I hate married quarters,' Claire informs me. 'I hate grills and I hate brown corduroy sofas.'

One couple living near by make love every lunchtime with the windows open. The husband's name is Frank.

'Oh, Frank, Frank!' shrieks the woman for all the road to hear. Claire develops a sudden interest in gardening. She hangs around outside where everyone can see her so nobody will think she's shrieking to her Frank.

I pretend to forget her twenty-first birthday. I get dressed and go to work. Actually, I've taken the day off. I sneak back to the shed where I've hidden chocolates, flowers and champagne and surprise her with them. Then when we're out on a job for the night, I buy her a big soft toy the first time the Range Rover stops for petrol.

'What the hell is that?' say the other lads.

'It's for Claire.'

They groan.

'You've only been away from her for about six hours. What's it going to be like when you're away for six months?'

Soon we'll find out. I'm beginning a course which will start in Hereford and end in Oxford.

There are a number of skills which the Regiment teaches to a very high level and each patrol should have a good cross-section of these skills. The first one everyone learns is signalling. Of course, I already have that and it means I'm generally appointed patrol signaller. But now, to my delight, I'm sent on a course to learn another skill. I'm going to be a medic. When I've completed it I can be patrol medic and watch someone else do the signalling. At last. Escape from the radio and a small hint that the Regiment is investing in me as a soldier, not someone who'll scamper back to the Signals Corps at the first opportunity.

The course is over three months long, run by paramedics with doctors participating. We learn how to carry out operations on casualties in the field, all about infections and drugs, including their side effects and contra-indications, stings, bites, fevers, gunshot wounds, and trauma. We do the work over and over and over again. There's lots of hands-on casualty simulation. We treat chest wounds and insert Heimlich valves. Every day we wrestle with problems.

'Frank, you're in the jungle on your own with this casualty, there's no helicopter to save you. He's unconscious. Keep that man alive. Now, what do you do?'

'Check his airway. Make sure it's free, check for obstructions. Check his breathing—'

'He's breathing but it's shallow. He's coughing blood.'

'I listen to his lungs with my stethoscope.'

'Good. You hear blood in the lung.'

'I lie him on the side of the injured lung in the recovery position.'

'What's happened to him?'

'His lung's punctured. I should check his ribs to see if they're fractured, that might have caused the puncturing.'

'What else do you do?'

'Blood pressure. I keep monitoring this and his pulse.'

'How frequently do you take observations?'

'Every five minutes.'

'His blood pressure's dropped to seventy-five over thirty.'

'That's bad. It means I'm losing him.'

'Still coughing blood. Obviously his lungs are filling up. You're going to lose him soon.'

'No, I'm going to try something else. I'm going to make a Heimlich valve to drain off the blood. I cut the finger off a rubber glove, take a hypodermic needle, I stick it in between the third and the fourth ribs . . .

I've done this only recently, using an orange instead of a human. Oranges and humans have a lot in common. The orange skin is more rigid but I've injected through it and practised stitching on it.

'What about pain relief?'

'Not necessary if the patient's still unconscious. But if he starts to come to, I'll give him morphine.'

'And if blood pressure falls still further?'

I reply mechanically, 'Close chest cardiac massage.'

'Are you sure about that?'

'Well . . . no. He's got broken ribs. I have to weigh up the danger of the injury I can cause after the trauma to his chest.'

I remember the picture we've been shown of a soldier who's had half his jaw shot away. The instructor said, 'How will you give him mouth to mouth, he hasn't got one?' Then he showed us how to insert an airway in the throat.

We practise again and again. Question and answer. Dummies and photos. For the final month of the course we are attached to hospitals. I'm sent to the John Radcliffe in Oxford with my former housemate, Jake. We wear white coats and carry stethoscopes in our pockets and the patients all think we're doctors. A little badge says: 'Mr Frank Collins, Medical Assistant' but this is half-hidden by my lapel and no-one bothers to read it anyway. Jake and I walk around trying to look confident and doctorish. I wonder about some of the other lads in other hospitals, though. There are two Scots lads with strong Glaswegian accents, huge Mexican moustaches and love-hate tattooed on their knuckles. I wonder what their patients will make of them.

We head straight for casualty where the consultants are pleased to see us. Our boys have a good reputation, it's the run up to Christmas and there are too many accidents for the doctors to cope with. Within days we're completely integrated. I'm soon running my own fracture clinic, anaesthetizing the patients, manipulating and setting. Only the jealousy of some members of the nursing staff reminds us that we're not real doctors sometimes.

153

One freezing night a pretty blonde girl comes in after a car accident. Her cheek is completely split.

'Frank, you know what to do. Suture her, please,' says the doctor.

I stare at him and then ask to speak to him outside.

'What's the problem?' he asks me in surprise.

'Well, she's a pretty girl and it's important that she isn't left with a scar right across her face . . .'

'I agree. You can manage that.'

'Don't you think you should do it?'

'Frank, who's the duty doctor tonight?'

'You are.'

'I'm going to be rushed off my feet. A suturing job like this takes time and you've got all night. Just go slowly. Take as long as it takes and call me if you have any problems.'

I return to the patient. She really needs plastic surgery but there's no way she'll get it late on a Saturday night.

'This may take a while because I have to go so carefully,' I warn her. It takes over three hours.

I follow her progress when she returns for appointments over the next few weeks. I have the satisfaction of seeing a perfect heal. Her face is almost unscarred.

A Lebanese chemistry student comes in with acid burns on her face after an explosion in the lab. A woman needs suturing all over her leg after she runs for the bus, the door closes on her hand and she is dragged beneath it. And, one freezing, snowy night, a teenage girl kills herself. She has taken off her clothes and lain down naked in the snow. Her parents have found her and brought her in and tried to warm her. They rush her in to casualty and we try slowly warming the body. Her body never does get warm and she soon dies. The parents are devastated. We are all too busy to spend any time with them. I'm horrified that no-one can comfort them. They sit without even a cup of tea, lost and shocked.

I see a baby born and fight back tears. I visit the morgue. The smell is unforgettable.

When a young Sikh hockey player is brought in with a split head, Jake is busy and hands him over to me. I walk in and he's lying down with his hockey stick. His eyes are shut and he's moaning quietly to himself.

'Are you all right, mate?' I ask nervously.

The man says yes but doesn't want to talk any more.

So I clean his scalp and, while I'm chatting to him, I cut off his pony tail. I razor round the edges of the scar. The skull is covered by a thin membrane like elastic clingfilm and it has to be pulled back. Beneath it is bone. The needle makes an awful scrape against his skull as I anaesthetize him before sewing him up, a sound so horrible that it makes my knees tingle. This is quite a quick job as I don't have to worry too much about scarring on his scalp.

The sister comes in, gasps, and gestures to me to come outside quickly.

Once we're out of earshot, she whispers, 'What are you doing? I told you not to cut his hair!'

I blink at her a few times.

'You didn't tell me—'

'I did! He's a Sikh! You can't cut his hair! And you have!'

I realize that she told Jake, not me. Jake had been briefed on the patient and then just handed him over to me without passing any of the information on.

As soon as I finish sewing the Sikh up I hide with Jake in the canteen.

'Oh yes,' says Jake casually, 'she did say not to cut his hair. I forgot.'

We sneak back only when we're sure the hockey player has gone.

'He was livid, absolutely livid!' says the sister. 'I had to tell him it was a new doctor who didn't know much.'

An accident victim is brought in. He's been hit by a motorbike and the pillion rider was carrying a Chinese takeaway. The victim, as well as his other injuries, is covered in Chinese food. Jake and I have the job of sewing him up. Every fifteen minutes we take his pulse and blood pressure.

The man's X-rays are displayed and I notice something interesting on one of them.

'Look at that line across his X-ray. Didn't they show us something like that on our course? Haemothorax or something.'

Haemothorax is blood on the lung.

'Can't be,' says Jake, 'he'd have low blood pressure if he had haemothorax.'

So I check the patient's blood pressure and, sure enough, it's dropped considerably.

I hit the panic button.

'What is it?' asks a hassled and annoyed doctor appearing in the door.

'Er, well, his blood pressure's dropping and that line on the X-ray . . . isn't that haemothorax?' we ask.

The doctor takes a look at the X-ray.

'You're right!' he says. The patient is taken straight into theatre.

Jake and I look at each other.

'Would we really spot that in the field?' I ask. 'Without an X-ray?'

'You might suspect but you'd need a lot of bottle to do anything about it,' he says. We know the Heimlich valve improvisation routine, but Jake's right that it would take a lot of bottle to shove one into a casualty if you didn't have an X-ray to reassure you.

We scrub up, put on our greens and join the others in theatre. Not only is our diagnosis proved correct but the patient is found to have a ruptured spleen. We watch as it's removed. We return to see the patient the next day and he's sitting up in bed enjoying his lunch.

Once a week the consultant gathers all his doctors to go through cases. At the next meeting, he slaps the Indian's X-ray up on the wall.

'What do you notice here?' he asks.

Silence. All the junior doctors study the X-ray without speaking. Finally he points to the line.

'Come on, what's this?' he says impatiently.

More silence.

The consultant starts to shout.

'These army medics have been on a three-month course! They've learned medicine for three months but they picked it up and all of you have missed it!'

He tears into them for some minutes. Consultants can be like sergeant majors. Of course, the doctors have been studying medicine to a terrifically high theoretical as well as practical standard, whereas we've just been dealing with the practicalities, and recently too.

The junior doctors look after us well. They take us to their parties and encourage us to take time off during slack periods. We take bleeps so that they can call us if there's a major road traffic accident.

Claire visits me in my hospital flat and gets snowed in there. When she returns to quarters in Hereford she finds water everywhere and six burst pipes. It's the last straw for Claire. She moves into our sanitation-free cottage. Since there are no pipes, at least there's no danger of any of them bursting.

My medical course ends soon afterwards and I join Claire at home before leaving for Belize. I'm soon off to my tropical paradise, leaving Claire to live with the sulky woodburner and the sacks of cement which are piled up on the living room floor.

There's always a troop out in Belize and it's our squadron's turn to man it. We stay at the camp I've been staying at since my first visit to Belize as a young signaller, only now we're in the sergeants' mess.

Our staff sergeant is Kev who is famous in the Regiment for his religious beliefs. Not only is he sure he's right about reincarnation but he knows he was, in a former life, a Viking. And, like a Viking, Kev loves to fight. He's a member of a close-combat club, which I often attend. A fight with Kev is bad news because he is handy with the rice flails and any other weapon you can name. He's already been chucked out of the Regiment once for fighting, but he's now back.

One morning Kev wakes up with a blistering, thumping hangover.

'Oh, Taff,' he says to his best mate, 'oooooh, my head.'

'I'm not surprised,' says Taff, quick as a flash, 'after what happened.'

Kev sits up. 'What happened?'

'Don't you remember? You must do.'

'I don't. What happened?'

'You beat that bloke up.'

'I didn't. I don't remember beating up anyone.'

'You did. You gave him a right good hiding and then you came back here boasting about it.'

'You're joking.'

'Nope. You really thrashed him.'

'Who?'

'Some bloke in the sergeants' mess.'

Groaning, Kev lies down again while Taff joins us for breakfast.

'Listen to what I just told Kev . . .'

At that moment, into breakfast walks a guy with big bruises all over his face and a cut on his eye.

'It's him!' we roar.

Taff rushes straight up to him.

'What happened to you?'

'I had a few too many last night and fell in a monsoon ditch.'

'Well, listen, we're stitching up a mate. Would you mind pretending that our staff sergeant beat you up?'

The guy, who's in the RAF, laughs and agrees to play along.

Taff sprints straight over to the military police, tells them the story, and asks them to pretend to begin an investigation into Kev.

The military police phone Kev, because he's our commander. They say, 'There was trouble in the bar last night and a lad got badly beaten up. None of your blokes involved, were they?'

'No, no, none of my blokes!'

Kev finds Taff.

'I've had the bloody military police on the phone, Taff!'

'Oh no!'

'They think one of our blokes might have been involved in a fight last night. What am I going to do?'

'Oh, Kev, I've seen the lad and he was beaten to a pulp. I saw him in the mess at breakfast. He looked terrible.'

'Oh no!'

Kev deals with this problem by keeping out of the way. He gets Taff to bring his food to his room, rather than going to the mess.

'Where's Kev?' we all ask, laughing over our food.

'He won't come out!'

Finally, Jake goes down to the ops room and discovers Kev with a big pile of money. We have money in case war breaks out. It's escape money for us if we have to go behind enemy lines. There's gold sovereigns, US dollars, Belizian money.

'What are you doing, mate?' asks Jake innocently.

'Counting it . . . I don't know why really.'

'You're not thinking of going somewhere?'

'Well,' says Kev miserably, 'to be honest, I might as well. As soon as word gets out that I've been in another fight, it'll all be over. I'm thinking of running for it.'

Jake thinks this stitch might have gone a laugh too far. After all, Kev's been suffering for a couple of days now.

'Time to stop,' we all tell Taff, but Taff insists he can push his friend a bit further.

He catches Kev in the ops room with the money.

'Come on, mate, it's not that bad.'

'It is. I might as well go now.'

'They don't know who it is. I mean, not really. Well, only . . .'

'What? What, Taff? What do they know?'

'Apparently they reckon it's a . . .'

'What?'

'Oh, nothing.'

'Tell me, Taff. You have to tell me!'

'Perhaps it's better if . . .'

'Taff! What do they know?'

'They think it's a . . . a bloke with a moustache.'

Kev nearly melts on the spot. As a reincarnated Viking he is not only big and burly with wild hair and staring eyes, but of course he has a bandit moustache.

Kev goes straight back to his room and shaves.

We all agree that it's been a good stitch but we should wind it up now, before Kev does something serious. We tell the military police and they visit Kev.

158

'Kev, this injured RAF bloke does think it was a man from your company who beat him up. He wants an ID parade. Er . . . didn't you used to have a moustache?'

'Oh no, no, not for quite a while,' Kev says hastily.

An identity parade is set up on the tennis court. There are two military policemen. The whole troop is lined up and Kev's too nervous to notice that we're all wearing trainers with go fast stripes on them. No-one wants to stand next to him. Taff finally agrees to risk his life by doing this.

The military policeman comes up with his big board and reads us the caution from it: 'Gentlemen, you've been called here in accordance with Queen's Regulations, paragraph ten. I must warn you that anything you say may be taken down and used in evidence against you. Anybody identified at this parade as the guilty party will be placed under arrest immediately and subject to court martial . . .' Of course, this isn't a real caution. It's a horror story, concocted by the military police, who are having a good time with our little joke.

Another policeman appears with the unfortunate victim of the alleged brawl. Now that I'm a medic I've been given responsibility for bandaging him up, putting his arm in a sling and, when he doesn't look damaged enough, I've even persuaded the man to let me draw some blood out of him and to cover the bandages. He really looks like the walking wounded when he's led onto the tennis court.

The RAF guy walks slowly up and down the parade, studying all our faces. Kev is sweating. He walks past Kev, back behind him, straight up to the military policeman, turns, and points at Kev.

The policeman starts to walk towards Kev, who, astonishingly, snaps forward, one two, in a drill movement of the kind we never do in the SAS.

'Sir! It's not me, sir. I'm telling you, sir, I was not there! Please believe me that I have no— '

'Stop, stop,' says the policeman. 'Staff, stop! I've got something to show you before you say any more.'

He produces a piece of paper which he waves in front of Kev's face. Kev is standing to attention but he can read the words: RUBBER DICK. This is one of our expressions for you've been had.

Kev passes through a series of rapid emotions. We know because his face works its way across most colours of the spectrum. We have about five seconds to enjoy it before it's time to start running. We run as hard and as fast as we can. The military police run. The wounded man runs. Everybody runs.

We hear the bellow, 'Taaaaaffff!' but by now we're at the perimeter of the jungle. This is Kev and we know that he's capable of killing us. We hide in the jungle, whispering, 'Where is he? Where's he gone?'

That night, Kev appears in the mess.

'You bastards!' he says but he's calmed down by now. It's to his credit that he takes the joke, and takes it well.

This is a good tour. We're in the jungle, continuing our hearts and minds programme in the villages during the week. At weekends we fly back to base where we enjoy ourselves.

I snorkelled as a boy and learned scuba-diving when I was at army apprentice college, and now I start again. We go out in an inflatable on a Friday, find an island, set up our hammocks between some trees, gather some coconut husks for our barbecue, do some diving, have a few beers, cook our fish.

The diving is spectacular. The colours of the coral and the rocks and the sea creatures are intense. On one occasion I get the strange feeling that I'm being watched. Water is an element I know well now. It's in constant motion and so am I but sometimes it rearranges itself in ways that don't feel right. It's the equivalent of a shadow falling across the sun.

I turn and there is a wall of fish right behind me. They are tuna fish, immense creatures, five feet long but their size is magnified by the lens of the water. There must be hundreds of them. They stare at me with their bulgy eyes and they don't move. I stare back at them. I know they are harmless but the massive size of the shoal is disconcerting. Suddenly, with no warning at all, they turn. Every single fish turns simultaneously. There is no leader which the others follow and apparently no communication between them. Somehow, they swim off in unison. Within a few seconds the water feels normal again, just as if they were never there.

I receive a letter from Claire. Nothing unusual about that. Before I met her, there were never any letters for me, now there's one every day, numbered so that I can tell her if one's missing. They're lovely letters and the other lads are green with envy.

She writes about the secretarial course she's started. She has to walk miles to the bus each day. There's just one bus home from Hereford in the evening and she has to catch it. When she gets back the cottage is freezing. There's a lot of snow at the moment, making life doubly difficult. The woodburner's still playing up. What surprises me is the news at the end. She's pregnant.

'But don't worry,' she concludes, 'I'll sort the problem out, just like

160

I have to sort everything out around here. Hope you're enjoying your-self in the sun. Love, Claire.'

Claire's pregnant. Claire's going to have a baby, our baby. We'd planned to start a family – but not for at least another four years.

There's only one way to deal with the tide of emotion that engulfs me, both at the news that she's having a baby and the news that she's not going through with it. I get drunk. Roaring, cursing, wildly drunk. I then stagger from the bar to the medical officer who tries unsuccessfully to have a coherent conversation with me.

Eventually, he tells me to come back when I'm sober. The next day I find a message telling me to ring a Hereford number I don't recognize. Maybe, just maybe, Claire's managed to get a phone installed in the cottage at last.

I ring, and Claire's voice answers. I'm so happy to hear her that for a moment I don't speak.

'Hello? Hello?'

For a while we don't talk about the subject on our minds. Her letter has taken so long to arrive that I'm beside myself with fear that she'll already have organized an abortion. But I'm determined not to tell her she has to keep a baby she doesn't want.

Finally I pluck up the courage to ask her and am relieved to find out she hasn't taken any action yet. We talk a bit about how she's feeling and gradually I realize that she wants this baby. She's offered to get rid of it because she thinks I don't want it. Somehow, eventu-ally, our feelings spill out and by the end of the conversation it's agreed that we're keeping it.

For the next few months, far away from home but knowing I'm going to be a father, I'm excited. Claire sends me a pair of baby bootees which I hang on my wall. I lie in bed staring at them. In the autumn there will be a tiny pair of feet wearing those bootees. The feet will belong to my child. There is a rush of emotion every time I look at them. I have a renewed sense of my own childhood back in Newcastle. I remember the twins when they were babies. I think of Mam. I wish she were here to be a grandmother.

Long before our baby is born, war breaks out.

The Falklands War is declared against Argentina in April 1982, when I'm nearing the end of this tour of Belize. We return to the UK, excited at the prospect of some real action at last.

To my disappointment, Claire's not looking particularly pregnant yet, although she's sick most of the time. I'm excited by the war and the whole country is in the grip of Falklands fever but it just leaves Claire cold.

The British have sunk the *Belgrano* and we're at the May Fair in Hereford when we hear that HMS *Sheffield* has been hit by an Exocet. We bump into one of the lads, who asks us, 'Have you heard what the effing Argies did to the *Sheffield*?'

Claire surveys him coolly.

'Well, did you say that about the *Belgrano*?' she asks.

He can hardly believe his ears.

'A lot of blokes were killed on the *Belgrano* too,' she says. 'And they've all got mothers and fathers just like the boys on the *Sheffield*.'

The Regiment lad finds his tongue.

'Well, they shouldn't have started a bloody war, should they?'

His tone's nasty.

'Come on, Claire,' I say, and steer her away.

Only the counter-terrorist team will remain in Hereford. Most of the rest of the Regiment is already out in the South Atlantic, or they're on their way. We learn about our mission. It has been masterminded by the Regiment's brigadier, Peter de la Billière, and it is daring to the point of recklessness. Not that we care about that. Claire would care, but of course I can't tell her about it.

The squadron commander is relieved of his command and a highly respected senior NCO resigns because they both say that this is a suicide mission. It's a brave gesture but nevertheless we take off from RAF Lyneham, the 'Ride of the Valkyries' playing over the intercom, then 'Bat Out of Hell', then 'Cool for Cats'. The music adds to the mood of sheer excitement. It seems to me, and to most of us, that what is happening is the pinnacle of our careers. We spend our lives training, until we are arguably the most highly skilled soldiers in the world. But our skills are seldom used in real conflict. Here, at last, is a war, and we have a mission to test our courage and ability. The odds are stacked heavily against us and that's how we like it.

It's a long flight to Ascension Island, where we refuel. Before we can take off again we're told that there's a delay. Then we're told the job's been put on hold. The RAF, who stood to lose an aircraft and crew, is relieved. We're disappointed and, if we're honest, a bit relieved too.

We're stuck on Ascension Island now. The job gets changed, delayed, changed again and delayed. As the scenario keeps changing we put in the appropriate training, practising on the Ascension Island airfield. We're frustrated and relieve our feelings with heavy firing.

This is a weird place, apparently just a big, black pile of lava in the sea. But go up a hill and through a low, dark tunnel in the lava and suddenly you're in another world, a damp, luxuriant tropical rain forest.

Out on the beaches we go crabbing and fishing. Mostly what we do, though, is drink and party and make wild plans for attacking the Argies.

Ships go through on their way to the conflict. We say hello and goodbye and when they get to the fighting a week later we hear what happens to them. This is frustrating. We want to fight too. Since we can't fight any Argies, we content ourselves with fighting each other. Nightly punch-ups break out in the bar. Something strange happens to one of the lads back in the UK. I don't hear about it until later. Jock is a hard lad. Imagination isn't his strong point. He's well-known to the binmen of Hereford because he placed a small explosives charge in his dustbin to scare the neighbour's dog away from the rubbish. Unfortunately, it went off when the binmen came round and a major incident followed.

Jock's watching TV with his wife. She goes upstairs to bed and he carries on watching television when suddenly he realizes that his closest friend has come in without him even noticing and is standing right by him. Jock's not pleased, because his mate's soaking wet. He's dripping all over the carpet. Jock's about to tell him to get onto the mat when he realizes that his mate's not supposed to be in England. He's in the Falklands.

He turns to his pal and says, 'Tony, what are you doing here?'

Tony has all his kit on, including his gun, and he's very, very wet. He looks at his friend and says, 'Jock. What have I done, Jock? What have I done?'

Then before his eyes, Tony fades away.

The next day Jock goes into camp and straight to the regimental sergeant major. There's a meeting going on but Jock takes the boss aside and says, 'What's happened?'

'Nothing.'

'Some of the blokes are dead . . . at least Tony is. I know that.'

The RSM looks him up and down. Finally he takes him further off to one side.

'Who told you?'

'I just know.'

'But nobody knows yet. Only the CO and me. There's been a helicopter crash. Most of the boys on board are dead. I don't know how you found out but don't tell anyone else.'

That's how Jock finds out the bad news about the crash of a Sea King helicopter. On our rock, we're called together to hear by more conventional means. The helicopter was transporting members of G Squadron and their signallers from one ship to another at night. The assumption is that it was shot down but this is soon ruled out. Another theory is that a ship was discharging its rubbish under cover of darkness. This attracts gulls, which might have got caught up in the rotors and brought it down.

Almost everyone is dead. A few manage to get out and survive the cold waters until they're picked up. One is a medic. He doesn't remember much, just the pushing, shoving and kicking to escape once the helicopter was in the sea. He has a broken arm and a broken collar bone and he thinks this is from other men's kicks. He gets out and it's a long, long way to the surface. He thinks his lungs are going to burst but eventually he gets there. With a broken arm he's helpless. He can't swim, he just has to stay afloat somehow until rescue comes. We don't know how many of the lads actually made it to the surface and then drowned waiting for rescue.

We all of us have friends on that helicopter and there is a shocked silence when the squadron commander breaks the news. All we want to do is get off Ascension Island and down to the Falklands and avenge our mates' deaths.

Later, in the bar, after a few beers, grief starts to take its toll. People talk about their religious beliefs, or lack of them. Most people don't believe God exists but now they're angry with Him anyway, just in case. Others believe in reincarnation. Paranormal experiences, first- and second-hand, are exchanged.

We're sent off to do ambushes and to practise our patrolling skills and tactics. Night on Ascension Island is absolutely black. It's hard to watch the man in front, and very easy to forget about the man behind you. The rule of patrolling is that if you lose the man behind you, it's your fault. That way, no-one falls off the back of a patrol. I'm following Terry, who's much older than me and has been in the Regiment much longer. But we keep losing him. When we find him again, he says, 'Where have you been?'

I say, 'I'm waiting for the guys behind me. You slow down!'

Terry says, 'Look, keep up, will you?'

Some people just can't grasp that the patrol moves at the speed of the slowest man. We repeat this exchange again and then a third time. Finally Terry explodes at me, 'Why can't you keep up?'

That's it. We're at each other, hammer and tongs, thumping and punching and kicking.

164

'What's going on?' ask the others. But they know. The level of aggression, with nowhere for it to go, is almost unbearable.

The attack we've been planning is called off completely. So here we are with a war on, stuck miles away on a lump of lava with nothing to do but top up our suntans.

At last, we're leaving. We're going to see some action, reinforcing D Squadron, who are taking part in attacks on the islands. We're going to fly down there in two Hercules C130s so that the Argies can't get all the special troops with one hit. We'll parachute into the sea and be picked up by ships in the area.

The flight is 13 hours long. We sprawl around on the canvas seats and sling our hammocks up to get some sleep. Sometimes we climb up to the flight deck and watch what's going on there: occasionally the co-pilot lets us fly the plane. We all have a go. Sitting in the back we feel the C130, known as Fat Albert, suddenly keel to the left and then the right. That means one of our boys is having fun at the wheel.

Finally, the plane loses altitude. By shoving our heads into the portholes, we see our ships far beneath us. We're ready in our wetsuits, our fins tied to the sides of our legs, all our equipment packed and ready to go. We've had P minus 20, P minus 15, P minus 10. We can't see the other plane but we know it's ahead of us. We circle. We circle again. We're ready to go but suddenly we're gaining height and flying off. Flying back in the direction we came from.

The jump master appears, waving his hands.

'It's off, no jump, sit down, sit down.'

We're returning to base. If I could hear much over the noise of the engine I know I'd hear a collective groan now. We've been trained to wait and not to ask questions.

Some of the lads are sick as dogs. They're young and trigger-happy and they want to get out there. I've passed this stage but I'm disappointed. I've never fought in a real battle and, like all the others, I want to be blooded. Freddie Porker, the great Regiment veteran who left for a few years to earn big bucks and has now walked through selection to rejoin the Regiment, isn't bothered. He's seen enough action in Oman and Northern Ireland to know what it's like.

Back at Ascension Island, after 26 hours' flying, we're told that we have 6 hours before we reboard the aircraft with a new crew to return to the exclusion zone.

We learn why we've been sent back. The first boys jumped. Their equipment fell straight out of the aircraft and into the sea.

165

Their bergens, weapons, personal belongings, everything went to the bottom of the South Atlantic. The equipment was, unusually, parachuted separately and the riggers had obviously made an error with these parachutes. Since their errors are generally consistent, it's a safe bet that our equipment would have met the same fate. We have 6 hours to give the riggers a hard time, and we do.

We also hear that the boys jumped wearing red noses and carrying waterpistols. This is just our troop humour but apparently the Royal Navy who picked them up to get them onboard HMS *Glamorgan* didn't think it was funny. They've had a sense of humour failure since their ship was hit by an Exocet. She has a gaping hole in her bow but, since she's an old-style steel-plated cruiser, she can carry on.

So, 6 hours later we're on our way back to the Falklands. There's no Wagner playing this time. We're weary with inaction. A whole day later, we're back inside the war zone.

Once again we start to lose altitude and we see below us our ships. Once again we're in our wet gear, fins at the ready. Once again we circle the area. And circle again. And again. The possibility that we won't be jumping has begun to occur to me but I dismiss it. After a total of 39 hours' flying time, it's not likely that we'll return to Ascension Island again without getting our feet wet.

We circle a final time. We're ready to jump. But we're starting to gain altitude. We're heading back to Ascension Island. Word gets passed back from man to man. The war's over. The Argentinians have surrendered.

I look around at the others. This is the worst news we've had in a long time. So, the Argies heard we were coming and decided it wasn't worth fighting any more, we conclude.

We all get gongs just for being there. It's a campaign medal and I can't help feeling I didn't do much to deserve it. And yet, preparing to carry out that mission is still the most exciting thing that's happened to me.

Claire greets me then goes straight to the bathroom to throw up. Her sickness hadn't eased as the baby got bigger the way the books promise it would. Her family have rescued her from the horrors of our half-renovated cottage and she's been staying in Wales.

Some of the boys have been through a lot in the Falklands and the colonel gathers us together once we're all home and tells us that they've organized a little reward for us.

'You're all going to . . .' Big dramatic pause. 'Hawaii!'

We say: 'Wow!'

Soon afterwards we're gathered together again.

'Boys, you may remember that we promised to take you to a tropical island?'

We look at one another.

'No, boss, you didn't promise a tropical island. You promised Hawaii.'

'Well, actually, now Hawaii's spelt C-y-p-r-u-s.'

It's the same thing, only different. The lads are not impressed. There are no American dolly birds on Cyprus. No hula skirts, no flowery garlands, no warm tropical seas.

We're scheduled to go to Cyprus to perfect the techniques we were practising for the Falklands War but never used there. Unfortunately, the baby's due the very week we're supposed to go. I am determined to be there for the event. I ask to be dismissed from the tropical island excursion and am told that I can delay my departure by one week at the most.

Claire visits her doctor and asks him to induce the baby and Charlotte is born. It is the most wonderful experience of my life. I am so excited by the miracle of birth that I won't leave the hospital and have to be thrown out. I buy a tiny brush for the baby's long, dark-red hair. I take it back to the hospital and brush her hair very gently. I won't let the nurses bath her. I do it. Finally, they throw me out again.

I leave the hospital saying, 'I'm a dad. *I* am a dad!' I can't believe it. I'm amazed. The whole world seems a different place. I go home without noticing how I got there. I want to tell everyone about Charlotte. I become a baby bore. As soon as I can, I go back. I am very possessive about the baby. I watch her visitors with beady eyes. I get jealous when Claire's mother holds her for too long. For the first time, there is something in my life which might, just might, be more important than the Regiment.

When we get our new baby home I hear a knock at the door, then voices. A few minutes later, Claire's calling me.

'Frank, someone's here!'

Downstairs is a white-haired vicar. I don't really know how to talk to vicars. In fact, I don't really want to talk to them at all. However, he introduces himself and we shake hands just as if we're both normal people. The only furniture we have is two red corduroy bean bags. I puff one of them up.

He says, 'I've come to arrange the christening.'

I'm surprised.

'Er, what christening?'

'Your baby's christening!' he says, laughing good-humouredly, although he must already sense trouble ahead.

'We haven't asked to have Charlotte christened, have we?' I say, looking hard at Claire. She shakes her head.

'I thought I'd save you the trouble,' says the vicar. 'So I've come to you.'

'Well, we don't want to have her christened.'

The vicar is taken aback by this, or he pretends to be.

'Not christened! Have you thought about the implications of that? Of not being a Christian?'

I am amazed that he has walked into our home and is starting to lecture us on a subject which we don't want to know about. His dog collar is no protection, more like provocation. I let him have it. I remind him how 'Christian' militiamen are slaughtering Muslims in Beirut. I point out all the wars that have been fought in the so-called peaceful name of Christianity.

'And,' I finish my tirade, 'I didn't invite you here. I wouldn't have let you in if I'd answered the door. You've got no right to impress your views on us and I'd like you to leave. Now.'

The vicar keeps his cool. His kindly, smiling manner is unswerving. He gets up off his bean bag with difficulty.

'Well, it's up to you. Good luck, and God bless!'

That cheery 'God bless' rings in my ears after he's gone, irritating me.

'You were a bit hard on him. He's an old man,' scolds Claire.

'Well, he shouldn't have come round here force-feeding us his views.'

# 13

A WEEK AFTER CHARLOTTE'S BIRTH, I'M OFF TO CYPRUS. HAWAII IT AIN'T. We're practising our attack technique against an RAF airfield. The game is to infiltrate and then take it without the RAF knowing, even though they've been told to expect some kind of SAS attack this week.

There is one little bush in this otherwise coverless airfield. It is right in the middle and next to it the Phantoms are lining up to take off. They wind up their engines to an incredible pitch, ease up the brake and fssssssshhh, off they go, up into the sky.

Freddie Porker and I penetrate the airfield. We infiltrate the camp, get through perimeter security, past the dogs and out onto the airfield using the shadows. The airfield is as flat and open as a billiard table except for that small bush.

Freddie says, 'Let's stick our necks out, Blondie. Let's be really necky and get in there.'

Freddie's suggestion is very necky as the rule is that you don't pick on the most obvious cover you can find. But Freddie's usually right. We scramble inside the bush and then spend the day watching. We log what's happening, where the patrols are, where the weak spots are, where the sentries and the guns are. We can find out everything we need to know from our little bush.

After dark it gets cold and we know the attack isn't coming until 5 a.m. It's a dawn raid. At about 4 a.m., Freddie says, 'Blondie. Are you cold?'

'Yeah, Freddie.'

'Then stick this against your neck and it'll warm you up.'

169

'What is it?'

'Never mind. Just have it.'

I take it. I smell it. I feel its warmth. Freddie hasn't been playing a nasty trick on me. He really hands me his bag of faeces because he thinks it'll warm me up. You soon get used to putting your own faeces in bags, tagging it, and carrying it with you. If you don't, it will give away your whereabouts to any passing dog. Carrying your own isn't so miserable. When junior members of the patrol are asked to carry all the bags, that's miserable.

Porker and I have about twenty tin cans. Shortly before the raid is due to start, we sneak out to the runway and line up our cans, fill them with dirt and pour in petrol. When we're told that the attack is five minutes away we start at one end and run down the runway, lighting the petrol-soaked earth in each can. They're hard to see unless you're above them and make ideal secret landing lights.

Our two aircraft land successfully on the runway. The tailgates are already open and as soon as the plane screeches to a halt two Land Rovers, bristling with machine guns, two motorbikes and men on foot zoom out of the back and down the runway taking out the various targets, including the control tower. Porker and I get into one of the jeeps and play cowboys and Indians with the machine guns. Of course, there's no real ammunition used. Dummy explosives are planted on all the Phantoms and umpires agree when a target's been 'hit'.

The raid is so successful that we even manage to get into our planes and fly off again before the RAF can react to our presence. They are taken completely by surprise.

Back at Hereford it's counter-terrorist training for us again. A new boy joins our troop. His name is Alastair Slater and, like so many of the lads, he's ex-Parachute Regiment. So we know he's a good soldier.

Al is tall and bony. He's very quiet but it doesn't take us long to get to know each other because he's keen to improve his free-fall skills. He comes from Scotland and he went to public school. Probably he could have been an officer, but he's chosen to be a trooper.

We go to Shobdon together to get some jumps in. Tentatively, I introduce him to Claire and Charlotte. Claire tends not to like the boys in the Regiment but she likes Big Al immediately.

We all go to Peterborough Parachuting Centre. Charlotte's birth has not stopped us from rushing off with our parachutes almost every weekend. Claire isn't just a Category Ten but she qualified in record-breaking time.

This weekend we meet Al's parents. This is the first time I've met the parents of anyone in the Regiment. Al is clearly the apple of Peggy and Ira's eye. They swell with pride as Al prepares to go. As they watch us from the ground with Claire, she talks them through.

'Where are they? I can't see them!' says Al's mother.

'You'll see them when the parachutes open.'

'Which one's Alastair?'

'He's got the blue and red canopy.'

'But . . . where's that?'

Where indeed? Claire notices that everyone else's parachute is open but Al's.

'Where's Alastair? Where is he?' asks his mother in an increasingly hysterical tone.

'Well . . . he's that one . . .'

'The one without a parachute! It hasn't opened!'

Peggy's right. By now it's clear that there's been a malfunction on Al's main canopy. He's going to have to use his reserve and he's going to have to use it fast.

Al whistles past me, falling like a stone.

'Cut away, cut away!' I yell.

He disconnects his chute and hits his reserve and with a boom his little round canopy appears.

On the ground, Claire breathes a sigh of relief.

'That's his reserve. He's OK, you don't have to worry about him.'

But by now Peggy is nearly fainting.

Al lands safely.

'That was brilliant! That was amazing! Let's do it again!' he says. He is flushed with excitement. The man they're already calling Mr Grumpy because he's so quiet is unable to contain his excitement. I know how he feels because I've used my reserve once at Shobdon. When your main canopy fails to open you brush with death. There's a rush of adrenalin, and then you save yourself with your reserve but the adrenalin leaves a euphoria behind.

His father pretends to be nonchalant.

'Did you think you were going to die, Alastair?'

'Naaah . . . it was brilliant!'

Peggy is still white and speechless with horror.

'I wish I could do it again!' says Al. But you can't. It takes a few hours to pack a reserve, especially a round one. And you can't pack a malfunction into your main parachute. You just have to wait for it to happen to you.

Back at Hereford, I receive unofficial notification that I'm expected to return to SAS Signals soon. I protest vehemently to various officers.

171

They all understand why. Their life is the Regiment, too. But the rules say that the Regiment's signallers only get to play soldiers for a few years.

I decide that I'd rather leave the Regiment than go back to an ops room. It's possible to leave the army any time if you've met the terms of your original agreement and I signed up for nine years, which I've completed. To get out, all I have to do is pay £300 and give a month's notice and I can go on Premature Voluntary Release.

I visit the regimental sergeant major.

'My transfer's through soon,' I tell him, 'but I'm not going back to Signals.'

His face wears the same pained expression that everyone else's has.

'It's Regiment policy—' he begins awkwardly.

'Don't start, I've heard it all before,' I say. 'But if they insist, I'll resign. I'll go on PVR.'

He stares at me.

'Do you mean that?'

'Yes.'

'Others have threatened PVR, Frank, but they've always gone back to Signals.'

'I won't go back.'

He studies my face and then nods.

'You really mean it.'

'I really mean it.'

'OK. Then I'll support you.'

My turn to stare.

'What?'

'I'll back you up, all the way.'

This is something, really something. The RSM is right behind me. For a minute all those self-doubts which I feel so often and hide so well, they all vanish. I'm flattered. I must be a good soldier if he's prepared to do this.

'We'll wait for the transfer to come through. It won't be for about six months. Then we'll fight,' he says. I nod. The RSM himself is going to back me. There's a chance I'll be able to stay.

I wander out dazed and bump into one of the other lads. I know him because he's a very keen free-faller, like me. He's just come back from an attachment to an élite American special operations unit, the US equivalent of the SAS.

This lad says, 'Frank, you've got to get out to North Carolina. It's for you. The free-fall is amazing.'

It is a crack outfit but none of us feels they can possibly be as good as us. So the work isn't attractive. What's enticing is the idea of all the free-fall I could do in North Carolina.

'You pay just a dollar a day and you can jump as often as you like! It's terrific.'

I say, 'I wish there was an attachment on offer right now—'

'There is! Check it out!'

'But I didn't know about it.'

'They've probably kept it quiet because they can't spare anyone to go. But if you say you want to, they'll have to let you.'

He's right. I discover that it's a five-month vacancy. That will just about take me up to the time when my transfer's due. I might as well have this last fling before I resign.

I ambush the boss.

'Excuse me, boss, this American thing . . . is anybody going?'

'Nobody wants to, Frank.'

'I'd like to.'

'What's taken you so long to decide?'

'I only heard about it yesterday.'

'But you should all have been told months ago.'

'Must have missed that one, boss.'

'Well, we'll see what we can do.'

A few weeks later I'm on my way to America. I fly on progressively smaller aircraft from New York to Charlotte to Fayetteville in North Carolina and finally to Fort Bragg, home to the All-American Airborne division.

I'm introduced to Karl, a member of my fire team, whose job it is to look after me. I say I'm planning to bring my wife and daughter out and he at once invites us to stay with him. Then I meet the rest of the five-man team. One of the lads wears glasses which wrap around his face. There are few special forces soldiers with glasses but out here he doesn't stand out because everyone wears them for eye protection when shooting. He smiles at me lazily. He's chewing tobacco. There's a lad who's small and looks very young. He barely has a moustache. There's Karl, who's a little taller than me, stocky, with the regulation moustache. And there's our leader, Big Kevin.

Every morning we have physical training. On the notice board for today it says UBRR. I ask Kevin what this means.

'Upper Body Round Robin.'

'Er . . . what?'

'It's just your upper body, Frank. You know, weights and bench presses for the whole hour.'

I have already noted that there is a difference in the level of physical

173

fitness between the American boys and us. Selection tests our endurance, there's a lot of marching, running and weight carrying. But there's no specific test for the upper body. It isn't important to us like it is to the Americans.

Big Kevin takes me outside to look at a 30-foot rope. He says, 'You have to be fit enough to climb that rope.'

'No problem,' I say. I know I can climb it.

'Without using your feet.'

'Without using my feet?'

'Yup.'

I try, and manage to get about 10 feet off the ground before I fall off. Then I watch Kevin pulling himself up by his arms, up and up like a circus gymnast.

I decide to start training. I'm not sure if I'll ever manage to climb that high without using my feet.

Life in North Carolina may be improving my upper body strength but I'm fairly certain they have little else to teach me. I'm not worried when we're scheduled to spend a day at the ranges. In Hereford I've helped train royal bodyguards and am on the shooting demonstration team for visiting VIPs. That's fancy pistol shooting. We fire two shots quickly, one immediately after another, a technique called double tapping. It's crucial when you use small 9mm ammunition and we've perfected it: we do two shots standing, two kneeling, two lying down, two on one knee and two standing again. That's ten shots at the target and all in the white patch. To do that you have to train, train, train.

The first day on the ranges here, I find they use .45s, and the larger, heavier ammunition means there's no need to double tap. This makes a part of my expertise redundant. I'm still not worried. After the first round I think my group is pretty impressive: the holes are all within two inches of the centre of the target. When we go up to inspect, I'm happy with what I see.

One of the lads wanders across and takes a look.

'Not bad, Frank.'

Something in his tone makes me wonder if he really means it. He sounds as though he's being kind and it seems to me that kindness isn't called for. So I stroll over to his target.

I can't believe my eyes. His group is at least half the size of mine. But I'm not going to get intimidated. He's probably the company crack shot.

I decide to reassure myself by walking along all the targets and seeing how everyone else has done. The next one is pretty impressive too. Obviously another first-class shot. But there is a tiny and familiar maggot starting to chew away inside my stomach. Self-doubt. I walk along to the next target and swallow hard. Yes, another exceptional group. By now, I can't fool myself that this kind of result is anything but the norm. I don't even need to reach the end of the row to realize that I'm completely outclassed. After my years of training, day in, day out, these men are shooting me off the range. They are all, every single one of them, shooting at least twice as well as I am. They are within an inch of the centre of the target in spite of the fact that they're using big bullets.

With some difficulty I decide to ask them how it's done. Their response is generous. They have a different shooting method and they'll teach me. I don't want to admit that my shooting has in fact been second-class all these years and I certainly don't want to train from scratch again but I want to leave America shooting as well as they do.

Their method is hard to learn because it's the psychology of shooting, not the physical skills, which determines the results.

The first lesson the teacher loads the gun and hands it to me. I take aim, pull the trigger and . . . no bang. There's nothing in it. However, I have to agree that the gun jerked just as if it were loaded. It wasn't the gun that was jerking, it was my hand, reacting to something that wasn't there. If there was a bullet, you wouldn't see the jerk, but it would still be there. The ball and dummy method eliminates the jerk. You just have to convince yourself there are no bullets in the gun.

When you're training the instructor hands you the gun over and over again. Over and over again you take aim and nothing happens. You end up with the gun not moving a whisker. Then, unknown to you, he puts a bullet in and it goes straight through the centre of the target, spot on. You're delighted – but now you've heard a bang you start to jerk again. So you keep training, with bullets, without bullets, not knowing. You're brainwashing yourself into believing there's no bullets in the gun.

The instructor assures me that after a few months of training you can say to yourself no bullets, no bullets, no bullets as you draw, even when you know the magazine's full, and believe it. And all the bullets go through the same hole.

I am also taught the Weaver method, a new arm position, a locked position. You fire side on, lock the arm and pull it across the body, dropping your head onto the arm. That, combined with the no bullets approach, works.

Claire and Charlotte arrive. We all live with Karl and his family in

175

their large house. Claire is disconcerted to find a gun in every room of the house.

'Frank, Frank, look, there's a machine gun under our bed!' she calls. Actually it's a M1 Carbine automatic .30 calibre, fully loaded with a 30-round magazine.

We don't have to ask him to know why he has so many guns. We know that racial tensions run high here. There are black soldiers inside the special operations unit and they're accepted because they're soldiers. But there are not many of them. The rigorous swimming requirements are allegedly the reason that more black men don't pass selection. Back home, things are a little better, but not much. There are a few black soldiers in the Regiment, more since an active recruitment campaign in Fiji.

It soon becomes clear to us that Karl's marriage, his second, is troubled. Karl wants to go out drinking every night and he wants me to go with him. At first I try to keep up but it's soon clear to all of us that I'm not going to be one of the gang. Our fire team turns out to be wild. They're hard-drinking, womanizing lads. I know I don't want to join in the things they do and Big Kev makes it easier for me to refuse. He's only a few years older than the rest of us but he plays dad. He shakes his head over the boys' tales of hellraising and whoring. But they all respect him. He was runner-up in the Mean Man of the County Bare Knuckle Fist Fight Championships. But there's something strange about Kev. He may be the best fighter for miles but he's also a committed Christian. This sounds like a contradiction to me but I'm not sufficiently interested in Christianity to ask him about it. Luckily Kev isn't one of those who shoves his beliefs down your throat.

While I'm at North Carolina I wear a US army uniform. It doesn't bother me that I'm wearing someone else's uniform until we come to the UK to work with an SAS counter-terrorist team on an exercise. Here I am in my camouflage brown, my peaked cap, my brown T-shirt and my jump boots. Everyone takes the mickey mercilessly. I become known as Frank the Yank.

After some training at Hereford we go up to the north-east for the exercise, which takes place at Kielder. We have to rescue about forty hostages. If we're captured, the Americans will be subjected to a British interrogation.

We're flown up to the north-east in Chinooks. We fly so low to avoid radar that we're almost skimming the surface of the sea.

When we arrive, we send some boys out to find and recce the target, a camp in Kielder Forest, and then all of us, our American special operations forces unit and 22 SAS, carry out a camp attack. We rescue our hostages and are then told that our aircraft have gone out of action. We have to escape on foot.

There are two lakes at Kielder, joined by a narrow bridge. It would take days to go around the lakes, there are no boats and it's too cold to swim. We know we're being given no choice but to cross the bridge and be captured. This seems unfair. My fire team are holding a group of five hostages, which includes a major. He turns to me and says in a southern drawl, 'Collins, I understand you're indigenous to this area. Fix this one for us, why don't you?'

The major is not going to understand that being indigenous to Whitley Bay does not mean you're indigenous to Kielder Forest. The Americans' grasp of British culture is lamentable. One captain has looked on a map and noticed that Kielder is near Newcastle. He has discovered that Newcastle United is the local football team. He has bought himself a black and white pompom hat and scarf and presented it as his disguise. I tried to explain to him that it is only a disguise on Saturday afternoons. If he wears it at any other time, his cover is blown. But the captain is unable to understand this because he knows that Chicago Bears supporters wear their hats every day.

With some misgivings, I phone my brother Gary. I ask him if he'll come and pick us up but he fails to appreciate how serious the situation is. He's just off to a fancy dress party with Michael.

'What are you wearing?' I ask.

'We're both wearing Fozzie Bear outfits,' he tells me proudly. The idea of my brothers in their Fozzie Bear outfits saving America's most élite force from certain capture is almost more surreal than I can stand.

Gary promises that he won't drink at this party so that he can drive out afterwards to pick us up in his van. I can't give him a grid reference because that would be meaningless to him, so I describe in detail where we'll be hiding. We spend the whole night lying at the road junction but there is no sign of Fozzie Bear. The major keeps saying, 'When will your brothers be here, Collins?'

Finally I put on semi-civilian clothes and stroll nonchalantly down to the phone box again, whistling and being very British.

Gary answers immediately.

'What happened?' I squeak.

'I was there!' he says. 'Where were you?'

'There!'

'You weren't.'

'We were!'

Fozzie Bear went to the wrong road junction.

The following night Gary turns up in his little works van at the right road junction, although sadly without his bear suit. He pulls up by a bush and we jump out with our hostages and bergens. He shoves the six of us into the back of the van and sets off. I ask Gary what happened last night. He says that he and Michael had arrived at what they thought was the rendezvous. A group of soldiers had stopped them and asked them who they were. They wanted an ID.

'But what ID did you give him?' I ask.

'I got out of the van and told him I was Fozzie Bear.' Michael got out too in his Fozzie Bear suit but since he's in the army himself now he wanted nothing to do with our escapade and he just stood by the side of the road refusing to co-operate. Tonight Gary drives us all the way around the lake, dropping us off right over the other side and saving us a three-day walk. We stop at a garage to buy some sand-wiches and drink. Gary goes back for the others. We're out with our hostages, and we've escaped interrogation.

Back in North Carolina, Claire and I are feeling the strain of living with Karl. The tension in his marriage is nerve-racking and he expects me to collude in the lies he tells his wife. It's agreed, without animosity, that we'll move in with Big Kev instead. He has a large wooden house in a pine forest. His wife's a keen tennis player and there's a swimming pool in the garden. Claire and Charlotte have a wonderful time.

There is, however, another side to the high standard of living enjoyed by the white Americans we know. Security is a constant problem. In the short time that we're living here, two people shoot their neighbours. One wounds a black man who is escaping after stealing from a house. The other has been suffering from petty thefts for some time and catches the intruders – he shoots one with a .357 Magnum dead and wounds another. The dead boy turns out to be his neighbour's teenage son. No-one questions his action. It's generally considered justified.

Despite his wonderful house, we have some hesitation about moving in with Big Kevin because he's a Christian. He's still hard as nails and such a good soldier that this is almost forgivable. I have great respect for Kev, although I'm embarrassed when he says grace and a prayer before each meal. Claire and I dutifully bow our heads, but we're actually thinking to ourselves that he's out of his tree. He has little tapestries hanging around the house saying things like: God is Master of this House. Thankfully, these are fairly unobtrusive. His daily prayers at mealtimes are for the return of his wife's first husband, who is missing presumed dead in Vietnam. After hearing this prayer a number of times I say, 'How can you really mean it, Kev? What would happen if this man really does return?'

And Kev says, 'It's up to me to pray for him to come home safe each day. God will sort out the rest.'

I go to church with Kev once. A man in our unit has been killed by a bomb in Beirut. I borrow some suitable civilian clothes and when I get there I wish I looked smarter because the Americans are all dressed immaculately. The women are in hats and gloves.

The coffin is carried in with the dead man's boots on top, highly polished, and his upturned rifle and his medals. The service is very emotional and uplifting. Both men and women are in tears. At our own Regiment funerals, men don't cry.

There's a sermon from the chaplain. I've already noticed that, whereas a chaplain in the British army is seldom taken seriously, here he is held in high esteem. He starts to speak and this is not the kind of sermon I'm used to. He's no wimp, for a start, and his language isn't archaic, incomprehensible Church language. He communicates. He speaks of love and hate and life and war and peace. He assures us that the dead man's sacrifice was not in vain. He tells us how Jesus laid down his life too. He reminds us how this man died fighting for the President of the United States, representing the American ideals of liberty and justice for all. I can almost imagine God in an Uncle Sam hat welcoming the soldier to heaven. The remarkable thing is that there is nothing corny about any of it.

I'm not used to religion, and I'm certainly not used to the idea that a religious service can have such an effect on the congregation. But the Americans, I acknowledge, are good at this. They know how to pull the heartstrings.

Apart from Kev, I meet one other Christian. Claire's unwell and I've asked for some time off. I've just taken her to the base doctor when a soldier walks up to me.

'Hi! I just want to introduce myself.'

He offers his hand, which I shake, and says, 'I heard your wife's ill and I want you to know that we're praying for her back home.'

I think this is very weird but I make the right noises and he walks off. Some of the others have overheard and say, 'Don't worry about him. He's a born-again Christian and he's way over the top. But, he's a good soldier.'

They tell me that his name's Larry and he's ex-Rangers. In fact, his résumé can't be faulted. But he's a Bible-thumper.

I nod if I pass Larry in the stockade, but I try to avoid speaking to him again.

With the Americans I do High Altitude Low Opening parachuting from big jets. Galaxies and Starlifters fly much faster than anything I'm used to. Jumping out into the slipstream is like being hit by a cricket bat. I'm going forwards at 180 m.p.h. in an arc until I slow down to terminal velocity at 120 m.p.h. Our four-man patrol flies in a diamond formation so that we stay together. We go on exercise in the Blue Ridge Mountains. We take off in Black Hawk and Huey helicopters. It's the 101st Screaming Eagles, the Air Cavalry, and the sky is dark with helicopters just like *Apocalypse Now*. We're dropped in the mountains where it is very, very cold and wet. We're carrying practically nothing but ammo, certainly not sleeping bags, so that we can move fast. We stink of vomit because someone has thrown up in the helicopter on the way out and this has been scattered all over us by the rotor blast.

We're told to target a US Rangers camp. They're our enemy. They're hunting us but we have to find their base location and take them out.

We're living off our belts, munching on the occasional chocolate bar and sleeping in a circle at night, although in these conditions we can't do much more than nap.

The Rangers are good. They're shaven-headed and gung-ho and they've been hunting us in-country for days. We manage to get through their forward groups and back to their base location, where we discover them sleeping in big green marquees. Each tent must sleep at least a hundred men.

We're outside waiting with our charges to hit the tents, about ten of us to a tent. When the word comes we pour our stun grenades onto the roofs. Although not high-powered explosives, these are strong enough to split the tent and send off at least ten bangs and flashes each.

Suddenly the Rangers aren't asleep any more. They're exposed in their underpants. As soon as the flash bangs go off, we burst in with our sub-machine guns and spray them with blanks. The Rangers are outraged. An officer, perhaps a major or a colonel, shouts, 'Stop, stop, it's all over!'

His tent is in shreds and some of his boys are pulling out their burning bedding, yelling, 'That could have killed us!'

'All stop now!' hollers the colonel.

We ignore him. Someone fires at him. 'You're dead,' they inform him.

180

'I'm not!'

'You are!'

We kill everyone and retreat with big smiles on our faces. A thirty-man assault team has taken out 300 Rangers. Afterwards, Ranger high command complain that our tactics are too dangerous.

Out on the ranges I keep practising. I'm leaving soon and my shooting's a great deal better than when I arrived. And I keep trying to climb that 30-foot rope using only my hands. Finally, in the last week, I do it. I can climb hand over hand all the way to the top.

'The unit doesn't require you to use hands only,' says Big Kev annoyingly at this point, 'but we like to.'

I have a chance not just to see but to experience an air live fire exercise. This is the last phase of the élite unit's selection course and I'm invited to enjoy this experience with the young hopefuls. Everyone comes out to watch, including generals and visiting dignitaries. It's a remarkable demonstration of air power.

The scenario is that we are a four-man patrol working behind enemy lines which has got into trouble. We have dug ourselves into a shallow trench and we have called for the twentieth-century equivalent of the US cavalry to save us from the advancing enemy. And here it comes. Known as Puff the Magic Dragon during the Vietnam war and now just called Specter, a Hercules appears far above, at maybe 15,000 feet. It looks like an ordinary C130 but we know it isn't. It's a floating gun platform.

Over the radio we give our grid reference and the Hercules picks up our exact position.

'I have four whites showing.'

'Roger, four whites. Enemy at three hundred metres, twelve o'clock on a bearing of six hundred millimetres.'

The Hercules crew read this back.

'Inbound,' says the voice in our ears. The Hercules flies closer. We all think we know what's going to happen. We wriggle as far down in our trench as we can, close our eyes and put our hands on our ears. We know it's the only way to withstand the assault. Because the Hercules is going to rain fire all around us. Even from high in the air its computer can be accurate to one metre, a phenomenal advance on the usual shell-lugging artillery.

'OK, guys,' says the pilot, 'keep your heads down. We're going for saturation fire now and it's going to last five minutes. Just five minutes.'

And with that, he unleashes death. First, there's a rapid, constant burst of the small 7.62 chainguns. They're sweeping around and around us at the rate of 10,000 rounds a minute. Bullets hit the ground and bounce and glance. I look out and see a red thread running in a straight line from the aircraft to the ground and the red thread is fire. It dances all around us in a tight circle. The sound is deafening despite our ear muffs, the air is thick with smoke and the smell of explosives and the earth is shaking.

'Twenty mike-mikes coming now,' says the pilot. Joining the continuing chaingun fire is the less frequent but more booming 20mm cannon. The ground shakes more. It goes round and round and round us.

'Forty mike-mikes now, boys. Stay down. Stay down,' says the pilot. We sink down into our trench that last few millimetres as the constant bang and flash and shake is joined by another, deeper, more booming, more penetrating cannon fire which dances all around us. The air is thick with smoke.

'OK boys, one hundred and five mike-mikes coming. You have one minute left and we're going to give it all we've got. Just one minute left. One minute.'

We all need this reassurance. The deep base of the big booms joins the deadly orchestra. Closing our eyes is no help because the flashes somehow penetrate inside our heads until our whole being, down to the bone marrow, down to our souls, is helpless under the might of this fire. There's an earthquake, a massive, ongoing earthquake. One minute which lasts for ever. This is the minute in which men go mad and have to be restrained from rushing out into the fire, when men don't care any more and deposit their breakfast in their pants, when men surrender their whole being to terror.

When it's over we stay down in our trenches. There's silence out there but no silence in our ears. Behind our eyes we still see the flashes. The earth is pitted and scarred. It's over. We crawl out slowly. Slowly we reinhabit our old selves.

No wonder Specter is used as the final assessment in the Americans' selection process. There is no greater test of nerve. It's a great finale to my time in North Carolina. I make a mental note to suggest to the Regiment that they consider developing some similar test for selection back in the UK.

The free-fall here has been fantastic. For me, if not for Claire. Early on we went skydiving and agreed to do a four-way formation with a couple of Americans. Claire was apprehensive because she didn't know the aircraft, the drop zone, the parachute or the people we were jumping with. We'd left Charlotte with some acquaintances, sitting in her pushchair by the drop zone.

'She'll be fine while we're gone,' we assured them. 'Just rock the buggy a bit if she makes any noise.'

Claire jumped first and then me. When the third arrived we could see that he was coming down too fast. Too fast! Stop! But no, he crashed into Claire and crashed hard. He bowled her across the sky. I flew over to her but she wouldn't come back into the formation. She'd had a shock. Until now she'd been protected, to some extent, because she'd usually jumped with me or with friends. She'd clocked around eighty jumps and got her Category Ten and she was good.

We came back and watched the dive on video. Every dive was automatically videoed and when we started the playback we realized that we'd left Charlotte sitting right by the camera. In vision was our jump. In earshot was Charlotte. We could see Claire getting hit in the air. We could hear a six-month-old baby roaring throughout.

At the end of the video, Claire turned to me and said, 'That's it. I give up.'

I looked at her with complete incomprehension.

'You mean . . . you're giving up the baby?'

'No, Frank, I'm giving up skydiving.'

Claire giving up skydiving! This hardly seemed possible. She was a skydiver. She might as well say she was giving up being tall.

'You've had a shock. You'll get over it.'

'It's nothing to do with the crash. It's Charlotte. The drop zone's no place for a child. It's no fun for her just sitting waiting for us while we risk our lives and—'

'We're not risking our lives.'

'I'm a mother now and I can't go on doing it. It shouldn't have taken me six months to realize that.'

I felt sure that she'd soon change her mind but she didn't jump again that weekend, nor has she in the whole time we've been in North Carolina. I've kept jumping, hoping that she'll join me, but she never does.

Now it's time to leave and I'm beginning to feel cheated. Free-fall's one of the reasons we came to North Carolina and Claire hasn't done any. It costs precisely $1 a day and we'll never get a chance like this again. But she remains adamant. She's given up free-fall. I'm angry. I married a skydiver and now she says she isn't one. I still hope that she'll change her mind. We decide to take a month's leave and spend it touring America. I ensure that our route takes us to various parachuting centres. But Claire sticks to her decision to give up free-fall. Skydiving suddenly isn't so much fun any more, but nothing's going to stop me doing it.

In Pennsylvania I pay $10 a jump. On arrival at the club, the chief instructor inspects my logbook.

'OK, so what do you want to do? Eight-way?'

I nod.

'We can organize an eight-way . . . looks good from his log, put him third or fourth . . .'

I gradually advance from eight-man formations to sixteen until I'm finally invited to take part in a thirty-man jump. This is progress. I'm excited. This is a big jump.

Claire asks me to look after Charlotte for a few minutes. I agree, although we're busy organizing the dive. We've got a mock-up of the aircraft drawn on the ground and we're jumping out, pretending we're in the sky. You have to know when you come out of the aircraft exactly where you're heading for, where your place is, who's sitting behind you and what your docking order is. A thirty-man jump is complicated.

I am trying to do this with a squawking ten-month-old baby. People are getting annoyed. Concentration is essential because if one person gets it wrong that blows it for everyone. Some of the other skydivers are wondering how serious I am.

After what seems like a very long time, Claire comes over. I'm furious with her but even I notice that she looks lovely. She's been doing her hair and making herself look nice for me but all I can say is, 'Where have you been?'

She stares at me without speaking.

'Look, I'm busy here, I want these people to take me seriously and I've just been left with a screaming baby . . .'

Claire takes Charlotte away and I know I've hurt her. I feel awful. The thirty-man formation is successful but I don't really enjoy it. I realize that for most of our holiday I've been having fun jumping out of the sky while Claire's been sitting watching me. I have a terrible realization. That one day I may face a stark choice: see less of my family or give up parachuting.

I take my new shooting skills and muscly upper body back to Hereford with me. The Americans offer me the chance to transfer to the US Army but, after considering it, I turn it down. The Regiment's still everything to me.

'The Yank's back,' say the boys.

I'm working hard on the counter-terrorist team when the transfer to Signals which they've been threatening for so long comes through.

I go straight back to the regimental sergeant major who is as good as his word. I only half expected him to fight for me because only half of me thinks I'm worth it. But he fights for me hard and battlelines are drawn between soldiers and officers over this issue. It's been bubbling along for a while now, the question of whether badged signallers should always be sent back to their parent company. Other men have refused and occasionally one escapes, but the majority are dragged back to glittering but dreary careers in ops rooms. Of course, other men who've been sent back are furious at my bid for freedom. Officers are angry. Signals protest. But the RSM is successful. He keeps me on the understanding that the Regiment will never do this again. From now on a signaller can only take selection if he agrees to return to the Royal Corps of Signals after three years. There are men walking around camp who almost hate me.

The RSM's way round the problem is to make me permanent cadre. This frees me from Signals for ever. It's an honour usually afforded only to staff sergeants and above. I'm just a corporal and the rules are bent for me. Suddenly, the long fight is over. I'm an SAS man through and through and the Regiment has displayed its belief in me.

Out on the range, some of the lads see my new shooting position and start laughing.

They say, 'Oh yeah, what's this, some weird American idea?' I just smile and carry on. When we go to check targets they don't believe I've fired all my bullets because there's only one hole. They tell me to do it again. I do.

They're impressed but it isn't easy for anyone to admit that our shooting methods have been wrong all these years. They argue that, in action, you'd go back to your old methods. You wouldn't, but they protect themselves by saying that.

Then a young squadron clerk helps me prove my point. He's about eighteen years old and has done almost nothing but pen-pushing in the office. His military skills are virtually nil. He has to learn about small arms because he's going to Ireland and the boss says, 'Frank, you take him and show him how to shoot.'

It's like writing on a clean sheet of paper. He's never held a pistol before so he hasn't got into bad habits, he has nothing to unlearn. I just teach him from scratch. Within two weeks he's firing better than most of the soldiers. Lots of the boys have been shooting for years and this unwhiskered little clerk pulls out a pistol and bang bang, there are two holes touching each other on the target. Most of the arguments against the Weaver method collapse but people still insist that it wouldn't work in combat. They see it as a crazy American idea and won't budge.

Out on the drop zone nothing has changed, but Claire and I have. She's not interested any more and the old round of parties and drinking and fun doesn't seem to fit now that we're a family and Claire's not jumping. I try to carry on but somehow I don't manage to get to the club so often.

# 14

TO MY DELIGHT I'M SELECTED TO GO ON ANOTHER COURSE. IT'S considered by many to be a plum: the close-protection course. In other words, bodyguarding. The SAS rarely actually bodyguards anyone: this course qualifies us to instruct bodyguards.

It's a useful course to the Regiment because the Government can hire us out as instructors to foreign governments for vast sums of money. It's useful to us because, when we leave the Regiment, SAS close-protection training is a passport to work.

I'm pleased that my pal Al Slater is also picked for this course, and a bit jealous that he's been chosen when he's only been in the Regiment a short time. But Al's good. He's just the kind of guy you want to work with and, if you're a VIP, he's just the kind of guy you want to guard you. Quiet, personable, unobtrusive, intelligent. By now I'm getting to know him well. He's a friend of Claire's too. He likes to come round to the house in the evening to play with Charlotte and have a few beers and he looks happy sitting there amid the family chaos while Claire gets the dinner.

'What do you think of Judy?' Claire asks him casually. Judy's a girl at the parachute club who she thinks might interest Al. She knows that he's not keen on one-night stands: he's too serious for that.

'She's nice.'

'Nice! Is that all you can say? Don't you think she's pretty?'

'Well . . . yes, I do . . .' He laughs in a big, embarrassed way. 'Are you trying to get me married off, Claire?'

'Yes.'

Al laughs again. Afterwards, Claire says to me, 'He needs a wife. Judy's just the right type. She's very intelligent.'

'Well, introduce them then.'

'I will.'

On the course, we're constantly writing notes and there are many written assessments. I do well in these. I like taking notes and rereading them and knowing my stuff and I'm good at it. I can't understand why I never felt this way at Whitley Bay Grammar.

For all of us, the psychology of bodyguarding is difficult. We all have a tendency to attack because we're SAS soldiers, but suddenly that's not the job. Our first priority is to protect our VIP, not to be aggressors. Defence doesn't come naturally to us but now we learn the three Ds. A bodyguard will deter by his presence, detect by his vigilance and finally defeat. But if you get to the third D, you've messed up. Most attacks are the result of a mess-up since they're nearly all detectable.

After the course I'm sent to Hong Kong to work as an instructor for a few months. I get back in time for a family funeral. It's Nan. She has survived Mam by two years. The funeral is packed but it is not a tearful occasion. All Mam's family are there, just like they were two years ago, and, just as surprisingly as two years ago, Dad is also there.

Nan died of a heart attack. She was with Michelle, who is very matter-of-fact and doesn't like fuss.

'I'm going, I'm going,' said Nan, clutching her chest. Michelle called the ambulance, calmed Nan down and then got on with her homework.

'Was there any sign of . . .?' I ask Michelle.

She shakes her head.

'No. No black pudding.'

After the funeral, which is organized by Michelle, there is food back at the house, also organized by Michelle. She is seventeen years old and has already informed the council that she expects to keep the house. Because she has a brother in the army who is entitled to a home to return to, they agree. She is undaunted by the idea of living in this house alone and looking after herself. She says she's done that for years anyway. She now works for Swan Hunter. Despite all attempts to dissuade her, she insisted on leaving school after O levels and taking a scholarship with Swan Hunter which enables her to work and study for her A levels. She's going to take a degree with them in Engineering and Ship Design. She knows what she wants. Michelle is cool, sensible and unstoppable.

Yvonne's husband doesn't go to the funeral. He doesn't come to any family get-togethers now and if he does he gets drunk, makes a fool of himself and leaves. I'm sure that Yvonne's having a difficult time with him.

I begin to feel for her what I felt for Mam. Helpless in the face of her sadness. There's only one way I know how to deal with this. I leave Whitley Bay as soon as I can. And this time, I'm leaving it far behind. I'm going to North Africa.

Just a few days later I'm standing in the desert. There is sand, sand and more sand stretching to the horizon. Occasionally there's a bush. Nothing else.

'Now. What do you see?' asks the African officer.

There are about fifteen of us and we look at each other and then at our African hosts.

'Nothing,' we say.

'Nothing at all?'

'Nothing at all.'

The officer yells something in Arabic and suddenly a man jumps up from the sand. He's not far away from us but he's been completely buried. This is part of the desert survival which the Africans are teaching us in return for some basic training. They explain that it's possible for a man to live under the sand in the desert without dehydrating. It's hard to imagine but the Africans assure us that it's even possible to sleep in these conditions.

We're told to form a circle and a soldier steps forward. He is carrying a sack. The sack's moving. He feels it very carefully, tracing the outline of whatever's in it until he's satisfied that he's holding it the right way. He is very dark skinned with a proud, prominent forehead. At an order from the officer the soldier pulls the string and the bag drops to reveal a big snake hanging from his hand. It's about four feet long. We all recognize it at once as a sand snake. It is highly poisonous. The soldier lifts the snake and suddenly thrusts its head into his mouth. His teeth close over the snake's head. He is biting it off. Then he spits it out, the body still thrashing violently from side to side. He uses his teeth to pull the skin off in one deft movement. The skin falls to the ground. The snake hasn't stopped moving but the soldier calmly starts to eat it.

We all nod and clap approvingly at his prowess. And take a step back.

'Now one of you has the opportunity to do the same.'

There is an awful silence as we realize what he's saying. He wants us to bite the head off a snake. He looks around from face to face. We know that British honour must be maintained and that one of us must

189

step forward. The lad next to me takes me surreptitiously by the elbow and shoves me. I can't giggle and step back like someone in mixed infants. I have to do it now. I'm going to bite the head off a poisonous snake. I wish I hadn't been in such a hurry to leave Whitley Bay. But, while the writhing bag is brought forward, I remember all the fish heads I bit off when I went snorkelling as a boy. I try to pretend that what I'm about to do will be just like that. But I can't convince myself. Plaice just aren't poisonous.

The soldier hands me the bag. I can see the snake writhing inside. It feels awful. I trace its body in the bag until I get to what I think is its head. Then I trace it all the way to the other end, just to make sure.

By now all the Africans are clapping and chanting and our lads are saying, 'Come on, Frankie, do it, boy!'

I take a deep breath and pull the bag down. The snake's head is in my hand. It is staring me right in the eye. The African sand snake is aggressive. It looks at me through its primitive, unfeeling eyes and there is no sign of fear. There is no sign of anything but the wish to kill me. It sticks its long, thin, forked tongue out. I don't know the Bible very well, I don't know it at all, but I know that snakes in the Bible are evil creatures and, now I'm eyeballing with one for the first time, I can see why. This is a creature which is ready to fight for its life.

Under normal circumstances, a sand snake bite probably won't kill. But a bite on the tongue certainly will. So what am I supposed to do with my tongue? I experiment, curling it up into various corners of my mouth. Wherever I put it, it's in the way. My mouth is dry, so dry that it's sticky.

The African chanting is getting frantic.

'Come on, Frankie!' say the boys. There is an urgency in their voices. They don't want to do it themselves, but they don't want me to chicken out either. Even though that's probably the sensible thing to do.

The snake looks at me. I look at the snake. All of a sudden, it's too late. I know I have to do it, and do it now.

I plunge the snake into my mouth and bite as hard and as fast as I can. My tongue's in the way and there's nothing I can do about it. It is pressing against the scaly snake head. I bite hard, and there's a scrunch as I bite through the bone. I tear with my hands and there is a ripping noise as my teeth sever the flesh. I can taste it now. Amazingly, it does taste just as salty as those fish back in Whitley Bay. It's hard to get through the flesh and the skin but I'm in a hurry. I tear harder with my hands and the second the body is severed from the head I spit, and spit hard. It's a relief to get the snake's head out of my mouth.

Now, off with the skin. It's hard and rough and old. I catch hold of the writhing body with my other hand and use my hand and teeth to pull the skin away like a tight glove. The Africans are cheering, the boys are saying, 'Yeah! Yeah!' They're glad it's me and not them.

I start chomping through the body. It's still moving. The flesh is thick and succulent and salty.

The applause dies down and the officer smiles.

'We thought you would all want to try this desert survival technique . . .'

The boys go suddenly silent. Soldiers are bringing forward fourteen more wriggling bags. They hand one to each of the lads. Some of them are really miserable but they know they have to do it.

Ross is cool. This kind of thing doesn't bother him. While everyone is feeling their way carefully around the bags, a variety of emotions written on their faces, Ross is relaxed. Too relaxed. When he pulls the string and the bag falls back, he finds he's holding the tail of the snake and not its head. The snake transforms itself into punctuation. First an exclamation, then a question and finally it twists its body into a figure of eight and rears up. It's going to bite him. He has no choice but to fling it away.

The snake hits the ground and moves along it, noiselessly, fast, scarcely leaving a trail. With skills like this a snake could be the deadliest of enemies. It dissolves into the desert and reappears a second later in a nearby thorn bush.

Ross is committed to killing the snake now. He can't just let it go. He approaches the thorn bush and, whichever side he approaches from, the snake's head pokes out at him, its black, forked tongue appearing then disappearing with deadly rapidity, a dreadful indication of the speed of its strike.

Ross finds a stick and somehow he bludgeons the snake to death. He's been quick, he's been resourceful and he's killed the snake. He thinks he's done well. But the Africans are not impressed. They stare at him in silence. One of them mutters a terrible insult which we have already learned means woman. They don't talk to Ross for the rest of the day. He killed the snake the cowardly way.

I'm still chomping through my victim, a treat which by now is tiring my tastebuds and jaw. The other lads are spitting out snakes' heads and peeling off skin. We'll all be glad when this is over.

Next, the officer produces some eggs. They're large, perhaps from

191

a hen. He cracks them on his head and the yoke runs down his face.

'What a wally,' mutters one of the lads.

'I'm not doing that,' says someone else. It's what we're all thinking.

Then he's handed a big, scruffy bird, some sort of desert chicken, flapping and squawking. He doesn't put the head in his mouth but he bites its neck until its head falls off. His mouth is full of feathers, they're sticking to the yoke which is all over his face and there is blood everywhere. The chicken still flaps. He then proceeds to eat the bird, feathers, guts and all until he is a yolky, bloody, feathery mess.

We clap and nod and look impressed. And, hardly realizing we're doing it, we once again take a step back. We wait, but to our relief we're not asked to do the chicken trick.

Later, back at base, we tell a doctor what we've done and he nearly faints.

'The African sand snake's poison ducts are just behind its head. You could have taken in the poison even after you'd bitten its head off.'

We agree that we've seen demonstrations of machismo rather than desert survival techniques. Ross's method of killing the snake may be womanly but, if you're trying to survive in the desert, it's a more sensible way of getting your food. And the egghead stunt is just indecipherable.

We do a lot of diving off the African coast, where there are a number of Second World War wrecks. The big ships lie 80 feet down, part-buried, home to thousands of fish. They are a strange and eerie intrusion in the underwater world. We scavenge for pieces of bomb and beautiful brass and glass portholes. One ship lies majestically on its side. All the top portholes have been stripped but lower down there are many left. To get them off, Al goes outside the ship and I swim into the wreck to undo the nuts.

I don't know whether anyone drowned in this wreck but it feels cold and dark in here like an old tomb. As I descend further and further, the light diminishes until I'm swimming through the blackness. I know that if I run into any equipment problems, getting out will be difficult if not impossible. This could be my tomb. I swim down staircases which men once ran up. The nuts are rusty and old and the man who put them in didn't ever expect them to be undone, not like this anyway. After initial resistance they give way. I manage to get four before it's time to retrace my route through the wreck. Each of the portholes weighs 30 lbs. The rope gets stuck when we try to pull them up to the surface and the boss, who is diving with us because he wants a porthole, goes down to try to release it.

When he doesn't reappear, I dive in again to check out what's happening.

Down into the underwater world again, where it's silent except for the sound of my own breathing. Something doesn't feel right. A slight rearrangement in the water, a strange displacement, odd behaviour patterns in the fish. A shape appears. It disappears almost immediately but I recognize it at once. A shark. I shudder.

Later, when the boss says, 'Let's do our swimming test in the Red Sea, instead of going round and round the baths at home,' I am unenthusiastic.

We all have to take an annual swimming test. It's only a mile and we'd all rather swim here than in Hereford's chlorinated pool early one morning. Except that there aren't any sharks in Hereford.

About sixty of us are dropped a mile off shore. We start to swim back. Nobody but nobody wants to be exposed to sharks at the back, and the sides aren't a very attractive option either. The only safe place to be is in the middle. We cluster together and there is a constant rotation as the men at the back push to the middle, and the men at the sides push inwards. We soon reach the shore. It is probably the fastest swimming test ever taken.

The Regiment places us all under constant and unrelenting assessment. We have to perform and perform well all the time. There's always a sense of competition. The only route is up. It's no use being a good soldier and wanting to stay a private. You have to get promoted or you'll cause a log jam for younger men coming in. I enjoy the work and one reason I'm so relaxed these days is that I can be fairly confident of my own competence but it's obvious that I can't stay here for ever.

I'm still a corporal but, here in North Africa, I'm given a chance to play sergeant. Of course, it's only a training exercise which is designed to assess my abilities. I'm asked to lead an ambush on a railway line. With my patrol, I have to make models of the demolitions we'll use and work out our strategy and timings.

We make a model of the bridge we're hitting. Or, to be more precise, Al makes a model. He's good at this. He uses wet sand, rocks, pieces of card for buildings, twigs for trees, parachute cord for fences. Before long he's produced a three-dimensional map of the area. He's trying to make an especially good model for me because he knows I'm anxious about this. When we close recce the target, everyone agrees the model was exactly right.

I ponder my strategy and throw it open to discussion. The lads study it carefully and most of them nod their heads but Steve, an

193

ex-para, pipes up, 'That won't work, Frank. Look, if the guys we're hitting break left and you engage them from here, your back-up comes from over here and there'll be crossfire here . . . this position could end up firing at their own men.'

He's right. He's absolutely right. All that pencil chewing and planning and I've still managed to get my men killed. It's taken an infantry-trained man a few minutes to see that. He's been living and breathing infantry since he came into the army. It's natural for him. And what's my background? Signals. I like to think that I've finally managed to break away from Signals, but now, suddenly, I realize, sitting with my patrol all around me, that I'll never break away. I could study infantry every day for ever and I'll never be an infanteer. I'm a signaller.

'You're right. I hadn't seen that,' I say, using my most relaxed tone. But I don't feel relaxed. My stomach's churning. I might never hack it in the Regiment. I can be the best shot and come first on my courses but deep down inside I fear that I don't have the skills to lead the men.

'So, what do you suggest, Steve?'

He stretches his legs out. This is easy for him.

'Well, why not move that gun group to there . . . that should do it.'

Afterwards I say to Al, 'I nearly blew it. If it hadn't been for Steve . . .'

He looks at me in surprise.

'Steve's an infanteer,' he says. He's trying to sound reassuring but there's an assumption beneath his words. The natural supremacy of the infantry-trained soldier.

I must look miserable because Al goes on. 'The whole point of the Regiment is that we've come from all over the army. Intelligence, tanks, signals, the infantry. Different skills for different situations. You know that.'

I nod glumly.

'When you lead men, it's not what you can do alone, it's what you can achieve together,' he reminds me.

My head knows this. But in my heart, old doubts return. They've been buried deep over the years, deep under successes and certificates, but they're still there and they'll always be there. I'm afraid I can't kick the ball. I'll have two tries and when I do it wrong the second time Dad will go into the house and he'll never play football with me ever again.

We make our explosives out of wood and plasticine. They have to be cut perfectly to size. Al takes this job on. He bends over his work, his face still with concentration. His big hands can move small things with precision until they take on the shape he wants.

We carry out our ambush and it goes like clockwork.

'See,' says Al, 'I don't know what you were worried about.'

'How did you know I was worried?'

He laughs at me. It's a nice laugh, deep and rich and unexpected, and I join in. For a few moments everything's all right. The boss comes over and congratulates me. My prospects of promotion in a few months look good. But soon that old feeling returns. I nearly blew it. Am I to go through this agony of self-doubt every time I'm in line for promotion? Years of worry seem suddenly to stretch before me.

Work goes on and, now I've been in for a few years, some of it begins to feel routine. Except that I know I'm under constant assessment, living in a relentless competition.

My next trip to Belize is uneventful. I get back to camp and am just leaving to go home for my reunion with Claire and Charlotte when I bump into someone I know. It's Larry, the born-again Christian who I met in North Carolina. The American special forces unit has sent him over for a few months. Perhaps because I've been in the jungle for a while, I'm pleased to see him. I greet him like an old friend and before I have time to think about it, invite him home for dinner.

Back at the cottage, Claire has cooked a special meal for my home-coming. I walk in with Larry. She's surprised. I suppose that afterwards I'll have some explaining to do, but not in front of Larry. We've been welcomed by many hospitable Americans in North Carolina and now Claire does the same. I hug and play with baby Charlotte, who's now almost eighteen months. She's running around and saying some words and I can hardly put her down.

After dinner, I talk to Larry about something that's previously been taboo in our household. Religion. Specifically, his religion. I tell him how impressed I was when I stayed with Big Kev by the way his beliefs formed such a quiet cornerstone in his life. But I didn't see how he could be such a good soldier and a Christian.

I'm doing the polite thing. I'm talking to a guest about his favourite subject. Is it good manners which leads me into the sort of discussion I don't normally have? I'm a macho twenty-seven-year-old and I'm not really interested in talking Christianity but here I am, challenging a Christian and arguing with him. We both enjoy it. That night, when I go up to bed much later than I intended, Claire says, 'You're not going to become a Christian, are you?'

I laugh out loud.

'Very funny.'

'Well, why did you keep going on about it tonight?'

'I have to talk to him about something.'

'Why did you bring him home at all?'

Here it is. I knew that sooner or later I'd have to explain why I let someone else in on our private family party.

'He was in camp, he's new to England and I wanted to be friendly. Think of all the people who looked after us in North Carolina.'

She nods and yawns.

'I did. That's just what I did think of. But you could have said, "Come over next week." Couldn't you?'

I pull the bedcovers over my head. Claire's right. I could have, but I didn't.

She yawns.

'I want to move house.'

I pull the bedcovers back.

'Move? From the cottage?'

She yawns again.

'It's taken me a long time to come to terms with it, but it's inconvenient being right out here. It takes me ages to drive Charlotte anywhere. And I'm always waiting for you to come home and get on with the next bit. That plastering in the other bedroom. The staircase. We'll never be finished, Frank.'

'You want to move from our little cottage? Our cottage we bought when we got married?' I suddenly feel sentimental.

'Goodness, Frank, you should hear yourself. How much home-brew have you had?'

'Not much. I'm just tired. We can move if you want to. You're here more than I am.'

'OK, I'll start looking.'

'Where?'

'In town.'

'You want to live in Hereford? You said you wanted to live in the country!'

'Frank, I've changed my mind. It's one of the things that happens to people as they get older. They change. It's called growing up.'

I lie in the dark disagreeing. I'm thinking: it's one of the things that happens to women. It's called changing their minds and they do it all the time, however old they are. Men, however, are different. Because one of the things we don't do is change.

# 15

IT'S MARCH. WE'RE FLYING SOMEWHERE OVER GERMANY IN A C130.
Outside it's dark. We can't see much through the portholes, just the
occasional lights of towns. Mostly we don't bother to look. It's so
noisy that mostly we don't bother to talk either.

We head for the door, shuffling and hobbling because our bergens
are strapped onto our legs.

We're ready to go now. My eyes are fixed on two small lights. The
red light's on and we know we're going to jump at any moment.
Everyone's watching for the green. Five of us are standing in a row,
lined up at the door like infants in the dinner queue only, unlike
infants, we're carrying our meals for the next two weeks. We have all
our kit plus bombs. We all weigh 300 lbs. I'm carrying my own body
weight, 150 lbs, in my bergen, while Al, who weighs over 200 lbs with
his parachute gear on, carries nothing much heavier than a handbag
in comparison. I glance at him. All our bodies are taut as we wait for
the light but it seems to me that Al's stance is less alert than usual. He
has flu. It's hard to know how ill he's feeling as self-expression isn't
his strong point, but I think it's bad.

The aircraft's banking as it weaves around the valleys, flying low
and then rising up to height to drop us. My heart's beating fast. I'm
hot and somewhere inside me is not the fear but the knowledge of a
possibility. The static line may not work. I could jump out into the
night, into the forest, with a parachute which doesn't work.

We feel the plane swing round. Our bodies sway. The door opens.
A rush of cold air, a black hole. We all watch the lights with big eyes.

Suddenly there is a red light. A green light, and the RAF jump master shoves us each in turn, one, two, three, four, five. I feel his hand on my back and my leg muscles are levering against the floor of the plane and then the plane's gone. Receding at 140 m.p.h., dropping rapidly back below radar, it's gone and I am tipping into a dark silence, the cold air whipping my face.

My body's seized by a howling wind which is so strong that it's practically solid. My legs fly away from me. I'm being swept away through the air. I might be upside down. It's impossible to tell. I'm powerless. I can see nothing, I have no idea where the others are. The air throws and swings me like a rag doll.

On my head a heavy helmet, on my back my parachute, on my front the small reserve parachute. My bergen is strapped to one leg. I can't regain my sense of which way is up. Wherever I look is pitch-black. Then I catch a glimpse of lights, a small group, like a village, far below and over to the left. Suddenly, understanding comes. I know where earth is. I'm falling fast towards it. I look up to watch my chute open like a big, graceful night flower. It felt like for ever but it's been precisely three seconds since I jumped from the plane. I'm safe. Now there's the landing still to dread.

I release my bergen from my leg. It's still clipped to my harness and it jerks me a little as it reaches the end of its rope.

Far beneath me I can see the occasional flash of the torch. The drop zone. I pull my risers to propel myself forward. I'm aiming to land as close to the torch as I can. It's impossible to judge exactly when the ground's going to come but those distant village lights give a clue. Quite a while yet. The canopy should have opened at 800 feet so I calculate that I have less than a minute before I touch something solid. I start to relax. With my parachute open and my equipment released, I can enjoy the madness of falling. About 30 seconds to go, I estimate. I get into position, just in case. My body's ready but my mind isn't. Suddenly, with a speed which is too overwhelming for thought, the ground's rushing up to me.

Bump, my equipment touches down. Crash, now the ground's hitting me. I grunt and roll and tumble. My helmet and legs are knocked and buffeted by Germany. It's hard and unforgiving, this land. My parachute flutters a little, dragging me behind it for a short way until I can get onto my stomach and grab the lines. I pull one hard and the parachute collapses. I gather it towards me and lie on the silk.

Shocked and badly winded by the suddenness of the fall, I go through the landing routine mechanically. I push the quick release buttons to undo the parachute line and remove my harness. Then I pull my equipment up, take my rifle out and load it. That's always the first thing. I pack my parachute. And then I set off towards the rendezvous.

It's about a mile away. One by one, we all arrive. Ross is leader. I'm still awaiting promotion and I play second-in-command in this patrol. Then come Joe, Al and Larry. At the rv, we establish that it's been a bad landing for most of us. Ross has some broken toes and a twisted ankle, Al has a twisted ankle and is feeling thick-headed with flu. Joe has injuries to his shoulder and feet.

We divide the kit up. We're supposed to dig in our parachutes but because of our injuries we agree to hide them in a culvert, making a note of the grid number so the RAF can collect them the next day. If this was a real war, we'd bury them. But it's not a real war. It's the scenario NATO plays out here every year: the Russians have invaded the West and we have to take out vital strategic points, like bridges and nuclear power plants. This year, it's the Americans' turn to pretend to be the Russians.

Our faces blacked, night sights on our weapons, we make slow and hobbling progress towards our first rendezvous. Across farmland, through woods, along hedgerows. We're led by Joe because he seems most badly injured and we want to set our pace to our slowest man. He keeps stopping, because he's vigilant and he has to look around, but perhaps also because he's hurt.

Only two men are OK: me and Larry. Usually we work in four-man patrols and the four of us have been working together for years now and know each other well. Because of the demolitions equipment required for this job, though, we needed a fifth man to spread the weight. Nobody wanted Larry. He may be a good soldier but since he's from America he's an outsider. What's he doing in our squadron? How has he managed to get into our patrol? He's in the UK to work on the counter-terrorist team but they gave him security clearance to take part in this exercise and Larry was passed from patrol to patrol. Everyone's suspicious of him, including me, and, since he's been out to our house a few times now, I'm probably as close to him as anyone. People find his born-again Christianity hard to take. This, more than his nationality, means that he can never be one of the lads. He's a short-haired, blond, upright Mr Clean. He probably has a sense of humour but it's not our sense of humour. He's not the kind of man you want in your patrol.

Eventually, painfully, we reach our laying-up point before daylight. This is where we'll sleep until darkness falls again, in a closely planted tree plantation where the carpet of dead branches is so dense that the woods are almost impenetrable.

When the first glimmer of dawn arrives I study faces. None of the injured men look good. Joe is creased up with pain. Ross is exhausted with the effort of walking all night on broken toes. Al looks very ill. He's shaking a bit.

We discuss the bad landing in whispers. Most people hit trees as they came down. Probably the guy with the torch guiding us in was standing in the wrong place. Soon we stop talking, but we don't start sleeping. Too tired, too much pain. When we sleep, it's in deep fits and starts. I lie awake wondering how we can get to the rv with three ill or wounded men.

The following night, when we've cranked ourselves back up into action, we head for a farmhouse which is nearby and isolated. Joe and I go forward. Joe, because he's injured and we hope people will feel sorry for him. Me, because he's too hurt to be charming.

Cross the farmyard, knock on the door. It's opened cautiously and the face which peers round it jumps back in horror at the sight of two men in muddy uniforms with their faces blacked. I flash him my most winning smile but he looks even more startled.

In bad German, English and sign language we explain that we're on an exercise and some of our men are hurt. I gesture at Joe and he looks very pathetic. The farmer nods. I wave at the others to come forward. They're trying to look pathetic too. Ross's limp has got noticeably worse for the occasion.

I show the farmer the map and indicate the point we're heading for. Joe, who speaks a little German, says that there's a British field hospital there. Can he help us? There are enemy troops all around so we have to be careful.

He shouts to someone else inside the house, an older man, who comes to stare at us. They know there's a NATO exercise going on and as they talk it's obvious that they like the idea of playing resistance fighters. Finally, the farmer smiles. He's going to take us. He is a big man with a long, bony face and horse teeth. I just hope he doesn't just turn us in to the enemy but he loads us into his estate car, indicating that he'll have to make two journeys.

He drives us about fifteen kilometres to the outskirts of the woods, where our final rv is. It's inside the actual attack area and the whole district is crawling with enemy troops but no-one's checking civilian cars. As we drive through the road checks, I wonder if he's just stringing us along so he can turn us in at the first opportunity. That would be a monumental and embarrassing failure for our patrol.

The farmer's amazed to drop us in the middle of nowhere. From our story of army hospitals he's at least expected to find some sort of military complex instead of a deserted wood. We indicate that the hospital is hidden deep inside the plantation. He looks at us doubtfully. However, he goes back for the others.

When we're all at the rv together, the first thing I notice is that Al now has an acute fever. He's sweating and he looks awful but he keeps saying he'll be OK. He may be right. He's just come back from the Far East where you pick up bugs which cause bad fevers for a couple of days. As patrol medic, I'd say it's either malaria or dengue fever but Al insists we wait and see if it passes. Of course, we can't really go around blowing things up. The bombs are plasticine and we've already made them as we're given details in advance of the targets. Demolition is a precise art. If the bridge is made out of girder sections, we've already crafted charges which fit the girders perfectly. We've cut and shaped them so that they're thin and lightweight: it's taken us weeks. Our aim is not to bend a bridge but actually to sever it, in theory by dropping the middle section.

It's soon obvious that Al has to go. I'm sure he has malaria. By the time he stumbles off with a pair of umpires, he's gibbering uncontrollably. Ross and Joe stay, although there's little they can do but wait in the wood for Larry and me to come back.

When night falls the pair of us sneak out and hit a target and log it. The log goes back to exercise control who send out the umpires to check. Because we're two men doing the work of five we take short cuts, like reaching a power station by following the power lines. Most nights we return to the rv, some nights we sleep elsewhere in the forest, close to our target.

Larry and I have a lot of time to talk. Our bergens are already heavy but Larry never goes anywhere without a weighty Bible. I think this is absurd. When light permits he'll sit under a hedge reading it, an irritating habit. Sometimes I tease him about it, sometimes I ask him. He answers my questions seriously, making constant reference to his Bible.

'Well,' he says, 'let's see what the Lord has to say on that subject.' And he shuffles around inside the thick brown covers until he finds what he's looking for. He produces it like a conjurer producing a rabbit. He reads me some passage which is supposed to answer my question and then looks at me as if the subject's closed. But it's not closed. I find it incomprehensible. He's getting bored with my questions but I'm compelled to keep asking them. I want to know the answers.

We're going to take out a bridge. The troops have been warned that we may turn up. They're guarding it. They're vigilant. On the first night they're looking everywhere. They don't see us. We're watching to see when they change shift. We establish that they have two hours on guard duty, two hours off. Dogwatch, the worst watch of the night, is two to four o'clock in the morning and it's the best time to catch them unawares.

The second night, they're less alert. After that, they get positively slack. They all sit under the bridge smoking and laughing.

The third night we get in and put the bombs on the target without them ever knowing that we've been there. We smile as we cut silently back through the forest to the hedge where we've left our sleeping bags. They'll learn from exercise command that the bridge has been blown up and they're all dead and they'll wonder how.

That night, Larry reads his Bible as usual. Tackling him on this has become quite a habit. He's beginning to look exasperated. My questions boil down to three basic points which I return to again and again.

First, everyone knows about evolution so how can Larry seriously claim that God created the world? Second, if this God loves us so much, how can he allow so much suffering? Finally, the question I've been asking since I stayed with Big Kev in America. How can Larry reconcile being a soldier and being a Christian?

Larry reads me little nuggets from the Bible which are supposed to mean something and when I press him harder he tries to explain. I'm not impressed and I show it. Finally, he tires of me. 'Frank . . .' he drawls. 'When we get back to England I'll try to find someone to answer your questions. But now, let me go to sleep. And if you want to know more about God, ask him. Just pray.'

It's dark. It was already cold but while we've been talking the cold night has closed in on us. I crawl into my green maggot. At first it feels cool and unwelcoming but as I lie there warmth spreads all over me. I suppose that Larry is lying in his sleeping bag saying his prayers. At that moment I envy him his close relationship with God. Sometimes I feel I don't have a close relationship with anyone, not even Claire. This is my choice, I seldom feel the need for closeness. But I catch myself envying Larry now.

Into the night I say, quietly and without moving my lips, 'God, if you really exist and you really are out there listening to me, then please give me a sign of some kind. If you don't send me a sign tonight then that means once and for all that Larry is talking a load of nonsense.'

I roll over in my maggot. I remember school assembly.

'Er . . . God . . .' I add, ' . . . Amen.'

I lie there waiting. Everything is still. There is no breath of wind in the forest to shake the trees, no rustling of night creatures in the grass, no distant aeroplanes. Nothing. No sign. Just a void. I wait. Occasionally I open my eyes and glance around sneakily. Just in case an angel's standing there, glowing in the dark and looking holy the way they do in old masterpieces. But there's no angel. There's nothing. I go to sleep. See. It's all just a load of nonsense.

I wake up once or twice in the night. I force myself to open my eyes, even though I'm tired. I'd hate God to send me a sign and for me to miss it. I find it's so dark it makes no difference if my eyes are open or closed. I drift back to sleep feeling warm and satisfied. No sign. Am I disappointed? A little. Who doesn't secretly want to see an angel? But it would be dreadful to become a Christian and start believing. That's not what Collinses do.

Dawn's about to break. The forest is still calm and silent but there's a distant glimmer of light over to the east. A few far cloud formations are visible. Weirdly, I feel rested. Larry is asleep. I send our signals back to base, confirming that we've blown up the target. I can do this without even crawling out of my maggot. Then I tune the radio to the BBC World Service. I lie feeling peaceful in my headset, listening to the news. I'm about to turn off the radio when the next programme is announced. It will be an interview with someone who was in Bomber Command in the war. Larry is still asleep and the darkness has hardly begun to lift. I decide to hear about Bomber Command.

From the introduction it becomes clear that today is Sunday and this interview is going to be a religious one. I groan to myself. But I keep listening.

The interviewee turns out to be a metallurgist. He's being challenged on how he can reconcile his life, as an ex-bomber and a scientist, with his religious convictions. He's going to be asked three questions, the interviewer explains, the questions most often asked about Christianity. How can God have created the world in a few days when, as a scientist, he must agree that it evolved over aeons? How can he believe in God's love when he has seen so much suffering? And how can you be a soldier and a Christian, when Christians don't kill people and soldiers do?

I lie in my maggot as if electrified. My three questions. This man is going to answer them. The possibility crosses my mind that here is the sign I asked for. I dismiss the thought.

First the man says that there's no contradiction between the Bible

and the scientific evidence for evolution. Our scientific understanding is frequently wrong or incomplete. Often so-called
certainties have been disproved by subsequent discoveries. All we
can really be sure about is the extent of our own ignorance. The Bible
explains why the world was made. Science is just beginning to
suggest how. When, at the beginning of the Bible, God makes the
world in six days, there's no attempt to suggest that a day is 24 hours.
A day might be an aeon, as evolutionary theory suggests.

In my sleeping bag I don't nod or move or speak. But I understand
what the radio is saying and acknowledge its truth and feel the fight
begin to drain out of me.

Next, the man talks about evil and suffering. He asks just how
much suffering is the result of human evil rather than the absence of
God's love. Even some large-scale natural disasters could, he
suggests, have been averted if man was prepared to invest resources
in doing so. He talks about the benefits of suffering. How it's only by
knowing pain that we can experience real joy. How without the
threat of suffering we humans couldn't learn to exercise responsibility towards one another. If God intervened to avert all pain,
our human world could not function. Pain is a necessary part of our
existence.

I lie listening to him. He's saying nothing new, nothing I haven't
heard before from Larry, but the rightness of what I hear almost
pushes me out of bed.

If a man dropped his hammer on someone else's toe and, for some
reason, God intervened to change the hammer's course and save the
toe, then that man will never be responsible about his tools. He'll just
keep dropping hammers. I know that this is obvious but I recognize
it now with a sense of discovery, even revelation.

Finally, the question which has bothered me most. How can a
Christian be a soldier? The speaker gives various examples of the way
that soldiers play an important role in the New Testament. He speaks
of the need for soldiers as God's agents to ensure submission to
authority and the common good. The soldier is appointed to carry out
God's punishment on evil-doers.

I feel a deep sense of satisfaction at his words. I have for many years
believed that the SAS exists to fight evil and that's exactly what this
man is saying. His words have made soldiering the noble, important
job I believe it to be.

I switch off the radio but I don't get up. I can't get up. All last night's
fight, the urge to challenge and argue, has gone. I am submissive. I
recognize the rightness of everything which has been said. I am sure

204

now that God has sent me a sign. He has sent a sign through a modern method of communication in language which I understand. This voice on the radio has been speaking to me. God has answered my questions through it and now I must surrender to the extraordinary, powerful feelings which are encompassing me.

For the first time in my life I have a sense of God. He is there, He is all around me, He is in every leaf and every tree. There is a massive presence and it's so physical that I can't believe I've been blind to it until now. I remember how I tried to hug my mother once and she pushed me away and I half fear that same rejection again, but I know it won't come. God is wrapped all around me and I'm His son. A foolish, arrogant, wilful child, but His son nevertheless.

I am happy. Not ecstatic, but glowing. Dawn is spreading through the forest. A dull light is breaking through the clouds and shining in muted shafts through the trees. I'm in a cathedral. I'm warm in my green maggot and God's here with me and I am overwhelmed by His love and my own sense of awe. I recognize my smallness. I recognize that my life will never be the same again and I don't want it to be. Overwhelmed by the majesty of God and His holiness – words I have never before considered using – I get up and wake Larry.

He stares at me glassily.

I say, 'Pray with me!'

He asks no questions. He sits up in his sleeping bag and prays. I repeat each line after him. I apologize for the way I've lived my life until now, I say I understand that it's been all wrong and that I've been selfish and hurt many people and turned away from God and His ways. I ask God's forgiveness. Please help me live according to your laws, Lord. I know as I say these words that nothing will ever be the same again and the things which I thought mattered are unimportant.

I look at the forest. Every leaf and every twig is a work of art. I remember that day I came home to find my father had made that perfect piece of skirting board and how, suddenly, I could see crafts-manship in something I hadn't even noticed before. That's the nature of true craftsmanship.

Everything is jumping up at me waiting to be noticed now. All my senses are heightened. I marvel at the ordinary.

We have a few days left before the end of the exercise. A couple more bombs to detonate. We do well. We succeed in blowing up both targets and large numbers of men. I am professional and efficient but, for me, everything has a sense of unreality. I am a Christian. Everything is different now. How did this happen to me? I was a sceptic and I always have been and suddenly, out of the blue, I'm a believer. It's hard not to feel I've been selected in some way.

I try on a few occasions to talk to Larry about what's happened to me but he's strangely cool. I realize he doesn't really believe I'm a convert. I don't try to convince him. Mostly I don't talk. I'm too frightened by what's happened. I'm scared I'm not me any more.

At our final rv all the lads in the squadron meet up and another Fat Albert flies us back to the UK, where we await transport. I sit staring at everyone as we wait. I examine the faces of these big, tough, young men with their swearing and their cigarettes. God's all around them, and they don't see Him. A couple of the lads are spitting and talking dirty. Something about a Hereford woman they all know. They break into raucous laughter simultaneously. They throw back their heads. They're just small, wayward children, despite all their swaggering. They cling to the Regiment instead of forming lasting, deep relationships. They are lost. I was lost too, until a few days ago, and now I understand that my life is part of a larger plan. Why me? Why am I destined to be different?

What am I going to do about all this when I get home? I turn to Larry. He's reading his Bible. I wish I had a Bible to read.

'What am I going to do now?' I ask him. He looks at me and blinks. 'I mean, do I have to go to church? Which one? Do I have to see the vicar or do I just . . . I mean, what do I do?'

Larry says it's a maze out there. He's a Baptist, but that means something different in America. He'll help me through the maze, as soon as he has time, but he's going straight back on the counter-terrorist team and he's going to be busy. I feel a little reassured. He tells me I won't have to start saying thee and thou when I pray. Don't let language come between you and the Lord, Frank. That's a relief.

I walk into my home knowing that I'm not the same man who walked out. But Claire surprises me by staring at me long and hard.

Her very first words are, 'You've become a Christian.'

So it shows. I can't help smiling. I want to tell her all about it. I want to talk and talk and talk about what's happened. I want to tell her how I was getting everything wrong before and now I'm going to try getting everything right.

I ask her, 'How did you know?'

'I've seen it coming for a while. It's happened, hasn't it?'

How could she have seen it coming when it took me so by surprise, when I went down fighting and objecting and challenging and arguing? I ask her and she just looks knowing.

'No, come on, tell me,' I insist.

'Well, you admired Big Kev so much and he's a Christian. Then you went to that funeral in North Carolina and came back full of how the minister had said this and that. And look at the way you keep arguing with Larry about it all the time. You wouldn't do that if you didn't really agree with him.'

Women's logic. Warped and incomprehensible. I know that something amazing has happened to me and it's happened out of the blue.

I've hardly taken off my coat and hugged Charlotte before I start to tell Claire my story. It all comes bursting out of me with a force and momentum of its own. Claire listens. But she doesn't sit there with rapt attention the way I'd like. She starts getting on with some wifely sort of thing like cooking dinner or chopping stuff up for the baby.

I keep talking and I realize I'm following her around. Then I realize that I'm following her because she keeps moving away from me.

'Will you keep still?' I say.

She looks at me and then her glance gets caught up elsewhere, by Charlotte or the stove. I'm talking about the most extraordinary experience of my life and my wife doesn't want to hear. Charlotte starts yelling. I interrupt myself to pick her up. For a few minutes there is silence between us. I wait for Claire to prompt me into continuing but she doesn't. She doesn't want to hear what I have to say.

Over the next day or so I try again and again but Claire remains unresponsive. I take a new delight in Charlotte, in her perfection. I love the way she's altered in just a few weeks. I love her bandy-legged way of walking. I'm awed by God's power of creation when I look at her. I keep praying, talking to God about what's happening to me. I say, please make Claire understand. At night when Claire's tiredness makes her less resistant and I try again to tell her how I'm feeling, she lies in bed looking up at the ceiling with no expression at all on her face. Finally she says, 'I want to go to sleep now.' She switches off the light. We lie side by side, not touching, in silence.

In camp I've tried to catch up with Larry a few times but it's obvious he's too busy to help me. I'm having cosy one-sided little chats with God, but where should I go from here? I know that I have to find out more about Christianity and the Bible and Churches but I have no idea where to begin and Larry just isn't available. I feel a sense of urgency not only because I now believe most of my life has been wasted but because the whole squadron's leaving for the Far East in a few weeks' time. I don't want to leave in the same state of ignorance and confusion in which I returned from Germany.

I drive into Hereford and walk around. I look at a few churches from the outside. I don't go in. It's hard to see what these grand old buildings have to do with me. I try to remember when I was last in a church and can't. Probably a funeral. Finally I pass a bookshop. I always knew it was there but it's the sort of place I wouldn't previously have noticed. It's a religious bookshop. Inside there's a man with a beard who glances up as I walk in. I saunter round. Occasionally I look in his direction hoping that he'll catch my eye and start talking to me but he's bent over one of his books. The shop's very quiet and I move around it trying not to make a noise, which is how I imagine people behave in church. I feel I've been big and noisy all my life. I suspect Christians are quiet people.

Which book should I buy? I pull a few out and look at them. They seem to be written in some other language. I want one called *What to do if you are in the SAS and have just become a Christian*. But I can't find that book.

Finally I choose something and creep up to the bearded man. He looks up, puts his own book down and takes my money. Now he's wrapping the book up in paper which crackles far too loudly. I thank him and I hear my voice sounding small and hoarse as if it hasn't been used for a long time. He hands me the book and I force myself to speak.

'Er, can you tell me, is there a book about the Churches in Hereford?'

He dips his head and looks at me over his glasses and says nothing. Finally he asks me what exactly what I want to know about the Churches in Hereford.

'Well, the Churches, they all seem to be different and I don't understand . . . I'm not sure what they all . . . how they all . . .' I fade into complete incoherence then silence.

The man is expressionless. He is still staring at me over his glasses. Then he says, 'Are you a Christian?'

My turn to pause. We're having a pausing competition.

'Well . . . yes. Yes, I am.' My face is hot. He studies me for a few moments more and then says, 'Would you like a cup of coffee?'

Gratefully, I accept. He introduces himself. I forget his surname at once but his first name, Rupert, makes me squirm a little. I've never known anyone called Rupert before and if I had known any, they'd certainly be officers. I know everything is going to be different now but I hadn't guessed the future would include Ruperts. A long vista of Ruperts stretches out before me. I try not to think about it.

He finds me a seat and I watch him with his small kettle and his bag of sugar and his jar of instant. Prompted by him, I try to explain a little of what's happened to me but I'm careful. I don't want to give

208

away too much about myself, I don't want him to know what my job is or where I live or my name or anything too personal but I'm trying to tell him about the most personal thing which has ever happened to me. Difficult.

Luckily, no-one comes into the shop. He listens to me and then tells me that he thinks I should speak to a man called Peter Wood. I nod. Peter Wood sounds fine to me. He's vicar of St Peter's, explains the beard. I feel slightly, very, very slightly, crestfallen. He's a vicar. Sticking-out teeth, braying laugh, a posh accent, another Rupert.

Pull yourself together. You're a Christian. That means vicars.

At that moment, the phone rings. When the beard, Rupert, hears who's calling, he raises his eyebrows.

'I was just talking about you,' he says. It's Peter Wood. He told me to phone Peter Wood and the phone's rung and it's Peter Wood. It seems remarkable that he has called at this moment. Even if he rings this bookshop every day. I discern God's work here.

The beard talks to Peter Wood about some book and then he tells him a little about me. A young man . . . religious experience . . . guidance . . . possible to visit you . . . But Peter Wood's reply is discouraging. I still can't tell a thing from the beard's expression but his voice is a bit clipped when he says, 'I see. Yes, of course. I see, I'll tell him.'

He puts down the phone. My eyes have been fixed on him throughout the call and now his eyes meet mine.

'St Peter's is a church with many civic responsibilities and Peter Wood's very caught up just now in Princess Margaret's visit.' I already knew about her visit. She was dropping by on the Regiment while she was in town. Or maybe she was dropping by on Hereford while she was visiting the Regiment.

'So, he won't be able to see me?' I ask. Thank you, Your Royal Highness.

'Not immediately. I tried to indicate that you'll be going away soon and are in urgent need of guidance and he suggested that you go along to St Peter's tonight. There's a Mission England meeting there.'

St Peter's. Mission England. This isn't sounding very me. I'm not even sure which church is St Peter's. The beard tells me it's close to the cathedral in the centre of town and I immediately know which one he means. Today I wandered right past it. But Mission England . . .?

'Have you heard of Billy Graham?'

Billy Graham. That ranting, raving American. But now I have to remember that what he rants and raves about is Christianity and

I am a Christian. I'm cautious. 'I've heard of him, yes, but . . .'

'He won't be there in person. But you might very well find his Mission England has something to say to you. It's a good starting point. Seven o'clock at St Peter's. And I'll give you Peter Wood's number so that you can contact him when Princess Margaret's visit is over.'

I get up to go. I'm so grateful I almost forget the book I bought. I'm determined to get to St Peter's tonight. Rupert the Beard thinks they'll have something to say to me.

'By the way . . .' I'm almost out of the door but I have to ask, 'does Peter Wood ring this shop often?'

The beard is frozen for a moment.

'I don't think he's ever rung before,' he says. We look at each other significantly and I close the door. I've got to get to Mission England. God told Peter Wood to phone just at that moment and he told me about the meeting and that must mean God intends me to go. I discuss this with God in the car on the way out of town. As the houses fall away I start to feel happy. God's showing me the way. The sun's shining in a weak, early spring fashion and it's warm, far warmer than it was in Germany. Things are growing. The hedgerows are beginning to bud and blossom, in one or two places the outrageous green of spring has started to rip through the brown winter landscape. In previous years I've hardly noticed this. Now it seems little short of a miracle.

By the time I arrive home it's already late afternoon and Claire's busy. She hardly looks up as I walk in. Charlotte toddles over to me and I pick her up and swing her around.

'How is she?' I ask Claire. Charlotte had a runny nose this morning and red eyes and now she starts to whine a little.

'I think she should see the doctor.' Claire's tone is a reminder. This morning I promised that if Charlotte didn't get better I'd take her to the doctor tonight.

'I have to be in Hereford at seven o'clock.' Careful. The ice is thin here. Claire's been getting more and more brittle since I returned home from Germany and one false step and it's going to crack. I've already eased up a little, but only a little, on my God talk. At first she just stared at me like a stranger. Then she avoided me. Then, whenever I cornered her, she began to look as if she was in pain. And now her jaw's set and she's angry. I just want her to see. I just want her to understand and what I really want is for her to have the same experience. I'm going on a journey and I want her to come with me. But she's angry and she doesn't want to understand.

210

'Oh yes?' she says. Anyone who didn't know her might think this was conversational but I know she doesn't just mean oh yes.

'There's a meeting . . . '

'In Hereford. At seven. What sort of a meeting?'

'Well, some American Christians are over here . . . that's all I know.' She's slamming plates around now. 'Oh, so it's about God, this meeting.'

'Why don't you come?' I ask innocently. She stops and turns to face me. Danger. Stand by, stand by.

'Because', she says, 'I'm too busy to waste my time talking about a load of nonsense.' Slam, bang, wallop, is she setting the table or mutilating it? 'Because someone has to look after the baby and do all the work around here while you go off and have experiences.' It's not nice, the way she says the word experiences. But that's how she sees my conversion.

'Obviously,' Claire continues, 'it's more important for you to go to this . . . meeting . . .' Ouch. The meeting's been pierced and mortally wounded. 'Than it is to take your own daughter, who hardly ever sees you anyway, to the doctor's when she's ill. Obviously, that's far more important. And it's far more important to go to the . . . meeting . . . than to get some dry wood in so I can light a fire because they say there's going to be a frost tonight. Obviously.'

'I'll take Charlotte to the doctor's. I'll get the wood in. And then I'll go to the meeting,' I say. My voice is calm and I'm all sweet reason.

Claire looks up at me again and her face is triumphant.

'You won't get into Hereford by seven,' she says. 'The doctor's surgery doesn't start until six and there's no appointments system. You just have to wait your turn. And probably the queue's already forming.'

I sigh. I'll be lucky to get to St Peter's by 8 p.m. But I know I have to go. I start to fetch the wood.

Charlotte and I arrive at the doctor's surgery just after 6 p.m. and Claire's right, there's a queue of people sitting all around the outside of the room, sniffing and leafing through old magazines. I count the people, estimate 10 minutes per person, add up the time it takes to get home and into Hereford and calculate I won't be there until 8.30 p.m. I make swinging cuts to the National Health Service and allocate just 5 minutes per person. Then I give up calculations. If God wants me to get to the meeting I'll get to the meeting. Simple.

A patient comes limping out waving his prescription and the doctor buzzes the next patient in. An elderly woman. She stands up and then hesitates.

'You go in now, young man,' she says. She's looking at me. I gape at her and she beams back. 'You go in next. I'm sure no-one will mind if you take your baby in at once, it's not fair to keep them hanging around, is it?'

I stare in disbelief at the other patients. To my amazement they are all nodding at me and Charlotte, who is sitting on my lap gazing at them. Yes, they're saying, you go in next. This has never happened to me before and I thank them several times before we get into the doctor. The doctor takes a few minutes to look into her eyes and her ears and listen to her heart and then he writes a prescription and tells me not to worry about her. I can't believe it. We're leaving the surgery about 5 minutes after we went in.

There's a swagger to my walk when I enter our living room. Claire's sitting by the fire. Her face is a picture.

'But . . . didn't you go to the doctor?' she asks.

'Yep, here's the prescription and he said not to worry, it's nothing.' I hand over sleepy Charlotte.

'See you later,' I call over my shoulder. I'm already on my way to Hereford. It's half an hour's drive and I know I won't get there at 7 p.m., but very shortly after. But as I enter the city my courage fails me. Do I really want to go to some kooky American meeting? Maybe I won't bother after all.

I enter the Hereford one-way system. The turning to the church is a little way ahead and by the time I've reached it I've convinced myself that I just want to go home.

On the corner of the street is a wine bar, a popular place with the Regiment. Just as I'm reaching it, the door opens and one of my mates comes out. He's dead drunk. He just falls out of the door and collapses onto a lamppost, where he begins to vomit. Then he slides gracelessly down the lamppost to the pavement.

I think of Dad, never rolling drunk but often drunk. I think of lampposts I've slid down. I think of all this in a split second and it seems to me that I've seen not one of the lads in the street, but a snapshot of myself.

I know God's saying to me, 'You can turn left for the church or you can carry on through life like that.'

I hit the brakes, lean on the steering-wheel and swerve down the side street.

I'm late at the church. I hang around outside, nervous of going in and then nervous in case the door squeaks. Me, the storm trooper, scared of a squeaky door.

Finally I go in. Sure enough, there's a squeak, squeak and then the door closes behind me and I'm actually standing inside a church. I have come to church and now I am standing inside it. This seems incredible. I play with the idea of turning around and going out again but I feel sure everyone's looking at me. However, I soon see that they're mostly intent on what seems to be a play at the front of the church. I am on the point of sneaking out when I catch sight of Larry among the audience. Instead of braving the squeaky door again, I edge over to him. He nods and then turns back to the actors. I try to concentrate, but it's hard. I'm in church.

Gradually I get interested in the drama. It's about a man with an unpronounceable name who is horrible and everybody hates him. He wants to watch Jesus go by but he doesn't want anyone to see him so he hides in a tree. Then Jesus comes along under the tree, stops, and says to him, come on down! I'm coming over to your house tonight. Jesus even knows his name. The man is converted and becomes nice and repays all the people he's cheated and robbed.

Just in case we miss the point, an American accent stands up and explains to us that God knows our names and may call us any time, no matter how wicked we are. I sit there thinking that I am just like the ugly little guy who hid in the tree.

The American tells all the audience to stand and pray together. I hope it's nothing more complicated than the Lord's Prayer. With a superhuman effort I've managed over the last few days to recall all the words to this prayer, but I don't know any others. However, the American's using his own words and we repeat them. Then he tells us to shut our eyes.

'Now,' he booms over the microphone, 'some of you think that God has been speaking to you tonight. That God has a personal message for you.'

I remember the way all Claire's obstacles have been swept aside and how my mate slid down the lamppost just when I was going to drive past the church. I think, yes, that's definitely me. God has definitely been speaking to me tonight.

'If you feel God has been sending you a message, please raise your hand. Only I can see you. Everyone has their eyes shut, so it's safe for you to put your hand high in the air. Please raise your hand if God has spoken to you tonight.'

I hesitate but remind myself that, apart from Larry, no-one I know can possibly be here. Keeping my eyes tightly shut, I raise my hand.

'Oh yes,' the preacher is saying, 'oh yes, I can see many hands going up . . . yes, there's a whole lot of hands in the air . . . yes . . .'

My eyes are still shut. I think it's nice God has spoken to so many

213

people. At last the preacher stops trying to drag the last shy hand into the air.

'Well,' he says, 'now I've seen you and God's seen you. That's been acknowledged by us both. Now I want you to be real brave. I'm going to ask everyone else to sit down. But if you put your hand up, I want you to remain standing.'

Very clever, I think. How can I sit down now, when I've had my hand in the air? I can't. But for all I know, there might be a thousand people standing up, or I could be the only one. This thought is so chilling that I nearly sink down into the pew. But, my eyes still tightly closed, I force myself to remain standing. A part of me is annoyed. Who are they trying to catch? Anyone who's genuine doesn't need forcing in this way.

'Now, if you're sitting down, please reach out to someone standing and say this prayer with me for them.'

So everyone else has opened their eyes! I blink into the light and look around with relief. There are many others standing. Larry puts his hand on me, and someone on the other side and someone behind. Ugh. All these people touching me. I don't like it. This is weird and I wish I hadn't come. My head's spinning.

After the prayer the preacher says, 'Come forward, all those standing.'

There's a surge from behind. A large proportion of the audience is moving up to the front of the church. I'm carried forward with them and find myself standing in one of many lines. There are about ten in each queue and my hesitation has placed me almost at the back. When I work my way to the front an elderly man with white hair and glasses explains to me that they're so overwhelmed by the response tonight that all they can do now is take my name and number. They'll contact me very shortly, he promises. Something almost stops me from giving my name. I never give my name, let alone my number, to anyone. I don't even tell the dry cleaner. And now I have to watch while someone writes my name on a list. I hesitate. The man looks up and smiles at me kindly. I remember how much I need his help.

'The name's Frank Collins.'

I give Larry a lift back to camp. When I arrive home, there's an outside light on and a hall light and the rest of the house is in darkness. Claire's already gone to bed. I creep in. The stairs creak. I hope I don't wake the baby. In the bedroom I say Claire's name softly. There is no reply but there's no sound of deep, sleepy breathing either.

'Are you asleep?' I ask the darkness.

After a moment a voice whispers, 'No.'

'Can I turn on a light? Can I talk to you about what happened tonight?'

There's a sigh. Eventually she says, 'All right.'

An agreement, although without a trace of enthusiasm.

I switch on the bedside light. It's dim but it still makes Claire wince. She looks up at me, shielding her face behind her arm. I sit on the side of the bed and start to tell her all the things which have been happening. I'm burning to talk. It's almost two weeks now since God spoke to me in the forest and I'm still wrapped up in the strangeness and awesomeness of it. I'm aware that I'm not talking like my old self. I used to be laid-back, now I'm talking with a burning intensity that Claire doesn't recognize. I know, because she's looking at me as though I'm a stranger again. We can try to pretend everything's normal during the day when we discuss the smoking fireplace and how many pounds of potatoes I should buy from the farm down the road but now it's night and we're alone. I try to tell her about this evening. She rolls over.

'Why won't you listen to me?' I ask in desperation.

'You were a nice guy. You weren't nasty to people. You lived a decent life, well, as decent as anyone in the SAS. Why did you have to go and become a Christian? I liked you before,' she says. And she won't say any more.

I wait the next day and the next for a call from the elderly man who took my name at St Peter's Church. No call comes.

A few days later Princess Margaret's been and gone and I arrange to visit Peter Wood. For some reason I imagined he'd be about my age but he's nearer my father's. That's all he has in common with my father. Educated, flowers in the hallway, a study full of books, half of them on the floor.

I can't hide my enthusiasm. I've discovered his religion and am full of excitement and amazement for it. He's been a Christian for years and, without him being at all discouraging, I can sense that my enthusiasm leaves him weary.

I ask a lot of questions. About God, about prayer. Then he talks. He gives me some pamphlets to read. One of them is about becoming a Christian and is very basic, like the Highway Code. I read it and read it again and leave it lying around at home where I think Claire can't fail to pick it up.

'Did you happen to see that little booklet I left on the kitchen table?'

'Oh, I think I must have put it away somewhere.'

'You didn't read it, by any chance?'

'No. I didn't read it.'

We already have a copy of the Bible, a big family Bible of Claire's from Wales. We've never even opened it before. Now the pamphlets direct me to certain passages and I leave the Bible lying on the hall table, its pages open at a place I've been reading which may capture Claire's attention. She just ignores it.

# 16

I LEAVE FOR THE FAR EAST. WE'RE DOING JUNGLE TRAINING BUT OUR presence is also intended to act as a deterrent on the northern borders where there have been some insurgency problems. At one point, medics like me are lifted out to win hearts and minds in certain villages with our skills and medicine. Then it's back to our patrols.

Much of this jungle is different from the Belizean jungle. It's primary, with enormous, breathtaking, hardwood trees. Their trunks are ribbed and at the bottom they fan out into cathedral buttresses. The canopy they form is thick and dark and the undergrowth is sparse and easy to move through.

We're carrying everything with us. We have one spare set of clothes for night wear, the rest of the time we're in smellies. We don't wash or shave.

The nights are long and, as we're not operational, we can read. Everyone takes just one book. I've bumped into Larry again who has finally been convinced that my conversion's genuine and has given me his Bible. It's American and the language is understandable. This is the book I take with me. But which bits to read? I try to be directed by some of the pamphlets and references which Peter Wood's made but it's a big, baffling book and it often leaves me confused.

The lads bring one book each and then, after a week or so, they start swapping them around. This is difficult. What do I do now? I know from Larry that it's important to tell people about my faith but I'm not ready to start telling the lads anything, not yet.

One of the boys, Harry, comes over and says, 'What you reading, Frank?'

I mumble, 'The Bible.'

He's a big man, a really wild man. I was already a lance corporal when he joined and we've never been that close but I've always liked him. He roars, 'The what?'

So I say, a little louder, 'I'm reading the Bible.'

He stares at me in a bulgy-eyed way.

'No! Get away!' Then he snatches it and sees that I really am reading the Bible. He stares at me and gives it back. Then he lopes off.

'Yeah,' he says over his shoulder. 'Yeah, well, let us have a read after you've finished.'

All our hammocks are more or less interconnected and he passes on the word to the next hammock until it's gone around the encampment like wildfire. The next morning everyone knows I'm reading the Bible.

People say, 'Read any good books lately, mate?' and I say patiently, 'Yeah, I'm reading the Bible, that's right.' And they back off. It's lucky that I'm a corporal. If I'd been a trooper I would have taken even more flak but the lads accept that I've done a lot of soldiering by now and they respect me for that.

So, now they know. Ever since that day in the forest I've half waited for this and now it's happening I feel a mixture of relief and trepidation. Relief because I've been secretive. I've been hiding the most amazing thing ever to happen to me. Trepidation because I know that from now on things really never will be the same again.

Ever since the NATO exercise in Germany I've been a different person but on the surface of my life there's been barely a ripple. Regiment, house, wife, daughter. I've stopped swearing and drinking and no-one's even remarked on it. But now the lads know I'm a Christian I'm not completely one of them any more. In my heart, without forming the thought to myself, I've known that since I sat watching the lads when we left Germany. I was seeing them in a new way, and it was a detached way. I began the separation then. Now, whether I want it or not, they'll complete the severance. You can't be a Christian and one of the lads.

Their attitude is disbelief, a low-key joshing, but it escalates into challenges.

'So, if there's a God, why did John's daughter die?'

'Here in the East people don't have the same God. They're all wrong, are they, and you're right?'

218

I can't answer most of their challenges. Sometimes I try. I recognize their tone. It's just the tone I used to challenge Larry.

'Oh, Jesus Christ!' people swear. 'Oh my God!'

I've never bothered about swearing before but now this grates on me. Do they know the power and importance of the words they're bandying around?

'Look, have you ever stopped to think what you're saying?' I try interrupting once or twice. People stare at me and take a step back. Sometimes they say, 'Sorry, mate.' Other times they get aggressive, 'Well, you never minded it before. We've all got to watch our language now you've come over all godly, have we?'

When we sit around the fire at night there's all the usual banter and joshing. Talk about this girl or that.

'Watch it, lads, the God squad's here,' someone will suddenly say, and there's a silence. I should fill it with something but I don't know how to respond.

Somebody destroys a leech with mosquito repellent.

'Oooooh, thou shalt not kill!' say the boys, eyeing me playfully.

My relationships are different now, some fractured, some strained, some more distant. Only with Al are things just the same. He doesn't join in when the lads challenge me and when I try to talk to him about what's happened, he listens. I detect slight, very slight, signs of embarrassment. I understand that. I know he's had a religious upbringing but that for him, with his public school background, religion is something private, not something you talk about.

We're joined by a new boy, a cocky Cockney of about my height and build. He's clearly a good soldier but he's too keen for us. His last experience of the jungle was on selection where everyone does everything right and you're under constant pressure. Now he's all eyes and ears: 'Watch out . . . what's that over there? Look out!' But this isn't selection. There's work to do and we set ourselves targets which are realistic. Experienced soldiers are at one with the jungle. We melt through it leaving no trace of ourselves. We don't use machetes, we just bend branches out of our way. We come across big animals, an elephant perhaps, only feet away. It looks at us and then turns and disappears noiselessly into the undergrowth. A big, unhurried creature which moves silently, at the right pace for the terrain. That's how we should be. But the new boy's always in a hurry, like all new boys.

'We could get there faster if we do this . . . let's use our machetes, OK, mate?'

We grimace at each other.

'Calm down. You're not on selection now. Just get at the back of the patrol and watch what we do.'

The lad's name is Andy McNab. McNab's just into the Regiment but I see that it's already occupying the number one position in his life. His ambitions, his skills, his soldiering, they're everything to him. And I'm moving the other way. Suddenly being a soldier is just a part of a much bigger picture. My family, my new faith, other things matter now.

One night, I write a letter to Peter Wood about it all. The effect this new faith is having on my life. How hard it is for some people to take on board other people's faith.

Back in England, it's a wet and drizzly July and Claire's jealous of my suntan. When she looks at me I can see she's hoping that there's been some change. She's searching my face for a return to the old me, but the old me's gone. Charlotte says some new words and I clap heartily. She laughs and says them again. It's almost like old times, except that Claire is on edge. I know that she's tense because she doesn't want me to start talking God talk at her. I'm careful. I want to convert Claire, but I've already grasped that haranguing her isn't the way to do it. Gradually, she relaxes.

She takes me into Hereford to see a house she wants to buy. It's a rambling old red-brick town house with an immense Aga-warmed kitchen and two sitting rooms and a mish-mash of different levels and bedrooms.

'Thinking of opening a bed and breakfast?'

'It's just the sort of house I want, Frank.'

'But the maintenance . . .'

I've inspected the rotting windows, the sagging roof beams, the missing tiles.

'It could be wonderful.'

I suspect the house reminds her of the enormous home she lived in when she was small, before her father left.

'You wait,' says Claire, 'a clean-up, a coat of paint and some new carpet and it'll be lovely.'

Her mind's made up. Our cottage, half-finished though it is, sells rapidly, and for a good price. A contract on the new house is quickly signed.

In camp, it's Northern Ireland training again for my squadron. I've been through this before but it doesn't matter. Back to basics for everyone. Taking the gun apart. Parts of the weapon. Dry practices. Then out onto the ranges for daily firing. For the new boys it's vital training and the rest of us still follow it with the same commitment and concentration that we did the first time around. Nobody ever gets lax about this kind of thing in the Regiment. And for me, although I'm changing and my priorities are changing, it's as important as ever to do well. More important, perhaps. Now that I'm a Christian, I have something to prove to the other lads.

'You have to be the best soldier for God,' Larry told me, and that's what I'm going to be.

We practise ambushes, house assaults, close target recces, vehicle surveillance. All the training situations which are set up for us are realistic and we play them for real. That's why as many boys die training as fighting. Before most Ireland tours we do specialist training. Last time I was a sniper, this time, a photographer. I learn to take pictures from a helicopter, or through a window or from a long way off with telephoto lenses.

Training is intensive but I still find time to visit Peter Wood. We're moving any day now, and will live quite near him. He thanks me for the letter from the Far East. I feel that because of it he takes me more seriously. He tells me to come to church on Sunday and I say I will, resolving to myself that I'll persuade Claire to come with me.

To my amazement, Claire agrees. There's a truce, an unspoken one. I'm going to ease up on the Godspeak and she's going to come to church.

Early Sunday morning and we're wondering what to wear. I have a good supply of check lumberjack shirts. Not suitable. I want a white shirt. Between us we manage to produce a white shirt from deep in the wardrobe where the clothes hang too close together. I even find a tie. Claire's mother's looking after Charlotte and you can feel her disapproval of the whole enterprise. Claire can't find her handbag. I hope she's not going to make us late. I go outside to start the car and she runs out and gets into the car in a breathless, businesslike way. She's making it all just like an early morning rush into the office. It's Sunday, and I'm going to church with my wife. I don't want to belt down the lane like Monday, but time's short and I'll have to.

During the prayers I kneel and shut my eyes tightly and try to communicate directly with God. I'm aware all the time of Claire next to me. I try not to look at her but I know that when she leans forward to pray her body is too loose and that when she bows her head there's nothing pious about it. She sings the hymns with surprising gusto. A throwback, I assume, to her school assemblies.

The truth is that I'm as baffled as she is by this new language I'm hearing, by the ritual of communion, by the church itself and even by the clothes here. I'm an outsider. This place isn't bringing me closer to God, it's coming between us.

At the end of the service Claire catches my eye. I know she's going to start behaving as though she's got a bus to catch. She's going to be first to leap into the aisle and shoot out through the door, so before she can move I put my hand on her arm. While some of the congregation are leaving, many of them remain in their pews. I explain in a whisper that there's coffee now. Peter Wood's already told me about this.

'Coffee!' she says, far too loudly. 'Is that what they all come to church for? Coffee?'

I say, 'Shhhhh.'

At coffee in the church hall, Claire shudders as a few beaming members of the congregation try to make us feel welcome. I'm hungry for information about the Church in particular or Christianity in general and I take people aback by jumping in quickly with too many questions. Sometimes they ask me about myself and my faith. When they learn I'm a soldier they say, 'Oh, you're the young man who wrote the letter!' I learn that Peter Wood has read out to the whole Church parts of the letter I wrote him from the Far East, about the reaction of the other lads to my Christianity. I'm half shocked and half flattered.

Next to me, Claire is trying to look wifely but I can tell that she's tense every time a Christian beam is turned on her. She jumps when people ask her if she'd like more coffee. She's scared that they'll start asking her about her faith. She wouldn't like to confess, in this company, that she doesn't have one.

Driving home in the car she says, 'Frank, admit it, that was awful.'

I explain that I'm looking for the right church, and you have to start somewhere. Privately I'm sure she'll think any church is awful but I agree with her when she says, 'That's not the place for you. You don't talk that way. You're not like those people.'

I wish she'd said 'us' instead of 'you'. But she's right. I spent most of the time I was in church trying to do the right thing. To sing at the right volume, to kneel the right way in prayer, to ask the right questions and give the right answers. To fit in. I'd felt people taking a step back from me when they learned I was a soldier.

Ever since my conversion, and for the first time in my life, I've been led by feelings. I have a direct relationship with God now. But nothing I saw or heard at St Peter's seemed to have anything to do with these feelings. And, despite visits to Peter Wood, I've been left

222

with a thirst for knowledge about Christianity and the Bible which St Peter's does nothing to quench.

I persuade Claire to give St Peter's one more chance but the following week things are much the same. To myself alone I admit that I can't turn into one of these people, with their well-modulated middle-class voices and their Christian language which doesn't have the words to express the emotions I feel.

I call by at the bookshop to see Rupert. We chat for a while over coffee. We talk about the commandment: 'Thou shalt have no other gods but me.' I've been reading about it. It seems to me that my collection of little gods probably has to go. I discuss this with Rupert. I explain to him that over the years, as I've travelled, I've collected little wooden gods. Even on this most recent trip to the Far East I picked up a gorgeous carved spirit of the jungle, an old man with big wooden earrings. But I also have a little Hindu elephant god, a Buddha, some interesting painted masks . . . Rupert agrees with me that they have to go.

Can you just put Buddha out for the dustmen to take away? That doesn't seem the right thing to do. I imagine the spirit of the jungle in the trash along with the old orange juice cartons and the potato peelings. Finally, I go into my workshop and take a saw to them all. I cut up Buddha, the spirit of the jungle, the Hindu, all the masks. I saw them into small pieces and when I go back upstairs and find Claire has the fire alight I fetch the little lumps of black and brown wood and I burn them. I watch them hiss and burn blue and red and yellow and I have a feeling of satisfaction, of service to God.

'What's all that?' asks Claire.

I tell her and she rolls her eyes.

# 17

'IT'S FANTASTIC,' SAYS AL, LOOKING AROUND AT OUR NEW HOUSE.
Claire's organized the paint and the carpet and it does look good.

'I like it,' Al says, nodding approval at Claire. 'And this is a great
part of town.'

Al has a neat new house on a small development out of Hereford.
I bet he had a big, rambling home as a kid. His family are Scots and
they lived by the sea. He spent his childhood fishing and crabbing
and swimming.

'It's really convenient,' Claire says. 'And the people are nice around
here.'

The new house is in a professional area. Some of the owners are
new and they're upgrading their homes. There are builders' skips on
the pavements, mums pushing baby buggies, brightly coloured front
doors.

'Why don't you look for something around here?' Claire suggests
to Al. She's happy tonight, cooking things at her enormous farmhouse range.

'I might do that,' he agrees.

'Well, hurry up. Prices are rising.'

'You'll end up babysitting,' I warn him.

He smiles. Al doesn't mind babysitting, which is good, because
we're expecting another baby.

Within a short time he's found somewhere near by and his own
house is on the market.

'Now we've sorted you out with a house, I have to find you a wife,'

Claire says. Al laughs, that big, surprising, open-hearted laugh of his. But he doesn't tell her not to.

'I wish you'd get to know Judy . . . why don't you ask her out?'

Al says he might do when he gets back from Northern Ireland.

In camp, we're given a full update on the current players in Ireland. We hear their histories, see their photos. Some of them are the same terrorists we followed before, who've managed to escape death or arrest. Sometimes I feel I know these people like I know my friends. Their houses, their families, their mates, their pubs, their routes to work. But I've never even spoken to them. And there's no way we could ever be friends.

A few are men we saw jailed on an earlier tour.

'What's he doing here? He was put away!' we say when a familiar picture comes up.

'Sorry, lads, he's out again.'

We groan. Weeks of surveillance and close target recceing to pin him down, and he's out again in a year or two.

Just before I'm due to leave, Peter Wood loans me a book about Dietrich Bonhoeffer. He says I'll enjoy it but the first few pages are heavy going and the picture on the front cover is discouraging. Dietrich Bonhoeffer is a small guy with glasses. German. Do I want to read a book about him? I know I have to if I want to see Peter Wood again and I have to see Peter Wood again because I've no other Church to go to. I take the book to Ireland.

Our base is a stockade within the confines of a well-protected army camp. It's basically a big warehouse. There are no windows. The lights are on constantly. We sleep in Portakabins inside the warehouse. There's an area for vehicle maintenance, a stores with special equipment, and a lock-up for our own personal weapons. There's a small firing range where you often can't fire because people are asleep in the Portakabins.

I have a room to myself. Al's sharing with someone next door. I know he's there because I can smell coffee. Al's taught me a lot about coffee. Before he joined I was like the rest of the lads. If it was hot and wet I drank it whatever it was. Al, on the other hand, has his own small coffee machine and little silver bags with a different coffee in each one. He's a coffee connoisseur. He introduced me to the tastes and smells of real coffee and now I want to drink it too.

One night Jake and I drop off a patrol to do a sensitive task in the borders. We're both corporals, which is some indication of the importance of the job. But, as the drivers, we don't know anything about it, not even who the target is. We just know the drop-off point, the pick-up point and where to get them in an emergency.

We're driving a Ford Escort van and we drop off a three-man patrol a few kilometres from their target. We drive out of the area, but not too far, and park until we're told to pick them up.

We're fully armed. Jake's driving and I'm covering with my weapon. It's a sub-machine gun, a Heckler-Koch 53 folding stock short barrel job. There's one magazine cocked and loaded. Another spare 30-round magazine is clipped next to it. In the bag at my feet I have another 4 magazines and another few in my pockets. The worst thing is to run out of ammunition. On my belt is a pistol and spare magazines for that. In the bag are some more magazines for the pistol, some smoke grenades, some field dressings and, most important of all, a big flask with a brew in it. Not, on this occasion, one of Al's specials, but some sludge from the cookhouse.

We're ready for trouble but we're not anticipating any.

We park up a little track. Shortly afterwards, a car drives past the track. It's driving very slowly. Its headlights are dipped. It crawls up the lane past our track and then turns around and comes back very, very slowly. There are a couple of figures in it. They grind to a halt near our turning, look towards us, and then drive on again. My heart starts to beat faster. Jake and I agree that it's time to move on now that we've been seen. Almost certainly there was a courting couple in the car, and almost certainly that's what they assumed we were. Almost certainly.

We get on the radio. 'Possible compromise, we're moving out, heading towards red alpha . . .' This is the pick-up point.

We slide out onto the lane. The car has turned around and now it's coming back. It starts to follow us. It's not a courting couple. Pulse rate up.

'Hmmmmm,' says Jake.

We're right on the border and it's a very hostile area. Probably it's a routine check by the other side to see who we are.

We drive on and the car stays with us. We get to a T-junction and turn right. At this point, a second car has joined the first. They are both following us and they have both switched off their headlights. They are on sidelights only. This is very strange.

We accelerate. They accelerate. We slow down. They slow down. They're driving very close behind us now. My gun is on my lap, a reassuring weight.

I tell the radio that there are a couple of cars behind us and they seem to be hostile. But, no panic, we're OK. We're touring the

226

area and when the boys are ready we'll pick up the patrol.

No panic, but we're excited. Jake's a good driver. He takes us up to a junction, giving no indication whether he's going to turn right or left. At the last minute he swings right. They turn right too. There never was much doubt that they're after us but now there's none at all. I'm watching them. We know that there could be a hail of bullets any moment. We're ready for anything now.

When the road widens, the car behind suddenly accelerates to come up alongside us. It's an old orange Ford.

Jake says, 'I'm going to let them come up. We'll get a good look at them.'

My safety catch is off. My whole body is tense as the car rolls up parallel with us. Inside are two masked men. All we can see are their eyes and their eyes are looking at us, scrutinizing, assessing. Who are we? We have long hair, old clothes and do not look like anybody in the security forces. On the other hand, we might be. And if we are, which force? Their eyes are crawling all over us. I'm looking at them, looking for guns. If I see guns I can shoot. I'll blast their heads off. But I don't see guns.

Jake puts his foot down. He's anxious for them not to overtake because then we'd have one behind, one in front. The van spurts forward and we take off, roaring away with the orange Ford and its mate in hot pursuit.

We're moving at speed, our hands sweating and our hearts racing. Suddenly, as we approach a junction, a third car swings towards us and tries to block our path but Jake swerves and passes. This third car joins in the chase. They've obviously radioed for help. I'm on my radio too, watching and giving a running commentary. For the next ten minutes we swerve along the lanes, turning to the right and the left and the right again. We're travelling in a big circle, zooming down the same roads twice, three, four times. Gradually the aggressors are joined by more cars, until there are six of them chasing us. That's a minimum of twelve men, probably more. Jake's throwing the wheel around. He's flinging the van around corners, its engine roaring. Things are getting sticky now. We're excited. Something's going to happen tonight. We want to pick up the boys and get out of here alive but there's no word yet from the patrol and there won't be until the job's finished.

We continue our mad dash into the night, escorted by six more sets of roaring gear boxes and screeching tyres. Suddenly we round a bend we last rounded perhaps ten, fifteen minutes ago and piles of rubble have been strewn across it. Somehow Jake gets the van through this makeshift roadblock and, as we do so, word comes that the patrol's ready for us.

I remind base that the patrol must know we're being hotly pursued. We'll try to lose this group for a few moments when we get near them, but they'll have to be fast. Very fast.

As we hurtle towards the pick-up point, Jake and I both realize that, with the other boys in the van, we'll be in a different position. Instead of being hopelessly outnumbered there'll be five of us, fully armed, against twelve of them. What looked like bad luck is turning into a wonderful opportunity. This could be a fantastic head count for us.

The circumstances are mad but we stay cool enough to make a plan. We radio to base that the patrol should be warned we'll be taking on some players on pick-up. When we get round the next bend we'll disembark into anti-ambush drills and open fire as their cars round the bend behind us. The rules of the game say that we are being chased and are therefore on the defensive. With our reinforcements we have every right to go on the offensive.

We have to get a lead over these cars to give us enough time to pick up the patrol. Jake's always a good driver. Now he's turning into a demon. The van's fishtailing around bends, wheels spinning, tyres objecting. Jake's throwing it at the road and I'm sitting in the back with my gun on my lap, operating the radio with one hand and reading the map by torchlight with the other. Somehow, amid this madness, I have to know exactly where we are.

'OK, in three hundred metres we'll be coming up to a track, there's a sharp bend to the right . . .' It's like navigating for a rally driver only we're being pursued by six cars and I have to be ready to shoot back if they open fire. By swinging the other cars off at the corners we gain the lead we need. We screech to a halt at the pick-up point, and the guys jump in the back.

They bring a breath of cold night air into a van which is hot with tension and sweat.

I radio, 'Pick-up complete. Send the QRF.'

'What the hell's going on?' say the lads.

'We've been chased for the last half-hour.'

'By who?'

At that moment the other six cars come screeching up behind us. The lads just stare.

'By them! But it's OK, we've sent the password and we're going to take them on.'

Adrenalin's shooting around all over my body. We're going to take them on and within a few minutes the QRF is going to be here. The

Quick Reaction Force is on constant standby with helicopters, Land Rovers, whatever's necessary to get to a conflict within ten minutes. From the moment I gave the word I know it'll be no more than three minutes before the helicopter takes off, no more than five before it's overhead, and less than ten before we'll be joined by at least twelve fully armed marines. We have a chance of taking out twelve, perhaps as many as twenty IRA men on the ground. It's going to be a terrific contact.

'OK,' I say to the lads, 'what we're going to do is—'

'Just a minute,' interrupts a voice, 'I'm in charge.'

It's the voice of the staff sergeant. He's been with the patrol and he's two ranks above me and Jake. And now he says, 'Just get us straight out of the area.'

'But we've been chased for half an hour!' I say. 'And now we've got a chance to take out upwards of twelve players—'

'Forget it.'

Jake and I can't believe our ears. We say, 'You're joking. You must be.'

'Take us out of the area. Now.'

The six cars chase us for another fifteen minutes and then we're clear. Jake concentrates on his driving but I can see from the back of his head that he's livid. I'm silent with rage. As soon as we're back at base we turn on the staff sergeant.

'Why?' we yell.

He says, 'It's my job. You were just the drivers on this one and I was in charge.'

I'm still angry, very angry. I know we've missed a significant opportunity because a colleague panicked. He didn't have the full picture and didn't take the few moments necessary to find it out.

We're called to give an incident report to the chief RUC constable of the area. He listens to our story and then double-checks. 'You say masked men came up alongside you and they were driving aggressively?'

'Yep.'

'Well, if one of my officers had been in that situation and hadn't opened fire, I'd sack them.'

We explain that we had a job to do and for us at the time it was important to pick up the lads. Plus, it so happened that by doing nothing, we'd amassed a whole collection of IRA men which could all have been dealt with at once. Except, they weren't.

Later, intelligence gets back to us that we'd run into a big IRA bomb team. They had watchmen out checking the area and it just happened that we turned up. The first car which had spotted us parked up the track was the patrol car. Because of us, they pulled off their job and so the bomb wasn't planted that night.

A whole IRA bomb team and we could have had the lot of them. But we didn't.

But our colleague's mistake wasn't the only mistake that night. Big Al Slater was on QRF liaison at that time. This means that he's living in a little block on the helipad listening to the radio and kitted up and ready for any action which might arise. He'd been listening in to the whole story and as soon as we gave him the password to send the QRF he was up and yelling for everyone to get going.

But the QRF commander, an officer, stopped him. He said, 'No, we can't go yet, there hasn't been a contact.'

Al said, 'There's a contact situation going on.'

'Well, have shots actually been fired?'

'Not yet, but it's imminent. There's six cars full of players and we've got one patrol there.'

'I'm sorry,' said the officer, 'I've got my orders. No QRF until there's been a contact.'

Al got shirty. He said, 'Stuff your orders. We have to go now. The boys are on the ground and they're heavily outnumbered.'

The officer said, 'No.'

Al said, 'Get your boss, then.'

The officer phoned his colonel and said, 'Look, I'm on the helipad and I've been told by the SAS liaison officer that he wants a QRF, but there hasn't been a contact yet. Do I go?'

The colonel, without finding out more about the situation, said, 'No, you don't go. The Quick Reaction Force rule is that you only respond to an actual contact.'

If we had got out of the van and opened fire, it would have been another ten minutes before the helicopter arrived, and that might have been too late.

The next day Al returns to camp and puts in his report. It goes straight to the top. Al, as man in charge of QRF liaison, is summoned up to tell his story to one of the Northern Ireland generals, and I, as man in charge of the van, am summoned with him. The general listens to the whole story without saying anything but I can see his jawline working on its own, as if he's chewing on something. I realize he's chewing on his own anger. By the time we finish, I can see that he's livid. He makes us tell him the story again.

Then, surprisingly, he says, 'Would you like a beer?'

We stare at him. 'Er . . . a beer?'

He reaches into a fridge for two tins of Heineken and takes the top off them both with a fizz. He says, 'Here you are. Two beers.'

We say thanks.

He says to Al, 'Now, would you like to put your feet up?'

Al is speechless.

'I'm serious,' says the general. 'Do put your feet up.'

'Put my feet up where?' asks Al. I have an almost uncontrollable urge to laugh when the general pats his desk.

'Here please. Just put your feet up on my desk, Al.'

It's first names. We're sitting with a general drinking his beer and Al's got his feet on the general's desk. Whatever next?

The general picks up the phone and tells someone to send in a colonel. It's the colonel who refused to send the QRF. The colonel comes in and he looks scared. There's me and Al relaxing with the general and no-one offers him a drink. The general keeps him standing there while at his request Al and I retell our stories. The colonel knows he's in trouble. His face begins to hollow out as we speak. When we've finished he looks at the general like a dog waiting for his master to hit him.

The general says, 'If this man, or any of his colleagues ever, ever, speaks to you again, it's me speaking to you. Do you understand? When they speak, you jump. Got it?'

This man is a colonel and he's looking at a couple of corporals and all he can do is splutter and say, 'Yessir.' It's a nice moment for me and Al but it does nothing to ease the frustration we both feel.

At a debriefing session back at base, we tackle the staff sergeant who pulled us off the job. He says he took the decision that his patrol's task was more important than anything Jake and I wanted to do. We couldn't judge that, since we didn't know what the job was at the time, but when we find out it's clear that there was no way it was more important than taking on a whole IRA bomb team. The staff sergeant simply didn't weigh things up. He couldn't see further than the end of his own job. I feel raw with fury. Al's the same. We're overwhelmed by the frustrations of working in this petty, bloody conflict.

'It makes me want to leave the Regiment,' I say.

'Me too,' says Al.

I'm not sure if either of us really means it.

We even discuss something which makes us feel better. We could take out some leading players ourselves, quietly, without telling anyone. We'd be unrestricted by the rules and regulations which we feel have given the terrorists such an unfair advantage. We'd do it unhampered by other people's bungling.

231

Are we the first to talk this way? How many other men, out of sheer frustration, have hatched plans they've told no-one about? How often have our boys gone out into the night to become terrorists themselves? Of course, there's no evidence that anyone has done more than talk about it.

Eventually, we reject the idea. Every time we start to think about it we go for a run instead.

'Did you mean what you said the other day about leaving the Regiment?' Al asks as we run around the perimeter of the big army base.

'Of course I've thought about it.'

'I had an offer recently,' he tells me. 'Good money.'

The security companies are always trying to recruit from the Regiment for close-protection work or military jobs overseas. For highly trained professionals, the turnover in the Regiment is remarkably high, and one reason is the money we can earn.

'It was good money, but not as good as the security company rake-off.'

The gap between what they charge for your services and what they pass on to you is legendary.

'It would be an easy market to undercut,' he says.

'You mean charge less?'

'Charge the clients less and pay the lads more. It's a bubble just waiting to be burst.'

'Let's do it,' I say, only half joking. 'Let's leave and set up our own security company.'

On the next job that comes up, Al and I put on camouflage. A mortar attack is expected on a security base and we're to lie in wait for the men who are planting the bomb. We'll see them coming and pull out the rest of the boys, who'll be nearby.

Al takes a light machine gun, I have an M16 Armalite. We arrive at the site, which is right on the border, just as dawn is breaking. On one side of us is the wall of the security enclosure, on the other open countryside. And I mean open. We can't find any cover at all except for one tiny area of trees. After a lot of whispering and sign language, we hide ourselves in this little copse, but with misgivings. It's too obvious a hiding place, because it's the only one.

We lie down in the wet leaves and damp earth. It's a drizzly November morning and there's a smell of fungus. But the weather doesn't bother us. Goretex is the big new thing. It's supposed to be completely waterproof and we're wearing the wonderful jackets we've heard so much about, so we know we'll be dry.

The rain stops drizzling and starts pouring. I think I can feel water dripping down my neck. It works its way down between my shoulder blades and then into the small of my back and then soaks its way through all my clothes. Al confirms in a whisper that he's getting wet too. So much for the mighty Goretex, we think.

Just after daylight comes, so do footsteps. They're sloshing down the muddy track towards us. Voices. Men, carrying something. I tense, guessing that this is it. The men come right up to our bush. I am rigid, not with fear but with anticipation. I feel vulnerable. The problem with digging yourself in like this is there's no cover from behind. There's nothing to stop them coming up from the right angle and shooting you without you even knowing they're there. So Al and I are on the alert, safety catches off. The men sniff around a bit, messing about in the very bushes where we're hiding. We lie still on the outside but inside everything's moving fast, my brain, my heart, my blood. The men seem certain to find us. But they don't, they just walk off.

We get on the radio and tell the boys to stand by but they say there's a problem. It's going to take them an extra 20 minutes to get to us because they have to go around a roadblock. We say, 'Twenty minutes!' We know the team we're up against consists of eight to ten heavily armed men.

Just then some more men arrive. They also mess about in the bushes and go away again. Every time they appear we say, stand by, stand by, with sinking hearts because we know it will take the boys 20 minutes to get there. But the men just disappear again. We don't know where they're going and we can't move to watch them. There's always the feeling that they know we're here and are going to attack from behind. We lie listening until our ears hurt with listening. We tell the boys to stand by at least four times, until they just say, 'Oh yeah?'

At midday, when we expect to get out of our hole, we're instructed to stay until night. We have one pack of hard tack each to eat and that's all. There are five biscuits in a pack and we guess we have to make them last. Luckily the packs are waterproof. That evening we ask for permission to come out but are told to stay here all night. So we do, lying in our cold wet pit and munching on our tack. Once or twice in the middle of the night we manage to sit up noiselessly and it feels terrific to stretch and curl the different bits of our bodies which haven't moved for hours. Apart from these moments, we're just lying motionless. We have to be ready for attack all the time and after 24 hours of being so alert we're shattered.

Whenever we ask for permission to leave, we're told to stay longer. We find ourselves here for another night. This time we try to take it in turns to sleep, half an hour on, half an hour off. On a few occasions when we're both supposed to be awake and on the alert I begin nodding off on my rifle. My nose keeps coming down on my rear sight. Al sees this and bites into his hard tack biscuit and the noise of the scrunch wakes me up instantly each time. He thinks this is very funny.

We're still here on the third day. By now my foot, which has never recovered from the trenchfoot I suffered during selection, feels completely detached. I assume it's there but I don't have any proof. We're so drenched that we're past feeling wet any more. Whenever I feel my legs stiffening up, I roll, very slightly, onto one side and wiggle my toes, the ones I can't feel, just to keep the circulation going. Then I do the same on the other side. These movements are minute but they're so satisfying.

The thing to look forward to, apart from getting out, is a good shiver. This is a terrific feeling and it's completely involuntary. You just have to lie there and wait for it to happen to you. It's a deep shiver of your whole body and it generates heat. You can feel your body moving frantically and warming itself, and you can actually feel the blood flowing down your arms and legs. Your teeth chatter too, which can be a liability when you're hidden. We've probably had about three or four good shivers each by now.

We can't talk much but know we must maintain some communication so that if either one of us gives in to exposure the other can tell immediately. You can't diagnose your own exposure. You just don't know it's happening to you. Your skin goes pale, your speech gets incoherent and you're overwhelmed by lethargy, but you don't realize any of this until after it's all over. If you survive, that is. So we whisper a little, when it's safe to do so.

On the fourth day they send another lad to join us in the middle of the night. He goes behind to cover us and that's a relief: a three-man team is a good fighting team.

'Have you brought any food?' we whisper.

'Well, no, but I've got my hard tack . . .'

By this time, hunger has passed. I just don't feel it any more, or the cold or the wet. All these things have become a norm. We're well past the irritation stage as well, where you have itches in places you can't reach to scratch. My thinking, which at first was fairly wide-ranging, has also become more limited. After the fourth day, I'm not sure if I'm thinking at all, certainly not about terrorists or bombs. Lying in our hole, waiting and watching, has become an end in itself and the psychology of this over time is that you lose any wider sense of why you're there. At first I talked to God a lot in my head. Now, it's hard to concentrate on even the simplest of prayers.

We end up staying in our hole with our biscuits for six days. At last we're pulled out, stinking, shattered, hair all over our faces, soaking and freezing. But we're happy. This has been six days of hard soldiering and that's what we like.

We go straight to the bar, get a dozen pints down our necks and off to bed to sleep solidly for about a day with no-one bothering us.

Later, we learn that the squadron storeman ruined the Goretex by putting all the new jackets into the washing machine with detergent on a hot wash. Intelligence tells us that the men who so nearly found us on our first day weren't terrorists but people crossing the border and hiding goods to avoid customs.

Our next job is sniper work for me. I'm covering a road where we know that an IRA hit team is planning to murder a UDR man on his way to work. As a safety measure, the UDR man has been prevented from leaving home that morning, and none of us has been allowed to impersonate him. The chances of catching a hit team when there's nothing for them to hit seem low but I'm dutifully in position, 200 metres away, on a hillside. I'm covering a road junction with another sniper. He's far away to my left. If we both fire at the target, our bullets will intersect at right angles.

A car drives up to the road junction. It stops. It waits. It doesn't drive off. But its engine is running. The driver appears nervous. He's looking all around him.

I am convinced, without even looking through my sight, that this is the getaway car for the hit team. And when I look hard, I can discern his face. I think I recognize him. I believe I know his name. He looks like a player. A bit player, not one of the really tough hitmen, but a terrorist all the same.

I want to shoot. But do I know for sure, 100 per cent, that this is a terrorist? It's unlikely, but possible, that it's a civilian who's waiting for someone.

The car remains there for fifteen minutes and for fifteen minutes I agonize. Of course, I don't get a command over the radio to shoot. No-one wants responsibility for a shot like this. The other sniper isn't the kind of guy who would work on his own initiative. Should I?

I lie on my hillside weighing up the problem. If he's a civilian he might have a wife and family. That would be a terrible mistake. I'd

235

get ten years for murder, but I'd be out after five. What about my own wife and family in that situation? What about my career? But if he's a terrorist, shooting him would be the right thing to do. I believe this as a soldier and as a Christian. Killing this man might prevent many more deaths.

Eventually, the car drives off.

'They just don't want to tell you to shoot. None of them wants to take responsibility,' I moan to Al later.

'They don't take responsibility even if they do tell you,' he reminds me. This is true. A soldier carrying out orders is still responsible in law for his actions. In theory, you have the right not to shoot. In practice, you must shoot. If you really disagreed with the order, you'd have to shoot to miss.

'I came very close to firing.'

'You could always have said it happened by mistake. It's cold, you were wearing gloves, the trigger's sensitive.'

'They'd still put me away.'

'If he was the getaway driver, he wouldn't have been a major player anyway. Just a fringe guy,' Al points out.

We switch on the Belfast evening news and learn that a UDR man has been killed at work. A car drove into the factory. The gunmen were hiding under blankets in the back seat. They shot their target, got away in the car and then abandoned it. There is a description of the car.

I groan. 'That's it. That's the car and I had it in my sight! And all the time there were two gunmen in the back seat under blankets! I could have had them too!'

'It was at eight forty-five a.m.,' says Al. 'What time did they pull away?'

'Eight thirty.'

'Very quick. Just fifteen minutes to change target when our man didn't show up.'

All this is confirmed when intelligence comes through. The Provos can't resist boasting about their exploits down at the pub. It's important to most terrorist groups to have heroes. Even apart from ideology, the need for hero worship is an important part of terrorist psychology and the pubs provide this in Ireland, making them a good source of intelligence for us.

Sometimes I wonder how much we have in common with these bad guys. I have no problem, as a Christian, believing that they are bad. That they attempt to thwart the democratic process with violence and a ruthless disregard for loss of life. That they must be stopped before they kill more innocent people. But I also wonder if their motives are so very different from ours. Ideology. Heroism. Death or glory. And I know enough Irish history to suspect that, if I'd been born a Roman Catholic here, I'd possibly be one of them.

# 18

EVER SINCE THE EXERCISE I LED IN THE SUDAN I'VE BEEN WAITING FOR
my promotion to sergeant and now I'm next in line. I'm made up to
acting sergeant for a few weeks to see how I get on. Another test in
the Regiment's relentless assessment process. As operations sergeant
I'm based back in the ops room. It reminds me of my signalling days:
the boys are out on the ground doing the job and I'm shuffling around
pieces of paper and listening on the wrong end of the radio.

I'm given a big job to organize. I'm in charge of 16 SAS men, 4
helicopters, 2 detachments of the Royal Ulster Constabulary and 100
regulars. I run around liaising and organizing briefings. I've lost my
feeling that I'm just a signaller and I can't do it. This time, I know I
can. The job is a success. But when our lads talk about it in the bar
afterwards, I'm miserable. I just wanted to be out there with them.

I'm relieved to be a corporal again. When I hand control back to the
ops sergeant I say, 'Keep your job, I don't want it.'

On my return, I'm sent out with another sniper to recce a rooftop.
Intelligence tells us that a gang of gunmen is going to hide up here
and fire at an army patrol.

'There's nowhere we can hide on that roof to ambush them,' we
report back to the boss. 'But we can lie low on surrounding roofs and
shoot from four hundred metres if they're fully armed.'

'No closer?'

'No closer. There's no way we can arrest them or challenge them,
only fire.'

'Forget it, boys. If you can't arrest, you can't fire.'

238

'Even if we can see their weapons? And they're pointing them at an army patrol?'

'No way.'

'So it's OK for them to go up and spray our boys with bullets, but we can't do the same to them?'

'Rules are rules.'

Al and I go for a run around the perimeter. I'm frustrated by this last job and when I tell him about it he says, 'I've been thinking about that idea we had for setting up a security company.'

He hasn't mentioned it for so long that I assume he's forgotten it. But typical Al, he's been thinking.

'We'd need capital. Maybe my dad would loan it to us.'

Al's dad is an engineer who set up his own company.

'Are you serious?'

'Yep. Are you?'

'Especially since I was ops sergeant. If that's all I've got to look forward to in the Regiment . . .'

'You'd only do it for a year,' Al reminds me. 'Then you'd be staff sergeant and back on the ground with the boys.'

'Not for long. After that it's just a change of office every time you get promoted. Weight gain. Big bellies.'

We accelerate a little.

'Corporal's the best rank,' agrees Al, who is one too. 'You've got some responsibility but you're still one of the lads and there's almost no paperwork.'

'Can't stay a corporal for ever.'

'If we had our own security company, we could pick which jobs we wanted.'

'Will you really talk to your dad about it?'

'Yes. When I go home for Christmas.'

Days follow of waiting in our windowless warehouse back at base. Sometimes we're waiting for a job, sometimes we're waiting for darkness. Waiting's frustrating. Working in Northern Ireland, our actions hampered by rules which wouldn't apply in a real war, is frustrating. People spend a lot of time in the bar. Small irritations blow up into big arguments that are settled on the squash courts. Not with a game of squash. With a full-scale punch-up. The squash courts are the only place you can fight in private.

We have a few days of good weather and I try to get some free-fall organized. I finally arrange a helicopter to take us up. I go around the boys asking who wants to jump. One of the other lads has been trying to organize a rugby game and I poach some of his people.

'We'd get an effing game of rugby going if it wasn't for your effing free-fall,' he growls at me when we find ourselves walking past the PortaKabins together.

'I thought we were a free fall troop,' I say, and carry on walking. He stops and starts abusing me. I yell back. Within seconds he's grabbed me and I'm punching him, then he's punching me back. It's just a scrap and a couple of people soon pull us apart. 'Come on, grow up.'

We retreat, snarling at each other.

The free-fall is fantastic. It's unusual to get such a clear, windless day so late in the year and after being penned into our hangar for so long the flying comes as more than a relief. It's a burst of joy. I look at Al's face and see he's experiencing the same thing. Freedom. The pleasure of using our experience, fitness and skill in this element. But the pleasure isn't unalloyed. We fall knowing that we're easy targets for a sniper's rifle once we're under canopy, and consequently we fall fast.

I start some serious woodwork out in an old shed. We run a lot. Sometimes Al and I break the days up by buying coffee. We go to a small shop where the coffee is arranged in sacks around the edges of the room.

'Get ready for the smell,' says Al as we walk in. He stands there, breathing coffee for a few moments. A helpful assistant approaches. She smiles at Al. A lot of women smile at Al.

'What's the Kenyan like?' he asks.

She discusses Kenyan coffee with him. She invites him to try a cup and he accepts. The silence in the shop is broken as she grinds the coffee. While she busies herself, Al moves from bag to bag, sniffing at the beans.

'Do sit down,' says the young woman. She has a pretty face and long auburn hair.

We taste the coffee and Al buys some. The assistant measures it carefully and puts it in a small silver bag which she folds and tapes. We agonize some more and then buy some Colombian too.

'You only had to ask her,' I tell Al as we drive back to camp, 'and she would have gone out with you.'

He laughs, as he usually does when the subject of girlfriends is raised.

'Claire's finding you a wife,' I remind him. 'You could always find yourself one first. Don't you ever think about getting married?'

'Do you recommend it?'

'Yes. And I recommend having children. When Charlotte was

born . . . well, I just can't tell you what I felt. I can't describe it. There's nothing else like it.'

He nods.

'I'd like to get married. I'd like kids. I just don't seem to meet . . . erm . . .'

Al's a soldier. He doesn't talk about his emotions much, except perhaps to his elder sister, to whom he's very close. But I know what he's saying. He's saying that he's waiting for someone special and she hasn't come along yet.

'Anyway,' he adds, 'what's the hurry? How many boys in the Regiment have happy marriages?'

'We're leaving the Regiment next year, remember?'

We talk about the security company we're going to set up and I sense Al relax. He's more at ease talking about this than about wives. He doesn't much like talking about religion either. I think of ways to convert him, search for sections of the Bible which will speak to him. I want him to be a Christian like me. I've learned from Larry that as a Christian I have to spread the faith and I want to do my friend a favour and spread it to him. Maybe even to some of the other lads.

But the other lads are hard work. Their lethargic mood is catching. They lie around in the Portakabins reading. I start the book Peter Wood gave me and after a chapter or two I'm hooked. Dietrich Bonhoeffer was a Christian who participated in the unsuccessful plot to kill Hitler. He was imprisoned and, out of sheer spite, executed just before the Germans lost the war. The cover shows a fat, bespectacled little guy of the sort you knew you could fight with and beat in the school playground. But he was a remarkable man, who believed that Christians must fight evil in the world. He condemned the German Church for not standing up against the evil of Nazism. Churches, he said, are attempts to make concrete the difficult and indefinable concept of faith. Building high, glorious cathedrals is easier than wrestling with the sheer simplicity of Christianity and God's love. Churches are unnecessary. All you need to be a Christian is a Bible.

Of course, I read the Bible every day, but I know I need guidance. I'm stumbling blindly through it.

At last, there's some action. An attack's imminent on a part-time member of the security forces. The Provos are likely to hide outside his isolated house in the country and shoot him as he leaves. We have to get into position there before them, but when we arrive we find no cover except for one group of bushes. Once again, we have to compromise good soldiering to circumstances and hide in the

241

obvious place. Of course, it's possible the terrorists are already here, watching us from the bushes.

'Er, what should we do?' asks my lance corporal.

I say, 'You stay here and cover me.'

I walk towards the bushes. They are 300 metres away across open ground. In them lurks a terrorist. His gun is trained on me, his safety catch is off, his finger is ready to make the tiny movement necessary to kill a man and that man is me. He doesn't want to do it yet. He wants as full a picture as possible and only time, these valuable seconds, can give him that. He wants to know how many of us there are, where we are, why a single man is walking across open ground towards him. Perhaps I appear unafraid. Perhaps he thinks I am very, very stupid. Perhaps he thinks I don't know he's there. He's sweating. He doesn't understand but he knows that he must kill me and in so doing will kill himself. It isn't easy to kill people, even if you're a terrorist. But you believe you have to do it.

I am afraid. I'm afraid that he'll shoot me in the face. With every step my body waits. My eyes are fixed on the bush and although I know I'm moving towards it I feel frozen with anticipation. In a few seconds, I could see God. In a few seconds I could know the unknowable. It's this which makes my heart beat faster. These are long seconds, as long as a lifetime.

Finally, I get to the bushes and he still has not fired. I reach out and part the branches. Any man here, reluctant to shoot, sizing up the situation, waiting, waiting to kill, can wait no longer. I brace myself for the impact of the bullet but none comes. Silence. There is no-one here. No terrorist. No gun. Nothing.

And now our positions are reversed. We take up our places in the bushes and when the gunmen arrive and they cross open ground to reach this cover, they'll experience the same horror as they walk to the bushes.

We hide here for several days, waiting. But the gunmen do not come. Finally we leave the man, the bush, the house.

When we return to our windowless shed, one of the guys goes berserk. He's been sitting in a bush for three days seething with anger. His anger has fuelled him through the long, still nights. Back at base, that anger erupts in a torrent of shouting and abuse.

'What the hell did you do that for?' he yells.

'What?' Have I kicked him getting out of the van or closed the door on his fingers? But no, the last few days, without speech or movement, haven't happened for him, and he's still watching me walk across that 300 metres towards the bushes.

242

'You're insane. What were you doing, just walking up to cover like that? You were asking them to shoot you! You could have died! What the hell were you playing at?' He swears at me and his anger swells his face.

I say, 'I can't be killed.' I speak calmly, my voice low.

'What!' he barks at me, after a silence.

'I can't be killed.'

'Who do you effing think you are, Jesus effing Christ?'

He is bawling now, and a small crowd of lads has gathered round to watch. I say, making sure my tone is in marked contrast to his, 'I can't be killed. I believe that I'm guaranteed eternal life.'

He is speechless. There is a terrible silence. Into it, I continue, 'If one of us has to be killed, it should be me, because I'm a Christian and therefore I'm guaranteed eternal life. I'm the best one to die, that's why I did it.'

'Are you saying,' asks someone else, a threat in his voice, 'that we're scared and you're not?'

'No. I'm saying if any of us die, it should be me.'

Actually, I know they're right. As patrol leader, I should have told a trooper to check out the bushes. It was a trooper's job, it had to be done and there was no way to do it without risking someone's life. But I felt I couldn't put a trooper into that situation. I wasn't being brave when I crossed that ground. I wasn't afraid to die, I was excited at the prospect. And I believe that God has a purpose and, if he wanted me dead, that's what would happen. I remember my intention to spread the Christian faith whenever possible but now I look round at the undisguised anger and hostility in the boys' faces and I ask myself if I haven't gone too far this time.

The boys all start arguing, there's a lot of shouting and indignation. It's almost impossible to extricate myself amicably from this level of hostility. Somehow I escape to the target shed and get on with my woodwork.

At eleven, as usual, I stop and go to the bar for a couple of pints.

'Ah, here's Joseph,' someone says, without affection.

The lads often challenge me. The bar is a place of thrust and parry for me because the boys have been mugging up on texts which are supposed to disprove the New Testament.

Tonight, because they're angry, they're not challenging me on my faith but on my soldiering now that I'm a Christian. They know that I'm ready to kill terrorists, they acknowledge that I'm one of the fastest runners and most would agree that I'm probably the best shot. But, because of my faith, they've begun to doubt me.

They develop hypothetical situations to test me.

'Let's say someone's found an arms cache. A kid. A farmer's son. It's been reported and you're observing it now to see who turns up. In the night, someone does come . . . when do you shoot them? Do you challenge and risk the life of your patrol?'

This situation isn't so hypothetical. It's well known that two members of the Regiment found themselves in court because they fired at a figure they believed to be a terrorist. This figure had gone straight up to an arms cache in the middle of the night. The correct procedure, unless lives are endangered, is to challenge three times. The lads claimed they challenged and the figure spun round and pointed a gun at them. This was hard to believe because the figure turned out to be the farmer's teenage son, who'd originally discovered the cache and reported it and was sneaking back to take a look at it. The lads were found not guilty but the judge clearly doubted their insistence that they'd challenged.

'What would you do, Frank? As a Christian?'

'Challenge. I have to challenge because I mustn't kill the wrong person.'

'But if you challenge a terrorist in that situation he has time to pick up a fully loaded weapon and blow you away. And the rest of your patrol.'

'Yeah, better to be tried by twelve than carried by six!' someone else says. This is an old Regiment chestnut.

'I'd be too quick for him. I've got a gun trained on him already, remember.'

There is a heated argument. The lads are trying to prove my morality is endangering my good soldiering and possibly their lives.

They stare at me with red, beery eyes and glassy hostility.

'Someone could get hurt,' they insist. 'We're not all effing Christians with a little cloud waiting for us up in effing heaven.'

Al usually keeps quiet during these exchanges but, to my surprise, he speaks up for me.

'Someone could get hurt! That's what they said when we had a wagon full of terrorists and the QRF wouldn't come in. We're in the SAS, boys, we expect to get hurt. If you don't want to get hurt, join the Brownies!'

His intervention doesn't stop the argument but it takes the heat out of it. They carry on talking and I look around at their faces. What a strange bunch of individuals we are. They all think my Christianity's a form of madness but they're all mad in one way or another. There's Kev, who knows he's a reincarnated Viking. There's Si, who only reads books about the paranormal. Trevor's addicted to physical fitness like some men are addicted to drink. Only a few of the boys are normal, but they're so normal that they're weird. What a bunch of crazies we are. And we go out with our lethal weapons every day.

'Thanks,' I say to Al as we make our way back to our rooms. He shrugs. He doesn't want to be thanked.

'If you get hurt . . . if you die . . . what do you think happens, Al?'

He looks at me and I can tell he wants to groan. He wants to say, 'Don't start now, Frank,' but he's too nice.

'Well . . . I do believe there's more . . .'

'You do believe in God?'

He's standing outside the door of his room now. He wants to go to sleep and I'm asking leading questions about his faith.

'Yes, Frank, but I think it's personal. You're not helping yourself or anyone at the moment.'

I take a step back.

Al continues. 'I think you should lay off the lads. Not just tonight. In general. I mean, is it true you tried to give McNab a Bible? No wonder you got some flak.'

'But he might actually read it.'

'Well that's up to him, isn't it? Don't force it on people all the time.'

He leaves me thinking about his words. Of course he's right that I'm annoying people, and probably annoying him too with my attempts to convert him. But all through history Christians have annoyed people. They annoyed the Romans so much that they got thrown to the lions. Dietrich Bonhoeffer annoyed the Nazis. Christians must stand up for what they believe.

I go to my room and pray. I pray for myself and I pray for the lads. I pray a lot, but now I have acquired a new habit. I pray before each new job.

When the next job comes up I load my magazines, an act of hard aggression, and then I kneel on the floor by the bed. An act, I hope, of humility. I know this job is extremely dangerous. I tell God that I don't want any of our boys to be killed, not unless it's really necessary. I say, if it means that we don't kill anyone on the other side either, then that's better than losing one of us.

I pick up my weapon and leave.

This time Al and I are to be involved in close-protection work. We're guarding the UDR man who didn't leave his house the morning that I was sniper and watched his hit team waiting. Now intelligence tells us he is again going to be receiving the Provos' unwelcome attention.

This time he'll leave for work. Only he won't be in the car. Al will be at the wheel impersonating him and I'll be cover man, hiding in the back seat with a sub-machine gun. At first light I creep out through the dismal winter greyness and take up my position under a blanket. I nod off in my sleep-alert mode. I know the area has been staked out by our boys. I know there are armoured cars waiting to help us. I'm not excited, not yet.

The radio tells me that Al's coming out of the house. I wonder if wearing someone else's clothes is making him walk like that person. I wonder if, despite the pistol he's carrying, he's managing to look like a man on his way to work. It's a different walk from a man coming home from work, or a man going out for a drink or a man going out with a gun.

He gets into the car. I know he doesn't look at me but he greets me without moving his lips. I have an uncontrollable urge to laugh but Al is all eyes. He's looking for the vehicle which might contain the gunmen. He sets off, giving me a commentary, when suddenly he pauses.

'It's there!'

He starts to swear at the boys who've done the drive past. There's some kind of van, looking suspicious, and they haven't even noticed it.

To me he says, 'Up, up.'

I rise out of my blanket with my Heckler-Koch like Excalibur rising out of the lake. There's a red pick-up approaching with a tarpaulin covering the back. My safety catch is off and I see the van clearly to my right. I cover it . . . and nothing happens. It just drives past. False alarm.

'But how did the lads miss that one?' I ask.

'Go down again, I'll call you if I need you,' says Al, and I sink down under my blanket. For some reason, perhaps because our adrenalin has been pumping, the anticlimax makes us laugh. We know our lives are in danger and we must be ready to act fast but we are both convulsed with laughter. Al can't even give the commentary he's laughing so hard.

We get ourselves under control and Al turns back into a UDR man on his way to work. I feel vulnerable. I am completely dependent on Al. As a soldier I need my eyes and ears and now I have neither, I have only Al. I would rather depend on him than anyone but I still don't like it. I sit tight wondering where I am and what's out there. I keep asking Al, what's going on? And he says, nothing, I'll tell you when something's going on. How could I have been laughing just a few minutes ago? Now I'm scared. It's an old fear returning, the fear of being shot in the head, of not seeing the bullets which hit me but feeling them penetrate my face.

I start to sweat under my blanket. The atmosphere in the car is electric. We know they'll pounce soon and the further we drive the more sure we are of it. One of our cars is ahead and another waits to pull in behind us, both heaving with lads and weapons. We know this, but it doesn't help.

And then it happens. Al says, his voice taut, 'That's it. Up!' And I know from his tone that this really is it.

I come up again with my gun and the radio. A yellow van has just completed a slow turn from a side road in front of us and it's driving along far too slowly now. I tell the radio, 'Yellow van, yellow van, up, up.' I put down the radio now because I need both hands for my gun.

The van crawls along. We keep our distance. We have strict instructions not to get closer than 200 metres. My gun is over Al's left shoulder. We expect the lads to respond to our call any minute but so far we're on our own. The rear windows of the van are blackened and suddenly they move. Plates are dropped down. Inside are the hunched bodies of men holding weapons. We know that this is it. Everything in our bodies, our eyes, our ears, our arms, our toes, every cell is focused on the van in front. Finally the van stops in the middle of the road, indicating that it will turn right into a junction. There is no oncoming traffic and nothing to stop it from turning but it stays in the middle of the road. It is waiting for us to get closer. I imagine what the men inside are saying. They are swearing at us, willing us to approach.

We do. We have no choice. We know that we've passed the 200 metres safety zone and slowly, very slowly, we near the van. Al is angry. Where are the boys? Why aren't we going for it? Somewhere there is a car full of lads, fully tooled, who should have swung past us, but for some reason, perhaps because of the earlier false alarm, they aren't there. The men in the back of the van are getting bigger.

Then, surprisingly, the van turns right. We move past it but it turns around and comes straight back up behind us. This manoeuvre has, finally, alerted the team leader in one of our cars. As the van accelerates to overtake us – it has to fire from its rear windows – our boys emerge in hot pursuit. At last.

The boys open fire through their front windscreen. Bullets are flying everywhere. The terrorists in the van return fire. Our other car sets off in pursuit.

247

But the team leader has spent too long training bodyguards.

'Protect the VIP!' he yells over the radio, instructing me and Al to pull in.

'What!' says Al, who wants to join the action. 'What's he talking about? I'm not a VIP!' He's forgotten that Al's an SAS man impersonating a VIP.

Our boys roar off down the road, to the sound of gunfire.

'I don't believe it! I just don't believe it!' says Al, his voice a mixture of fury and disappointment. Despite the order, we follow them.

Our lads engage in a wild chase with the terrorists for the next twenty minutes. We give chase but we never succeed in getting to the thick of the action. We can hear cars screeching and the sound of gunfire. The firing is almost constant. It is hard to imagine that there isn't a bloodbath.

Finally, the terrorists manage to get far enough ahead of our boys to lose them at a T-junction. The Provos turn right, our boys turn left. By the time the lads find the yellow van again it is abandoned, along with some of the terrorists' weapons. The men inside have legged it across a field and stolen a car from a nearby farm. They've escaped, all of them, as far as we know, unhurt. Amazingly, none of our boys is killed either. But a civilian has been caught in the crossfire. He does not survive.

Back at base, we go over the whole incident. Intelligence has told us that these are top terrorists, heavily armed. We could have taken them out. Al is livid. He and I have measured the distance which eventually lay between us and the terrorists' van as 30 metres. If the killing zone starts at 200 metres, that's ridiculously close and we still find their failure to fire baffling. As we were driving very slowly it accounts for many seconds when action could have been taken by our boys but wasn't.

Al wants to know why the team leader waited so long before attacking. The boss says that he wanted to see what would happen after the earlier false alarm.

Al keeps saying, 'But why didn't you go for it?' until he's told to calm down. It's not that the boss's reticence risked his life. That doesn't occur to Al. It's the failure of the boss to act, and act at the right time, which galls him.

'And what was that nonsense about "Protect the VIP"? Why did you try to pull us out?'

Ross, the patrol leader, begins to look uncomfortable. He's a career man, identified early by the Regiment as someone who'll do well, and

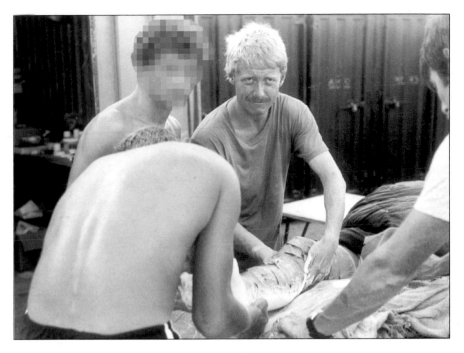

Me as a patrol medic, having escaped the Royal Signals at last, plastering a damaged leg in Africa. Its owner was a training casualty and had to be airlifted back to the UK.

Lying on a pole bed in the rain in the Far East in 1984, shortly after I became a Christian. The lads spotted me reading my Bible here and suddenly they all knew about my conversion.

The Far East, 1984. The new Christian separates the wheat from the chaff (Matthew 3 v.12) with the locals, all part of the hearts and minds programme.

Al Slater with parachute in the summer of 1984, six months before his death.

Going under. Pastor Phil Thomsett from Elim Pentecostal Church baptizes me in the River Wye in Hereford, August 1985.

Me looking discreet, behind Sir Ralph Halpern and his daughter, Jennifer. *(Rex Features)*

Mountain climbing, 1989, when I was a theological student.

White-water canoeing, another way of escaping the books and learning while I was a student at Oakhill Theological College.

Moments after being ordained, Hereford Cathedral in the background.

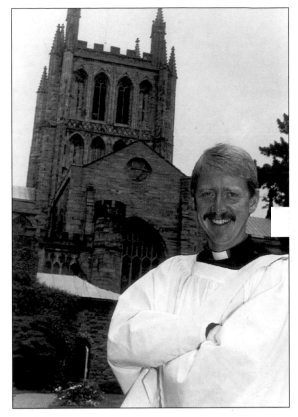

Perhaps a certain awkwardness here: it was the first time my family from the north-east saw me wearing a dog collar. From left, Michael, Dad and Gary were sitting in the garden with me after my ordination.

Family photograph, taken when I became a curate in 1992. From left, Francis, me, Claire, baby Nathan and Charlotte. Only our third child, Lucy, is missing . . .

Lucy with Mum and Dad.

The climbing curate poses for the local press in 1993.

# The Regiment Collect of the Special Air Service Regiment

Oh Lord, Who didst call on Thy disciples to venture all to win all men to Thee, grant that we, the chosen members of the Special Air Service Regiment, may by our works and our ways dare all to win all and, in so doing, render special service to Thee and our fellow men in all the world, through the same Jesus Christ Our Lord, Amen.

The special prayer 'Collect' of the SAS.

he's been promoted fast. Too fast, Al and I have privately agreed. Ross has one eye on his career and another on the job and that's no way to work.

Although the UDR man is still alive, a civilian is dead. We both feel the whole job has been bungled. Eventually Al walks out of the debrief.

Afterwards I find him in his room. There's no nice smell of coffee today. He's getting out his running gear. I can see he's still furious. When he's angry his whole face seems to close up behind his anger. His movements are noisier than usual. I say I'll go with him and I meet him outside a few moments later and we start to run. I'm angry too and his fury infects me until we're both stomping around the outer perimeter of the base, banging our feet against the ground, taking it out on the Irish soil. We run round and round the base like a couple of mad horses.

'I'm deadly serious about leaving now,' says Al. 'I mean it. We can set up something to go to and I think we should do it.'

'Would your dad really help us?'

'Yes. I want to do it.'

It was the seed of an idea and somehow, over these last few months, it's rooted. There's decision in his voice and it comes from weeks of thinking, not from a moment's anger.

'I do too.'

It needs almost no more than that for the decision to be made. We're going to leave the Regiment. We won't just be mates, but partners.

We run on and on and on until fatigue begins to take the edge off our anger.

As I run I think how incredible it is that no-one involved in today's action was killed. The cars are shot up, shot to pieces in fact. The number of bullets fired was remarkable. Whole magazines of Armalite bullets were flying around but none of us died. I'm sure that when the terrorists got home to their wives and children they wondered too how it was that they didn't manage to kill any of us.

Suddenly, I remember my prayers. How, before we went out on the job, I'd asked God: let us all live, God, even if that means the other side surviving too. I realize that I got exactly what I prayed for. None of them killed and none of us. The civilian I hadn't bargained for and hadn't mentioned. It seems to me that God is doing just as I ask and this is scary. I resolve to be very, very careful in future prayers.

I tell Al all this as our feet pound the turf to mud. But Al is still angry.

He says, 'Well, tell God to keep his bloody nose out of our business in future.'

I wish Al hadn't said that. I really wish he hadn't said it.

I'm sent back to Hereford to brief the boys there and help answer questions about the yellow van incident because our failure to produce results is so embarrassing. I take some flak. This is part of an annual meeting where jobs are reviewed and discussed. There's usually a visiting dignitary who comes in to give a speech and this year it's the secretary-general to NATO, Lord Carrington.

He gives us a woolly but interesting overview of world politics and potential areas of conflict. Afterwards there are questions. To everyone's horror, Gorilla's hand goes up. Gorilla is a big wild man. Everyone hopes that Lord Carrington won't pick on him but he says, 'Yes, yes, the big man over there with the moustache.'

The room is deadly silent. Everyone's waiting for something awful to happen.

Gorilla says, 'Well, you've talked about politics but what about wars then?'

Lord Carrington hovers over his papers.

'Er . . . wars?'

'Yeah. Wars. We just want a war. That's what we really want. We just want to get out there and kill people.'

Lord Carrington looks at Gorilla with incomprehension. All the officers are muttering, 'Shut that man up!' A rustle has gone down the room as men shuffle around trying to look as if Gorilla isn't in their troop. But Gorilla is unstoppable.

'Well, I'm sorry, sir, but we're not interested in your politics. We just want to kill people.'

Lord Carrington is lost for words. He flounders. He moves on to the next question. There are red faces all round.

'It's true, isn't it?' Gorilla's saying to anyone near him who'll listen. 'It's true.'

I go home after the briefing for a day or so. Claire's looking very pregnant now. She's still throwing up. I drive her to the hospital for a check-up.

'Do you realize', I say to her, 'that if this car crashes now, I'll go to heaven, Charlotte will go to heaven, our unborn baby will go to heaven, and you won't?'

'Thanks,' she says.

250

I go to see Peter Wood at the church.

'I love the Dietrich Bonhoeffer book,' I tell him. 'I've read it twice. I've made notes all over it. Can I buy you another copy?'

He's taken aback but agrees. I return to Northern Ireland with Dietrich Bonhoeffer.

# 19

A FEW DAYS LATER I TALK TO GOD IN MY PRAYERS ABOUT ANOTHER JOB. But what to pray? I can't ask God to protect us from being hurt. As Al says, we're SAS men, not Brownies. I can't ask God to help us kill as many terrorists as possible. Carnage doesn't seem a Christian thing to ask for, it's the sort of request that Gorilla might make. But the idea of saying, 'Lord, protect us as we kill these other people . . .' is uncomfortable. So, carefully, I choose my words.

'Lord, we're more than halfway through our trip. Whatever's going to happen, let it happen tonight.' Then I surprise myself by adding something which might be foolish.

'I know, Lord, that if we lose one of our boys, we'll get at least two of them.'

Some of the boys judge the success of a tour on its body count. This may be terrible but it's a fact. They're sheepish about that last incident, where we fired so many bullets without killing a single terrorist. Next time they don't want to miss.

This job is very similar to the last. An active service unit is planning to take out another UDR man. This time intelligence isn't sure exactly who the target is. Al is dressed in green army gear and working with local units on a list of possible, although unlikely, targets. He's not delighted. Close observation accompanied by a platoon of excited local infantry with little chance of seeing action is not his idea of a great night out.

My patrol is looking after the prime target, a man in his sixties. He lives in a remote farmhouse with a Sterling sub-machine gun with which he answers the door. There are four of us, plus an officer. The officer is a new boy. Before leaving I've been pulled aside by the boss and asked to take the officer along.

'He's a good guy, Frank. He needs to broaden his experience.'

'No way, boss, not tonight. We should take him out on something harmless. He'll only get in the way tonight.'

'Come on, Frank, he's from the Paras, he knows what he's doing, he's got Falklands experience.'

So the officer has come with us on the condition that he stays out of the way.

We no sooner arrive at the farmhouse than there's news from intelligence. The terrorists are driving a blue van and it's packed with explosives for an attack. All change. We're all pulled off our jobs and told to find the blue van. I think how pleased Al must be.

We've been dropped off and so have no vehicle. We borrow the old man's van. I drive. McNab is one of the boys in the back. It's December. The weather is that Irish speciality, freezing fog. It lies waiting in the dark, a thick veil, its white knots leaping out at the car headlights. The road is a sheet of ice. I feel the van slipping from under us once, twice, but somehow I always manage to stay on the tarmac. We're listening to the radio and travelling slowly, very slowly.

Al's team of four reports that they've seen the blue van, parked in a lonely country road. We're heading in their direction, in fact we're only a couple of miles away, but whenever I accelerate I feel the car running away from me.

Over the radio, we learn that Al's patrol is turning around and stopping at the end of the road where the van's parked. The others are getting out, Al's staying with the car . . . then the lads are challenging someone. The rest is confusion.

We don't need the radio to pick up the sound of gunfire. It's carried to us loud and clear in the cold night air. There's shouting over the airwaves and then someone is yelling for a helicopter. There's a casualty. The helicopter can't take off in this weather. Get a helicopter, now. Confusion. Yelling. People call for an ambulance but ambulances won't come out where there's a terrorist incident still going on.

The name of the casualty is confirmed. It's Alastair Slater. They don't say how badly hurt he is but there's shock and anger in their voices.

Al's been hit. I don't feel anything much for a while. I'm numb. I'm just driving the car. I don't entertain the possibility that Al might be dead. I don't think about anything except that we're heading to the place where Al's lying and we're going to find the terrorists who've shot him. My mind, my whole body, is focused on getting us there.

I'm driving at a snail's pace through this white night, slithering and sliding and skidding. And when we arrive, what will we find? In the car is silence, except for the radio. McNab is tense. He tells me to slow down. Outside is irregular gunfire. The area is being cordoned off. There are terrorists lurking somewhere in the fog, fully armed.

Over the radio there's still an argument about the ambulance. Finally a voice says, 'Don't bother. He's dead.'

Al's dead. This news, this night, is surreal. Al can't be dead.

We know we're getting close to the action because we're stopped and challenged by another SAS patrol. It's that sort of night. No-one knowing anything for sure, not who their mates are, not where the terrorists are, not what's happening twenty yards in front of their noses beyond a wall of wet whiteness.

When we arrive I get out of the van and see the body of a dead terrorist.

'Get down, get down,' one of the lads hisses at us. 'There's terrorists about!'

I say, 'Well we're not going to find them lying down there, are we?'

'They're around here somewhere!'

'If they were, they'd have opened fire on us. Come on, let's find them.'

'Just get down you idiots.'

I say, 'If you don't want to get hurt, join the Brownies. Now, where did you last see them?'

'They were over there.'

I take young McNab and try to find them. He stumbles with me into the night and the fog. He's a first-rate soldier but I can sense his lack of enthusiasm for this. We end up following a swollen river bank. I'm the corporal and he's the private and I put him in front, covering him from behind. As the new boy he doesn't argue. He would probably prefer to stay dark but after all that shooting we're tactically overt with bright lights and flares. There is a deep, foggy silence, broken occasionally by distant sirens or more local gunfire. The skin of my face tightens and numbs in the cold air. My eyes are every-where, looking for terrorists. My thoughts are full of Al – not anything in particular about him, just a glimmer of an acknowledgement that he might be gone, the dawn of a grief which is going to be fierce.

We find nothing, and return to the others. We stop and search a few cars and then pull off.

Back at base we go to the bar.

Al's dead. I can't fully comprehend that he just doesn't exist any more. Al's too big to die.

In the bar, and over the next three or four days, we learn the full story of that night.

The road junction where Al and the boys stopped their car was an ambush site. Explosives were hidden there and four hitmen lay in the bushes. They planned to phone the police and say there was a bomb in a local hotel, then when the police car came they would blow it up with the explosives they'd planted, and annihilate it with gunfire.

They'd just got their bomb in position and hadn't even finished setting it when a car full of long-haired blokes turned up. Who was it? IRA? UDR? That's the game in Ireland. No-one's sure who's who on the ground and there's always a period of indecision while everyone tries to work out whose side everyone else is on.

One of the men had parked their blue van and was walking back to join the hitmen when two of our lads walked up the road and challenged him.

The terrorist said, 'It's OK, it's only me.'

Either he genuinely thought that he was talking to one of his own boys or he was buying himself time. He must have been in no doubt who he was talking to when they said, 'Halt, stand still!'

At that point he started to run for it and our boys opened fire over his head to make him stop. When Al heard, 'Halt, stand still!' he went to the back of the car and got out a Schermuly flare. As the lads started firing, the Schermuly went up and everything which had been hidden and secret and dark was suddenly lit up. It's unlikely but possible that at this point Al saw the hitmen. They certainly saw him. They opened fire on him at once. He was shot a number of times and killed instantly.

The fleeing Provo had halted to save his life and was being searched when Al's body was discovered. The terrorist then took advantage of the situation and tried to escape again, drawing his pistol. The rules say that in this situation you can shoot, and he was shot dead. Despite the security cordon, the other terrorists managed to escape, but one was killed in the process. He drowned trying to swim across the river. I like to think that McNab and I flushed him into the river, but I don't know if we did. The other two hitmen were picked up by the police the next day, suffering from exposure.

Some of the lads who were with Al feel guilty about his death. You do. You ask yourself, could I have done things differently? If I'd done this, would he be dead?

I say, 'At least Al went down fighting and that's what he would have wanted.'

The others say, 'No. He was just shot.'

But I'm insistent. I'm convinced that's how Al must have gone. He was a soldier through and through and no ordinary soldier. A lot of men, even in the SAS, won't give 100 per cent. They're not cowards but they're still short of 'Who Dares Wins'. They don't want to be hurt. But Al thought that not getting hurt is for Brownies. The others just shake their heads.

A few days later, forensic confirm my conviction. Al did, indeed, go down fighting.

'Slater's weapon had been fired. He'd fired off five or six rounds.'

So he had known they were there. Maybe he heard something, turned and engaged them. Maybe he saw them starting to run when he put up the Schermuly. No-one knows, except the surviving terrorists, and they aren't telling.

I remember how Big Al had said God should keep his nose out of our business. And I remember my prayer. Sure enough, two of them had died and we had lost one man. Al.

I don't make close friends easily and Al meant a lot to me. He was a solid, dependable guy in a world where there are many wild men. I always knew I could trust him. We'd spent a lot of time together. We'd driven many miles. We'd operated very closely. We'd had good laughs. He was a man with a conscience who thought about the moral side of our work. There are few such soldiers.

I phone Claire. I don't want her to hear it on the radio news. She starts to cry immediately. I fight back the tears. What can I do to comfort her on the end of a phone when I can barely speak for fear of crying? What can I say to make it less terrible that Al's dead?

I ask to be the one to clear out his locker. It's a sad and a dangerous privilege, locker-clearing. Your job may be to protect others from what you find there, and to protect the dead man from other people's knowledge. But no-one protects you. You may discover something about your friend you'd rather not know. Or you may find something which makes you wonder if you ever really knew him at all.

Al doesn't let me down. I find a Bible. There's nothing significant in that, lots of the lads keep a Bible in their locker as a sort of lucky charm. But Al's is thumbed. He also has a prayerbook which has been well-used and tapes of Christian music, a whole series of them. They are out of their cases. He'd been listening to them. Al was a quiet Christian all along. Not like me, hot with the experience of my conversion. Just steady and quiet about it, the way Al was steady and quiet about most things.

I sit on his bed, feeling embarrassed. I tried so many times to convert Al, and he was already converted. For a moment, I'm angry. Why couldn't he have talked about his faith to me? Just once? Why did he have to keep his thoughts and feelings to himself so much?

Wearied by emotion, fighting back the tears, I compile all the little things which make up a life. The toothbrush. The comb. The half-read book. The bag of half-used Colombian coffee. I start to list whatever I find. I put everything in a box. The box smells of coffee.

'He liked his coffee, didn't he?' says the lad who shared Al's room. I nod.

I learn that we can't be spared to go to the funeral.

'I'm going,' I tell the boss.

'I'm sorry. I'm very sorry. But you're needed here.'

'You'll have to get someone else over.'

The others agree with me and at last replacements are brought in to cover for us so that we can go back to Hereford.

We never cry at funerals. We're SAS men.

Claire weeps buckets. On the way home she says, 'I don't understand it. Most of the men you work with are animals.'

She means this. She doesn't like your average Regiment man. She's sobbing again now. The tears fall down onto her belly.

'You're dripping tears all over the baby,' I say.

She ignores me. 'Most of them would be no loss. It wouldn't matter if they did die. Why did it have to be Al?'

The death of your closest mate of course makes you more aware of your own mortality. On the one hand I feel that now I'm a Christian I'm ready for death, on the other, seeing the effect Al's death has on Claire makes me understand how awful for my family my own death would be. I don't want Claire to be another SAS widow, telling my children what a nice guy and a good solider I was.

'Al and I were thinking of leaving the Regiment,' I tell her.

She looks at me.

'We were talking about setting up our own security business. He thought his dad would put some money in to start us off.'

She turns away and stares out of the car window.

'Well, that's all over now,' she says. It doesn't occur to her that I might still leave the Regiment, without Al and a business to go to. But Al's death has strengthened my resolve.

Over Christmas, I'm given a short break. I tell Claire I'm resigning. She's always wanted me to make the family more of a priority and now I am, but I sense that she's not delighted. She doesn't say, 'How will we pay the mortgage?' But I know she's thinking it.

'I'm doing this at least partly for you,' I tell her.

'I don't want you to make sacrifices for us,' she says. She's often complained that I'm off having fun in sunny places while she's coping with all the family responsibilities. And she's usually been right.

'It's not a sacrifice.'

If I stay in the Regiment my future's in an office. That's not much to sacrifice. I'll be tested and assessed and all those deep insecurities, about not being an infantryman, would keep on surfacing. That's not much to sacrifice either.

'I know you haven't been as happy at work lately as you used to be,' she agrees. 'Maybe it is time for a change.'

I nod. My mind's made up.

'I know what's going to happen,' she adds, looking mischievous.

'What?'

'You're going to become a missionary or something like that. You'll probably drag us all off to Africa.'

I stare at her. This is her hormones talking now.

'Claire, what are you on about?'

'You've got religion and you're not going to dabble in it, are you? That's not you.'

'You're crazy.'

'Here you are, trying to find your way through it all, sort it out, get on top of it. That's you. You won't be satisfied until you can teach other people, like a pastor or a missionary. Everything's a challenge for you.'

I leave, shaking my head. For an intelligent woman, Claire can be amazingly stupid sometimes.

I visit the sergeant major at home to tell him that I'm leaving. He's not surprised to see me.

'How's it going, mate?'

'I've had enough. I'm going to bin it.'

'Right. OK.'

I am half hoping he'll argue with me. Perhaps he will ask what's wrong, why I want to leave, if there's anything to put right? But he doesn't. He doesn't even remind me that about eighteen months ago I caused a furore by refusing to leave soldiering for signalling. He doesn't remind me how the Regiment made me permanent cadre, an honour which it will now seem I'm snubbing. I feel bad about that, but he doesn't mention it. He just tells me to get the forms from the squadron clerk.

Word soon gets around that I'm leaving. There are phone calls from the security companies about job possibilities. Nothing definite yet, but it's enough to put Claire's mind at rest.

'It's not really like leaving at all,' I tell her, 'it's just moving into the civilian wing of the Regiment. I'll be doing the same sort of work with the same lads. It's like another squadron.'

'Except the pay's better,' she reminds me.

I sign my forms in the clerk's office. I'm thinking to myself: the Regiment is always so desperate to recruit good men, it invests a fortune in training them and then when they say they're going to leave there's no attempt to discuss their decision.

The clerk just nods and takes my forms.

I leave the office knowing it really is all over. I'm going to complete this tour of Ireland. Then, in March, the boys will go on to some other job in some other place, and I'll stay behind in Hereford. I won't be one of them any more. Occasionally over these few days, walking along a cold street or in the night, when Claire's snuggled up to my back and the baby wakes me with its kicking, I'm overcome by regrets. I won't be one of the lads any more. I have to remind myself of all the arguments there have been in the bar over my faith. I have to remind myself that, as far as they're concerned, I'm already not one of the lads.

I wonder what God has lined up for me next. I still don't have a Church. I arrived home hoping that perhaps there would be a message from the nice white-haired man who took my details at the evangelists' meeting all those months ago but there is nothing and I accept that I won't hear from him now.

I visit the vicar of St Peter's again, Peter Wood. We begin our talk as usual, with me appealing for guidance. We end our talk on an agreement. I'm going to visit all the Churches in my area, even the Methodists, and see what I think of them. Without my saying anything, he has understood that I don't fit in at St Peter's. He isn't throwing me out, he's just throwing me to see where I'll land. He seems to understand that I have a spiritual journey ahead of me and that St Peter's isn't going to be my ship. I nod agreement. I'm anxious to start this project at once. I only have a few more days before I return to Ireland.

I wonder where to try first.

'What about the Roman Catholics?' suggests Claire naughtily. She knows that nothing would drag me into a Catholic church. I still retain that sense of secrecy and shame about my father's being a Catholic. Catch a Catholic, kids used to say, and give him a good hiding. I am emphatically not going to visit a Catholic church.

The nearest church is Holy Trinity. I phone the vicar and there's no reply. I am running out of days anyway. Holy Trinity will have to wait until I return in March.

I visit the Methodists. I find out the name of their minister and she comes to the door, a small, anxious, grey-haired woman. She has flour all over her hands. I explain that I've recently become a Christian and am looking for a Church and she brushes back her hair with her forearm so that flour doesn't fall into it.

'I'm so sorry,' she says briskly, 'I'm so very busy just at the moment. Can you possibly come back another time?'

'Well, no . . . I'm in the army. I'm going to Ireland in a few days and I won't be back until March.'

This ought to get me inside the door but her face is set now. 'That's all right,' she says, 'I'll still be here in March.'

I decide the Methodist Church is not for me.

It's time to return to Ireland and nothing has been resolved but I feel stronger. I've started the first leg of my spiritual journey and when I return to the UK I'll keep trying all the Churches until I find one. It occurs to me that I'm already attempting to replace the Regiment with some other kind of support structure. If I need such a structure, why not just stay in? Flying over to Ireland I'm seized with a desire to rescind my resignation. It was a crazy decision, taken when I was still confused by grief. But when we get back to our Portakabins and I see Al's empty bed, my decision seems again to be the right one. I'm ready to move on from this. God will take care of me.

Sure enough, within a few days a call comes inviting me to start work in Sri Lanka next April. The employer is one of the big security firms, and the money's much better than my Regiment salary. I accept the job.

The rest of our Ireland tour is uneventful. I do a lot of close-protection work for an MI5 man who claims to be doing a good job infiltrating the Provos. He was recruited when he left university about ten years ago and only now is he sufficiently integrated into the community for the terrorists to accept him. But this man is scared. He meets the heavy mob at their houses and in pubs and he likes to know I'm near by, with a back-up car available if I need it. I'm the guy hanging around at the bus stop who's flummoxed when a bus actually arrives. I'm in the phone box outside the pub. I'm at the next table.

'I feel completely safe when you're here,' he tells me. He's fallen for the Regiment mythology. I don't tell him that, if six terrorists decide to take him outside, there's very little chance that I'll be able to save him.

When he hears I'm leaving, MI5 approach me. I think about their job offer but turn it down because of the long hours and days away from home.

On our return there's a couple of weeks' leave. Then the boys are preparing to go off to Africa. Without me. I get ready to go nowhere while the boys get ready to go south. They're packing their gear, organizing their mosquito repellent, getting briefed on the job. I'm immersed in the bureaucracy of leaving.

I'm given a clearance chit. I have to go round each department getting a signature. The quartermaster has to sign to say I've brought back my gear. Then there's the pay office, the medical office, the dental office, the families officer, the RSM. The chief clerk signs for my ID card. They all have to sign me out. I traipse from hut to hut.

'You're off, then?'

'Yeah, time to move on.'

'Got anything to go to?'

'Out in Sri Lanka.'

'What's the pay like?'

'Good. Very good. Tax-free.'

I have known some of these people for the last nine years and such an exchange of pleasantries is a routine part of our existence. But this time, because it's the last time, it has a significance for me which they don't feel. I wish one of them would ask me a searching question. 'Is this really what you want to do, Frank?' but the conversation is light, the mood jovial. I play the game. I smile.

The day before the boys fly out, we have a farewell drink. It's a low-key affair. We're hunched over our pints when the boss calls us to order and makes a speech. I say a few words and a small bronze statuette of an SAS soldier is presented to me, as gracelessly as you'd expect, by Jake. There's an awkard silence as people turn back to their pints, then the murmur of men drinking and talking continues. As I drive home it's the silence I remember. The next day I get to camp and everybody's gone. The squadron offices are so empty that they echo.

The last thing I do is hand in my belt kit. It's a gut-wrenching moment. I've worn it for so many years in so many places that my sweat and movements have moulded it to my body shape. It feels uniquely mine. I keep the white plastic containers which we use for our first aid kits but I hand back everything else. It'll be dismantled now. Bits of it will be issued to other people. But basically, my belt kit won't exist any more. I leave camp feeling as though it's me which won't exist any more, not the belt kit. I don't look back.

I stop down the road, at the church. I stand outside the door, wondering whether to go in, and then decide against it. I walk among the graves, recognizing the names, until I find the one which is most freshly dug. Alastair Slater, says a temporary wooden marker. I stand looking at the turf-covered mound of earth. A big mound for Big Al. I feel that hard, numb place inside me which I've learned to recognize as grief. I know I'm not just grieving for Al but for myself and everything I've lost.

I glimpse another figure in the graveyard. Another ex-soldier, I can tell from his gait. He's much older than me. He's haunting the gravestones, visiting old friends, reliving old times. I'm seized by a desire to say something to him. I want him to tell me that there is a life after the Regiment. When I look round for him, he's gone. I'm alone in the graveyard.

The next day, when I wake up, I'm still numb. There's nowhere for me to go. No drive to camp. No prayers. No lads. I know, with a clarity which frightens me, that I've made a mistake. I shouldn't have left the Regiment. But I can't admit this to anyone. I'll have to pretend, to myself and others, that I made the right decision. The only person who'll know I've made a mistake will be me.

# 20

WAITING FOR THE BIRTH OF THE BABY, WE VISIT MY FAMILY IN THE north-east. I've told them all about my conversion and they avoid the subject if they can. I brace myself to discuss my faith but part of me is relieved when they don't want to know.

We visit Dad and Joanna and stay with Michelle. She's still alone in the big council house but, although she has the right to buy it for a knock-down price, she's leaving.

'I don't want it,' she says simply. 'I'd have to stay here another three years if I bought it and I don't want to. I want a flat of my own.'

Michelle always knows what she wants. She's started on her degree course now.

Michael stays at the house when he's on leave from the army. He gets drunk and brings girls home and Michelle's fed up with it. She's house-proud and she doesn't want him vomiting on the leatherette sofa.

Gary's doing well in the security business. He got married in a small, impromptu wedding last year and now we meet his wife for the first time. She's a keen spiritualist and when she tells us all about this, Gary shuffles about looking apologetic.

'I'm not sure if that marriage is going to last,' I say to Claire.

When we get back to Hereford, I continue the search for a Church which I began at Christmas. I phone the vicar of Holy Trinity. This time he answers. I explain that I recently became a Christian and am looking for a Church. He seems surprised by my call.

He tells me, 'Well, we have a service at ten o'clock every Sunday.'

I say I'll go but he senses this isn't enough and finally offers to visit. He's in no hurry. We fix an appointment for the middle of next week.

I ask Claire to visit Holy Trinity with me. After St Peter's she's not enthusiastic. I tell her that, since she's nearly eight months' pregnant, no-one will expect her to kneel and, to my surprise, she agrees to come.

We wear our smart clothes and tell Charlotte she's on her best behaviour and walk down the road to Holy Trinity. We wedge Charlotte between us and look around. The place is chock-a-block with clergy and they are all dressed up to the nines. Some are in big hats, some are in red, others in white, most have big gold ponchos. Charlotte is wide-eyed, thinking this must be something to do with Father Christmas. There are few ordinary members of the public like us.

The clergy parade around the church, a few of them carrying crosses so immense that they could pass as offensive weapons. They swing a big ball which seems to steam like a witch's brew. Puffs of smelly smoke are released, which waft all over the church.

'Incense!' hisses Claire in my ear. 'That's what Roman Catholics use! This place is Roman Catholic!'

'But it doesn't say so on the board outside!' I hiss back helplessly.

'Baby,' says Charlotte loudly, pointing to a small person hidden amid all this regalia. The baby is christened. We wonder if this is a special service of baptism or if they christen babies here every Sunday. We don't understand a word they're saying. The service might as well be in Greek. Occasionally I glimpse Claire giggling out of the corner of my eye but I know that, no matter how much she'd like to laugh, she's too shocked by all this to enjoy her laughter. That will come later.

Finally, a piece of paper we've been handed tells us it's time for Communion. This is Claire's cue to leave but I point to a discreet sentence. It seems to have been written just for us. It says, if you haven't been confirmed, please come forward for blessing rather than Communion. In order for the clergyman to know this, please carry your blue hymn book.

Determined that this Church and this service must have something to offer me, I say, 'Come on.'

'No way,' says Claire.

'Yes.'

'No, no, no!'

'Yes, yes, yes!' shrieks Charlotte delightedly.

'What will we do with Charlotte?' asks Claire through clenched teeth.

'Take her forward with us.'

'No!'

'Yes!'

I make a move, pulling Charlotte into the aisle, and Claire pulls her back. Charlotte giggles, perhaps nervously, in the middle. I am being a Geordie male and insisting. Claire is furious. People are beginning to look at us and this is probably what makes Claire give in. We go to the front of the church, clutching Charlotte and our blue hymn books. We kneel at the rail like the others and the minister, who is dressed more grandly than any Christmas tree I have ever seen, reaches Claire first. I wonder if this is what he'll wear when he visits us in a couple of days. If he does, the neighbours' curtains will certainly be twitching.

The man is carrying in his hand a disc of thin cardboard. He has been putting one in each mouth opened for him along the altar rail. When he reaches Claire, she offers him her hymn book. He is surprised and holds out the paper in response. Claire closes her mouth firmly. He rolls his eyes heavenward, looks exasperated, and tries to put the cardboard in her mouth anyway. She shakes her head. The man's expression changes from confusion to insistence. Maybe he is a Geordie male too. He does not want to pause long at this awkward woman. He wants to put his cardboard in her mouth and that is what he's going to do. With a well-practised movement, he stuffs it between Claire's reluctant lips. She glares furiously at him.

He reaches Charlotte and waves his hand at her. Charlotte is transfixed by this. I realize that he is blessing her and, despite everything, this gives me a warm feeling. Except that I know I am next for the cardboard. I am hoping that he's got the idea by now and thrust my blue hymn book at him but going fifteen silent rounds with Claire has only made him more determined and he shoves the cardboard into my mouth before I can put up a struggle.

The paper is thicker than it looks. It tastes of absolutely nothing except perhaps the wafer which used to come with ice cream at the cinema. It sticks to the roof of my mouth. I really want something to wash it down with and I see with relief that a drink is being passed around in a cup. This time it doesn't occur to me to resist, nor Claire. We take our sips meekly.

As soon as it is possible to do so, we leave the church. Claire virtually runs. Outside we walk briskly down the street, without looking back.

'I am never, never going there again,' says Claire when we are far enough away to slow down a little.

I say, 'Neither am I.'

By now I am beginning to wonder if there is any Church in Hereford, or anywhere, which speaks my language. It seems to me that everything which has happened in Holy Trinity, the words, the clothes, the rituals, is designed to come between me and God, not to bring us closer.

I'm interested in the Pentecostal Church. My friend at the bookshop, Rupert, is a member of just such a Church, but to his credit he's never tried to recruit me. However, I've learned enough from him to interest me. On the other hand, Larry has given me one piece of advice and it's to beware the Pentecostal Church. Larry, however, is from the Southern Baptist Bible belt, and to him Pentecostal means black. It is possible, given his background, that somewhere deep down inside Larry is a racist. So I decide to ignore his warning and visit the Pentecostal Church anyway.

I go in the evening hoping to get the name of the vicar from the board. The church is an old war prefab situated in a red-brick terraced street on the edge of town. I jot down the vicar's name and number and then hang around outside listening to the singing. There's a spontaneity and energy in there which attracts me and embarrasses me at the same time. People are shouting hallelujah. There are drums and guitars. I'm fixed to the pavement by it all. This Church couldn't sound more different from the smooth, orchestrated rituals of Holy Trinity.

I slink away but the next day I call the minister. To my delight, he offers to come round straightaway. It's the first really warm response I've had.

However, the Church of England vicar from Holy Trinity beats him to it. He arrives in a long black cassock edged in red. Quite a surprise when I open the door. He is not the man who administered communion.

'Hi,' I say, 'I'm Frank Collins.'

He hesitates before he says, 'Will Jewell.'

I say, 'Hi, Will . . .' and, sensing his disapproval, I add, 'can I call you Will?'

He's perhaps ten years older than me, in his late thirties, and he shuffles a little in his cassock before he says, 'Well, most people do prefer Father.'

I say, 'I think I prefer Will.' He's sitting down now and occupies himself with his cassock to hide his displeasure.

I ask about the service on Sunday without wanting to give away the fact that I took Communion without having been confirmed. I think this is probably some kind of sin and I'd prefer Will not to know my sins. He explains it was an unusual service. His curate is married to a bishop's daughter and we were witnessing the baptism of their first child. The place had been packed with clergy from out of town and the child's grandfather himself had taken the service.

So it was a bishop who had shoved the cardboard into our mouths and blessed Charlotte. A bishop from some other place who hadn't known about the local blue hymn book etiquette.

But Will Jewell is waiting for me to speak. I have summoned him here, he's waiting to know why.

'I very recently became a Christian—' I tell him, and he raises an eyebrow.

'Er . . . you became a Christian . . .' he interrupts. 'So, you weren't baptized?'

'Oh, no, I was baptized as a baby but that doesn't count.'

Will looks amazed. 'Why doesn't it count?'

'Because I was a baby and I didn't know what was happening . . . I mean . . . I've only just had this experience of conversion . . .'

Will is cool. He says, 'I don't understand this at all. If you were baptized as a baby then you've always been a Christian.'

Conversion is not a word that Will seems to comprehend. It doesn't take long for us to establish that we are poles apart. One God, but so many different theologies and understandings. When he leaves we shake hands again and stare into each other's eyes, both baffled. Christianity has, for some time, been a muddle for me, and the vicar has done little to help me find my way.

Shortly after Holy Trinity leaves, the Pentecostal arrives. Claire gives me an old-fashioned look. It seems to her there's a long line of vicars at the door. But she listens to what this man, Phil Thomsett, has to say. We get him a cup of tea and within moments, all of us, even Claire, have relaxed. He seems to be talking about God in language I can understand. I try to explain what's happened to me and he nods a lot. When he speaks, he reassures me.

I find myself telling him all the things I need to know. Why did Christ have to die? What's Passover? Cain, Abel, or the New Testament . . . I read the Bible but I'm lost with it. He smiles and nods. That's normal. Everything which has happened to me is normal. I feel relief wash over me. The minister explains that his Church runs many classes and study groups as well as Wednesday and Sunday worship. It's a teaching Church. It gives its flock experiences of many different sorts and part of that is the experience of discipling. I like the sound of this. I like the word experience, I like to think of myself as a disciple. I have found my Church.

I go to a service at Elim church. The double doors have frosted glass in them. I hover around studying the frosted glass for a few minutes before I can make myself plunge inside. Better to do this quickly. I am scarcely in when I am confronted by a guy of about my own age in a denim jacket, a young down-and-out who I've seen playing his guitar around Hereford.

I say, 'Hi, I'm Frank.'

He says, 'Hi, Frank. I'm George. Are you washed in the blood?'

'Pardon?'

'Are you washed in the blood of the lamb? You have to pray for the blood of Jesus, Frank.'

This is strange.

I make my way into the hall. There is a small band playing shakily at the front, an assortment of instruments including a drum, guitar and mouth organ. No-one is listening. The congregation are all chatting loudly to each other. There are children running over the seats. It is extremely informal. People immediately start talking to me. I smile a lot but my replies are not informative. Then the instruments get loud and self-important and the chatter falls away and the children rejoin their families. It is obvious something is about to happen. Phil Thomsett appears through a side door and the service begins.

I am both exhilarated and embarrassed by the emotional level of what follows. Somehow, the words of the pastor, the energy of the singing, the sheer abandon of the prayers, the yelling and the shouting, are almost overwhelming. At one point people begin to talk in languages I don't recognize and others translate for them. There is clapping and some crying. I must be the only silent person in the room. I realize that I have my hands firmly in my pockets and that they're stuck there. I don't take them out until I open the door to leave.

At home, Claire is lying down and looking very pregnant.

'How was it?' she asks. She is more interested in my faith these days. I try to describe all the details for her, including the foreign languages.

'Were they foreign?'

'No more foreign than you.' This is a trick answer as Claire likes to believe being Welsh makes her foreign.

'I think,' says Claire wisely, 'that they're speaking in tongues.'

How does she know so much about the Pentecostal Church all of a sudden?

'It's like this. They're not speaking real languages. They think they are but it's gobbledegook.'

'That's how it sounded. But how could these other people translate gobbledegook?'

'They aren't. They're making it up.'

I believe that there's probably a more religious explanation for what I saw tonight but I can't expect Claire to give me that. I resolve to ask Phil Thomsett.

In no time at all I'm involved in the Church. I become an enthusiastic member of the new learners' group and a Bible study group and I go to two services a week.

'I thought being a Christian was supposed to make you spend more time with your family,' says Claire. 'But we're more left out than ever.'

'Come with me, then.' To my amazement, the next week she does. She shuffles her feet and looks embarrassed through most of it.

'I know what you're thinking,' I say as we go home.

'That woman at the front. In the hat. Waving her arms around and shrieking in weird languages . . .'

'I call her Mrs Hat. They're not all like her. The pastor's wife's very nice.'

'Hmmm.'

'I bet you don't come again.'

'Maybe I could help with the Sunday school.'

I'm surprised and pleased that Claire's so keen to help. We make our offer to the elders, who ask Claire to attend church a few more times before they decide. She is offended by this, but agrees. Then they tell her she's not acceptable because she isn't a Christian.

'I'm not sure if I'm going back there,' she says.

She's very ill with a stomach bug and lies in bed reading and waiting to give birth while I look after Charlotte. I make sure she has a lot of the right sort of pamphlets and books to read. One day I go up to her room and find them spread all over her bed.

'Frank . . . this stuff . . .' she gestures around at it.

'You've been reading it?'

She nods. Then says, very softly and shyly, 'I believe it.'

I'm brisk with her.

'What do you mean?'

'I'm starting to believe it.'

I shrug.

'Good.'

Is she trying to tell me she's converted? I'm sceptical. All that hostility wouldn't just evaporate.

'Have you had some sort of religious experience?' I ask her coldly.

'Well . . . not like you did. It's just been a sort of gradual process.' She doesn't look at me. And I don't believe her.

'This book . . . someone at Elim gave it to me. About a vicar's wife. Her husband came home one day and said he was a Christian. And in the end, she converted too. All the things which have been happening to me are in the book . . .'

'That's nice.'

I still don't believe her. I remember, fleetingly, as I leave the room, how Larry hadn't really believed me that morning in Germany either. Claire's got a tummy bug and a baby about to be born. She's not herself.

A lady from Elim visits me to give me tapes of Christian music to take away with me to Sri Lanka. She says she'll remember to pray for me and that she'll work on Claire while I'm away, so that Claire can be saved too. She's already started this process. Claire hears her high heels on the path and runs upstairs to hide. Even now she claims she's converted, Claire refuses to speak to the high heels.

My visitor's talking about something I don't understand now. She wants me to visit the pastor, and ask to be baptized in the Spirit.

I flounder. 'Er, pardon?'

She repeats everything and I still don't understand her.

'Baptism in the Holy Spirit', she explains, without a trace of impatience, 'is something you really must do. Without it, you won't be able to speak in tongues.'

I've been watching closely those people who suddenly break into other languages and I'm convinced that they're sincere. It's been explained to me that God is speaking through them. Speaking in tongues is a miracle and the gift of understanding and translating what they say, the prophecy, is another.

'But what do I do?' I ask.

'Just see the pastor and tell him you want to be baptized in the Spirit.'

I go along to the normal Sunday service and there's the lady, bobbing up from nowhere between the seats.

By now I know that the pastor is praying with his elders in a little coffee room at the front of the church. I am reluctant to disturb them, and anyway I can't do so without everyone seeing me, but the lady is insistent.

'Have you asked him?'

'Well . . . no . . .'

'Come along now, you're not scared, are you?'

'No . . .'

'Just go and ask him.'

Finally, I am persuaded to go up the blue carpet to the front of the church. I give a very small knock at the door and Phil opens it.

'Oh, Frank, ' he says, 'do come in. What is it?'

I'm sure from his tone that the lady has already visited him about me.

'Er, I'm going away soon, and er . . . well, it's about this . . . baptism in the Spirit . . .'

Phil says, 'Right. You want to be baptized in the Holy Spirit.'

I try to sound decisive. 'Er . . . well, I do.' Not very decisive. 'I do, yes I do.'

'Right. Well, we'll be out in a minute.'

I go back along the blue carpet sure that all eyes are on me. I am thinking what a wally I am. I know I've let myself in for something and I don't know what.

All through the service I wait. Every time the pastor pauses I expect something is going to happen to me. Phil doesn't just announce the hymn, he leads up to it with a long preamble.

'Brothers, our God is a great God, a holy God, He calls us today . . .' and it finally builds up to, ' . . . and now let us praise almighty God. Let us stand and worship Him with our hearts and with our voices . . .' There are no hymn books. Either everyone knows the words or there's an overhead projector. I've already begun to enjoy this thickening of the atmosphere before each new chapter of the service but today it fills me with horror. I'm sure each build-up is going to end in my name. But I'm wrong. To my relief there's always a hymn or a prayer.

I seem to have got through the whole service with nothing awful happening to me. I have been actually praying this will be the case and it seems my prayers have been answered and the pastor has forgotten all about me.

Then he says, 'We've had a good service today, brothers, we have worshipped and praised the Lord but just before we end . . .'

I know this is it.

'Just before we end, we have a young man here . . .'

This is it. I'm that young man.

'Frank. Frank's going to come up and we're going to pray for him to be baptized in the Holy Spirit.'

Bright-red, thanking my lucky stars that Claire isn't with me, I walk forward. He calls the Church elders to the front as well and the whole church starts to pray for me and in a few moments the room has erupted into a frenzy of praying and shouting. I stand transfixed at the front of the church as the pastor puts his hands on me, and then the elders. Members of the congregation yell at me in tongues. I realize that something is expected of me but I don't know what.

The pastor says, 'Start speaking. Let the words come. For the Lord has spoken to you.'

I open my mouth. No words come out. I close it again. What can I say? My failure to do anything has sent the room into an even greater frenzy. I am surrounded by a cacophony of noise. People's eyes are bulging, their mouths are distorting, they are like big birds throwing giant morsels at me. This is not me. It's someone else. Just let me evaporate.

The longer my silence continues, the more frantic and undignified the yelling and praying has become. I just want it to stop and finally the pastor raises his hands and it does.

He says, 'Friends, I believe that the Holy Spirit has come upon Frank and in his own prayer-time things will develop. Praise God in all his glory, praise him!' And there is a howl of hallelujahs.

I return to my seat, red-faced, shocked, confused but with an over-riding sense of failure. I was supposed to do something and didn't. Afterwards, the pastor comes to me.

'Something did happen, didn't it?' he asks.

I say, 'Well, yes, it did. It was quite an emotional experience, having people focus on me like that.'

At home Claire glances up as I come in but something in my appearance arrests her and she does not look down again.

She says, 'What's happened?'

'What do you mean?'

'Something's happened, hasn't it?'

Maybe I came in too quietly. Maybe I'm shocked and it shows. Or maybe she can see that something really has happened tonight.

I explain, 'Well, I was baptized in the Spirit but I can't really feel anything and I get the impression I was supposed to speak in tongues and . . . well, I didn't.'

She looks at me and I tell her the whole story. I have her attention throughout. She doesn't find some other distraction while I'm talking to her about the Church, the way she used to. But at the end she only says, 'Hmmmmmm.'

'Well, what do you think?'

'I don't know what the Bible says about all that.'

I search her face for some sign that she's being sarcastic.

'You said that the Bible has all the answers,' she reminds me, gently. No sarcasm, just humility. 'We should ask Rupert, he knows his Bible well.'

'Have you been talking to Rupert?'

'He dropped by to see you when you were out and we had an interesting chat. I may go along to his church when you're away.'

'Claire . . . are you really becoming a Christian?' I ask.

'I told you I am.'

'Yes . . . but . . .'

'But you didn't believe me. You shouldn't have spent so long preaching at me. If you'd been a bit more subtle, it probably would have happened earlier.'

Our baby is born. A boy. I am ecstatic. I have a son and both his parents are Christians.

Claire suggests that we call the baby Francis Alastair. The third Francis Collins in a row. I like the sound of this family tradition but there will be no other similarities between this father and son. I'm not going to be a detached, distant, difficult figure like my dad was to me. I'm going to be loving and available.

I like the sound and smells of a baby in the house again.

'Let's have lots more of them,' I say.

'You must be joking,' says Claire.

# 21

OUR PLAN IS THAT CLAIRE AND THE CHILDREN WILL JOIN ME IN SRI Lanka as soon as I can sort out suitable accommodation. She's looking forward to moving to an island paradise but before she even has a chance to start packing, I'm home again.

'It's not a ghost,' I say, walking into her quiet evening. Charlotte's in bed. Claire's reading the Bible and nursing the baby. 'It's really me.'

I assume she'll be surprised or shocked but instead she's anxious. She's been expecting me.

'I rang you out there and they said you'd left . . . Frank, you've only been gone a few weeks. What's going on? They didn't sack you, did they?'

I nod.

'Sort of.'

'Oh, Frank!'

'I had to go. They wanted me to be a mercenary. I couldn't help them fight against the Tamils, Claire.'

I went to Sri Lanka to help train the Sinhalese army. The involvement of a British security firm in this training was sanctioned by the British government but when I arrived I found I was expected to wear army uniform and join in their war against the Tamils. Through a church I attended in Colombo I learned more about the war. I was introduced to Tamils who had been the victims of oppression and atrocities. I'd finally agreed to fight – but for the Tamils, not the Sinhalese government. The security firm decided to send me straight home.

'But I don't understand . . .' says Claire, closing the Bible on her lap. 'When they hired you they told you that you mustn't, under any circumstances, wear army uniform in case you were taken for a mercenary.'

'They don't care what happens when you get out there. They just want the money the Sri Lankan government pays them for us.'

'How much?'

'The Sri Lankans were paying about three times as much to the security firm as they were paying me.'

Claire whistles.

'That's a big rake-off. No wonder you and Al thought of starting your own firm.'

'They accused me of Bible-bashing. That's the official reason I was sacked.'

Claire grimaces.

'Did you?'

'Never once. I read it in my room, that's all. Didn't even talk about God.'

'What are we going to do now?'

'I'll just have to get another job. There's plenty of them around. Bodyguarding work might be best. Then I don't run into the mercenary problem again.'

But whatever jobs there are around, they don't come to me. The security firm has spread my unfair reputation as a Bible-basher and no-one wants to work with me.

I sign on the dole, a wretched humiliation. I shuffle to the front of a queue with people who have never worked, people who haven't worked for so long that now they can't work, people who have given up hope of work. The officials ask me my qualifications. I'm a bodyguard, a bodyguard instructor in fact. And what was my last job? I was a mercenary. Yes, well, they'll keep in touch. Later, they do offer me work. As a chef at McDonald's. I decline this politely. They give me milk coupons.

'What are they?' asks Claire when I show them to her.

'They say, give them to the milkman.'

'Good! Free milk, that's something at least.'

'We can't use these milk coupons. They're like something out of the war,' I tell her.

'Why can't we?' There's a hard note in her voice.

'We have to give them to the milkman. We don't want him knowing I'm unemployed.'

'Why not? Millions of people are unemployed.'

'He'll tell everyone, that's why.'

Another two weeks pass with no prospect of work and I give in. I sidle up to the milkman with my coupons. Out of the side of my mouth, I say, 'Er . . . do you know anything about these?'

'Milk coupons!' he says in a voice which is louder than it should be at that time of the morning. 'No problem. Loads of people use them.' He takes the coupons and hands over the milk.

'Free milk,' I say to Claire, carrying the clinking bottles inside.

'Well, it tastes just the same,' she says.

It's May now, a time of year I usually like. I suspect I'll be spending the whole summer at home. This would usually be an inviting prospect but not when there's no knowing when and if there'll be an end to it. I might be spending the autumn and winter at home too.

I pray a lot. For God to give me strength. For God to give me a job. I try to take advantage of the situation by getting on with the work which needs doing on this big, old house. There are outbuildings which need reroofing, doors which need replacing, a garden which needs digging. I have decided to treat this as a job and set about the tasks systematically. And I go to church.

I still can't speak in tongues and my failure becomes a real worry to me. People talk to me about it in Church meetings and some visit me at home. I begin to think there's something wrong with me. Why can't I do it? A Church elder suggests that there must be some unconfessed sin in my life and I spend hours trying to work out what it can be. Someone else goes way back to my childhood. Did I ever play the Ouija board? Yes! I'm told to repent it and we pray, 'Lord, please release Frank from the spirit of the Ouija board.' There are other suggestions. My whole life, a catalogue of unrepented sins, is examined, but no amount of repentance seems to give me the gift of speaking in tongues.

'Some people', says a Church elder gravely, 'never do.' I presume I am destined to be one of those people. I am disappointed.

My career may have hit the rocks but my faith is developing and deepening by the day. Through church I meet interesting Christians and am inspired by their faith. They, too, have been through bad times, and God has brought them through these periods wiser and stronger. They say, don't worry, God will bless you. Their words give me a deep-down reassurance, a warmth that comes from inside me.

Gary phones to say that I have to come and talk to Dad because they don't know what to do with him. Joanna has thrown him out, presumably because she's tired of getting home from a hard day's work and finding him asleep on the sofa, having drunk ten pints at her expense at lunchtime. He has gone to Michelle's new flat in North Shields. Michelle is twenty and she's been independent for a long, long time. She doesn't want Dad vetting her boyfriends and throwing them out of the house at ten o'clock. There have been arguments. And now she says he has to go.

'Gaz, what can I say to Dad? I'm not sure I've ever talked to him in my life.'

'Someone's got to say something.'

'But you talk to him more than I do, Gaz, you and Michael. You see him at the pub every week.'

'Can't you come and help us sort things out?' He's appealing to me as a big brother and I can't refuse.

I meet Dad in the pub, the same old pub in Whitley Bay where he always drinks. It's strange walking into the Ship again. I used to come here with my schoolmate, Daniel.

There's Dad, standing at the bar in his usual place. I'm shocked by his appearance. He looks unkempt. His hair's long. His sideburns are bushy. His flat cap is pushed down hard. Pencil behind his ear, he's watching the racing, as usual.

He greets me as if he last saw me yesterday.

'All right, bonnie lad?'

'Hi, Dad.'

'Pint of Ex?'

This is more of a command than a question. He whistles to the barmaid, something you wouldn't dare do in Hereford, and she pulls me a pint. Dad drinks up so she pulls him one too. I pay. Dad hasn't paid for a pint for years when his boys are around.

I ask myself why, if I'm going to talk to Dad, I've come to the pub. Dad doesn't talk in pubs. He drinks in pubs and studies the form in the *Sun*.

Without even thinking about it, I slip back into the old rituals. As soon as Dad's glass is empty the barmaid gives him another, however busy the pub is. He turns and looks at me and I down the rest of my glass, even if it's half full, so that I can join him in this next round. There's no question now of stacking them up. I have to keep up with him. It's expected.

Before long my bladder says that I want to go to the Gents. I remember all the old discomfort of drinking with Dad. You don't, you just don't, give in to your bladder. You are not the first one to go. Dad is the first one to go and that's near the end of the session.

I make a decision which seems almost revolutionary. It is so subversive that I can hardly go through with it but I know that if I'm going to do it, I have to do it with conviction.

When Dad's glass is empty, instead of throwing back the rest of my pint, I say, 'I'll miss this round, Dad.'

The effect is immediate. It's all in the body language. He tips back his hat a bit, looks at me in a way that says, you nancy, and tips his hat forward again. He also looks quickly around the other drinkers to make sure that they haven't noticed his son isn't keeping up.

I nearly give in. I nearly drink up and say oh, OK then, when the barmaid approaches. But I don't. It's not important to follow these rituals any more. It was drink and horses which pulled our family down and drink and horses are not what being a man's all about.

The next time I go to the pub with Dad, I'm joined by both my brothers. Michael's doing well. He's going to be personal chef to a general. We talk a little. Dad doesn't join in. He thinks the pub's for more serious things.

I miss a round again and Michael and Gary both stare at me in disbelief. It's as if some great weight has turned out to be a feather and I've just flicked it away. They start missing rounds as well. Dad doesn't say anything. He looks at his watch just before closing time and the barmaid brings him another pint and a double whisky. He drinks the pint, all except an inch. Then he downs the whisky in one gulp. Then he pours the last inch of bitter into the whisky glass, swills it around and drinks that. Then he goes to the Gents. It's a ritual and it doesn't change.

On my next visit to the pub I find myself suggesting to Dad that he comes down to stay with us. I'm working intensively on the house and I ask him to help. He likes the idea and accepts.

'Oh no!' says Claire. Her mother's been staying with us for some months, waiting to move into her new house in Hereford. I wonder how Jean and Dad will get on. It's a big house but I suspect there isn't a house large enough in England for the two of them.

But to our surprise Dad strikes up a friendship with Jean. They are joined together in mutual disapproval of our faith in general and me in particular. They are heard muttering together in the living room and caught giving each other knowing looks when Claire or I say anything religious. Sundays are tense. So are evenings, if we go out. They both want to babysit. I actually hear them arguing over Francis.

My father starts work on the rotting bay windows, replacing the bad oak. He'd like to do more but he has arthritis in his hips and some days even walking is nearly impossible. However, if he can persuade Claire or me to give him some money he somehow manages to walk to the pub. Perhaps because of his lack of finance, he consumes astonishingly little alcohol.

'He's no trouble!' Claire tells me, surprised.

Claire and I are going out for a Christian dinner. The meal won't be a very grand affair – we're really going to hear the after-dinner speaker, a healer. Tentatively, I suggest to my father that he comes too.

'The healer might be able to do something about your arthritis,' I say. But I still have misgivings when he accepts the invitation.

The dinner is held in a big ballroom. There are several hundred people. My father sees the jugs of water on the tables and says, 'Where's the drink?'

'There's only water, Dad.'

He groans and makes some stupid joke about how we should be able to turn it into wine. I begin to wish we hadn't come. I remember how we were chucked out of a nightclub once because of my father's behaviour. There was a hypnotist on stage and my father had volunteered to go up and be hypnotized and it all ended with him leaping up, calling the hypnotist a fraud and trying to punch him. The bouncers arrived before my brothers and I could get him off the stage and my dad started fighting with them. All the way home Dad kept waving his fists around and saying, 'I'd have had those bouncers if you hadn't stopped me!'

I have a terrible feeling that tonight will be the hypnotist all over again only there are no bouncers here to stop Dad turning the Christian healer into a punchbag. I ask him if he'd like to go home but by now he can smell blood and he refuses. He's already convinced that healing's a con and he's squaring up for a fight.

The speaker tells us the story of how he became a Christian and then he says, 'If anyone here tonight would like to experience God's healing power, please come forward.'

My heart's in my mouth. I am praying Dad will keep quiet. The healer asks for anyone suffering from headaches or neck problems first and Dad jumps up.

I hiss, 'Sit down, Dad. It's not your neck, it's your hips!'

Dad says, 'Oh no it's not, it's my back, and my neck's part of my back.'

He hobbles up towards the speaker. The room is completely silent. When he's about halfway across, he suddenly turns around, points at me, and roars in a voice everyone can hear, 'If this doesn't work, I'll belt you.'

Claire and I try to pretend we don't know him. But by now he's up on the stage. The healer says, 'Are you a Christian?' and my dad says, 'Well, I'm as good as any of you.'

The healer says, 'Do you know Christ?' and my father says, 'Huh! How can anyone know Christ?'

It's clear to everyone that Dad's getting difficult and the healer says quickly, 'Let's pray.'

He prays and puts his hands on my father's shoulders and says, 'Can you feel that?'

Dad admits that he can feel something and the man tells him, 'Well, that's you being healed.'

'I wouldn't say that,' replies Dad. I can tell he's going to start arguing and brace myself to drag him off the stage, but the healer laughs and says, 'You can feel something, though, can you?'

'I can feel a heat,' says Dad, 'but I wouldn't say I'm being healed.'

'Well, now let's see you walk.'

I hold my breath while Dad walks across the stage. He's still hobbling, though perhaps less than usual.

'See,' he says. 'See, I'm not completely healed.'

The man prays for him again and then tells him he's completely healed. Dad walks again. His walk is more upright and balanced than it has been for some years.

'I'm not sure about that,' he says. 'I'm a lot better than I was, though, so thanks very much.'

His voice was raised before, but now he's mumbling. He comes back to us and sits quietly. I'm just relieved that he hasn't punched the speaker.

When we leave about half an hour later, I open the car door and try to help my dad in. This is probably the first time I have actually touched him for years and he slaps my hand away.

'I don't need your help. God's healed me.'

I can hardly believe my ears. He jumps into the van. He has a pile of Christian literature which he holds onto tightly. The next morning he's up with the lark. He's already told Jean what happened last night. He describes her face as she realized that she was losing her ally. She has taken her handbag and gone out for a walk. Dad tells me the story. He is actually talking to me. He has been a dominant figure in my life since my birth and I can't remember him ever talking to me like this, stringing whole sentences together and recounting an incident.

As we laugh, I reach out and touch his shoulder. It seems a brave and frightening thing to do. You don't touch Dad, or any Geordie male, unless you're fighting.

'Right,' he says, 'let's get to work.'

He goes into the garden and all day he heaves big barrows of soil around until he's virtually relandscaped the garden. We all watch him in astonishment. Even Claire and I, who believe in healing, are amazed at how well it has worked on Dad.

Over the next few weeks we work, and as we work together we talk. For the first time in my life we have a proper father-son relationship.

At one point we're working together on the roof. We're taking the old slates off and we find a hammer that the roofer had dropped there years ago. It's a small hammer, and my father picks it up and hands it to me.

'Now then, lad, that's for you,' he says, 'a nice little hammer for you, just about your size.'

I am several inches taller than him, a grown man with children of my own. But to him I am just a small lad. Maybe he will always see me as just a little boy. Or maybe I'm a little boy to him now because we are capturing the relationship we should have had all those years ago. I'm still not sure. I just thank him for the hammer.

We take him back to the north-east for the funeral when one of his brothers dies. There are still three other brothers living and they all suffer from arthritis of the hips. They're waiting in their black ties at the house for the hearse to arrive.

I'm expecting quiet handshakes when Dad walks in but his first words are, 'Boys, watch.' And, with a dramatic gesture, he bends down and touches his toes.

Before anyone can open their mouth, he says, 'Watch again.' And he touches his toes again.

Uncle Norman says, 'Oh, so you've had the operation then?'

My dad says, 'Nope. No operation.'

Uncle Norman says, 'You must be on drugs then?'

'Nope,' says Dad. 'My son Frank . . .' and he gestures at the corner where I'm trying to make myself small, 'is a born-again Christian.'

They all look at me with a mixture of curiosity and hostility and I shrink into my corner. Dad goes on, 'I went with Frank to a meeting and God healed me.'

There's a silence. His brothers are struck completely dumb. I smile apologetically. Dad starts to tell the story of how he was healed and he gets to the bit where the healer puts his hands on Dad's shoulders.

'Er, let me get this right,' says Uncle Norman. 'This man. He put his hands on your shoulders. He put his hands on you and you were healed.'

'Yep, that's it,' says Dad. 'His hands were on my shoulders and this heat went through my body.'

Uncle Norman says, 'Well, I'll tell you something. Any man who puts his hands on my shoulders, in my book, is nothing but a poof.'

And that's that. That's healing disposed of, completely and utterly. No more discussion. They all take their arthritic hips off to the funeral.

Joanna, seeing that he's now a changed man, agrees to take Dad back. He returns to the habitat of the Geordie male and in this environment his old habits gradually return. He wants to tell everyone about God's healing power and of course the place to tell is the pub, and the rest is inevitable.

'How's Dad's hips?' I ask Gary whenever we talk.

'Not as good as they were when he came home, but not so bad as when he went away,' comes the reply. 'It's still working, Frank.'

# 22

THE BOYS ARE BACK FROM AFRICA. I'M LOOKING FORWARD TO SEEING them again. I want to hear what happened out there. I want to know what I missed.

I meet up with them for a drink at a pub in town. We greet each other jovially and settle down over our pints.

'How was Sri Lanka?' they ask.

I shrug. 'It didn't work out.' They don't ask any more questions. Perhaps they've already heard on the grapevine what happened. Perhaps they know I'm out of work now.

My turn to ask.

'What about Africa then?'

Jake slides around in his seat. 'Good. It was good,' he says.

I wait, but no-one adds anything. So, what were they doing there? Was it a successful trip? Who did what? And how did one of the lads get killed? They answer my questions but their answers tell me nothing. I'm not in the Regiment any more. They're not allowed to talk to me about their work.

I get home feeling acutely, painfully, alone. Not being in the Regiment is a state of mind and I realize that I haven't even begun to adjust to it. Until tonight. Now I have to recognize that my troop has already moved on and moved away from me. For the lads and everyone else in England, it's high summer, 1985, and for me it's still the day I left at the end of March. Time to get a life of your own, Frank. But where? How? Doing what?

At church I am recruited to join a small fund-raising choir. There will be a band and we'll go to Hightown, in central Hereford, where we'll sing and raise our hands to the Lord. The elders are keen for me to come. My ex-SAS status has already won me admirers among the younger members of the congregation and the elders argue that if I'm there the teenagers are more likely to come.

I know it will be hard for me to do this. Praising the Lord at Elim church is one thing, praising Him in front of a sceptical public is another. I remember how I used to cross the street to avoid people like me.

Saturday morning and here I am in Hightown. We're singing Jesus songs loudly and raising our hands. Mine are in my pockets and they just don't want to go up there. Somehow I defy gravity and raise them. I try to sing enthusiastically and look as though I'm enjoying myself.

The public are there in droves. Inevitably I notice first one lad from the Regiment and then another. They walk up the street, look at what's happening and see me. Aaaaaaaagh. It's Frank! Red-faced with embarrassment, they look the other way and walk quickly past with their heads down. I'm embarrassed too, but I'm determined not to show it. I sing all the louder.

Soon afterwards, I join a special early morning prayer session. To my horror, there are just three of us. The pastor, one other man who, it emerges in conversation, is a Church elder, and me. I wish I could think of an excuse to leave but the other two are unperturbed. We arrange our chairs in a little circle and start to pray.

We take it in turns to pray for different people and things. I'm rigid with fear that I'll run out of things to pray for. My turn keeps coming round all too quickly. I am increasingly tense and then, as I sit in the group praying, something happens. Inside my head I see something. It's a detailed picture of startling clarity. I am above the River Wye in Hereford. I'm standing on the Victoria Bridge and beneath me is the river bank, which looks like a gravelly beach. I know this place well but today, in my head, the beach is full. There are crowds of people standing around in the park, it's a beautiful sunny day, the grass is gleaming and the river's sparkling and people are being baptized in the river. I know about baptism in rivers because I've read about John the Baptist, but I've never actually seen it.

I watch this picture inside my head and as I do so I hear the pastor, Phil Thomsett, speaking. He says, 'Somebody here's got something to share.' I'm rocked back to reality. I'm angry with myself for letting my mind drift. As the new boy, it seems best to shut up about what I've just seen. I say nothing and Phil Thomsett insists, 'I think someone's got something important to share.' I still don't open my mouth. We carry on praying. All the time I'm wondering how Phil knows that I've seen something. On the other hand, what have I seen? Is it something I've imagined or is it a vision?

We finish our prayers but before I reach the door I feel I must speak.

'Phil . . .'

'Ah!' cries Phil. 'I knew it was you.'

'I saw the strangest thing. In my head. You're not having a baptism today, are you?'

Phil says, 'Go on.'

'Well I saw a big baptism. It was like a party. There were lots of people there, a crowd in the park. It was a beautiful day and there was a baptism in the River Wye . . .'

The pastor's face lights up. He says, 'I wrote to the bishop of Hereford last week about it, Frank. '

'About what?'

'About holding a baptism in the River Wye right there in Bishop's Meadow. I wrote last year as well and he turned me down but now I think he'll agree. I think there really will be a baptism in the River Wye this summer and what's more, Frank, I think you should be baptized.'

I stare at him blankly.

'But . . . I was baptized as a baby.'

Phil smiles. He's a neat, clean-cut man with a wide smile, American style. He says, 'Frank. I think God's saying that you should be baptized.'

When I get home I tell Claire and she agrees with Phil that maybe God really does want me to be baptized. The next question is: should Claire be baptized too? Unlike me, this didn't happen when she was a baby. We agree that we should be baptized together.

Sure enough, a letter soon arrives from the bishop telling Phil to go ahead with the baptism. It offers not just his approval but his blessing. I am confident that I have had a vision and that events will transpire exactly as I have seen. But when the day fixed for the baptism arrives, the weather is terrible. We drive to the church that morning with the windscreen wipers slapping. The rain is torrential. The wind howls.

When we get to Elim the Church elder who was there when I had the vision is practically dancing with excitement. He says, 'This weather's going to break, Frank. You've promised us a sunny baptism and that's what we're going to get.' I think: some faith.

After lunch we leave Charlotte and Francis with Claire's mother and say we're going for a walk. We don't mention a baptism. She

285

would regard it as ridiculous anyway but if she knew we were going into the river in this rain she'd hit the roof.

We drive down to the Victoria Bridge in my van, park it, and walk towards the river. The appalling weather has kept almost everyone else indoors. When we reach Bishop's Meadow there's a team wrestling with a tent in the wind. They're trying to erect it so people will have somewhere to change. They're all convinced the weather will break. This makes my stomach feel queasy because they're basing their faith at least partly on my vision. Phil is there, telling us that he has informed Central Television about the baptism and they're probably sending cameras from their local news programme. This makes me feel queasier still.

The baptism is scheduled for three o'clock.

Just before three, the wind suddenly stops and the rain lets up. The clouds break almost immediately and in a matter of minutes there is sun everywhere. The wet grass gleams, the river sparkles. People who've been stuck indoors all weekend take advantage of the change and come to the park. They see a gathering and come over to find out what's going on. The crowds build. There is a party atmosphere. Claire and I are both baptized. Later, we hear the Central Television reporter commenting on the remarkable change in the weather. The local paper prints something similar, along with a photo. I cut out the photo. It is the photo of my vision.

# 23

IT IS EVENING. I AM IN A CONCRETE ROOM. THE SOUND OF GUNSHOT IS so loud that it doesn't deafen my ears, it annihilates them. Bullets are dancing off the ceiling, the walls, the floor. Big men, fully armed, are standing on the tables. Everywhere I look there are 9mm Berettas. I am praying quietly to myself. It is possible that I won't escape this encounter alive. But at least I'm working.

I was hired by one of the security firms to work here in Athens for Mr Vardis Vardinoyannis. He's the richest man in this part of the world and he's under constant protection. There are frequent threats against his life. There are conflicting reports that he made his money by shipping oil into South Africa at a time when such exports were embargoed. I only know that his family now owns and runs Motoroil. Left-wing extremists have already assassinated his brother.

Before I left, Claire said, 'Do you think it's OK to take this man's money?'

I'd already been chewing this one over. But I had no way of knowing if he really had sold embargoed goods and, anyway, he wan't asking me to do it. I said, 'Don't let's judge him on rumours. Besides, I'm a bodyguard. Find me an employer with clean hands.'

Claire accepted this. By now we were anxious for me to be off the dole and I'd promised that I'd get her and the children out to Athens as soon as possible.

My job is to sharpen the skills of Mr Vardinoyannis's bodyguards. When I arrived at Athens airport I was met by one of the two ex-Regiment men already out here. They're actually bodyguarding so

287

there's little overlap in our job descriptions but I get the distinct impression that they aren't pleased to see me. Both are older than me, both served their full time in the Regiment and both are dismissive about my early departure. Shaun, who was a sergeant major, makes it clear from the outset that he resents my presence.

I've met the team I'll be training. Mr Vardinoyannis is from Crete and he only trusts Cretan men. So he's surrounded by black handlebar moustaches. They already think they're pretty good at close-protection and Andreas, their leader, has indicated he feels I have little to teach them. However, they're friendly enough and have taken me out tonight for a welcoming evening in a taverna. And this is how it ends. In a traditional Crete shoot-out with retsina galore and men dancing on the tables. Probably it's OK to shout and yell and fire pistols indiscriminately in old Crete but here in Athens the modern buildings are all made of concrete. I try to look as if I'm having a good time as I duck bullets.

I've spent a day or so recceing and setting up the training programme, then it's down to the ranges with my close-protection team to start working on their shooting technique. Shaun comes too, although I haven't invited him. I have barely opened my mouth when Shaun has muscled in. He's about fifteen years older than me and left the Regiment before anybody knew about the new no-bullets technique. He starts to demonstrate his techniques to my team. He dinnerplates – in other words, a dinner plate can just about cover all the holes his bullets leave in the targets. There is a murmur of appreciation from the Greek onlookers. They think that Shaun is a good shot.

Then it's my turn. I give the usual display. It's the one we used to do when Mrs Thatcher visited us with foreign dignitaries. The old routine feels good again. Draw, up, fire two shots, down onto my knees, two shots, roll over on the ground, fire two from the rolling position, back up onto my knees and fire two more, back up to standing, two more. This is five series of two. I drop the magazine off, put a fresh one on, and put away the loaded weapon. The whole thing has taken about five seconds and the bullets all go through one hole.

I enjoy the sensation this causes. The reaction is always the same: for a few moments the audience is perfectly still while they replay the routine in their minds. The Greeks do not move a muscle. They just stare and stare at the target. Their mouths are frozen open. The 5 seconds I was shooting have done more than hours of talking could ever do. Their attitude to me is completely revised. Any resentment they might have felt towards the Englishman who thinks he can teach bodyguards to bodyguard has evaporated. Shaun slinks away quietly.

Later, someone says, 'How can we shoot like that? Will you train us to do it?'

I know I can improve their shooting skills, although I can't take them to the same standard as me in the time available.

I say, 'If you want to shoot like this, it helps to have faith in God.' They stare at me but over the next few weeks get used to this line in my teaching. Greece is a very religious country but it is more wedded to the rituals of Christianity than to individual faith. However, the boys respect my beliefs and even discuss them. I have some small Greek gospel tracts ready to give them. I always carry my Bible and sometimes refer to it when I am teaching them close-protection skills. They find this novel, but they tolerate it.

Word about my shooting gets back to Vardis straightaway and soon afterwards he says, 'Frank. You know how to shoot.'

I say, 'I know how to shoot, sir.'

'You got a gun?'

'No. I don't need a gun, I'm training your bodyguards.'

He says, 'You stay with me, OK?'

He gets me a gun right away, a 9mm Walther, which is the sort James Bond carries.

From now on, I'm one of his close bodyguards. My team of handlebar moustaches is working with him anyway. They have to escort him from his big white, vine-covered mansion by the sea to the office each day. Once he's in the office he's safe, surrounded by external security. So then I take the close-protection team away and work with them until it's time for him to come home again. Leaving the office he has a ring of steel around him: six Cretan men, fully armed, and me.

Working together every day gives me a good opportunity to observe their skills and improve on them. Andreas is right, the boys are good. But it's always possible to improve vigilance. The client comes out of the door and you walk in front of him, moving from side to side, looking for a threat and putting yourself between the client and any possibility of attack. If there's a window you're not sure about, you have to make certain that anyone at that window can't shoot the client. He can shoot you, but you're wearing a bulletproof vest.

We always have one man in the street who cordons it off whenever Mr Vardinoyannis leaves the building. Chauffeurs bring the cars up, we surround him as he gets in and then we jump in the one behind.

We are as fast and discreet as it is possible to be, but this is heavy security.

One day Mr Vardinoyannis is leaving the building and I am lead man. There are two of us, walking either side of him, when a man in a black mask breaks through the crowds in Constitution Square and throws a petrol bomb. We swing into action. We knock down Vardis and I draw my pistol. But I don't fire. Something is wrong. This feeling lasts only a second. I have seen the petrol bomb go over our heads and explode behind us onto a wall in a ball of flame and I am certain it would be wrong of me to fire back.

We hustle Vardis into the building. He's nettled. He's a hard man and he loses his cool with me. He keeps saying, 'Why didn't you shoot him? That bastard tried to kill me and you didn't shoot him!' I say, 'No, I don't think he was trying to kill you.' But Mr Vardinoyannis is too angry to listen. Back in his suite he gives security a rocket. How was it someone on the street knew we were coming? This would certainly have been a big mistake but it soon emerges that the man hadn't known we were coming. This is a time of widespread rioting in South Africa and the man had been trying to protest by lobbing a bomb at the South African airline office next door: it was sheer coincidence it happened just as Mr Vardinoyannis appeared.

I am vindicated. I could have fired my pistol and I believe that most bodyguards would have done so. But something about the arc of the bomb, something that wasn't quite right about it all, stopped me from shooting. I'm pleased that I haven't lost my feeling for these things. I suspect that for Mr Vardinoyannis this is an academic point and he wouldn't have minded if I'd shot the protester anyway.

A few days later he calls me in and asks me about my family. He himself is a family man and he tells me to bring Claire and the children out to Athens. They are to join me in my five-star hotel. I phone Claire and she starts packing right away.

Most of my Cretan men are good at their job, but not all of them. And members of the team who aren't from Crete get a hard time and usually end up leaving. Crete has never been conquered and the men from that island are very proud. On at least one occasion I suggest that someone should leave the team and meet a wall of defiance. That someone is family. It's very difficult to move him. But I know he's not good enough to be on such a high-level close-protection team and eventually I ask Andreas for an appointment with Mr Vardinoyannis so that I can discuss the composition of the team. Andreas agrees, without enthusiasm.

Mr Vardinoyannis agrees to see me at the very end of the day, when his security men are milling around everywhere waiting to take him out of the building. I sit in the outer office feeling distinctly shabby in my old sports jacket. The security men are immaculate, perhaps because their employer buys their clothes. Finally I'm called in, past banks of secretaries.

The men outside were amazed that I got an appointment and now they're even more amazed that I'm actually going in there to talk to the boss.

The boss gestures me to sit down. He's sitting in an immense leather chair behind a desk which seems as big as a tennis court. In front of him is a box of cigars. That's big too. In a glass case nearby is a model ship.

With some apprehension, I outline what I think is the problem: family ties are overriding his personal safety and the hostility of the Cretan men to outsiders is losing their team some good men. He nods. He tells me to wait for a moment because he needs to make a phone call. He presses the buttons on his expensive telephone and then picks it up. From the moment he starts the call, he is yelling into the receiver. I'm amazed by the scale of his anger.

'How dare you speak to me like this . . . what sort of a fool do you think you are talking to?'

I feel sorry for whoever's on the other end of that line. They are really getting chewed out. Finally he finishes ranting and slams down the phone. He looks up at me and says sweetly, 'Thanks very much, Frank. I'll give this problem some thought.'

It's only as I'm leaving that I realize there wasn't anyone on the other end of the phone. He put on the entire display for the benefit of the guys listening outside the door. He wants the Cretan men to think that I've been torn off a strip and that's just what they do think. No matter how much I try to tell them that he was shouting into the telephone and not at me, they don't believe me. Our talk isn't wasted, however. Having made this concession to their national pride, the system is changed in accordance with my request.

Once Claire and the children have arrived I really start to enjoy myself. We try three different Churches in Athens. We start with an American Episcopalian Church for the ex-patriot community. It is too posh for us and we know immediately that we don't fit there. We try an Anglican Church but after Elim at home it seems a little downbeat. Finally, Claire spots a small ad in the English newspaper. It says, 'Born-again Christian spiritual fellowship here in Athens.' It gives a phone number. We call and speak to the Greek pastor and the next Sunday we go along. We receive a warm welcome. This Church is mostly attended by Greeks, by Filipino maids and by Africans but there is a fair smattering of people from all around the world. The women all wear long dresses, mothers and daughters dressed identically. They have long hair and we learn that they never cut it. This proves to be a Church of Jesus only. They don't believe in the Holy Trinity, that is, that there is one God expressed through the Father, the Son and the Holy Spirit. They believe that Jesus is all three and they are baptized in Jesus' name.

We like this Church very much and immediately feel at home there. However there is a point in the service when my heart sinks. The pastor says, 'Now we're going to have a time of open praise, when we can all praise God in tongues. I want everybody here to speak in tongues. I'll listen to you each in turn and, if you're not speaking in tongues, I'll pray for you.'

Speaking in tongues is still a sensitive subject with me. Despite the attempts of everyone at Elim Pentecostal Church I have failed dismally to do this. There is probably some appalling unrepented sin in my past but I've been unable to work out what it is.

I look at Claire. She says, 'I'm going to the crèche to check on the children.' She vanishes.

The entire church goes into gobbledegook and the pastor is walking down the rows listening to each person in turn. I am beginning to panic. From time to time the pastor says, 'Speak up, please!' and inclines his ear a little closer. However, whenever someone can't do it, he simply puts his hand on their head and prays for them. Suddenly I am refreshed by this approach. There's no mystery here about speaking in tongues. There's an assumption that everyone can do it. By the time the pastor reaches me, I am doing it too. I am opening my mouth and words I don't know are spilling out just as if they mean something. The pastor nods and passes on to the next person. I am thrilled to hear myself. I had half expected him to say, 'No, no, you're doing it all wrong.' Having gained his approval I gain in confidence. But a part of me is disappointed. I've read a lot now about the experience of tongues and you're supposed to be taken over by it. I haven't been taken over. It feels genuine but I can't help wondering if I'm making it all up. When you're amongst a body of people all praying like this it's hard to know exactly what's happening to you.

Claire and I agree that this Church is the one for us and we continue to worship there. At work, though, there are changes. I'm still on the boss's personal-protection team but I've completed training with the moustaches and have been moved to Mr Vardinoyannis's oil refinery at Corinth where I'll be training the security team for a further two months.

I am thrilled with the daily bus ride out from Athens to Corinth. This is the route that the apostle Paul took when he taught in Corinth. This road, winding around the mountains, is probably the very road he travelled. Corinth today is exactly the same as it was in those days: a place of low morals. Prostitution is rife there and this generally leads to other sorts of crime. The Corinthians should have taken more notice of Paul's warnings about human indulgence.

The oil refinery security force is also of a high standard. My interpreter is called Soterio, Greek for Saviour. He learned his English in a London kebab shop and it's excellent. Today I'm teaching unarmed combat on the beach. It's clear that Soterio is fielding questions on my behalf. Someone keeps interrupting and Soterio is getting more and more annoyed with him. Finally I ask what's going on. Soterio tells me not to worry about it. We're working on how to escape from a stranglehold if someone grabs you from behind. I continue, but there's another interruption from the same guy and this time I demand to know what's going on.

Finally Soterio tells me. 'This man is claiming the technique you're teaching doesn't really work. He says it's OK in practice but if someone really grabs you and tries to strangle you, you don't stand a chance.'

'OK. Tell him to come and try it.'

Soterio says, 'What?'

'Tell him to come here and try grabbing me from behind.' This is dangerous and I know it. Once, during a practice fight in Hong Kong, I was beaten by a black belt and I know that an instructor can lose a lot of credibility that way.

I'm trying to relax but I feel both nervous and tense. This guy is large and in a minute he's going to try to kill me. In front of an audience.

The big man comes around behind me and I'm ready to react but he stops and says something to Soterio, who is getting anxious, 'Frank, do you really want him to do this?'

I say, 'Tell him to try to strangle me. As hard as he likes. He has to be doing it for real, so let him try whatever he wants to do.'

I wait and in a few seconds the blow comes. He's hit me hard, very, very hard. I take half a second to think. I am going to use the exact technique I have just been teaching, the one he doubts. I lift my knees up to my chest, throwing my head forward to prevent my neck breaking from my own weight. The big guy thinks he has me but when my knees hit my chest he's suddenly holding all my weight and he can't hold me by the head. Momentarily he's off balance and I'm quick to take advantage. My hands go up and I grab him around the neck behind me so that he topples forward. I pull him over my head.

Unfortunately for him, I am wearing a watch and this catches his eye. He screams, 'Waaaaaargh!' in midair, then hits the ground. Bammmm. There's a second when he lies in the sand, his face covered in blood, before I jump on him.

I say, 'I won't kill you this time. But the technique does work, doesn't it?'

He says, 'Yes, it works. Let me go.'

The man gets medical treatment and his eye proves not to be seriously damaged. I am glad about this, but also glad that my watch made my victory look so dramatic. Word spreads around the whole oil refinery. After this, no-one else challenges me. The story goes straight back to Mr Vardinoyannis and adds to the mythology which has already grown up around my shooting. But I know how easily I could have blown things there on the beach. I am not as invincible as the Greeks believe.

I have a graphic illustration of this in December. Claire has already returned to the UK for Christmas and I am to join her there for a few days while my visa is renewed. By now I have finished training at the oil refinery and am working with the boss's house staff out at the glittering white mansion by the sea. There are Filipino maids everywhere and in the grounds is a nuclear fall-out shelter. It is a place of almost unreal luxury.

One day I come out of the hotel and, as usual, I am immediately surrounded by pimps. I should have got used to this in the months that I've been living at the hotel but they still annoy me. Daily they offer me anything I want and, even when Claire was with me, their list of lewd suggestions was endless.

There's one pimp in particular who approaches me tirelessly. He's a horrible, squat little man, who drips with sweat. One reason I dislike him so much is that he doesn't just talk to me, he paws me, saying, 'Hey mister, hey mister . . .'

On the phone to Claire I say, 'That greasy little pimp. Do you think God would mind if I thump him?'

Claire says, 'I don't think God would mind.'

I am actually on my way to a Church meeting in Athens when he comes up to me and, as usual, takes me by the arm. As usual, I tell him that I'm a Christian, I don't want his women, I just want him to leave me alone. He leans forward. He's matey. Conspiratorial. He says in a stage whisper, 'It's all right. I understand. I know your problems, I finally get your problems worked out. I can get you a boy. OK?'

I say, 'What! Get me a boy?'

I have time to think, 'God won't mind this . . .' before I hit him on the nose. We are standing in Constitution Square surrounded by Greeks hurrying home from work, tourists, people milling aimlessly about. Everyone stops in their tracks when they see what has happened. An Englishman has hit a pimp on the nose and the pimp has crumpled onto the ground.

All the other pimps rush over to us, and a crowd of onlookers gathers around them. I look down at the shocked man and say, in my shaky Greek, 'I told you to leave me alone. I'm a Christian.' The incongruity of what I'm saying and what I've just done occurs even to me. I add, for good measure, 'Don't you ever speak to me like that again.'

The little man jumps to his feet, holding his nose, and yells, 'Why did you do that?'

I say, 'Because you started offering me boys.'

He says, 'I'm not scared of you. I'm a boxer.'

With that, the little dwarf of a man takes a deep breath. He sucks his stomach right into his chest, he rounds his shoulders into a boxers' hunch and suddenly he's not so small any more.

I think, he's not kidding. He really is a boxer.

The pimp has turned into a beast. He is snarling, circling me now, his body taut and his fists up and ready for a fight. The other pimps are shouting at me and urging him on. I am in the middle of a bullring.

I have the uncomfortable realization that I am outside God's protection. I have hit this man and cannot expect God to take care of me now. For a few heart-stopping moments I have a sense of falling through a trap door into that other world, the one I came from, the one I thought I'd left behind over a year ago. A world without God. I look around me and think there is no way out of this situation. All the pimps are carrying knives. There is no sign of the police.

Suddenly the angry pimp stops circling me and jumps forward as fast as lightning. His fist comes out and he catches me on the side of the mouth. He has hardly touched me. It is a glancing blow but this is my cue. I yell, 'Oooohh, ooooow, OK, OK.' The pimp shouts something and all the other pimps yell and clap and cheer. They think he's taught the Englishman a lesson. They are probably right. I take my opportunity to shoot off.

I get to the church feeling terrible. I have experienced what Christians call being on the outside. I have placed myself beyond God's care. It's bleak, lonely and frightening. I am so shocked by this, and by my own behaviour, that I tell no-one in the church what has happened. I ask God's forgiveness.

Back at the hotel I phone Claire. Of course I blame her entirely for encouraging me to hit the pimp. She says, 'What a shame you weren't carrying your gun! Seeing that would have scared him off.' This is a typical woman's response. My gun is a working tool. I pick it up each morning at the guardroom of the house. I wouldn't carry a weapon unless I was working and, anyway, the golden rule is that you don't draw your weapon unless you intend to use it.

The next morning I walk out of the hotel and, unbelievably, the same pimp comes running up to me. I am speechless with amazement and try to walk past him as usual. But he says, 'Stop, stop!' He puts out his hand. I just stare at him.

The pimp says, 'Come on, we're friends.'

I say, 'We are?'

He says, 'Yes, and I want to shake your hand.'

We shake hands and he tells me, 'I'm sorry. I didn't understand that you're a Christian. You don't want women. You don't want boys. I understand now. I've told all the men, and we'll leave you alone.'

I look around and all the pimps lining the pavement are nodding and smiling at me. From then on I can walk out and the pimps just say, 'Hello, Frank.'

A happy ending, and one I don't deserve.

My time in Athens, unfortunately, does not have a happy ending. I go to renew the car hire, a routine enough procedure, and the firm says, 'No. We've been told you don't need your car any more.'

Baffled, I visit the boss's secretary, a Greek American. I say, 'Why don't I need my car any more?'

She's icy.

'Because you're leaving.'

I have been sacked and I'm never told why officially, although the grapevine tells me that foreigners are out of favour and the boss is sending us all home. I am saddened, but can't complain. I was originally sent out to train the close-protection team and have been kept on to work with more teams and do close-protection work. I've had fun in Greece. There's no job to go to but, all the same, it's time to go home.

# 24

I HAVE NO EXPECTATIONS OF EARLY EMPLOYMENT SINCE I'M STILL encountering my own reputation as a Bible-basher on the grapevine. But early in the new year a call comes from the security firm which sent me to Athens. I'm invited to work in London as a bodyguard. The client is called Ralph Halpern.

I haven't heard of him. The security firm explains that he's a very highly paid businessman – according to the tabloids he's Britain's most highly paid, at a million pounds a year. He is chairman and chief executive of the Burton Group. As a Jew, he apparently feels under threat because a radical splinter group from the Palestine Liberation Organization has issued threats against Europe's top Jewish businessmen. Since no threat has been issued against him by name, Scotland Yard aren't providing Special Branch. Burton's are going to hire us and foot the bill themselves.

The firm has put some lads on immediate duty in London. They've even provided more back-up at the Halperns' country estate but the London boys are desperate for yet another man to make up the team and give them some time off. Without anyone at the security firm saying so, I know that I have been asked to do this job because I am literally the only person available. I am booked to work for two weeks: presumably by the end of that time they think they can find someone with a better reputation.

The team leader is an ex-Regiment lad called Ben. He's tough and he likes to fight. He'll have heard that I'm a Christian and that I refused to fight in Sri Lanka and he won't be impressed.

My suspicions are confirmed when Ben drives over to the firm's offices to pick me up. He looks at my suitcase, which has small wheels on one side and an extra handle on the other so you can drag it through airport concourses.

'It's got one of those handles,' he comments, pointing at the offending article.

'Yeah, it's built in.'

'I smashed it off my case.'

'You smashed it off?'

'I smashed the handle off. Because I'm not having anyone thinking I'm a mincer who uses wheels on his suitcase.'

After that, there's not much to say. He drives us over to the Burton Group's headquarters in silence. Eventually he mutters, 'I hear you're into all this . . . er . . . religious stuff.' He can't even say the word 'religious' without embarrassment.

I say, 'What's the problem with that, Ben?'

He says hastily, 'No problem, no problem. It's just I heard . . .' But his voice trails away somewhere inside his big moustache.

'What have you heard, Ben?'

'Nothing.'

I say, 'Look, I know what you've heard. That Frank's a Christian and doesn't want to fight. Well, stop the car.'

He looks at me for the first time.

'Stop the car? Why?'

'I said, stop the car, we'll have a fight.'

'What do you mean?'

'Come on, get out, we'll have a scrap now.'

'What . . . now?'

'Yes, stop the car now. If you want to find out whether I fight, just stop the car.'

Ben is reddening. He shakes his head. 'No, no, I don't mean that.'

'Well, Ben, if you want to fight, just let me know any time.'

There is a long pause while Ben takes all this in.

'So . . . you don't mind fighting then?'

I say, 'I prefer not to but if you've got to fight as part of your job, then I will.'

'Ah,' says Ben. 'Well, that's all I wanted to know. Right.'

On arrival at the office, I'm taken upstairs to meet Mr Halpern. I have to walk past banks of potted plants. Behind them sit secretaries, and they are all stunning. They look like models and they wear beautiful clothes. They glance up at my crumpled suit with distaste.

Mr Halpern is a little smaller than me. He's lean and dark-haired.

298

He wears tinted glasses. His clothes look a million dollars. Double-breasted suit, tasteful tie, sharp creases, square shoulders.

He reads my cv, asks me a few questions, welcomes me to the team and then dismisses me. In the evening Ben and I drive him home. We see Mr Halpern inside and then I'm taken down to the small basement flat which we're all to share.

I introduce myself to Mac, the second team member. He's a red-haired Scotsman who is also ex-Regiment. There's a certain tone in his voice when he greets me.

'All right, Frank?'

I say, 'Yeah. Want to fight?'

Mac looks at me hard. 'Er, what do you mean?'

'Well, just in case you've been speaking to Ben here about me and you've got the same wrong idea as him. I want to make it clear that if you ever want to fight, I'm on for it.'

'No, no, I don't want to fight.'

'If you ever do, no problem.'

'Right. Well, let me show you where you'll be sleeping . . .'

On my way around the flat, I pass a brand new Samsonite with the handle smashed off.

'What's the boss like?' I ask Ben and Mac. They look at each other.

'Well . . . he's OK. Can be a bit tetchy, but he's basically OK.'

On Sunday morning I go to church in London. It's a huge Pentecostal church and there are thousands of people there. The preacher asks everyone wearing tartans or checks to stand up. They're blessed. Then everyone who thought of wearing tartan or check this morning but decided against it is asked to stand up too. They're also blessed. I decide that this church is too kooky even for me.

When my two weeks with Mr Halpern are over, no-one asks me to leave. I know the job well by now. I go into the office early to sweep it for bugs or any security threats. When the boss is due to arrive, I go out to check the street. Points of arrival and departure are potentially vulnerable. When the car pulls up, Ben gets out and shields the boss with his body and I move in to do the same. We manoeuvre around him constantly. This is called ballooning and it's designed to cause difficulties to any gunman who might be taking aim.

The Burton Group has security men on the doors at work, of course, but whenever the boss leaves the office, we go with him. The security firm has given him a VIP's course in threat evasion and he likes to check us out.

'Frank,' as we're driving along, 'has that car been following us long?'

'The red Rover, sir? It's only been there five minutes.'

'Frank, that blue car. It's been close to us for a long time.' Luckily I've noticed it and jotted down the number.

'I'm watching it, sir. If it stays around us much longer I'll run the number past Special Branch.'

There are cocktail parties, dinner parties, lunches and meetings. These are busy days for the Burton Group. The boss often features on the City pages of the newspapers. Sometimes there are meetings at Downing Street or Chequers. At Downing Street I wait at the end of the road with the car. The Special Branch lads who are hanging around are friendly.

'You're ex-Hereford?' they ask. We discuss work and salaries and they find mine enviable.

'If there are any jobs going with Mr Halpern, ring me,' they urge, handing me their cards.

At Chequers, chauffeurs and security men are ushered into a room downstairs where prawn mayonnaise sandwiches are laid out on trays for us. We're on duty, but the security here is already tight and there's not much to do but read the paper and nibble.

When it is time to visit the Halperns' country estate, the boss's chauffeur, who used to be a taxi driver and has the Knowledge, turns and dips his way there with scarcely a stop in the traffic. If we do stop, there's a voice from the back.

'Philip, why are we going this way? We went this way last time and we got held up then, too. Can't you find a better route?'

'I'll try another route next time, Ralph.'

People rarely argue with Mr Halpern, although they are often on the receiving end of sharp criticism. Ben, Mac and I have an agreement that if he sacks any of us, the others will let that lad hit him three times before we pull him off.

The country estate has a splendid new house, stables and a lake. On arrival, Mr Halpern puts on immaculate riding gear and rides his horse around his property. And he works. Wherever he is, he works. He is driven – by what, I'm not sure, although money and status are clearly immensely important to him.

The next time I'm in London for the weekend, I try another church. All Souls, Langham Place, is right next to the BBC's Broadcasting House. I'm hesitant to go because it's Church of England and most of the people I now know are Pentecostals who thoroughly disapprove of the wishy-washy Anglican Church. But since it's not far away, I decide to try it.

All Souls turns out to be beautiful. Pentecostals also disapprove of this, but when I walk in it's hard not to be disarmed by the beauty of the building. I'm also impressed by the size of the congregation. Not only is the place packed but I learn that there are a few hundred more watching the service downstairs on video.

When the service starts I'm worried that, because it's Church of England, it will be like that terrible baptism Claire and I attended at Holy Trinity, with robes and incense everywhere. I'm relieved when the minister isn't even wearing a dog collar.

He gives a brilliant sermon, in clear, direct language. The congregation worships God with energy and commitment but without waving their arms around, shrieking, or gabbling in tongues. I pick up a welcome card inviting newcomers to attend various meetings or just come for coffee. But I leave without talking to anyone.

It's a fine spring day. I walk back through the park and think about the service. At All Souls there were few demands made of God. No-one asked for a miracle or tried to make a prophecy in tongues. I wonder, fleetingly, why we have to yell so much at Elim.

Next weekend I'm back in Hereford and Elim seems normal and All Souls is a distant church in a distant city. I've given up trying to speak in tongues, although once I understood what someone else was saying.

My new job isn't the only change early in 1986. We've decided to move house. Everyone's moving house. Prices are rising and everyone's buying and selling. This phenomenon is replacing the weather as Britain's main talking point. Claire has finally agreed that our big old house is too time-consuming. The newspapers assure us that we should be spending three and a half times our salary on our house and I'm now on a good salary. The whole country has property fever and we're not immune to it. Our house is sold in a week and we choose somewhere sensible, a modern four-bedroom box on the up-and-coming Bobblestock estate. It's dull, but requires no work. All around us developers are busy and yuppies – a new word in the English language – are snapping up the new houses.

One of our last visitors in town is Roly.

'I don't want him coming to our new house,' says Claire. 'It's supposed to be low-maintenance but it won't be if Roly's there.'

Roly is a tramp. I've been bringing him home for over a year now. Since my conversion, I've felt differently about vagrants, the mentally

301

ill, the outsiders in our society. Before, I stepped over them in the street. But when I found Roly outside the church I felt genuine compassion for the first time in my life. He's a paranoid schizophrenic and during bad periods can be glimpsed sneaking and ducking his way through the town centre. I rarely see him during these bad times. I see him when he's drunk, or when he has a hangover.

Claire's been more tolerant of him since her conversion but she's never been enthusiastic about Roly's visits. At first I just brought him home for a bath and a change of clothes, but now he sometimes stays.

Our move takes place in late spring, with all the usual chaos. We stand in our new, neat kitchen, the children exploring the empty house, men lugging boxes in and out.

'I haven't prayed today,' I say to Claire.

'Neither have I.'

It's hard to know where and how to pray in the midst of this kind of disruption. It's too easy to forget to pray, or to be too casual about it. I feel such an infant Christian because I don't know the right way to carry out this simplest of acts. Usually these days I pray when I go running. I'm not sure if that's right.

When we're settled in, I go to Rupert's bookshop for a book about prayer.

'Why do you want that?' asks Rupert, looking at me over his glasses. 'Having trouble with your prayer life?'

'Sometimes I think I just don't know how to do it,' I confess. Rupert smiles.

'I'll help you, Frank,' he says. 'I'll pray with you.'

This is a generous offer, but my instinct is to find some way to refuse it. The idea of me and Rupert closing our eyes and bowing our heads in the bookshop is, like so much about worship, embarrassing.

'Why don't I try to call in on you first thing, on my way to the shop? We'll pray together, just for half an hour. You'll have a more disciplined prayer life and I'll be able to guide you through it.'

I know I can't refuse. The next morning I'm up at six, ready for Rupert's visit at seven.

'Want to join us?' I ask Claire. She's got to know Rupert and his wife Anna very well now. She even goes to their church with them when I'm not around.

'You're mad,' she says, pulling up the bedclothes. 'You're barking.'

I wish I could go back to bed too, but, at seven o'clock, Rupert and I have a cup of coffee and talk in quiet, early morning voices. We talk about ourselves but mostly about the news of the Chernobyl nuclear disaster in the Ukraine. Our talk drifts into prayer. We lean forward and close our eyes. We pray for our wives and our children and a few people in Hereford and then for the disaster victims in Eastern Europe.

Rupert and his wife Anna are members of a Pentecostal Church called Family Fellowship which has about thirty members and is actually a splinter group from my Church, Elim. Rupert was very careful, when I was trawling the Churches of Hereford, not to try to recruit me to his own, but now he surprises me by inviting me to join. He and his pastor feel Claire and I have a particular contribution to make to Family's youth work. At Elim the youth work is already well-organized, but Family is a newer, younger fellowship and I'm soon convinced that it can use us.

We leave Elim on good terms. There is just one sour note: someone warns me that Brian, the pastor at Family, is dangerous.

'What's that supposed to mean?'

'Well, he's a real one-man band.'

'Meaning what?'

They decline to elaborate.

Certain routines begin to slide. For example, the boss takes a lot of work home. In the morning he might have three briefcases and he expects his bodyguard to carry two of them.

'Ben, the bags please!'

'What are you doing, carrying his cases?' I ask Ben. 'You know you're supposed to have your hands free.'

He shrugs.

'I've told him that but he still wants me to.'

Ben leaves for more exciting work, another lad joins, and Mac becomes team leader. He does a good job until the boss has a dinner party in London. There's a different wine served with each course so bottles are being whisked away half empty. Mac sits in the kitchen drinking the leftover wine. By one o'clock he's tired and emotional.

He goes upstairs, where guests are enjoying their coffee.

'Right. Off you go, you lot. I've had enough of this. I'm not staying up all night. Get your coats and go.'

The tinkle of fine china and silver spoons stops, people freeze mid-munch, mid-sentence, mid-laugh.

'Mac,' says Mr Halpern, 'I think you've had too much to drink.'

'Are you calling me unprofessional? I hope you're not because I'm very fopressional . . . pofresh . . . profress . . .'

'Mac. Go downstairs please.'

'I'll go downstairs if you tell this little lot to clear off.'

'Downstairs, Mac, please.'

'All right, all right, I'm going. But remember, ladies and gentlemen, it's last orders now.'

The next day I arrive from Hereford to take over from Mac.

'Everything OK, mate?'

He nods but I detect something sheepish in his expression.

'Fine. Dinner party last night. No problems . . .'

'Good. Have a good break.'

'See you then.' Mac makes a hasty exit. I'm called to see Mr Halpern almost immediately.

'Frank, what am I supposed to think when my head of security arrives in the middle of my dinner party and tells my guests to go home?'

'Er . . . sir?'

He has to repeat the question so that I can take it in. Mac's sheepish look is explained.

Ralph tells me the whole story and I later get an even more graphic account from one of the waitresses.

'Frank, please phone the security company and tell them what happened and ask them what they propose to do about it.'

I know what they'll do. I'm next in line for the throne and within half an hour Mac's sacked and I'm given the thankless job of head of security. That almost certainly means I'm next in line for the axe.

We work three weeks on and one week off. I take one of the company cars, perhaps the black BMW or the white Mercedes, back to Hereford with me.

On my trips home I participate as fully as I can in the life of our new Church. The pastor, Brian, is in his late forties. He's small with a neat moustache and tight, curly hair. The congregation are like one big family. Everyone makes us feel welcome and it soon becomes clear that Brian is a gifted leader. He has the knack of getting people to do things. He manages to involve everyone and at his services there is real joy.

It's agreed that Claire and I will help run the Church youth group. Of course, I'm away in London half the time, so we couldn't run it without help. But at the very first meeting it's clear that we aren't running it at all. Brian's running it.

The meeting is held at Brian and Rita's house. They are helped by their daughter and son-in-law, and it soon becomes evident that their role, like ours, is to reinforce Brian's lectures. Today's subject is pre-marital sex.

'So,' he turns to his son-in-law, 'how did you feel about all this, Richard, when you were fifteen?'

'Well,' says Richard, with a shy glance at his wife, 'of course, Alison and I were very attracted to each other and it was very difficult, but somehow we managed to wait and we're glad now that we did.'

I hope Brian doesn't ask what I felt about sex at the age of fifteen. Richard gave exactly the right answer, but I know that I can't say what Brian wants to hear.

Claire and I hardly like to admit to ourselves after the youth group how disappointing we found it.

'Perhaps Brian will gradually hand over more control to us and we can do more interesting things with the kids,' Claire suggests. I remember that comment, before we joined Family, about Brian being a one-man band.

'Even if he doesn't hand over control, we can suggest some other things to do,' I say. We go home and make a list. Top of the list is a Christian youth camp.

Shyly, but confident that our ideas are good, we show the list to Brian.

'Wonderful,' he beams. 'These are good ideas. And a Christian youth camp would be great fun.'

We agree to organize it soon.

Back to London to that other world, where Ralph Halpern is living life in the fast lane. The Burton Group takes over Debenhams, whose flagship store is Harvey Nichols. His name is now all over the City pages. Soon afterwards, he becomes Sir Ralph.

As head of security, I discover that my job is to sack people. Sometimes they start work and they just look wrong – Sir Ralph doesn't want any gorillas – and I have to tell them to leave the next day. Sometimes they really do something wrong. And sometimes Sir Ralph imagines that they do. Before he left, Mac agreed that we'd all leave the security firm and work for the Burton Group direct. The idea is that, without the middle man, Burtons will pay less but we'll be paid more.

Before this happens, Sir Ralph gives the security firm one last chance. They say they're going to send over one of their senior and most trusted managers to troubleshoot the job and see how things can be improved. As head of security I'm offended by this but also relieved that someone else is going to be in charge of hiring and firing for a while.

The troubleshooter arrives in a sports car carrying a big briefcase. It is none other than Shaun, my colleague in Athens. He is charming and suave and managerial with everyone and I can see Sir Ralph is impressed.

Shaun has a meeting with Sir Ralph at the house and, just as he's leaving, Sir Ralph indicates a tarpaulin on the building next door. When the wind catches the tarpaulin it flaps noisily, day and night. He asks Shaun to do something about it.

'Certainly, sir,' says Shaun.

When Sir Ralph returns from the office, there's the tarpaulin, flapping away.

'Frank, I asked Shaun to see to that. Where is he?'

'I think he's already left for the day, sir.'

'Can you sort the tarpaulin out?'

'I'll certainly try.'

I get one of the other lads to help me. The building's four storeys but we climb up it and tie in the tarpaulin. Then I go back to Sir Ralph.

'The tarpaulin's all right now, sir.'

'Good. Thank you, Frank.'

Before I'm out of the room, he's on the phone to the security company. Shaun is fired.

Shaun phones me in fury.

'What's the problem, Frank? I don't get it!'

'The tarpaulin.'

'I spoke to the developers who're renovating that building. I went right to the top of the company. They promised to sort it out!'

But it's no good talking to some director in an office. You have to see to things yourself. As a lot of us have already learned to our cost, Sir Ralph wants results. We leave the security firm and become employees of the Burton Group, and I suspect that the firm is relieved to get rid of this demanding client. Sir Ralph runs the company on bonuses and incentives and now we're part of the company we're subject to the same system. Our salaries are good but there's a bonus of 10 per cent on top. But it can be cut for the slightest of reasons. Every month, Sir Ralph and I go over my team's bonuses, me arguing for and him against. I usually end up giving my own away rather than arguing over it. But sometimes Sir Ralph surprises me with a big and unexpected gift in my pay packet. He's an exceptionally shrewd businessman, but that doesn't mean he can't be generous. It's a nice surprise when he does this but I've learned that the only way to deal with the bonus system is not to expect it, rely on it or allow myself to care about it. Just like the no bullets system, I teach myself to think: no bonus.

Whenever the rota puts me in London at the weekend, I attend All Souls, Langham Place. I've been along to a welcome group there and a discussion group and met all sorts of people, from hospital consultants to mechanics.

Gradually my job evolves so that I'm working one week on and one week off. This gives me more time for involvement in the Church in Hereford. There are several services a week led by Brian, Bible study classes taught by Brian, and, of course, the youth group.

Brian becomes a close friend to Claire and me as he is to everyone. He provides good leadership and we enjoy his support. I don't trust people easily and I haven't been really close to anyone since Al died but I know I can trust Brian. I'm disappointed that, whenever we've tried to resurrect our youth camp idea, there's always been some reason why Brian thinks the time's wrong, but I still trust him.

Brian runs his own small manufacturing business in Hereford and a lot of people from the Church have left their jobs to work for him as well as worship with him. I am uncomfortable about this, especially as I have learned that wages in his factory are poor. However, as a friend and pastor I am confident that his care is second to none, and I assume this is true of Brian the employer too.

Very occasionally I find the family atmosphere at church, and Brian's domination of the place, stifling. He knows everyone's business and, before any change or decision is made in anyone's life, he expects to be consulted. This is known as heavy shepherding, and mostly we like it. For the first time somebody, apart from God, is looking after me. Fathers are supposed to do that but mine never has. And if it all gets too claustrophobic, the way families do, I can always escape back to London.

Now that Sir Ralph's busy trying to knock Debenhams into shape, he has a policy of swooping on stores. Sometimes we leave the city by helicopter and are met by a chauffeured car at our destination. The chauffeur has no idea where he'll be asked to go.

We climb in.

'Debenhams,' says Sir Ralph.

The chauffeur looks amazed.

'Did you say . . . Debenhams?'

'Are you deaf?'

We pull up outside the store in our grand car and walk in. By now, I've learned quite a bit about storesmanship.

'Well, Frank, what's wrong here?'

'The signing.'

'Certainly, the signing's very bad. What else?'

'The lighting.'

'Exactly. And why is it that when we walk in we find ourselves surrounded by duvets? How many customers are they boring out of the store?'

A hapless assistant passes and Sir Ralph halts her with the words, 'Get me the manager.'

This just isn't the way customers behave out here in the sticks, or probably anywhere.

'Er . . . sorry, sir?'

'I'm the chairman. Get the manager.'

A few minutes later the manager appears, straightening his tie. 'Mr Smith' is in his fifties and has probably worked for the company loyally since he left school.

'Er, how nice to see you, er, Sir Ralph . . .'

He's manager of a clothes store but he's wearing a shabby suit and his tie was a fashion statement ten years ago. I know that this isn't good enough and I fear for the man's future. So, it seems, does he. His smile is anxious. His brow is shining.

'Now then, Mr Smith. I'm a customer and I've just walked in and I want menswear.'

'Er, that's on the third floor, Sir Ralph.'

'Yes, Mr Smith, you know that, but how, as a customer, am I supposed to know it? I need to know where to go and how to get there. And, Mr Smith, it's nice if I take a scenic route so I can do some window-shopping on the way. Who knows, I might actually buy something then.'

Sweat begins to pour off 'Mr Smith' as he shows us around the shop and listens to Sir Ralph's comments.

When we leave, Sir Ralph says to me, 'Well, Frank, what do you think of that store?'

'It's not very good, I'm afraid, sir.'

'Not very good at all, Frank.'

I know that nice 'Mr Smith' has had it.

Sir Ralph turns to me.

'And what did you think of the manager?'

'Well . . . I liked him. He's a very nice guy . . .'

'Yes, Frank, he's nice, but we're running a business here, a business with a multimillion-pound turnover. Do we need nice guys or do we need managers?'

'I think we need managers, Sir Ralph.'

In one big store the manager bounces up to us looking smart and confident, his hand outstretched. He's in his early thirties.

'Good morning and welcome to the store, Sir Ralph. I've been here six months and I'd like to show you what we've been doing. I'm working on the following areas . . .'

Afterwards, the boss asks me what I think.

'He's good, one of the best we've seen.'

He agrees, 'Maybe the best.'

The next time we're in the region for a meeting, the manager isn't there. I'm surprised he's gone. Then he appears, as area manager. He's been promoted as a result of our store visit. And that's the way Sir Ralph runs things. You either get bonuses and promotions, or you're for the chop. There seems to be no middle ground.

Since we work together so closely it's inevitable that we know each other well. Sometimes I even call him Ralph. Occasionally we eat in restaurants at the same table. It's a strange relationship. His constant demands and complaints make him a difficult man to work with, but I can't help liking him. He's obsessed by his need to make money, to work, to be successful, to be seen to be successful. But is he a hollow man beneath it all? His faith plays an insignificant part in his life and he seems to have no real friends. His world is divided between his complicated, demanding London existence and his more simple weekends in the country with his wife and daughter. My own life has a similar division. I'm in London, mixing with the beautiful, rich, sophisticated people who surround Sir Ralph, attending one of the best-known churches in the land. Then I go home to that other world of small children and ardent Pentecostal worship. Sometimes I am lonely and feel I don't belong in either place. Maybe Sir Ralph feels the same way.

So we have dinner together. Two lonely men, the master and his servant.

When I next go back to Hereford I hear a rumour about Brian which I don't like. A member of the fellowship who also works for him was offered a better job elsewhere. Not only did he prefer the work, but the hours and the pay were also preferable. Of course, before he could leave Brian the employer he had to consult Brian the pastor and the pastor advised him in the strongest possible terms to remain in his present employment. Which he did. I find it hard to explain why this story disturbs me so much. I discuss it at an early morning prayer session with Rupert. Rupert is not defensive about Brian but very gently suggests that the employee needs the daily care and support which Brian can provide more than he needs the extra money. I'm relieved at this sensible explanation. But I'm beginning to dislike the power Brian exercises over his congregation.

# 25

SIR RALPH IS SUDDENLY CATAPULTED FROM THE FINANCIAL SECTIONS OF the newspapers onto the front pages. There is a sexual scandal. A young girl, Fiona Wright, has sold her kiss-and-tell memoirs to the media. Suddenly, the public is fascinated by 'Five Times a Night Sir Ralph'.

The rest of the team quits at once. They are taking the moral high ground.

'We're not staying here with all this stuff going on!'

'But you knew Fiona Wright was around a few years ago. She's not news. All that's changed is that the papers have got hold of it,' I argue.

But they leave all the same.

I manage to find some replacements fast. I'm sure the story is a set-up, since the Burton Group's results are due out next week. I suspect that Fiona Wright herself, who is barely out of her teens, is as much a victim as Sir Ralph. However, the press is enjoying the story. They are camping outside the house and the office.

'Where is he?' they keep yelling at me.

'I don't know.'

Of course he's inside the house. But I don't know where.

'Is he in there?'

'No.'

I mean he's not in the basement.

'We pay well for photos . . .'

'No thanks.'

We smuggle Sir Ralph out by a back route but some photographers catch sight of us and are soon running down the road after the car. At work, we've hired extra security but the cameramen are still thick on the pavement and the boys have to push them aside to get in.

This goes on for several days, until Burtons' annual general meeting in a London hotel. There's a lot of Burton security men on duty but somehow a photographer manages to find his way up to Sir Ralph in the foyer.

'I just want to take a picture . . .'

I get straight to him.

'Excuse me.' I don't even have to get physical because the photographer knows the score. I just shepherd him tactfully out. But Sir Ralph is not pleased.

'What was he doing here?'

'The perimeter's not my responsibility, sir.'

'It's just not good enough!'

Useless to tell him that it's not my fault. He's worried and nervous, but the meeting goes well for him. The scandal backfires on the media. A shareholder says, 'Anyone who can do it five times a night gets my vote!' and the whole room roars its support.

Afterwards, in the lift, another reporter manages to slip in with us. Sir Ralph is cool and gives him a comment but he says, 'He shouldn't have been there, Frank. It's really not good enough.'

The head of Burtons' security compares notes with me.

'I got three tickings off. How many did you get?'

'Only two this time!'

I find it hard to see why the other lads have taken the moral high ground over this sex scandal. Sir Ralph has bimbos, usually aspiring models, throwing themselves at him all the time and if he gave in to temptation with young Fiona it's only what most men would like to do. I don't feel I have the right to judge him because I have no idea how I'd behave in that situation.

Sir Ralph's enhanced sexual reputation gets him into some embarrassing situations. He's been having a business lunch with a woman who seems to have fallen for him. The posh London restaurant has an old and highly ornate lift to take diners back to ground level and after lunch it's full, giving this woman a chance to press closer to Sir Ralph than he wants her to.

Then the lift breaks down. We're stuck between floors. The liftboy frantically pushes buttons but we don't move. It's hot. Someone's going to faint and it's obvious who it will be. To the amusement of all, the woman gives a melodramatic swoon.

'Ooooooh, Ralph . . . help me!'

She's spent too much time at the local amateur dramatic society, this one. She may even have starred in the panto.

Sir Ralph looks at me as she starts to fall.

'Frank, do something!'

I catch her, and she's no lightweight.

'Can't you make it go?' demands Sir Ralph of the liftboy, who is now pushing all the buttons at once.

'I'm sorry, I only started here last week, sir.'

'Didn't they tell you what to do it if goes wrong?'

'No, sir.'

No help arrives. Sir Ralph gets out his mobile phone and calls his secretary. She phones the restaurant to tell them that one of their lifts is stuck.

'No it's not.'

'I'm telling you, my chairman's stuck in your lift.'

'Oh yes? Then why didn't he ring us? Why did he ring you?'

She calls us back to warn that the restaurant is being unhelpful.

'Do something, Frank,' says Sir Ralph, assuming control of the lift like the captain of industry that he is. Everyone else in the lift turns to me and their looks are saying the same thing.

Despite the crowd, I manage to lie the fainted lady down. There's only one lift door and I've noticed that there are two little catches on it. I undo them and the door slides open. I now have to do some acrobatics and climb down to the next floor. There's a brief moment of terror when I hang with the lift shaft gaping beneath me, all its greasy wires visible. My main fear is that the lift will move, trapping me as I swing out, but I get safely to the landing.

I wedge the lift in place with a big sofa I find in the hall and then use more furniture so everyone can exit without risking their lives over the lift shaft. The occupants start climbing out, passing the limp body of the fainted lady from one to another. She lands safely but is not so unconscious that she doesn't put out a modest hand to pull down her skirt.

The management appears.

'Just what do you think you're doing with that sofa?'

Sir Ralph and I escape from the crowd, the fainted lady and the lift and we walk back up Regent Street to the office.

'Are you all right?' asks his secretary.

'Fine.'

'But, what happened?'

Sir Ralph smiles winningly at her, 'It was no problem at all. I managed to sort it out.'

'Really, Sir Ralph?'

'A simple matter of a few catches, a death-defying leap over the lift shaft and some very quick thinking.'

I am agog at this but I realize that by now Sir Ralph really believes that he got us all out of the lift. Which, in a way, he did. By telling me to sort it out.

When Sir Ralph is in the country, we park the armoured BMW outside the house with the security cameras trained on it. There are cameras everywhere and if they spot something moving they beep. George, an amiable ex-Regiment man who is not far from retirement age and likes the country life, is on duty one night. Of course he can't stay up all night waiting for a camera to beep, so he's in bed. His night-time attire is a big pair of baggy underpants and a string vest. Not glamorous, but he probably gave up wearing silk pyjamas when he joined the SAS a long, long time ago.

Unfortunately, George has left the mobile phone switched on in the car. The battery gradually loses power. The car alarm is programmed to start screaming if any wires are cut and this is how it misinterprets the power failure. At 2 a.m., the battery runs out and the alarm is triggered.

Sir Ralph, lying in bed, wakes up.

'George left the mobile battery on again,' he groans to himself, and rolls over.

George, on the other hand, is in a deep sleep and when he hears the car alarm he leaps up. He's at the ready. Suddenly he's back in the thick of the action, and there's something going on out there.

He grabs his rifle. It's actually the bedside lamp but George is too busy rushing over to the house to notice. The front door is triple deadlocked and upstairs Sir Ralph can hear George fighting with the keys. He gets up and goes to the top of the sweeping flight of stairs.

Below him, the door is flung open. In charges George, string vest flying, baggy underpants akimbo, bedside lamp at the ready. He's an assault trooper and he's gained access to the embassy and now he's storming the stairs.

'George,' says Sir Ralph. 'Wake up! Wake up!'

George pauses.

'I said, wake up!'

George stops and stares up at his master.

'It's not the house alarm, George.'

George blinks, he blinks at the bedside lamp and then he blinks at the boss.

'It's the car alarm. You must have left the mobile on.'

I hear this story in some detail later from Sir Ralph.

'Frank, the most dangerous thing which has happened to me since I've had bodyguards is George running up my stairs in his underwear in the middle of the night armed with a lamp.'

We laugh but I know that George's days are numbered and, sure enough, when he's caught making a personal call on Sir Ralph's mobile phone soon afterwards, I'm told to sack him.

He accepts his fate placidly.

'It wasn't really the phone call. It was the string vest,' he mutters. And he's probably right.

By now, I warn anyone that I take onto the team that their days here will be numbered.

'This isn't going to be a job for life. If you stay six months you're doing well. It's highly paid and you get some great cars but no-one stays here long. Not even me.'

I receive a phone call from Claire. She has had some bad news. Her father has died suddenly from a heart attack. He took early retirement from his job as head of the Art Department in a big school only last September. And now, less than a year later, he is dead. Claire is devastated. She is also pregnant again, four months, and we've learned that what was thought to be a twin is in fact a cyst and she may require an operation later in the pregnancy.

I leave with her for her father's home in Wales but soon have to return to work. I'm glad that we're members of such a small, close-knit Church as Family. She'll receive plenty of support from Brian and Rita.

But Brian doesn't call. Claire waits. She needs his help. We've both developed some dependency on his shepherding and at a time like this she needs him. She telephones and he promises that he'll come to see her soon. But he doesn't come.

Later, some time later, he apologizes. He explains that his wife was too unwell to visit with him and he never, under any circumstances, visits a woman alone.

Claire says, 'I'm pregnant and my father's just died! What sort of threat am I?'

Brian shakes his head. He tells her that it's his principle and he never breaks it.

'I never put myself in a position where anyone can say anything against me.'

Brian's wife is suffering from depression at the moment. When she feels this way, he sends her off with £300 in her pocket to buy herself a new dress. I was incredulous when I first heard this, but Brian tells us that this kind of thing can keep your marriage alive. And he recommends all wives to buy sexy underwear to revitalize their marriages. Claire and I have often laughed disloyally at this advice. But now Claire's angry and hurt at Brian's failure to visit her and we aren't laughing any more.

Privately, guiltily, we start to reveal to each other grievances we have against Brian, like his vetoing of all our ideas for the youth group. We begin to suspect that we are coming to the end of our time at Family. We wonder exactly how it will end.

Then I lose my temper.

Two members of the fellowship have fallen in love and everyone at Family is delighted. Although the couple are very young, one of them has been married before. Jane divorced her husband when he turned out to be aggressive and now she has met Steve and we are all hoping their romance will turn out well. Except for Brian. He does not approve because Jane is divorced. To counter suggestions that he is too autocratic, he has appointed some elders to the Church and Rupert is one of them. Rupert is dispatched to visit Jane and Brian visits Steve. They go at the same time and carry the same message: that Jane was once married and therefore always will be and that the couple should discontinue the relationship immediately. I can't imagine that Rupert is happy to do this but he is loyal to Brian and, like most of the congregation, does not question the pastor.

I am very angry when I hear about these visits to Jane and Steve. The next time I am in Hereford I arrange to meet Brian at the fellowship office, which is now over the bookshop. I leave Claire talking to Rupert downstairs. A tape of Christian music is playing in the shop and the atmosphere there is harmonious. But I do not climb the stairs in a spirit of brotherly love.

Brian is sitting in the small office looking at some papers. He greets me warmly but there is a hint of aggression in his tone. He knows that he's about to be challenged.

'Brian, if our Church really believes that marriage is for ever under all circumstances, shouldn't we be told?' I say.

He blinks at me slowly and folds his arms.

'I mean, shouldn't we have some sort of written doctrine, if these are the beliefs we follow?'

At the word 'doctrine', Brian explodes. He's been waiting to. Perhaps I have too.

He says, 'We don't have doctrine in our Church! That's the problem with the Church of England, it's full of doctrine and empty of faith! You don't understand what it's like being a leader. I have to make decisions. It's not easy being in charge. You can feel isolated just by doing what you believe to be right.'

I say, 'You're certainly in charge. You tell us what we believe. Now tell me if it's true that we believe that marriage is for life, whatever the circumstances? And if it is, shouldn't people know this before they start worshipping with us and forming relationships?'

Brian accuses me of undermining his authority. There is an immense, shouting, undignified argument. Even while I'm yelling, I'm wondering if the real problem is that we are both leaders at heart.

Claire and Rupert downstairs can almost certainly hear every word. They've turned up the music but that won't drown us out. I know this but I am so angry that I don't care. Accusations are being hurled around. We are both hot and red-faced, as if we've been fighting physically.

'You've always believed I'm too much of a one-man band,' yells Brian.

'No!' I bellow back. 'That was someone else's comment. But I do think—'

'Oh, I know what you think. Rupert's been telling me! You've talked about me behind my back, that's what kind of a man you are!'

It takes a few moments for me to realize that Rupert has passed on some of the concerns I've aired at our early morning prayer meetings. I feel betrayed. We argue on until our anger has run its course. Then, strangely, we shake hands and wish one another good luck. Our hands are hot.

I go down to the bookshop and as I negotiate the steep stairs I find my legs are jelly. Down here, Claire waits, her face a deathly pale. Rupert, too, is extremely upset. He has heard his two friends arguing, and his own name has been mentioned.

Claire and I leave the bookshop. I say, 'We're free, Claire. Don't be upset.'

317

Claire repeats, 'We're free.' And the first emotion I experience is relief. I realize how Brian, with his advice, his expectations and his rules, has been dominating our lives. Even now, my heart still pumping with anger, I know that he's been acting from the best of reasons, but for me his heavy shepherding has become too much. I look back over the last eighteen months and it seems to me I've been trapped between two controlling men, Sir Ralph in London and Brian in Hereford.

'We're free . . . we're free!' Claire is still repeating with increasing pleasure.

Over the next few days we take more and more delight in our liberation. We begin to wonder whether we haven't been caught up in something like a cult, so dominating has been Brian's personality.

I visit Jane and Steve. They are going to stay together and leave the Church. I am also concerned about my friend Rupert, trapped helplessly between two angry men. I am disappointed in him for relaying so much private information to Brian but now I'm on the outside I see how hard it is to resist Brian's power on the inside, and I forgive Rupert. I phone him. It is clear he does not want to speak to me.

'Can't we be friends, still?' I ask.

There is silence at the end of the phone.

'Brian's asked us not to speak to you,' Rupert says, 'and I feel guilty even having this conversation.'

Rupert and his wife Anna aren't the only friends we've lost. Everyone at Family shuns us. Brian has told them to. This is a strange feeling, particularly on the following Sunday. It's odd not to be getting ready for church. We have learnt that Brian has already sent a letter to all local Church leaders warning them not to accept us into their congregations. We are, he says, black sheep who will come into your flock and talk against you.

We want to laugh at this but it's too painful. And we need a Church.

'What are we going to do about a Church?' Claire says several times.

I tell her that I may have outgrown the Pentecostal Church. The miracles, the tongues, the healing, the shouting: it was necessary when I first became a Christian. Emotion was the only language I understood then. I wanted constant proof of God's presence. I made constant demands on God in my prayers – look at all the lists of requests I'd issue to God before each job in Northern Ireland. I look back on that from here as I look back on all the foolishnesses of my childhood. I was lost then. I didn't know anything. I was just a jumble of emotions and confusions and, after Al's death, grief. My faith doesn't need all these outward forms of reassurance now, it's too strong. I try to explain this to Claire and she nods.

'You've been weaned. You're a baby which doesn't need breast milk any more.' That's one way of putting it. She is pregnant, after all.

'So,' she asks, 'where do we go?'

'The Church of England,' I suggest.

She guffaws. 'The Anglican Church! Are you joking?'

'No. Holmer's good.'

Holmer's our local church and the vicar is regarded as exceptional, even by Pentecostal pastors.

Claire says, 'We can't go to the Church of England, Frank. They don't really believe anything.'

I say, 'Well, if that's the case, let's try to change it.'

Claire looks at me carefully. My words have surprised even me.

'What do you mean?'

'I mean, let's try to get involved in the Church of England.'

'That won't change much.'

'It might. If I'm a minister.'

This is the first time such an idea has occurred to me. A Church of England minister. The words are out of my mouth before I've had time to think what this really means.

Claire doesn't argue. She just says quietly, 'I told you so.'

'Told me what?'

'When you were first converted. I knew you wouldn't be content just to go along to church on Sundays. I knew you'd have to become a missionary or a pastor or something. I told you.'

'I don't remember you saying that.'

'I've seen this coming a long time,' she sighs.

We phone the vicar of Holmer church. He visits us, expecting to hear that we'd like to join his congregation. We reveal that our intentions are even more serious than that. He explains the long process of application to become a minister. I'll have to be confirmed and the children baptized and then we'll have to attend church for several years. We nod.

Somehow, with little discussion, research or investigation, Claire and I have accepted that I'm to try to become a Church of England minister. We have no knowledge of the practices or traditions of this

Church and little idea how we've arrived at this strange decision, but we assume God must have guided us. I go back to London believing that God has at last shown me my path in life. Nothing Sir Ralph can say or do from now on is going to bother me.

# 26

GEORGE IS REPLACED IN THE COUNTRY AND WE ALL GO DOWN FOR THE weekend. On Sunday morning we're admiring the fluffy little yellow ducklings on the lake when suddenly there's a big splash and one of them disappears.

Sir Ralph is shocked.

'What was that?'

'Well, I think it must have been a pike, sir. I believe they eat ducklings.'

He is horrified at the sight of nature in the raw. After all, he's spent all week in the rag trade and likes to get away from it at the weekends.

'We must do something about this. We have to catch it, Frank.'

On Monday morning I'm dispatched to a ludicrously posh London shop to buy all the necessary equipment to catch a pike.

'May I help you, sir?' says the snooty assistant.

'Er . . . well . . . I want to catch a pike.'

'Don't we all, sir?'

'What have you got that will help me?'

Once the snooty one realizes that I'm a man with an AmEx card, he produces large quantities of expensive equipment, all of which he insists is essential. I also buy a book on how to do it, which I start to read.

The next weekend, Sir Ralph is looking forward to using his new toys. But it is very much in his character not to read the instructions. He just assumes he knows how to do it.

'I really do recommend taking a good look at the book, sir . . .'

'Just get the boat out, Frank. Those ducklings are disappearing at the rate of at least one a day and I'm going to get the culprit.'

We wobble aboard the little rowing boat with our expensive nets and lines.

'Row us out into the middle, Frank.'

I row. Sir Ralph sits at the back with his pike rod. I know from the book that he's done it all wrong and, not surprisingly, pike aren't racing up to his line to get caught.

'I used to fish a bit as a boy, sir. Not pike, of course. But I think you might find it's more successful if you—'

'There's nothing wrong with my technique, Frank. It's the equipment. You've bought all the wrong things.'

He's trying feathers, hook, weights, all at once.

'Sir, I think—'

'Row around the lake, Frank.'

The lake is not small. I row on in silence while Sir Ralph catches his hooks on branches and weeds. I'm lathered in sweat by the time he says, 'All right, let's go back. It's clear that you wasted my money on these lines. They're just not the right ones.'

I'm too exhausted by now to argue.

Sir Ralph commissions a report on his lake and a few weeks later the expert presents it. He says the lake is overstocked. The fish are small and undernourished and one very hot day could kill the whole lot off.

The expert says, 'You need to reduce drastically the number of fish in this lake.'

'You mean,' says Sir Ralph suspiciously, 'someone will remove them for me?'

'That's right. Then the others stand much more chance of survival.'

'But what will they do with them?'

'With what?'

'The fish they take away.'

'Er . . . I'm not really sure. You see, you've got too many.'

Sir Ralph shakes his head. They're his fish and no-one, but no-one, is taking them away. He always thinks people are ripping him off. He decides to get the local pike fishing club in to sort out his problem instead.

We return to town. We left one of the boys guarding the house while we were away and it's obvious he's been using the jacuzzi while watching the video and quaffing Sir Ralph's champagne. It's the high jump for him.

Sir Ralph's having dinner in a restaurant and I'm at a nearby table, when the mobile phone rings. I see his face pucker up with annoyance. He doesn't like the phone ringing in restaurants.

'Frank—' It's one of the other lads.

'You're not supposed to ring on this phone at lunchtime!'

'Frank, phone home at once. Now, mate.'

Sir Ralph's glaring at me but I ring Claire and hear her crying.

'I'm on my way to hospital.' She is six months' pregnant now. 'I'm in such pain that I called the doctor. He's getting an ambulance.'

Claire has very recently had an operation to remove the cyst which has been growing alongside the baby. It seemed to have gone well.

'What does the doctor think the problem is?'

'Something to do with the operation. I can't talk, it hurts too much.'

I go straight over to Sir Ralph. He's furious. I tell him what's happened and his anger vanishes.

'Take the car, Frank, go now.'

'I'll wait till someone comes to take over from me here.'

'Don't wait. Just take the car from outside the restaurant and go.'

The car is a big BMW and 150 m.p.h. is no problem for it. I phone the hospital on the mobile.

'Claire Collins . . . she was admitted this evening . . .'

'Ah,' says the nurse, 'I'm afraid your wife's very ill.'

'What is it?'

'Possible kidney failure . . . we're not sure. But you really shouldn't be wasting time on phone calls. If you want to see your wife again you should get here as soon as possible.'

Claire dying. Claire with possible kidney failure. The BMW flashes through the fading winter evening. I'm circling Oxford when a blue flashing light appears in the mirror.

'In a bit of a hurry, sir?' says the elderly policeman who bends over me.

'Yes, yes, my wife is very seriously ill and I'm on my way to the hospital . . .'

He smiles.

'That's what they all say, sir.'

'It's true!'

'Just step into our car please, sir.'

'But my wife . . .'

There's a second policeman now, a much younger man. He notes my agitation and looks at me sympathetically. He believes my story. But the first policeman has seen it all before.

'Please don't keep me here long. My wife could be dying. Phone the hospital if you don't believe me!'

'Just step inside, please, sir.'

'Look, I was trained to drive fast. Trained by the police. I used to be on a counter-terrorist team.'

'Yes, sir. Weren't we all?'

I have to wait while he writes out my ticket. His hand moves ridiculously slowly across the page.

'Hurry, please! I must get going!'

At last it's over. I run from their car to mine and set off again, only slowly. At least as long as they can see me.

When I get to the hospital I find the danger has passed. Claire's lying comfortably on a drip. The hospital doesn't know what caused the pain but they've established it wasn't kidney failure. She's going to be all right. I could cry with relief.

We are both worried about the effect of all this on the baby. Christmas comes and goes and a few days later, to our joy, Lucy is born, happy and healthy.

Among the flowers Claire receives is a bunch from Sir Ralph. But in the new year my relationship with him becomes strained. Maybe, now that I've made up my mind what course my life is to take, I'm less submissive. Maybe Sir Ralph is changing. The Fiona Wright scandal has affected his standing. He's not invited to the same parties. He's no longer a guest at Chequers or Downing Street.

Our usual arguments, over men's jobs and bonuses, grow acrimonious. By springtime I'm sure that I won't last much longer. Summer brings a release. Sir Ralph goes to St Tropez for six weeks. He comes back brown and relaxed and perhaps even happy.

The post-holiday mood is shortlived. Soon men are being dismissed and we're back to arguing over every bonus. One day Sir Ralph asks me to dismiss a good man for such a trifling reason that I refuse. There's a row brewing.

'This is it, boys, I know it,' I say to the other lads in the basement.

'Well, you've been here almost three years!' they say. 'It's amazing anyone's lasted that long.'

The phone goes and it's the boss calling me upstairs. The boys exchange glances.

Sir Ralph often works from his living room. The whole interior is the work of an exuberant lady designer and everything in this room is brand new and perfect. He gestures me to one end where the sofa and armchairs are leather and there's a writing bureau. He doesn't look at me. He's busy doing something, arranging the magazines on the coffee table, sorting out some papers. He's always busy, so that he doesn't have to look you in the eye.

'So, we've got a problem with Dennis,' he begins.

There is a long pause. Sir Ralph is master of the pause. He knows that the pause can be a powerful weapon and he's a black-belt pauser. But after all this time with him, I've learned a thing or two about pauses myself and I let this one go on. Finally, when it's clear he's not going to speak, I say, 'Well, I think he's a good man. But there does seem to be a minor problem.'

'Minor! You think it's minor!'

This is what I've been waiting for. A proper argument with the man.

I shrug carelessly, although my heart's beating faster, 'So, let's sack Dennis. Next week we can sack someone else. Let's just sack them all.'

'I don't like your tone, Frank.'

'I don't think we can just keep disposing of people this way. We've lost some good men.'

Gradually, as I refuse to give in, the discussion escalates into a row, more in tone than in content. Soon both our voices are raised. Only now does he look me in the eye.

Click, click, click, the alarm system keeps up its constant vigil for non-existent terrorists.

Sir Ralph does not lose control, because that is something he would never do, but suddenly he sits back in his chair and hisses in a tone that is low with anger, 'Frank, you've always judged me! You've always sat in judgement on me!'

I am taken aback by this. I've never really talked to Sir Ralph about my faith, but I know that because of it I've been a great deal less judgemental than others. Now it seems that, all this time, it's bothered him. It's bothered him to have a devout believer in his midst. It's made him uncomfortable.

'Sir Ralph, I've never judged you. And I certainly don't look down on you.'

'You do, Frank, you do.'

He's retained his cool now.

'Thank you, Frank. That's all.'

I go downstairs where the boys are waiting for me.

'Bad one, lads.'

'Did he sack you?'

'Nope, but he never does. Not face to face. He'll find some other way of doing it.'

The next morning, when it's time to take the boss to the office, he emerges wearing his shades. It's a foolproof way of avoiding all eye contact.

'Good morning, Sir Ralph.'

He grunts in reply.

The temperature in the car drops a few degrees on the way to Oxford Circus. Sir Ralph's on the phone and reading the papers but there's an atmosphere. The chauffeur, who knows him well, looks at me and winks.

We get to the office. I'm tense all morning as I wait for something to happen. It reminds me of the time my main parachute didn't open and I had to use the reserve: exhilarating and frightening at the same time. But by noon nothing's happened and my working week's at an end. One of the other lads arrives to take over and I drive back to Hereford as usual in the Mercedes. I drive very fast.

I say to Claire, 'Well, that's probably it with Sir Ralph.'

Claire doesn't throw up her hands in horror at the thought of the dole queue and three small children to feed. She just says, 'It's time for a change. All this sacking and the wife ringing you half the time: it was really getting to you.'

She's right.

'I'll miss the trips to London, though,' she adds. One of the perks of the job has been our use of a Burtons' flat on Oxford Street at the weekends.

I wait for a phone call and halfway through the week it comes. It's the head of Burtons' security. He's never rung me at home before.

'I know why you're phoning,' I say.

'Sorry, Frank.'

'I could see it was coming.'

I'm ready for this news and, as Claire says, I'm ready to leave Sir Ralph, but I still don't like it. I don't like being sacked.

'He's cutting back on security. Fewer men. You won't be replaced.'

'Uh huh.'

'Because of your long and very fine service, though, Sir Ralph wants to pay you off until the end of your contract. That's about ten weeks away. Only, you don't need to come into work.'

'What about my bonus for that ten weeks?'

Here's the only man at Burtons with a take-it-or-leave-it attitude to bonuses and, suddenly, I'm demanding one.

'Don't blame me, Frank.'

'He should pay it,' I insist.

'Sorry, mate . . .' I recognize his tone. It's the same tone I adopt when I've had to sack one of the boys against my will.

'What about the car?' I ask.

326

'Someone will be round for it at the weekend.'

'Why can't I keep it until the end of my contract?' I'm being bloody-minded now, but I can't stop myself. After almost three years with this man, three years of unswerving loyalty and even a friendship of sorts, he's getting someone else to have this conversation for him.

The head of security argues reluctantly over the car.

'It's OK,' I say at last, 'I don't really want it. I'm just fed up at the way he does things.'

Within a few days I have another job, working for the Egyptian millionaire Mohamed al Fayed, owner of Harrods and House of Fraser.

Before accepting me, he wants a sample of my handwriting for analysis. The lads assure me he does this to all prospective employees. He only takes close-protection people on personal recommendation and if he doesn't like someone he doesn't have to offend whoever recommended them: he just has to say the graphologist's report wasn't favourable. Mine must be OK because I get the job.

I'm to start in a low-grade position doing house security. As soon as a place opens on Mr al Fayed's close-protection team, I'll be moved up to bodyguarding. I live in a dingy basement room behind the Dorchester, take a drop in salary of one third and lose my company car.

I go for a few drinks with the Halpern security boys and announce my intention of getting my missing bonus.

'You'll never manage it,' they say.

'I will.'

I'm on nightshift at the moment, which gives me free time during office hours. I'm pretty sure I know where Sir Ralph will be at one o'clock today but I phone the lad on duty to check. This will probably be my last meeting with Sir Ralph, and I look a lot smarter than I did at the first meeting, largely because he gives away his old suits and I'm wearing one of them.

I wander up to Burtons' security with a wave and a smile.

'Er . . . hi, Frank,' they say nervously. They're not sure what to do when I slip past them. The expressions on their faces say, oh-oh! I hear them making a phone call. It's probably to the lad who replaced me as head of Sir Ralph's personal security.

Here's Sir Ralph in the gym as expected. He doesn't look pleased to see me. But he's at a disadvantage, sweating on his treadmill in his running gear, his headphones playing Dire Straits. 'Can I have a word with you, Sir Ralph, when you've finished?' I ask politely.

He agrees. What else can he do? I know so many details of his business and now I've moved up the road from Harvey Nichols to Harrods.

His bodyguard appears.

'Hello, mate,' I say.

'Hello, Frank . . . er . . . is everything all right, sir?'

'Yes, thank you, Simon.'

'There's not going to be any trouble is there, Frank?'

'No, no trouble,' I say, smiling.

Sir Ralph changes after his workout and meets me in one of the offices adjoining the gym. He doesn't want to take me up to the nerve centre of phones and secretaries and security because he already smells defeat.

'Now,' he says briskly, trying to seize control of the situation, 'I haven't got long, so be quick.'

'Thanks for saying how well I've served you over the last few years. I'm sorry my contract isn't being renewed. But when the message came that you'd been very pleased with my work, I was disappointed not to receive my last bonus.'

'Well, it's not up to me. It's up to the head of Burtons' security.'

I laugh but it's not a nice laugh and Sir Ralph begins to look worried.

'Come on, Sir Ralph, we both know the truth. For heaven's sake, it's not even your money! It's the Burton Group's money.'

Soon, we're both angry. In fact, I'm furious. I don't really care about my bonus, I'm here to rebuild my pride. I've been sacked and in an underhand way. We shout, and at one point I stand up. He shrinks back a little in his chair. He thinks I'm going to hit him. Of course, I'm not but the thought makes me smile a little. First George, half asleep in his underpants wielding a bedside lamp, and now me, angry and hurt.

Finally he agrees to the bonus. The atmosphere relaxes a little, at least on my side. I even look at him with something like affection. I've seen this man nervous and sweaty before making a presentation. I've seen him playing the tyrant. He's a captain of industry and I respect him for it but we're all a bundle of human failings and weaknesses, every one of us.

'Well,' I say, remembering that, despite it all, I've always liked and admired him, 'we've worked together a long time and spent a lot of hours together. I think we should part friends.'

He blinks a few times and I hold out my hand to him.

'Certainly, Frank,' he says. 'I wish you well.'

But his handshake is flimsy and he avoids my eye.

# 27

I HAVE A THREE-YEAR WAIT BEFORE I CAN BE CONSIDERED FOR
ordination into the Church of England. Despite this, and the long
selection process, I have a quiet sense of certainty about my future.
Not confidence. I've never been sure of myself. But I am sure of God.

To prepare myself, I read as much as I can. My reading now
becomes less that of a man who's lost and looking for guidance and
more that of a man who's trying to grasp an enormous subject. And,
of course, I throw myself into the life of the Church.

Holmer is a pretty, small, black-and-white church, typical of the
area, which is being engulfed by the new housing estate. But
the development is doing Holmer nothing but good because the
people who move in are attending services. Thanks to George,
the vicar, the church is filling. There's a buzz and an energy which is
exciting. And there's no hugging, hallelujahs or speaking in tongues.

Claire and I help run the Pathfinders, the youth group for eleven
to fourteen year olds. We organize outdoor activities, ice skating, a
taste test around the chip shops of Hereford, hiking, a tramps' supper,
dry-slope skiing and more. Claire becomes secretary to the Parochial
Church Council. I'm elected a member of the PCC and of Holmer's
mission strategy team, where we discuss ways of tempting new
people along to services. I bring ideas home from All Souls, Langham
Place. Not all of them transplant successfully. People are different
here. Whenever I get back from London, Hereford seems to be
moving in slow motion. But the Church itself is bursting with energy.

We make new friends and they're different from our friends at the

Pentecostal churches. They're doctors and engineers and executives and even a bank manager. The frenzied housing market is responsible for bringing so many young people to Holmer at this time. It didn't seem possible, after our last move, that prices could continue to rise. But they have, and we move again. This time we buy a trim terraced house in town, the sort which is hard to love but easy to let. We're anticipating that in a few years I'll be off to theological college.

'Do you realize,' says Claire, 'that we're yuppies now?'

One Sunday a familiar, craggy face turns up in church. It's Owen, a man who left the SAS shortly after I joined. I've noticed that, while lads in the Regiment move through life with confidence, ex-Regiment men can be unhappy, lost individuals. Many have never really left, in their hearts. One look at Owen tells me he's in need of help.

We agree to meet for a pint but Owen can't stop at one or even two pints. He has a drink problem, a history of job loss, divorces and unhappy, difficult children. It's a familiar story. Many of the teenagers best known to the Hereford police are the children of Regiment men.

Owen gets drunker and drunker. I try unsuccessfully to persuade him to go home. He wants to talk about my faith.

'Does God always forgive? Always?' he asks pleadingly.

'I believe that if you truly repent then God always forgives.'

He gets tearful.

'Not me, Frank. He won't forgive me.'

'He will if you ask Him. But what's so bad, Owen, that you think God will turn his back on you?'

'Things I did in the Regiment. Years ago.'

Slowly, drunkenly, the story comes out. The SAS was heavily involved in a dirty war in the Far East. This was all-out war, a situation in which there are few rules. Information was scarce and some prisoners did not respond to interrogation. They were flown up over the ocean in a helicopter to five, even ten thousand feet. Owen is told to start throwing them out systematically. He chucks men into the ocean until the remainder crack and agree to talk. He cries when he describes their screams and the way their arms flail as their bodies are tipped into the empty air. I look away from him. I know these people would have exploded on impact with the water.

'How many people, Owen?' I ask, hoarsely. 'And how many times?'

He doesn't reply.

Owen thought in those days that he was a hard man, unhampered by any moral guidelines. Now he finds he had a conscience all along,

331

but he has learned this too late, too late for him and too late for his children. We go home, agreeing to meet again.

Now I know what I'm going to do with my life, everything's simpler. Even getting sacked and starting a new job is less painful a process than it would have been, and I'm undaunted by the turnover of Mohamed al Fayed's security staff.

I now work for Mr al Fayed; Sir Ralph is just small fry.

Among Mr al Fayed's properties are a villa in the South of France, a house in Switzerland, a Scottish castle, a country estate close to town, a London house behind the Dorchester, a whole block of apartments in Paris and, a recent addition to his Paris portfolio, the residence of the Duke and Duchess of Windsor at the Bois de Boulogne.

House security is a grim job, just checking that doors are locked and the street is clear. A gap soon appears in one of Mr al Fayed's two personal-protection teams and I'm immediately moved up.

Once again I melt into someone else's life: their habits, family, routines and needs. Sometimes only my trips back to Hereford remind me of that other life: my own.

Occasionally I wonder if I could have stayed in the Regiment and found my way to this same point. Or, if I should have. Would it have been possible to apply for ordination from the Regiment and stay there until college? All the wilderness years could have been avoided. I miss the boys, the training, the demands and even the guns. I'm a great shot, but my skills are rarely used. I almost never carry a gun and I've traded my camaraderie with the lads for the aloofness of the al Fayed family.

Mr al Fayed has a grown-up son by his first marriage and a young family by his current wife. Mrs al Fayed, known by us as Mrs Heini, is a breathtaking Finnish beauty. She's warm and loving to her family and unassuming with everyone else, but sometimes she's a human iceberg.

The security operation around the family is extensive: perhaps there are eighty people in all. The bodyguards are just small cogs in this big wheel and intimacy is unlikely.

Soon after I join the close-protection team, the family goes up to their Scottish castle for a holiday. We fly up in the private jet. The story is that Mr al Fayed has the Koran sewn into this aircraft. When he sent his pilot along to check the plane over on delivery, he said, 'By the way, what's your religion?'

The pilot said, 'I'm a Christian, sir.'

'Then get the Bible sewn into the plane too.'

It's nice to know that we're flying with the Bible. When we arrive, our vehicles are there to meet us because another group of security staff drove them up here a few days ago.

The castle is magnificent with suits of armour lurking in the hallways. Outside there are forests where you can glimpse red deer. We're all issued with beautiful Timberland boots and Barbour coats.

I'm inside the house when Tom, our team leader, comes running up.

'Quick, get the butler's wellies on, Frank.'

'What?'

'Don't argue, just get his boots on, you'll need them.'

The butler's a big bloke and his feet are enormous. I decide that whatever I have to do out there I'm going to do it in my Timberland boots.

'Now come on, you have to get out to the cow field.'

I'm so new that I don't know where the cows are but one of the other lads, Jay, is rushing out too.

'Follow me, Frank.'

The cows turn out to be big, hairy Highland cattle with enormous horns. There are literally hundreds of them behind a big fence. I'm staring at them wondering what I'm doing here when I see the family party emerging out of the castle and walking up the track. There's the usual cordon of security around them. Some men walk ahead, Tom is with the family, there's a vehicle further up the hill and another far behind.

'What's happening?' Jay radios to Tom.

'Bring the cows up to the fence.'

'What!'

We see Tom pulling away from the family so that he can mumble into his radio unheard, 'They want to see the cows. Bring them over to the fence.'

In my career to date there have been encounters with sharks and bears but so far cattle haven't featured on my cv. However, Jay's leaping over the fence so I follow him.

'Do you know anything about cows?' I ask. The big hairies are putting up their heads and fixing us with their bulgy eyes now that we're moving in their direction. I wonder how much their horns weigh.

'Not a thing.'

By now the family is in position at the top of the field. Mr al Fayed is wearing his white hat and white wellies. He also horse rides in these wellies in Surrey. They remind me of the mortuary attendant's boots

333

at the John Radcliffe hospital but he thinks this is a good country look.

Jay and I go behind the cattle. They are staring at us, and they just know that we're incompetent in the cow department.

'Bring them closer,' says Tom over the radio.

We decide to sound confident.

'Ooooooh, yeeeeeh, uuuuuuuup,' we howl in a farmerish way that we've heard on *The Archers*. The cattle are surprised. They'd thought we were idiots and here we are sounding like genuine cowmen. They turn around and amble in the direction of the family.

'Well, this is easier than I thought it would be,' says Jay.

'Don't know what I was worrying about,' I agree.

As we get near the fence a few cattle start jumping about. We say, 'Oooooooh, yeeeeeh.'

Tom's voice comes over the radio.

'Stop the cows.'

We look at each other.

'Er, Tom . . . how do we . . .?'

But Tom's under pressure up at the top of the field.

'Just stop them. The children are frightened, one's crying. Just bring a few of them forward, Mr Fayed's saying, just a few.'

'Well, we'll try.'

We move up the sides of the herd and manage to cut in on a small group at the top end. We do this by walking right into the midst of the animals. I try not to look at their horns.

'Oooooooh, eeeeeeeeh, uuuuuuuup,' we say, but less confidently now. However, the cattle are speaking our language and sure enough the vast majority of them turn around and the thirty or so we've split from the herd amble on up the field. There's a certain amount of confusion as some try to go the wrong way.

'No, you cow, that way! Down there!' we yell. Finally, we've succeeded. We're good at this. We understand cows.

By now we're quite close to the family and can see them clearly. They are all laughing. Why are they laughing? One of the children is doubled up, pointing at me. I wonder why. Then I hear a thunder of hooves behind me. I turn and there is a beast, its head down, its massive pointies aimed like missiles, charging for me with murder on its mind.

I run. I have always been a fast runner but now I break my own record. I dive over the fence with seconds to spare. My first thought is that I'm glad I wasn't wearing the butler's wellies, because I certainly would have died in them. The family seems unperturbed by my possible demise. They are screaming with laughter. So is Jay, back in the field. He's laughing so hard he doesn't hear the sound of hooves.

'Jay! Behind you,' I yell. It's another mad cow. Jay dives for the fence and out of the field. He just makes it. More gales of laughter from the family.

We're dusting ourselves down when the radio crackles into life.

'Er . . . Frank. Do it again.'

'Pardon?'

I see Tom walk away from the family, hunched over the radio. He mutters, 'Mr Fayed says, do it again.'

'Get lost.'

'Come on, Frank. He really wants you to.'

'He can take a running jump.'

'Er . . . Jay?'

'No, Tom. No way.'

Maybe I'll be sacked for this but I'd rather be jobless and live. However, Mr al Fayed is good-humoured.

'Well done!' he says when he passes us. 'We enjoyed that.'

Mohamed al Fayed is a devoted family man, but he works very hard. He's in his office at the top of Harrods most weekdays but we can't relax while he's working because he frequently and unexpectedly makes forays into the shop.

Harrods is a maze, and he's always trying to lose us in it. He heads towards an elevator and one of us jumps onto it, then he swerves off in the opposite direction and we're forced to run round the escalator and up again.

When he walks he's looking at goods and prices. If assistants can't answer his questions, he brings out his greatest insult: 'You donkey! Do you know who you work for?'

'Harrods.'

'I own Harrods. You work for me!'

He sometimes fires them on the spot but actually personnel usually manages to find them a job at another House of Fraser store.

Every few weeks we fly to Paris, where the boss has bought the Ritz. I have travelled ahead to check out his apartment. Mr and Mrs al Fayed arrive amid a great fuss. The police have given them a blue-light escort from the airport and now chauffeurs are carrying cases and security men are buzzing around.

'What's happening tonight, sir? Are you going out?' Tom asks amid all this chaos. Mr al Fayed grunts that he isn't and Tom and Jock, the other bodyguard, heave a sigh of relief. That means they're off duty. Unfortunately, I'm on night duty. I'll have to stay awake downstairs in an armchair by the elevator. All Paris street life passes by the glass doors, from prostitutes plying their trade to drunks who urinate in the doorway.

Some food arrives and Jock and Tom get their jackets and ties off and have a few glasses of wine. Suddenly, I hear the top door open.

'Tom! The top door's gone!'

'What! Who is it?'

'Blue!' This is one of our codewords for Mr al Fayed.

'What!'

'They're coming downstairs, Tom.'

The boys throw down their wine, jump up and start putting on their jackets and ties. By now Blue's in the lift and his chauffeur's outside with the car. Tom rushes into the lobby, his jacket half on. Jock curses the chauffeur. He's new and doesn't realize he should have told security a car had been called.

'What's the matter, Tom?' says Mr al Fayed. 'Why aren't you ready?'

Mrs Heini is there and she is making no effort to hide her contempt.

'I didn't know we were going out, sir.'

'But, I told you! What's wrong with you? Haven't you even got a car?'

Mr al Fayed can be such a mumbler that Tom obviously misheard him.

'Tcccch,' says Mrs Heini, shaking her beautiful head. She is often the ice maiden but right now she's Arctic.

'Well, we're going to the Ritz. You come when you've sorted yourselves out,' says the boss.

I go out to clear the traffic and they drive off. Around the corner comes a taxi. I flag it down.

'Tom! Tom, there's a taxi here, take it! Don't wait for a car,' I advise.

He and Jock rush out of the building and into the taxi.

'Got any money?' he says.

I give him all my francs. We're allocated great wads of currency before we leave the UK, and we generally spend it all, tipping constantly to grease the wheels of the entourage.

'Follow that car,' they yell at the driver. He gestures and shrugs and obviously doesn't speak English but drives off in the right direction.

When the party returns, Tom is groaning with misery and Jock is saying, 'Oh, don't worry, mate, it'll be all right.'

'What happened?'

It turns out I was right about the taxi driver speaking no English.

'Er . . . that . . . er . . . *voiture* . . . follow that *voiture* . . .' the boys say.

336

Finally the driver seems to understand. He cuts through the Paris traffic, weaving dangerously in and out to catch up with the boss. The boys heave a sigh of relief as the car comes into sight, but the driver does not stop when he reaches the al Fayed car. He's swerving out and trying to pull in front of it. He misses the al Fayeds by an inch and charges once more, manoeuvering them into the curb. It's Highland cattle all over again, only with cars. Jock and Tom realize that the taxi driver has misunderstood follow that car for stop that car.

Jock tries to dissuade the driver from this threatening behaviour. Tom, who is sitting on the left side of the taxi, finds that he is inches away from Mr al Fayed, who is sitting on the right side of his car. There are an awful few seconds when they are face to face, Tom making helplessly apologetic gestures through the window. He can't hear the boss but he can see his face curled up with anger and his mouth forming the words, 'You donkey! What kind of a donkey are you?' And at his side, the iceberg shakes her head. The chauffeur is glaring and hissing and the taxi driver is swearing at the boys in French.

Somehow, they all manage to arrive at the Ritz at the same time. Tom leaps out of his taxi to be a good security man but Blue turns to him and says, 'Tom, stay away! You hear me? Just stay away.'

Mrs Heini looks straight through him.

'I've had it,' groans Tom. 'I've only just been made a team leader and I won't last long.'

We try to reassure him but we both suspect he's right. I wonder if people aren't sometimes safer without security.

One of our team has been stationed for the duration of the al Fayeds' stay at the Bois de Boulogne, in the Windsors' house, which is undergoing renovation. I decide to walk there one night and I phone Mike to say I'm on my way. It doesn't look far on the map and the Bois is a huge wood in the town, which ought to be a nice relaxing walk.

'Which is the best way?' I ask the *gardienne* of the apartments.

'Well . . . I wouldn't walk there tonight.'

'Oh, it's not far, just a few miles.'

When I reach the Bois, I become aware of figures moving behind the trees. As I go deeper into the forest, there are more people, people lining the pavement. At first I'm confused. Then a woman walks up to me and opens her coat. Beneath it, she's naked. I realize that I'm surrounded by prostitutes, male and female. And what prostitutes. Every kind of perversion is catered for. I haven't even dreamt of most

337

of them but, as I walk towards the palace, I lose my innocence. I know that now I've seen these things I won't forget them. I'm reminded of the time I was a young cadet in Germany and the men showed me their hard-core pornography.

The prostitutes offer themselves and I refuse. I try to look innocent, waving my map and asking the way. But they just shout and spit at me. They don't believe in innocence. They believe I'm just looking for the right prostitute and they want it to be them. Behind them is always a lurking presence. The pimps.

Finally I see an old bag lady sitting by the side of the road. She has long grey hair and must be nearer eighty than seventy. I walk up to her with my map to ask directions. She turns to me with a toothless smile and opens her coat. This is a horror show. I just want to get out.

I speed up but the faster I move the more I become aware of flickering shadows and movement behind me. Before, all the movement in the forest was independent of me but I know that now I have been noticed and that I'm a target. I am certainly going to be mugged and I have nothing to protect myself with except a Parker pen. I examine its point in my pocket. What would make a better weapon? A pen with the nib in, or out?

I'm not scared of a mugging, only scared of my wounded pride. The bodyguard who gets mugged. I imagine the way Mrs Heini would look at my black eyes and broken nose. Her disdain as she says, 'Tcccch.'

I speed up until I'm almost running. The figures are getting close to me now. I can hear them as well as see them. I have only a few minutes before they'll be upon me. What's a couple of miles' walk through a wood at night if you're an ex-SAS man? A problem, if the wood happens to be in the centre of Paris.

Suddenly, there's the palace ahead of me. I bang anxiously on the gate and a hatch slides open. Mike's face appears.

'Hurry up, mate, I'm about to be mugged.'

Bolts rattle and slide on the big iron gates. When he opens it I see that he has a big dog by his side.

'Didn't you get a taxi?'

'No, I walked.'

'You must be mad! This place is really dangerous!'

When they're in England at weekends, the family usually goes to their estate in the country. The house is gorgeous. It has an indoor pool with mosaics and fountains. Despite the size and beauty of the house, Mr al Fayed has a weird desire to spend his time in a tent. He has a small white marquee erected on the lawn, where he works. It has carpets, lovely furniture, a phone line, and is completely weatherproof, but it's still a tent.

He likes to ride and, especially, to walk in the country. He's small and stocky but he strides out purposefully. One day we're walking when he turns to me and gestures me to come closer.

'Frank. You have children?'

His English isn't always easy to understand.

'Sir?'

'Children. You have children?'

'Well, yes, I have three children.'

'Good, good. Children are good, yes?'

'Oh yes, sir.'

We stride on in silence and I fall back to my position.

That night, the chauffeur appears with an enormous bag.

'Mr al Fayed gave me these for your children.'

I open the bag and it's full of mini-computers, perhaps six of them. This is very strange. The boss doesn't even know the names or ages or sex of my children. But I know how generous he can be. His own children have the run of the toy department at Harrods and he can be kind to strangers' children too.

'You have that,' he says to a child who is admiring a particular toy.

The child stares up at him.

'It's OK, you have that. This is my shop.'

He signs to the woman who runs the department to sort out the receipt. The parents are usually gobsmacked.

'You mean . . .?'

'I own this store,' he reassures them.

Confronted by this bag of toys, I double-check with the chauffeur that they're really for me.

'Don't ask questions,' he advises, 'just take it.'

But I feel uncomfortable. Perhaps Mr al Fayed intends me to give them to someone else. If this is so, it would be embarrassing if I'd kept them.

I ask my team leader, Tom, for advice.

'No,' he says confidently, 'there's some mistake. The lion just doesn't do that sort of thing. You must ask him to clarify.'

The next day I sidle up to Mr al Fayed.

'Excuse me, sir.'

'Yes, Frank.'

'The chauffeur brought me some presents last night . . . are they for my children?'

He looks at me. He's not pleased.

'You think I'd give you presents?'

I flounder.

'Er, well, not really, sir . . . I mean . . .'

'I haven't given you any presents. Give them back.'

'Yes, sir.'

At first I am relieved. The presents weren't for me and I've discovered the mistake and returned them. The chauffeur apologizes and takes the bag of computers to the gardener's children, as instructed. I wonder. Perhaps they were for me but somehow I transgressed protocol with my blundering questions. Perhaps I should just have thanked him for them.

# 28

I CAN'T BE CONSIDERED FOR ORDINATION UNTIL I'M CONFIRMED. THERE will be a confirmation at Holmer in December when, I learn, the Bishop of Hereford will lay hands on me, confirming my faith and blessing me. As he does so, I'll receive the strengthening gift of the Holy Spirit.

Confirmation classes start in the autumn. I can't attend all of them because I'm in London half the time but George, the vicar, promises to fill me in on what I miss. The other students are some elderly ladies who want to be confirmed in case they die and some giggling thirteen-year-olds who have been told they have to be confirmed.

'You're not missing much,' confides George.

He's also concerned that no Church of England selector is going to be impressed by my complete ignorance of the Church and its ways. He suggests that a retired friend of his, Bishop Gordon Savage, has both the knowledge and the time to help me.

I thank him and agree that I need this knowledge but deep down inside I think Church lessons are ridiculous. I'm not interested in becoming a minister so that I can tell people about the Church. All I know about Gordon Savage is that he was embroiled in some old scandal. The Bishop and the Bluebell Girl, said the headlines.

Despite my doubts I like the bishop so much when I meet him that I am determined to be a good pupil. Gordon says with a chuckle that I'm not having Church lessons, I'm being Anglicized. I think this sounds good.

He's a small, round man in his eighties, enthusiastic and kind, a scholar of both Greek and Hebrew, which he teaches to Hereford's Jews. His wife, the former Bluebell Girl, and now a committed Christian, is in her forties. It's hard to imagine them both at the centre of a tabloid scandal.

We meet fortnightly. He lives in a big Victorian terraced house and we sit at his chipped Formica kitchen table with our cups of tea. He digs out a biscuit barrel with some half biscuits in the bottom.

'I'd like some exercise,' says Gordon on our second meeting, 'and since we're only talking there's nothing to stop us walking as well.'

After that we spend most of our time together walking the dog around the flood common. Back at the house, he picks books out for me to read.

'Tell me what you think of this one, Frank.'

One day, when we know each other well, I say, 'Gordon, I think I've seen you before. A long time ago.'

He looks frightened for a moment. He probably thinks I'm referring to the bishop and the bluebell girl.

'You took my name and address once.'

He's interested now.

I describe the American evangelists' meeting I attended at St Peter's soon after my conversion four years ago, when I was still glowing but lost. His face changes as he starts to remember. 'Yes, they did some sort of a play. And then everyone closed their eyes . . . And then they asked people to come forward . . .'

'Well, I was there. I came forward. And you took my name and address.'

He blinks at me. 'Did I get in touch with you?'

'No.'

'No?'

'I waited for your call. I didn't know where to go and I was desperate for your call. But it didn't come.'

Gordon is full of apologies. He explains that they had expected a handful of people and that he and the other counsellors were intending to pray with just one person. When they ended up with ten each they didn't know what to do, so they just took our details and got in touch at a later date.

'I don't know how it was that you slipped through the net. I thought I'd followed up every name on that list. Why, we could have been doing this years ago if I'd just made that call!'

We laugh. We both know that if he had phoned me, everything would have been different. We both think, without even needing to

342

say it, that for some reason God didn't intend that call to be made. I look back over my last four years of intense Christianity, how I've wandered through such a maze of people and Churches and religious experiences, and I don't regret one moment of it.

On one occasion in the early winter, when the wind's scudding around us and leaves are blowing into our hair, we walk over the Victoria Bridge. I look down at the Wye. It's full of dark winter rain and, although its flow is deep and purposeful, the wind is creating little waves. I remember my vision and how Claire and I were baptized in it that summer's day. I'd like to lean on the bridge and look a while longer but Gordon is deep in the Lambeth Quadrilateral. It is some kind of declaration of agreement by all the Anglican Churches – the Worldwide Communion of Anglican Churches. It sounds more like a dance.

At home afterwards I feel disloyal to Gordon when I tell Claire, 'I've just spent the whole morning on a load of unpronounceable drivel which has got nothing whatever to do with God!'

Claire says that even drivel comes in useful sometimes. She's busy trying to work out how she can get to my confirmation and Charlotte's nativity play at the same time.

As I wait in Holmer church for the bishop to arrive and confirm me, I pray. I'm thinking about my future, how I'm building it on the assumption that I'll become an Anglican minister. But supposing I've misread God's purpose? Supposing it's not going to happen?

I pray in a way that I thought I'd left behind. I thought I'd stopped asking God for signs and reassurance a long time ago but I say, Lord, when the bishop lays hands on me, please give me a sign that what I'm doing is right. Please speak to me.

When the Bishop of Hereford lays his hands on my head and prays for me to receive the Holy Spirit, I do feel something extraordinary. I feel a glow from his hands, a glow which I know to be divine and which fills me with warmth and hope and happiness. At the end of the service my sense of well-being leaves me in no doubt that something important has happened to me.

Claire has managed to get to both my confirmation and then Charlotte's nativity play. I quickly pick them up after the service and take them back to the reception. I am trying to explain to a confused Francis that the bishop is not one of the three wise men when George, the vicar, rushes up to me. He's breathless.

'Where have you been, Frank?'

'Picking up—'

'Frank, the bishop wants to talk to you.'

343

I straighten my tie and am introduced to the elderly bishop. He is tall and gaunt-faced with a shock of white hair. He says, 'I understand you're interested in being ordained. Come and talk to me about it. Phone tomorrow.'

I am almost beside myself with excitement. George is agog. He says this is a most unusual step. There should have been another two or three years before I discuss ordination with the bishop.

The following day, still excited, I phone his secretary. I explain that I'd like to make an appointment to see the bishop. She says, her voice cool, 'I see. What exactly is it about, please?'

'Well . . . ordination.'

'Ordination. Well, the correct procedure is for you to see your vicar first. Then you see the DDO. That's the diocesan director of ordinands. You don't come directly to the bishop.'

'I understand that. But I met the bishop yesterday and he asked me to come and see him.'

'Are you sure?'

'Yes.'

'Where exactly did you meet him?'

'At a confirmation service at Holmer Church.' I don't say that it was my confirmation service.

She's still surprised. She's going to check. 'Hold the line, please.'

A few minutes later she returns. 'Yes, the bishop says he will see you tomorrow. Can you come then?'

I tell her that, yes, I can see the bishop tomorrow. I phone Gordon. He has a cold and was unable to get to my confirmation last night.

'I knew it,' he laughs with glee. 'I knew God would smoothe your path. Everything's going to be easy from now on, Frank, just trust in God.'

'Gordon, what am I going to say to the bishop?'

'Well the first time you speak to him, you're going to call him My Lord Bishop.'

'I can't do that!'

'You can and you must. Now, I know it's going to be hard. Not the sort of words which trip off the tongue. So practise before you go. Practise on Claire. Practise on me. Practise until it sounds natural.'

'Right, er . . . My Lord Bishop.'

'Awful. Keep practising.'

When Claire gets home I say, 'Hello, My Lord Bishop.'

'Have you gone stark, staring . . .?'

I explain. I call her My Lord Bishop for the rest of the day. I'm happy because Gordon's words have filled me with confidence, 'Trust in God. Everything's going to be easy now.'

Later, the curate from Holmer church rings me with more advice.

'Be sure to accept a drink if he offers you one so that he doesn't think you're one of these weird fundamentalists who won't touch a drop.'

'Can I ask for beer?'

'No! Sherry. And if he gives you a choice, go for the dry. That's what he drinks.'

The next day the room is flooded with weak, welcome December sunshine as I pull out first one tie and then another. A suit? A jacket? A jacket. Finally I'm ready. I want to run down the road to the bishop. I feel that everything that is happening is happening because it's right.

The bishop's palace is a huge, grey-stone building. The waiting room is lined with books. There are three secretaries and one of them phones through to say I'm here. I wait, nervously, reading the titles of the books. Then, suddenly, the bookcase opens up. It's a door disguised as a bookcase. Standing there is Bishop John Easthaugh, wearing a collar and tie and a startling long white cardigan. He greets me warmly.

'Frank, my boy, do come in.'

'Good morning, My Lord Bishop.'

It's come out as if I've been saying it for years. He beams at me.

'Come in, come in.'

We sit down. He crosses his legs.

'Now, tell me all about yourself.'

That's a difficult one. I give him a short life history and he asks me questions about the SAS. He nods. He asks more questions.

'And do you pray?'

'Well, yes, I have quite a disciplined prayer life at the moment . . .'

I describe my routine. He asks me what I'm reading. At one point he gets up and heads for a decanter.

'Would you like a drink?'

'A sherry, please.'

'Dry?'

'Yes, please.'

We talk and it seems to me that things are going well. Then there is a long silence. The bishop studies my face. I look away from him. He seems to be very deep in thought. Finally he speaks. His half smile has disappeared.

'Frank, I take my job very seriously and part of it is selecting people for the ministry. I've enjoyed meeting you very much. Thank you for coming. But I'm afraid I don't believe that you're called.'

I stare at him in disbelief. I can hardly take in what he's saying.

'I don't believe you're called', he says gently, 'to serve in the Church of England.'

I am stunned. It is even possible that my mouth is open.

He prompts me to go. 'Thank you for coming, Frank.'

At this cue I stand up and walk mechanically towards the door. I am numb, robbed of thought, by shock. I cross the room. I am almost at the door.

If you touch that door handle, it's all over, I think with such force that instead of opening the door I turn. I say, 'My Lord Bishop, you're mistaken. I believe that I am called to the Church of England to be a minister. Everything fits into place if this happens. It makes sense. I can see how God's purpose and timing is right and . . . ' I run out of words so repeat myself lamely, 'and I believe you're making a mistake.'

A light comes into the bishop's eyes and he smiles. He says, 'I knew as soon as I met you that God had called you into His Church.'

He has been testing me, and I've passed.

He continues. 'I myself am going to ordain you. Come here, young man.'

In his office, with the desk and the books and the sherry decanter, he tells me to kneel. He puts his hands on my head. He says the prayer of ordination and consecration. I know there is much more to learn and do before I can be a minister but in my heart there is no doubt that Bishop John Easthaugh is ordaining me now.

I leave feeling lightheaded with joy and relief.

'Did he ordain you to be a priest or a deacon?' asks Gordon Savage, after whooping excitedly.

'A priest, I think.'

'That's wonderful. It's remarkable. He is a remarkable man. You can be a minister tomorrow if you want to be.'

'I couldn't . . . I wouldn't . . . '

'It's all right, he knows that. Now, you'll have lots of selection boards to pass but they're a mere formality because Bishop John is the old-fashioned sort of bishop who runs the diocese the way he wants to. So no-one can stop you now.'

'Will I go to college this autumn?'

'I imagine you will.'

The bishop has referred me to his diocesan director of ordinands. Walter's job is to oversee the selection and training of ordinands. He will visit Claire and me at home.

'Is he checking up that I'll make a good vicar's wife?' asks Claire.

'Yup. If you give him a weak brew, I'm out.'

Walter King's appearance is startling. He is late and rushes in wearing an anorak over his cassock. He peels the anorak off and sits down. He is wearing walking boots. They are only half-laced, and with pieces of string. Walter would not have a glittering career in the army.

He has already been told by the bishop that I am going to be a minister and he is still buzzing with indignation and concern about this when Claire hands him a cup of tea.

'I'm shocked that the bishop has said and done these things. I'm sure you realize that it is most, most, irregular. You have to be passed by the diocesan selection conference and then the Advisory Council for Churches' Ministry and I strongly advise you not to go into either saying that the bishop has already accepted you. It will endear you to no-one.'

I nod, and try to look humble. But he knows and I know that I am going to be a minister at the end of all this.

'What a very nice cup of tea,' he tells Claire. She smiles sweetly at him.

Once I was ignorant of the different theologies within the Church of England, then I was aware of them but baffled and now, finally, I'm beginning to work out where I fit in.

I'm an evangelical. Evangelicals are not to be confused with evangelists like Billy Graham. We are one large, and growing, wing of the Church of England. Evangelicals base their beliefs and actions on the Bible: it is our authority. We let as little ritual and tradition come between man and God as possible. Further down the spectrum are liberals who interpret the Bible loosely and therefore take human reason as their authority. At the other end are Anglo-Catholics, with their incense and priestly robes, their statues and elaborate altar cloths. The traditions of the Church itself are their authority. It's a hop, skip and a jump from there over the fence into Roman Catholicism which has the same religious trappings but takes as its authority the Pope.

So now I'm beginning to understand how the Church works, I can see it's like politics and can be just as tedious. But from this point, I assess everyone according to their place in this structure.

At Easter, the first selection board comes. I am in Malvern, where

347

Claire and I are helping to run a Christian youth camp. I teach canoeing. The weather is bleak, and each day we repeat the same lesson for successive groups of teenagers.

'Right, let's see who can get their life jacket on first!' I yell over and over, with progressively less enthusiasm.

This year, I feel defeated by the camp. The kids enjoy the canoeing and other activities but when we try to talk to them about Christianity they're sometimes hostile.

One evening, I drive to a large house in Hereford, where the selection board is held. There are three people, two ministers and one lay minister, sitting in three different rooms and we're sent around the house to talk to each of them individually. All the interviewers work hard to put me at my ease. Because I know I have the bishop's support I quickly relax. But I am careful in my choice of words.

'Don't talk about being born-again, please, please, please!' Gordon Savage has said.

'Thank you all for coming,' says Walter King. 'We'll phone you all in the morning to let you know what we've decided. Frank, can I phone you at youth camp?'

'No, I'll ring you.'

I spend the night alone at home and very early the next morning I get up to return to Malvern. The day is cold and grey and that's how I feel when I set off from Hereford. Another day of saying the same things over and over again about canoeing to a bunch of unreceptive kids. I wish I was still asleep in bed.

On this unpromising journey, in the grey morning light, alert but drowsy, I have a vision.

What I see is more palpable than the imagination. It is a vision and God is telling me something, I'm sure of that.

A shining figure is looking at me. His face is bright and luminous but still indistinct, because I can only stare into his eyes. They are compelling. They are full of love. They are moist with tears. The figure reaches down into the dirt and searches through it to pick out some bright, colourful jewels. He puts them into a crown. Still looking at me, he says, 'Everyone, everyone, is a jewel in my sight.'

The figure fades. I am still driving along the road so I assume, I hope, that the vision has lasted a split-second rather than the minutes it seems. I am moved almost to tears by it. I continue my journey feeling choked with emotion. I am in no doubt that the figure I saw was that of Christ.

When I get to the youth camp all the other leaders are having their early morning meeting. I grab a cup of coffee and join them.

'Well . . .?'

'What news?'

'How did it go?'

Claire just raises her eyebrows at me.

I want to be quiet after my vision.

I say, 'I think everything was OK.'

We discuss some of the children in our care. We pray and then I tell them about my vision. I must, because it is relevant to all of us, but describing it makes me shy. I can't even look at Claire. 'I've felt annoyed and frustrated with some of the kids at this camp. I've felt my enthusiasm flagging,' I admit. 'But I believe God was reminding me that however annoying or irritating the kids can be, each one of them is a precious gem in God's sight.'

'Yes, and of course it has special significance for you as you're hoping to become a minster,' someone says, with a little bitterness. Some people are sceptical, others jealous, and a few are awed.

'I feel this is an admonishment from God,' I say. 'Because I'm not taking my work here seriously. I've been too distracted thinking about myself.'

Claire says nothing. Does she think I'm a fraud? I decide to ask her later, but somehow the right time doesn't arrive.

During that morning's canoeing, I find extra energy.

'Right, let's see who can be first to get their life jacket on!' I roar with renewed enthusiasm.

When we break for lunch I phone Walter King. My heart is beating fast. I hear his voice, the pips start to whine, I shove my 10p into the slot.

'Frank! How are you?' he asks jovially.

'Walter . . .' We're on first name terms now, 'Walter, what did they decide?'

'Who? Oh, the diocesan selectors. Do you really want to know?'

He's teasing me. A good sign.

'Walter . . .?'

'It's unanimous, Frank. They selected you unanimously.'

I'm relieved. Even though the bishop has promised me he'll over-ride the selectors if necessary, I still wanted them to want me. And they do.

Having passed the diocesan selection board, I now have to face a national selection board, the Advisory Council for Churches' Ministry. My name goes on a waiting list and I start looking at theological colleges. The bishop is keen for me to go to one of the Oxbridge colleges but I'm convinced I'm just not clever enough. I

349

picture rows of thoughtful students wearing mortar boards on their heads.

The curate at Holmer is a graduate of a college he highly recommends. It's right for me because it's an evangelical college but it's in London. No good. I don't want to spend another three years in London, and I don't want to take the family there.

'No, no, it's not like being in London at all. You have to see it.'

Through him I visit Oakhill and get to know a few lecturers and students. The curate's right: it isn't like being in London. The college is a big Victorian house and, although it is close to the M25, its vast, overgrown grounds and high walls protect it from the bustling world outside. There is housing for married students inside its safe environment.

I go to a few lectures to see what they're like. One is called Family Perspectives. There are only about eight students in the class and the teacher looks up when I enter. 'Hello, are you joining us?'

'Is that all right?'

'It's fine, come on in and tell us a bit about yourself.'

I immediately wish I hadn't come. I hate telling a bit about myself. Not only do I have a thorough training in secrecy, I never know which bits to tell.

I stand up and say, 'Er . . . well . . . er, my name's Frank. I'm thirty-two years old. I'm thinking of coming to study here. I used to be in the army but now I'm a security consultant for the chairman of Harrods.'

I sit down again as fast as I can.

'Right, Frank, thanks for talking to us. But, just one thing . . . Are you married?'

'Yes, I am actually.'

'I see. Thank you.'

I remember the name of the module. Family Perspectives. I've just talked about myself and my job without even mentioning my wife and children. This is a clanger. I cringe for the rest of the lecture but I know that I've learnt something already and it's not book learning but that other sort of life learning which I never expected college would provide.

Soon I've decided that Oakhill is the college for me and after interviews I am accepted. I can start a two-year diploma course in September, which is just over three months away. But my place is provisional. I still have to pass selection by the Advisory Council for Churches' Ministry, which guarantees me Church sponsorship. As soon as I've passed we can move down to our new house at the college, even though my course doesn't start until September.

Unfortunately, all the ACCMs are fully booked until August.

'Look,' I say to the college secretary, 'the bishop's promised me that, even if ACCM rejects me, he'll override them and take me anyway. Can't you let us move in now?'

She looks at me strangely.

'Hmm, well we'll have to see,' she says.

I try this line on Walter.

'The bishop says I'm going to be ordained whether ACCM accepts me or not, Walter.'

And Walter gives me the same strange look.

'Frank, I know he says that, but he may not be able to. Don't count on anything. Just go through the process like everyone else.'

'We've been building plans on a false assumption,' I tell Claire. 'There's just a chance that we may not be going off to college this September. Or ever.'

'Oh no!' says Claire. 'We'll never get rid of Wei Lo if we don't go to college.'

Wei Lo is a non-paying lodger. She is a refugee from China. We've taken her in because we have two empty rooms at the top of the house and we feel it is our Christian duty to look after people. Claire points out that her Christian duty doesn't include liking all the people she looks after, and it is certainly hard to like Wei Lo.

She has been with us for about four months. Someone at church has asked us to sponsor her visitor's visa and Home Office conditions are that if we sponsor her, we look after her.

She is in her mid-thirties and has escaped from Communist China, where she was involved in the pro-democracy movement. She's also a Christian. It's hard to ascertain her exact beliefs because her English is poor and, anyway, that's not the sort of conversation you have with Wei Lo.

Her money has taken her as far as Malta, where a young, single man in our congregation happened to be holidaying. She latched on to him in the hope that he could get her into Britain. He thought of marrying her, but delivered her to us instead.

Wei Lo wants to work ('I strong! I work!'), but her visa doesn't permit it. We give her money and lodging but she does not see any reason to offer Claire her help in return. We accept that she is from a different culture and has had a traumatic time there, and we do not press her.

I am working one week on, one off with Mohamed al Fayed in London, but Claire has to put up with her all the time. Wei Lo hardly acknowledges Claire's presence. She treats her like a servant and totally ignores the children. She will communicate only with 'Mr Frank' to whom she shows the utmost respect. Unsurprisingly, this bugs Claire.

In the morning, Wei Lo comes down when everyone else has eaten and fries herself some cabbage for breakfast, cursing the stove.

'Cooker no good. No flame.' This is because it's electric. There's nothing we can do about that. She has a wok but it doesn't produce the desired results on our stove and so I make her a present of a nice non-stick frying pan. It is a big success, but all is still not well.

'Knife no good!'

Claire buys her a really sharp knife and is quietly delighted when she cuts herself with it.

Wei Lo was a chef in Beijing and now announces that she is going to cook us a meal. We are grateful. We spend a fortune getting the ingredients that she requires, all of which must be exactly right. This is one very expensive Chinese meal. However, it's authentic, and we're looking forward to it. She has smuggled out of China lots of little bottles of herbs and spices, which she gives us to understand are unobtainable in the West. We ask to see them and she shows us her greatest treasure, a jar of star anise.

'Herb only in China. Very special herb for very special chefs.'

Claire says, 'Oh, you can buy that in Sainsburys.'

Wei Lo looks daggers at her and Claire proves it by producing her own jar of star anise. It is clearly a blow to Wei Lo to find that China exports her little secret worldwide but she covers this with a haughty turn of her head.

'Wei Lo herb better.'

The meal takes hours to cook. We get so hungry while we wait for it that we snatch at the crumbs on the dining room table. At work, I often eat in the Harrods restaurant where a speciality is caviar and quails' eggs. When I'm in my dingy little Park Lane flat, food arrives from Anton Mosimann's Dorchester kitchens. And when I'm in Paris I quite often eat at the Ritz. After all the time, effort and money which have gone into Wei Lo's special dinner, I'm ready for her meal to be as good as any of these.

She serves it and we try to ignore the ugly mess in the kitchen but we have a horrible feeling that Wei Lo is not intending to clear up herself. Like our own top chefs, she just doesn't do that sort of thing.

Wei Lo clearly believes she has produced a winner. We are polite about the meal to the point of enthusiasm but the fact is that we can't taste the difference between this and a number 47 from our local Chinese takeaway. Afterwards, it takes Claire even longer to clear up than it has taken Wei Lo to prepare it. Fat has splattered out of the pan not just all over the stove but all over the kitchen. We agree that, if we price our time as well as the ingredients, it is the most expensive Chinese meal ever eaten.

In general, Wei Lo cooks her own meal, puts it in a bowl, and disappears with it to her room. Then, in the night, the banging starts. At first we think it is the central heating, then we wonder if she is practising some kind of martial art. It happens night after night. Time and again we are awoken by the sound of energetic and erratic banging.

Finally I ask her about it.

'Mr Frank, small fur animals.'

'In your room? Small furry animals?'

'Small. Fur. Very fast! Wei Lo has shoe . . . bang bang!' She mimes the awful thing that she is doing with her shoe to the mice. She drags her fingers through her long hair and curls up her face in distaste. 'Small fur animals in Wei Lo hair.'

'There are mice in your room and you've even had them run through your hair!'

She nods tragically. Then she mimes mouse genocide again.

'Wei Lo kill. Bang! Bang! Wei Lo kill!'

I go to her room and find that she has piled books along the bottom of the door to stop the mice from getting in. I set traps at once. I set them everywhere and tell her to stop taking food to her room.

Not one mouse is caught. This is because there are no mice in this house. Wei Lo is lying in bed in the dark. She imagines that mice are running all over her. She doesn't turn on the light, she just thumps and bangs at her imaginary mice. We don't know what she has suffered in her home country. Perhaps she has been jailed or forced to hide where mice run through her hair. But now, the mice are in her head.

'It's very sad,' I tell Claire. But Claire just draws her mouth into a straight line and does not look sympathetic. The truth is, we've both run out of patience.

Wei Lo is very anxious to go to London. She is in no doubt that all she has to do is walk into any restaurant in Chinatown and she will immediately be taken on as a chef. I warn her that the Chinese business community in London is a closed shop but she won't listen. So I arrange for her to spend a few days at a hostel run by a Church fellowship.

When I return to work in London, I take her with me. We wait together on Platform 4 of Hereford station. I am wearing my smart

353

suit ready to go straight on shift at Park Lane and she is in her baggy blue clothes. We are an odd couple and are already attracting glances. One train is cancelled and ours is an hour late, so the platform is filling up.

Wei Lo turns to me and says, 'Mr Frank, you hungry?'

'No.'

I've got used to her calling me Mr Frank and nodding deferentially to me at home. To Claire's disgust, I've even begun to like it. But, not in public.

She says, 'I eat.'

She reaches into her bag and brings out a family-sized pizza wrapped up in clingfilm. It has a reduced, half-price sticker on it from Tesco. It is uncooked. It is a doughy, gooey, tomatoey mess. People start to stare at her as she pulls off the clingfilm and, when she begins to demolish it, the whole platform is transfixed.

I try to look as if I'm not with her but she says, 'Very good, very cheap.' She waves it at me, her mouth full. 'You want, Mr Frank?'

I say, 'No thanks.'

The train arrives at last and Wei Lo has a wonderful journey. Everything amazes her, even the most commonplace. 'Mr Frank! Look, *look!*'

'Yes, Wei Lo, that's another train, it's quite normal for them to pass each other.'

Part of me is embarrassed by her, part of me is refreshed and enjoys showing her things. I am glad to drop her off at the hostel. I phone friends at the fellowship in a spare moment.

'How's she getting on?'

'Well . . . she's not the most popular person in the hostel . . .'

The hostel is supposed to be a small, self-supporting community. People staying there do chores and contribute to the community spirit but Wei Lo has refused to participate.

It's a busy week. We don't work shifts, we just work when Mr al Fayed does, and this week he works long hours. Even if he has a lie-in, we must be ready to leave Park Lane by 8.30 a.m. in case he decides to get up.

I take one of the firm's cars down to South London to pick up Wei Lo. She gets in grumpily. Only the hostel seems happy, and that's because she's going. She is in a bad mood because she has spent the week trawling Chinese restaurants for work and being turned away. I try to be sympathetic but my words leave her expressionless.

I bring her back to Central London to drop off the car and get changed. We now have 30 minutes to reach Paddington. We must catch this train because our tickets are not valid for later services without paying a large penalty.

It is a hot day. It is rush hour and there are no taxis. We can make it if we walk fast. We set off. Although big and strong and, when she wants to be, very fit, Wei Lo can also be extremely stubborn. She is carrying, among other things, her frying pan, the one I gave her when she first arrived. Maybe it's the weight of the frying pan, but she's walking very slowly. I am focused on Paddington and the train I must catch there which is going to take me home. In my mind I am far outpacing her, but only in my mind.

'Wei Lo, we've got to get there by half-past,' I say.

She scowls at me and walks more slowly.

Finally I say, 'Wei Lo, if you can't keep up, you'll have to take the next one.'

I am going to catch that train. I quicken my pace. I turn to shout over my shoulder, 'Just ask someone which train's for Hereford.'

I march on past the unmoving traffic. I gain a good 100 yards on Wei Lo. Then there is a shout from behind.

'Mr Frank! Mr Frank!'

I turn, without stopping. There she is. She is livid. Her face is red not so much with exertion as with anger, I can see that even from here. She has my frying pan in her hand. People in the street are stopping to stare at her, drivers are craning their necks to get a better look.

'Mr Frank. Your pan! Waaaaaaah!'

With this war cry and theatrical gestures she waves the frying pan in the air and then deposits it into a litter bin, the sort which is halfway up a lamppost.

Wei Lo thinks that I will be hurt because she is throwing away the pan I gave her. But to me, it is her pan and she can throw it away if she likes. To her, it is my pan which she is carrying for me. I shrug and continue walking. All I can think about is Paddington station.

As I arrive, she comes up, sweating, behind me.

'Mr Frank, Mr Frank . . .'

Mr Frank and Wei Lo have caught the train. They even manage to find seats, although happily not together, so that Mr Frank does not have to feel her angry eyes boring into him all the way home. I wish, quietly and guiltily, during the journey, that I could get a place at ACCM soon. If I pass it, we can move down to college for the summer and then, as Claire says, Wei Lo would have to go.

The next time I am back at work, there is a phone call from Claire.

'Guess what! There's been an ACCM cancellation. I've accepted on your behalf and you're going next week.'

I pass this final stage of selection. When I return to work, everything's different. In September I'll be gone. A new life is starting for me. It's going to begin in a few weeks when the family moves to London. For the rest of the summer, they'll be living in an idyllic wilderness at the end of the Piccadilly Line, just half an hour away. Everything's falling neatly into place, everything feels right. A long period of waiting and hoping and wondering is over.

We warn Wei Lo that the Hotel Collins is closing. We wanted her to go but we haven't given much thought to where, and now we start to worry about her.

I'm walking behind Mr al Fayed as he stalks across his country estate when suddenly he sinks onto a convenient bench and calls me over to him. It's a hot day. He's sweating a little. Overhead the trees are heavy with high summer leaves. The birds are quiet. Nothing moves.

'Frank. You're going to be a priest,' he tells me. He's known this for a while and he knows I know but he feels some acknowledgement is necessary.

'Yes, sir. I'm starting college this autumn.'

'I see. That's good.'

I'm dismissed, with his approval. I melt back among the thick trunks of the trees. I wait for him to stand and move on and while I wait I realize for the first time how much I'm leaving behind me. Not just a phase of my life but my whole life since the age of fifteen when I joined the boys' army. I've been trained to the highest level but from now on all my skills will be redundant. I have no skills, no training, no equipment for the future. When I get to college I'll be about as adept as a new-born baby.

'Frank, there are a lot of things you'd like to discard from your past. But God's taken you through all this for a purpose and the things you most want to throw out of the suitcase are those things which will one day be most useful to you,' the Bishop of Hereford said to me when he first met me. But suddenly I don't want to discard my past. I want to cling onto the handle of my suitcase, clutch it grimly to death. It's safe. I can move smoothly in this world I know. I don't want to throw it all away.

Mohamed al Fayed gets up and marches off across a field. I give up the shade of the woods reluctantly to follow him. I remind myself that I can't follow men for the rest of my life. I'm going to college to learn to lead.

356

Back at the house, there's a call from Claire. Another lodger has told her that she often hears Wei Lo on the phone a lot, speaking in Chinese. This can only mean that Wei Lo is phoning her Chinese friends in Malta. I have shown her how to use the phone to make local calls and she was amazed to be able to do this without booking in advance. Now she's discovered that international calls are just as easy. There is no point in Claire attempting to talk to her as Wei Lo still regards Claire as beneath contempt, so the problem must wait until I get home.

On my return to Hereford I go to Wei Lo's room and say, 'Wei Lo, you really mustn't use the phone to talk to your friends in Malta.'

Wei Lo shakes her head.

'Mr Frank, I no call Malta.'

'But you've been on the phone speaking in Chinese. Claire's heard you. You must not phone Malta.'

'No, Mr Frank. Not phone Malta. Phone Beijing.'

For a moment I am speechless.

'Did you say . . . Beijing?'

Wei Lo nods so emphatically that her hair falls all over her face. 'No problem, Mr Frank. After one o'clock, cheaper.'

I say, 'What!'

I get the phone book and there is no cheap rate to China. Not that it would have been affordable anyway. I learn that Wei Lo has been phoning her brother in Beijing for about two hours a day. I am beside myself with horror. I can't hide my shock and fury and neither can Claire. Wei Lo watches us and then her face gradually disintegrates.

Remorsefully, we try to tell her that it's all right because we know she didn't understand. But it's obvious even to the insensitive Wei Lo that things are not all right.

She has a return ticket to Malta and announces that she is going to use it immediately. We tell her not to, that we'll try to take care of her, that we'll cope with the phone bills, but Wei Lo, as usual, does not listen. She leaves. I feel we have done so much for her but finally failed her in some way. We receive postcards from Malta, then Australia.

'She must have had more money than we thought,' says Claire pointedly.

Finally, there's a card from Bulgaria. Then we hear no more. The massacre at Tiananmen Square takes place very soon afterwards, changing British policy towards Chinese refugees. If Wei Lo had only remained in Britain a little longer, she would have qualified for refugee status and been allowed to stay.

British Telecom agree to let us pay off the phone bill, which is just into four figures, in instalments over a year. We can't have a phone connected in our new house because of this debt but we aren't worried. Our house sale is scheduled to take place in a few weeks' time. In just a few weeks, our money problems will be solved.

# 29

WE ARRIVE AT COLLEGE IN DARKNESS. THE BURSAR TAKES US TO THE little sixties semi in the college grounds which is going to be our home for the next few years. It proves to be already inhabited, by slugs and snails. The last human occupants have left their creamy carpets behind and these glitter and glimmer in the dim light with slug slime. We tell the children that slugs don't bite and persuade them to lay their sleeping bags on the floor. The children aren't convinced but are so tired they go to sleep anyway. So do we.

The next day our furniture arrives and we deal with the slugs. Close observation leads us to an old freezer beneath which we discover a slug Ritz. We close the Ritz.

Our new home is in a cul-de-sac of council-style houses. It's surrounded by the vast, overgrown gardens and wild woodlands of the college grounds and the children are immediately delighted with everything. Behind these high walls, just out of earshot of the M25, we're living in the quietest, safest home we've ever had.

I ring my brother Gary.

'I phoned you and got number unobtainable!' he says. 'What's going on?'

'We've moved.'

'Moved! Where are you?'

'London. Gaz, listen —'

'Is that why you're talking with a funny accent?'

'What sort of accent?'

'Well, not a Geordie accent.'

'I still have a Geordie accent!'

'Not much, mate.'

'Gary, I've got something to tell you. I've been meaning to tell you ... I'm at college.'

Gary makes me repeat this, twice.

'I'm at college. Theological college. I'm training to be a minister.'

There is a long, long silence.

'What sort of a minister? The prime minister?'

'Very funny. A minister of the Church. The Church of England.'

'You're going to be a vicar!'

Gary's voice is half-shocked, half-mocking.

'That's right, Gaz. I'm going to be a vicar.'

'Well,' says Gary. He's looking for something to say. I can hear him searching for words. Eventually, all that comes limping out is, 'That's nice.'

I don't even want to think what my dad will say when Gary tells him. I don't even want to think about his face.

Our house sale falls through. The property market has completely crashed now and we have little hope of selling or letting. But for the summer months I'm still working and this income cushions us from the dramatic drop which we know is coming.

In September, college begins for me and school begins for Francis. I am terrified. So is Francis. Claire takes a picture of us in the garden. I'm wearing an ironed shirt and pressed trousers. My brand-new books are under my arm. We are both grinning with the same expression of sheepish apprehension.

I walk the few hundred yards to the imposing college building. Its door is enormous and today I am a very small schoolboy. I am aware that, while I finished my education at fifteen, most of the people here already have degrees. They're sure to know the Bible better than I do. I'll be writing essays when previously it was hard enough to write a letter. I could never even think of anything to fill the blue army aerograms: I'd write Dear Claire and then stare at the page for hours. And now I'm going to write essays which are thousands of words long. Part of me is ready for this change and hungry to learn and that part fuels me as I walk to my first lesson.

The beautiful building has little in common with Whitley Bay Grammar. Inside, it is a strange mixture of old and new: ornate fireplaces and Formica tables, oak panelling and pine benches. Some rooms are small and intimate, others echo.

One of our first lessons is designed to help us study. I sit at the back where I hope I won't be noticed. I realize that I'm less likely to be

360

noticed if I'm at the front under the teacher's nose, and resolve to sit there in future.

The teacher hands us each a book, which we are allowed to look at for one minute. Then we have to stand up and tell the class about it. Horrors. Mine is a German book.

'What can you tell us about this one?'

'Nothing. I can't read German.'

'Tell us something anyway.'

'Well . . . it's a big book. A big, old book. A big, old, German book . . .'

'That's it, we're getting there. How many chapters? Any dates? Can you pick out the author's name?'

I realize I know more about the book than I'd thought. The idea is to show us that we can evaluate books and their usefulness without spending a lot of time on them. The teacher tells us not to be afraid of books but to get inside them quickly.

I write my first essay. Incredibly, I get an A for it. I am over-whelmed. I have to go home right away and tell Claire. I am not thick. I am *not* thick. I can get an A for essays just like the middle-class eggheads here.

The term starts to move rapidly. There are lectures every morning except Wednesdays and the rest of the time is filled with studying and essays. I find to my amazement that I enjoy it. Sometimes I don't work. I go sneaking off into the grounds where I sit up a tree with a book. I don't read the book. I'm thinking. Five years ago I was in the SAS. Now I'm at college studying to be a minister. My life has moved from the physical to the cerebral. Everything has changed except my name and my family. My beliefs, my work, my friends, my house, my income, my vocabulary, even, I have to admit Gary was right, my accent. I've read that every cell in the human body renews itself: prob-ably not one of the cells in my body still remains from my SAS days. How can I still be Frank Collins? I sit up my tree wrestling with all this.

I am friendly with everyone at college but, as usual, form no close friendships. There are a lot of pot bellies and stamp collectors here. People who are years younger than me behave as though they're years older. I keep fit by running and many of the students regard this as an eccentricity. I can't shake off the feeling that I'm a trooper and most of the others here are officers. There is in fact an ex-army officer among the students who always wears brown brogues. It's impossible not to feel our old ranks.

Not everyone is middle class. There is Davy, who has a pony-tail and a wife who wears red lipstick and ghoulish eye shadow. He used to be a chef at McDonald's. Tony is an ex-lorry driver who was converted when his wife dragged him, against his will, to a Billy Graham meeting. He only went so that he could laugh about it afterwards but to his amazement he saw Jesus there. Jesus was sitting on the grass in front of Billy Graham and looking at Tony and saying, 'Come on, I want you tonight.' Tony thought it was a scary special effect. Then he realized that no-one else could see Jesus. When Billy Graham made the call, Tony ran down to him. Tony's life is changing, like mine did, from darkness to light. But he's still laddish, and a heavy drinker.

In the course of my first year there is devastating news. Bishop John Easthaugh is dead. He did so much to change my life. If he had died earlier, I wouldn't be here. I take time off from Oakhill to attend his funeral, which is a full Church mass. The singing, the robes, the ritual, it is all the very opposite of my beliefs but has been carried out at Bishop John's request. Whatever I think of his wishes, I must respect them. I sit through the long service remembering how much I liked and admired him.

I am attached to a church in Walthamstow. On Sundays I stop being a student and start being a trainee minister. Right from the start I feel that I'm not going to do well here. Everyone keeps saying, 'Do you know Theo?' Theo was the last trainee attached to this church and it is clear that he was adored by the congregation. They were particularly delighted with his music skills. My own skills are restricted to, for example, detailed knowledge of the working parts of sub-machine guns, and this is unlikely to delight the congregation. I am sure that they go home and say, 'That Frank. Well, he just isn't Theo, is he?'

'I've been coming here for eighty-three years!' says an old lady. 'How long have you been going to church?'

I say, 'Er . . . two years.'

Luckily she thinks I must be joking.

Others are shocked by how little I know about the Church of England. I try to be open about my ignorance but they prefer not to hear me. They want knowledgeable ministers, not men who confess their weaknesses.

Saturday nights become misery for everyone in our house as I write and rewrite my sermon. Claire learns to keep out of my way.

'Do you have to bring your sermon to bed with you?' she asks sleepily when I finally come upstairs at about two in the morning, placing my neatly typed sheets of paper on the bedside table.

'Yes. It'll help me to remember it.'

First thing in the morning, Claire is awoken by the shuffle of paper. She pulls the covers over her head as I mutter my way through the sermon yet again.

When I get up to deliver the sermon in church, there's a rustle as people drag out their pens and the yellow forms on which they've been asked to assess me. As I speak, I can see the congregation ticking little boxes on delivery, style, content and humour. I try not to watch them but my delivery, style, content and particularly my humour falter. Afterwards, I usually find that they've given me average grades.

The curate helpfully suggests I'll do better if I copy some of the vicar's mannerisms. The vicar makes a point, pauses, folds his arms and leans forward, takes off his glasses and waggles his finger at the congregation, making the point again. The curate has learned to do this too. It looks OK when the vicar does it but odd when the curate tries to copy him. I decide not to do any finger-wagging.

The more preaching assignments I'm given, the less confident I feel. I have a great sense of awe and responsibility, handling God's word in this way I could easily misuse it and upset people. Each time I have to stand up in front of the congregation I'm more worried. I gradually become convinced that, even if I pass my exams, I'll be a terrible minister.

Just once I'm asked to take a whole service alone. It's in a daughter Church, a black Church run by a minister who has returned to Africa for a holiday and mysteriously hasn't come home when expected. The church is an old mission building and services are Pentecostal in style. With my Pentecostal background I enjoy every minute of it. My sermon is punctuated by cries of, 'Hallelujah, brother! Tell it like it is, brother! Praise God!' and I soon get into my stride. It is terrific to have this response. I realize I've already become used to the blank stares of the congregation at Walthamstow.

I talk about healing, and I say that I'll be happy to pray with anyone after the service, although I'm not guaranteeing any healing. And, if I'm tied up, just see my wife Claire because she's sitting down there and we're a team. At the end I process out, with the Church wardens. Everyone is enthusiastic and pleased with my sermon (of course, on this occasion there are no yellow marking sheets). Members of the congregation come up to me, one by one, clasp my hand and shake it for a long time. I am unaccustomed to such kindness and generosity. I glance over at Claire and there she is in one of the pews surrounded by a crowd of people who want to pray with her.

A few days later we are shocked to learn that the reason for the minister's absence has been discovered: he has been killed in a car accident.

Our biggest problem here is money. We have dropped from my salary to a grant of £3,000 a year and are finding it difficult, if not impossible, to keep a family, buy books and pay off Wei Lo's phone bills on such a low sum. We have always been unable to save, and in recent years unwilling to do so. Three thousand pounds a year is all we have. We have still not sold our house in Hereford and there's no prospect of letting it either.

The Church of England loans us the money to pay our mortgage and month after month the loan gets larger. Over the year we revisit Claire's mother and our friends in Hereford. We pick up the junk mail at the house and wander around the cold, empty rooms. This place is a big, white elephant, and an expensive one.

Humiliatingly, we are forced to write to charities for coupons to buy children's clothing. We even write to Vardis Vardinoyannis asking for help, but we hear nothing from him. Sometimes I get so depressed with this situation that I decide to quit college for a year, go back to work and save some money. But somehow, we struggle on.

At least we are not alone. The college is divided into people who managed to sell their houses before the crash and those who didn't. The poorer members of the community all know each other and know each other's problems. We're in the minority. At Oakhill there are students' Mercedes lined up in the car-park. Whenever our shortage of money starts to pinch, I'm angry and resentful. This is a community of Christians and we are all the Lord's servants but there is only love and charity here up to a point.

Perhaps the wealthier people at Oakhill feel that we're feckless and should have saved our money for this period of poverty. They're soon bored with taking calls for us on their telephones. But Claire and I have decided that we don't think true Christians should save. We now see this as a test of faith. If you really believe you can trust in God to take care of you, then you don't try to amass funds just in case He doesn't. We even disapprove of pensions, although we know I'll be entitled to an army and a Church pension one day. How can anyone sit on their own cosy little nest egg when so many people out there are hurting? We decide that if we ever sell our house at a profit, we won't keep the bonanza to ourselves. We're going to be Christian about our poverty, we decide, not angry.

Sometimes, though, it's hard to contain my anger. One day I am making rabbit hutches for the children. I have bought some wood and returned home with it to find a builder's van standing across the parking space outside our house, and across two other spaces. It's a simple matter for him to turn his van side on so that he only takes up one space.

He's the college's occasional contractor. I've seen him around before, a big man with a bald jutting jaw. I go into the house in our cul-de-sac where he's working with a circular saw. He looks up at me in annoyance.

'Is that your van outside?'

'What of it?'

'It's parked across three spaces.'

'So?'

'So, no-one else can get in.'

Rolling his eyes, he throws the keys to an underling.

The van is moved and I park. I start work on the rabbit hutches but soon have to rush out to buy something I've forgotten. When I return, the van is parked across three spaces again. Inside it is the bearded builder. He is chatting to someone on his mobile phone. I wait, the windscreen wipers swishing in the rain, but when he finishes the conversation he just leaps out, slams the door, and walks into the house.

I get out of my car.

'Hey, mate! Excuse me! You've parked across three spaces again!'

He stops and turns to me.

'So?'

'So, no-one else can get in.'

'You got a problem with that?'

'No, you have. You don't know how to park.'

The big man comes striding towards me. He does not expect trouble like this at a theological college.

'You want to watch who you're talking to,' he says, 'or someone might rip your head off.'

That does it. I feel 15cc of adrenalin suddenly shoot through me like an injection. My fingers tingle. My hair stands up. I am angry, very angry, angrier than any minister should ever allow themselves to be, but I don't care that I'm going into the Church, I don't care about anything except that I'm a highly trained close-combat fighter and I am going to tear this man apart. I square up for a fight and whatever transformation has taken place inside me clearly shows. The big man is scared. He takes a step back.

'Move the van,' I say. My voice is pure, undiluted threat. The builder seems to be getting thinner. He takes another step back.

Another student who lives next door happens to come out at this moment. He sees what's happening and stops short, mouth open. But I am going to tear this man apart and I don't care who sees me.

'Move it!' I repeat, my fists up and ready.

'OK!' says the big builder weakly. 'OK, I'll move it.'

I watch him while he hastily reverses the van into the allotted parking place. He slams the door and goes rapidly into the house. I watch him until he's gone. My heart is still beating fast, the adrenalin is still racing around my body, the veins are still standing out on my arms. I don't even want to think what my face is like.

My neighbour says, 'Er . . . is there some kind of a problem, Frank?'

'Not now, Roland.'

Claire, inside the house, takes one look at me and says, 'What's wrong?'

'I'm going for a run.'

I run for fifteen miles until I'm very, very tired. I shower and then tell Claire what happened.

'I nearly blew it,' I say. 'I can't believe I nearly blew it! If I'd hit him, the police could have been involved, I might have been thrown out of college . . .'

I try to forget this incident. I try to be a nice Anglican teddy bear. But deep down I suspect I haven't changed as much as I think.

I often pass the builder at work in the hallways. He sees me coming and freezes, flattening himself against a wall.

'All right, mate?' I say in what I hope is a non-threatening way.

'Yeah, yeah,' he assures me hastily.

Finally, at the end of my first year, our Hereford house is sold for more than our mortgage loan. We use this windfall to pay off our debts. We get rid of our car and buy an old camper van which we'll use for holidays. Then we distribute the rest of the money, about £6,000, to people we think need it.

We give some to a poverty-stricken pastor friend and his wife before starting on the college needy. A group of us with money problems have been praying together and now Claire and I don't feel we can just put our cash in the bank knowing how hard-up these other people are. There's one neighbour who has told us about his credit card debts.

'How's the credit card problem?' I ask him casually.

'Mounting up. It's really depressing,' he says.

'We've sold our house, we've got a bit of money now. Give me the bills and I'll take care of them for you.'

I spend a few thousand pounds paying off the man's bills. He and his wife are thrilled. It's only later that we find out he has both a big house and a boat.

Originally I was on a two-year diploma course but I opt to stay for a third year and go for a degree. Part of me needs the reassurance of those letters after my name. Claire starts studying at the college too, and continues, even when she finds she is pregnant for the fourth time.

'I just don't know how we're going to manage. I mean, apart from the money. We'll both have finals next year and a small baby as well,' she says.

'We'll manage because we always do.'

I sell my parachute. I can't afford to jump any more and the parachute's valuable and I know it's foolish to keep it. But seeing it go is painful. This sale is the most poignant reminder for me of how much my life has changed.

There is another death. This time it's Bishop Gordon Savage. I am very miserable at the loss of this friend and teacher but I know that death held no fear for him. He often told me how much he was looking forward to seeing the Lord.

Before our final year at college, we are scheduled to visit the new Bishop of Hereford and learn what church, if any, I'll be sent to on leaving. As an evangelical minister I can only be sent to an evangelical church, and there are strong rumours that the diocese has no such vacancies.

Back to Hereford again. We drive up the big hill which leads to the city and at the top a magnificent vista stretches before us. Hereford looks beautiful in today's sunshine. It looks like home despite the fact that we have been living in London for three years. I can't enjoy this view without sensing the ghost of all those other homecomings, when I was in the Regiment and had been away for months. At this hilltop, someone would always say, 'Who's for the Horse and Groom?' Some of the lads preferred to go to the pub before they went home. They'd stagger back plastered, to angry wives and burnt dinners.

We stay with Claire's mother and for once Claire relaxes with her feet up, the way the books say pregnant women should. The next morning we go to see Bishop John Oliver. We are shown into his study and I have a sudden pang at the absence of Bishop John Easthaugh who looked after me so well.

The bishop starts to talk about St Peter's. We assume that he's talking about the last church the college attached me to in London but after some confusion it emerges that he means St Peter's, Hereford.

St Peter's is one of Hereford's leading Churches. It is in the city centre and it is the church I went to just after my conversion, when I hovered outside the door of the evangelists' meeting. It is the church of Peter Wood, who talked to me in those early days and introduced me to Dietrich Bonhoeffer. It is the church where Claire and I attended a few services five years ago and she told me I didn't fit in with these people. Well, now, it seems, I fit. The bishop is saying that I am about to become curate there.

It takes me a few moments to comprehend this.

'St Peter's!' I splutter at last, and he looks at me strangely. He doesn't realize that my spiritual journey has taken me in a complete circle. The vicar of St Peter's sent me out on this journey and now I'm coming back. The perfect symmetry of this delights me and I cannot stop smiling.

# 30

I STARE AT THE MIRROR AND REMIND MYSELF THAT I'M ME. A VICAR stares back. A vicar wearing a dog collar, a black cassock, a white surplice, a white stole. I try to smile. The vicar returns my smile nervously.

Around me the other ordinands are laughing and chattering. We're changing into our new robes in the bishop's palace, right next to Hereford Cathedral, and the level of excitement is high. We've all waited a long time for this.

We go downstairs, being careful not to tread on our robes. The bishop's chaplain is waiting for us in a high dog collar and panama hat. He inspects our clothes to make sure they're correct. 'Good . . . Nice . . . Lovely scarf! Look at that embroidery . . .'

He stops when he reaches me. He studies me, up close, with distaste.

24286081. Corporal. Collins. Sir.

'Well!' he says. 'Which college were you at?'

'Oakhill.'

He curls his face. Oakhill, I thought so. No wonder you look plain.

'Well, that stole's far too much like a piece of hessian. By next year I expect to see some embroidery on it, at the very least, young man.'

I know he won't see any such thing, because I don't believe in these flowing robes, these silky rainbow scarves, these priestly garments. I don't even believe in the same priesthood as this man. He likes mysteries and power and I think as little as possible should come between man and God. Not clothes, not priests. I'm being ordained

369

today and I've spent three years at college working hard for it, but I don't think it makes me special.

I say, 'Yes, all right.'

He passes on, shaking his head.

We go in a big, bleached group to the main door and process in from the bright sunlight to the dim coolness of the cathedral. As we move down the central aisle the people stand and sing. There are thousands of them. The walls echo and our hymn sheets shake. My heart lifts. I sing up to the roof as I pass friends, lecturers from college, Dad and my brothers and sisters, and finally Claire and the children. I am moved to see them here. My life to date. All here to witness my rite of passage. The cathedral resounds with our voices.

Over the altar hangs the great corona. It is a memorial to Bishop John Easthaugh. I think of the people who should be here and aren't. Bishop John. Bishop Gordon. My mother. Al Slater, who died when we were both such young men and so remains a young man while I age.

The service is moving, sometimes unbearably so. I read a lesson. Clergy lay hands on us, one by one. Then comes Communion. There are stations for this because the congregation is so large and I am sent to one of these to administer the chalice. I cup the wine for friends and strangers.

I baulk at the power of my position. The humility with which people receive Communion is humility to God, not to me, I remind myself. Heads down, hands up, they kneel at the foot of the cross. I'm not administering the wine. That would be a priestly thing to do. I'm just passing them the cup which it is their right to take.

'The blood of Christ keep you in eternal life. Amen,' I say to each one before I give them the cup. It's too easy for ritual to set me apart. It's too easy for ministers to hide behind all this.

One woman is strikingly attractive. Her head is not bowed. She looks me in the eye. Does she know me? I don't recognize her. There is unmistakable challenge in her look. Confrontation. She smiles at me but there is no warmth in her smile. No submission in the way she takes the cup. A coldness runs through me, suddenly and unexpectedly. I wonder, fleetingly, if she is a witch. I feel unhappy in her presence and glad when I have taken the cup from her. It's easy to forget, in the glow of today's occasion, that evil is a presence in the world. This woman has reminded me.

Afterwards, there is a party at the bishop's palace for the ordinands and their families. I stand apart watching them all.

Claire is talking to the bishop about the cathedral.

370

'We don't really need cathedrals and we can't really afford all this upkeep . . .' she's saying. The bishop is staring at her.

'Er . . . historic significance . . . tradition . . . ' he mumbles.

'Well, people who are interested in heritage should pay for it then. Not the Church,' Claire is insisting.

Gary and Yvonne and Michael and Michelle are standing together, embarrassed and unsure of themselves in this strange environment. Other people in the room have seen their fortress and are moving to break it up, bringing drink, asking questions.

A woman in a hat is talking to Dad. He is trying not to drink his sherry too quickly. His look has already indicated what he thinks of sherry.

'Well,' he's saying in answer to her question, 'he was a bodyguard. And before that he was in the SAS.'

The woman looks surprised.

'Really? That's quite a dramatic transformation.'

Dad nods.

'Yep, he was in the SAS and now he's going to be a vicar.'

'You must be very proud of your son,' she says brightly. I watch Dad for his reply. I scrutinize him. He pauses for a long time.

'Well,' he says at last. 'Well . . .'

I crane forward. Is Dad very proud of me? Is he really? I've worked hard and studied hard for this, Dad. It's been a long and often a very lonely road for me. I had to turn my back on everything I knew and just trust in God to take care of me. The last few years have been difficult and there have been occasions when I've nearly turned back. I've faced challenges which are greater in the classroom or in the Church than I ever knew when I was fully armed and ready to fight. Are you proud of me, Dad, for all this?

Dad adjusts his tie.

'Well I wouldn't say exactly, that I'm proud,' he tells the woman. She is looking at him with concern. Ludicrously, I feel a lump rise in my throat. So he's not proud of me. So he doesn't think I've achieved anything. So I still can't kick the ball. I may be wearing a cassock and a surplice and a dog collar but I am a small boy again and I want to howl with fury and misery at the unfairness of it all.

'No?' says the concerned woman.

'In my opinion,' says Dad, 'my son should never have left the SAS.'

I turn and walk away.

# EPILOGUE

I SPENT THREE WONDERFUL YEARS AS A CURATE AT ST PETER'S AND ITS daughter Church, St James'. Three years of youth groups, pastoral work, cups of tea, sermons, three years of listening and learning. Of course, in that time I bumped into a lot of boys from the Regiment and officiated at their various weddings and christenings.

One day a call came from America. It was the young major who'd been playing hostage during that exercise at Kielder, the one who told me to sort things out because I was indigenous to the area. Now promoted, he was asking me to come back and be visiting speaker at my old American unit's annual prayer breakfast. I went, and it was an uplifting experience. All the men attended. They wanted to be there. They saw religion as an acceptable part of military life.

Maybe that's what first gave me the idea of returning to the military as a chaplain. Or maybe it was the Territorial Army. I was approached by a former colleague – my troop commander in the Iranian Embassy seige – to become chaplain to 23 SAS, the Regiment's TA wing. At first I laughed. Part-time soldiering and the SAS seemed completely incompatible but eventually I did become their chaplain. The money proved a useful supplement to my income: it was tough for me and Claire keeping four children on a curate's salary especially when, for about a year, we actually fostered four more children from the parish.

I was impressed by the quality and commitment of the TA soldiers. The work, mostly pastoral, brought me into contact with a lot of the

372

lads from the Regiment. I didn't pine for the army but I did begin to see that I might have a future there: a very different future from the one I'd envisaged all those years ago when I left home for army apprentice college.

It seemed a natural progression to slip back into the military as a chaplain. I wanted to work with young people and I felt I had a particular understanding of young men in the army. I wanted to bring God into their lives in a way they'd understand. If they were on exercise at three in the morning, I wanted to turn up in their trenches with my coffee and my Bibles stuffed into ammunition pouches. I wanted to hear their problems and help sort them out.

So I came back into the army in 1994 as a chaplain. It's a long way from the Regiment but I won't pretend that the SAS wings I wear haven't sometimes helped me in my job. They can make the men more inclined to listen to me.

I've managed to maintain a good level of fitness and this is important. I still regularly run long distances but, now I'm forty, I admit that the years of heavy-weight carrying are taking their toll. My joints ache: my knees, my back, my ankles. But I'm not going to stop running.

Now I'm back in the army, I have the opportunity to free-fall again at last. I also ski and canoe and climb mountains. I used to think mountains were just large things which got in the way. Now, I really believe they bring me closer to God. I've climbed the Matterhorn. I want to climb K2.

I've kept in touch with a lot of old friends from the Regiment. Most of them are forty and out now, and, with the exception of Andy McNab, who became a writer, they're all working here or abroad in the security world. Claire and I see Al Slater's parents as often as we can. They're from tough, Scottish stock but nothing will ever really get them over Al's death. They've been good to us: it's thanks to some help from them that Claire was able to study at college.

My dad died in 1994 of lung cancer. The funeral was an emotional occasion as the wake moved around most of his old drinking haunts. His surviving brothers were all there, devastated, partly because, as one of the younger brothers, he wasn't scheduled to die until they had.

All my brothers and sisters have married, had children and divorced – except for Michelle. She's still married and she's left the shipyard now to look after her three children. Yvonne's still in the civil service, Gary has a good job in security and Michael's career as an army chef has been glittering.

It's difficult to end a book about your life when life keeps rolling on. I want a lot more to happen to me, but my route so far has been so unpredictable that I can't even try to guess what's next. I just trust in God to show me the path.